THE OBJECT

JOSHUA T. CALVERT

PROLOGUE

She dreamed of curiosity. Not that restless curiosity before tearing off the wrapping paper at Christmas, but the deeply felt desire for knowledge. As always, this desire, which was much more of an urge, was fed by a single fascination: the stars. They lay spread out before her, a sparkling sea of silence. Her mind was wide, so much so that its boundaries blurred. The myriad glow changed, became a complex puzzle of photons that sent heat at the edge of the measurable into the cold vacuum. They were the messengers of the past, relics of stars that had been using up their hydrogen supply for millennia, perhaps millions of years. Like a cosmic breath, they had expanded into red giants and collapsed into white dwarfs before shrinking into cold formations without luminosity as the last photons left them.

But nothing ever *died*, and so the massless elementary particles traveled through the cosmic void as ambassadors of their former hot origin and met her invisible retina here and now to reveal to it the intimidatingly all-encompassing structure of the stellar panorama.

An image for the moment, fleeting in place, constant in

the infinity of space and time. She looked down on the solar system she called home. No, she did not see it, she felt it, had a sense of each of its objects, and their relative localities. She saw the orbital mechanics before her, an only-seeming jumble of ecliptics and slightly curved orbits. She felt the bow wave of the heliosphere, where the sun's excited particles were slowed by the interstellar medium and piled up into a spray of particles that produced a surge of heat. With the ionizing hydrogen atoms having lost their electrical charge, they plunged into the heliosphere envelope and entered relative quiescence, far from the system's glowing central star and its planetary satellites, which rotated in faithful orbits around its gravitational center.

It was only a moment, a second perhaps, though concepts of time eluded the dream, and yet it struck her as such a complex image of a single point in time that it was enough to fill entire libraries. As her mind began to race, wanting to absorb it all and somehow store it all away, she knew that the harbingers of the fading dream were coming forward to withdraw it from her. Disappointment crept into her bones like a creeping infection, seeping inexorably into her mind and waking her body with a paralyzing sense of inadequacy, a violent reduction after the experience of grave greatness.

Melody lifted her head and blinked a few times before running her hand over her forehead, feeling a strange pattern with her fingers and triggering a surface headache.

Sighing, she moved away from the keyboard, which had acknowledged its misuse as a pillow with a warning on the screen that the Caps Lock key had been activated, and rubbed her eyes.

"Hey, Adams," she heard a voice with the typical Boston accent that rounded each vowel oddly.

"Morning, Winthrop," she greeted her cohort, punctuated by a mighty yawn that cracked her jaw joints. As the scent of fresh coffee hit her nostrils, she sniffed, like an animal catching a scent. "If all my colleagues started the shift change like this, I might just forget why I'm here and not in Houston."

Winthrop, a lean man in his 40s with a surprisingly full head of hair, considering that it was completely silver, grinned broadly and handed her the white cup with the NASA logo and the inscription 'I Need My Space.' He brought his own cup to his lips, sipped from it, and then nodded before pointing it at her monitor.

"Found anything exciting?" The fact that his question was rhetorical, merely inviting the obligatory denial on her part like an annoying ritual, disappointed her more than she wanted to admit. It was like a slap in the face to her fading dream and the far-more-real dreams that'd had nothing to do with the fitful sleep of a long night shift, before they had shattered.

"I fell asleep," she admitted bluntly, sniffing her coffee. "No sugar?"

"Black as your soul, and bitter as the expression on your face."

"Charming as ever," she grumbled.

"You look awfully tired," Winthrop observed in a conciliatory tone. "Maybe you should take a day off."

"I've never taken a day off and I'm not going to start now."

"You're not in Houston anymore, though."

"Clearly not." Melody didn't feel like having the ensuing conversation, which they'd had several times over the past two months, and the first time had already been once too often. So she tapped the spacebar with her thumb and entered her username and the associated password. "I've maintained the focal length, as discussed, and kept Pluto in view." She made an ironic gesture as if trying to crush her coffee cup.

"Our poor dwarf planet must have gotten a pimple," Winthrop noted, pointing to the nondescript columns of data on the analysis screen with its many lines, wave representations, and combinations of numbers along the x and y axes.

"Probably because he's still sad to be labeled a dwarf planet." She interrupted herself and furrowed her brow, which spoke up with a painful zing as the depressed key imprints shifted. "Wait a minute. That's an aberration."

"Probably a measurement error."

"Hmm," she responded absently, putting down her coffee cup, which her cerebellum reacted to with a wave of disappointment. In quick succession, she copied the relevant lines into a simulation program she had written in recent weeks during times when she had been bored.

"You still have to enter the factors for the focal length differences of the different time periods," Winthrop remarked, but she was already at it and ignored him. She only saw the numbers in front of her and felt the growing excitement in her gut, which she tried hard to shoo away and thus only intensified.

When she had everything ready, she placed both programs next to each other and compared the relevant data one last time before pressing 'Enter' and leaning back. A green loading bar showed her that the simulation program was busy generating optical equivalents from the raw data and scaling them up with constant powers.

"Pluto has a pimple," Winthrop said after 15 minutes, during which they both drank their coffee silently. "Told you."

Melody looked askance at her colleague with a mixture of indignation and irritation.

"That's not a freaking pimple, Winthrop. That's an asteroid!"

"An asteroid that looks like a pimple."

She rolled her eyes and looked at the preliminary image her program had spit out. A gimmick, sure, but a fairly vivid version of the data that roughly matched the optical spectrum of what the Gemini North telescope had thrown out in terms of observational data.

"Pluto is currently four and a half light hours away from us," Melody said mostly to herself. "That means we'll have to point the telescope at the same spot again to see how far our visitor has moved since then."

"What you're saying is that you want my faculty's observation time."

"This one could be an important discovery!"

"Adams, that *one*," Winthrop pointed with his empty cup to the image of dark Pluto with its 'pimple,' "is an asteroid. Possibly a rather large one, granted, but still an asteroid. You discovered it, so it's yours. Today is the third of January, so naming it will even be easy. But you can always do that tonight when my shift ends and yours begins again."

"Winthrop," she said, looking him seriously in the eye. It didn't bother her that she looked possibly ridiculous doing it, with the fading keyboard pattern on her forehead. She spoke very slowly now, as if trying to explain something to a child. She didn't notice that his expression was growing more disapproving as she did so. "Do you see this corona?"

Melody tapped against the screen, where the asteroid that had just emerged from behind the dwarf planet's terminator at the time of the shot appeared badly frayed. "It's brighter than the surrounding area, which is highly unusual, don't you think? It's also unusual for this celestial body to pass so close to Pluto without crashing into it."

"It must be very fast."

"Or so big that, even from our distance and perspective, it

looks like it's in close proximity to our degraded friend out there on the edge of the solar system."

The astronomer from Harvard's Department of Astronomy shrugged. "Pretty unlikely," he argued. "The chunk would have to be an appreciable fraction of the size of Pluto itself. But that's no lightweight, at just under twenty-three hundred kilometers in diameter. So you can do the math on the probabilities. Can't you?"

Melody did not respond to the provocation. She knew Winthrop wasn't intending to needle her; he was far too eager to set up a date with her. Rather, it was his personality that brought out constant teasing—and thus one of the reasons she would never date him.

"I wasn't just a fighter pilot, dear, I also got a Ph.D. in physics, remember?" she replied instead.

"I didn't. But you're not a computer scientist."

"If you want to say that my program is flawed—"

"—and thus, this representation," he interjected with an innocent look.

"Then..." She paused and clenched her teeth. "All right, then. A deal's a deal. Your twelve hours."

"Thanks. And don't worry about it. Worst case, you can tweak your program and it will run better next time. I'm sure it's just a minor error in the heuristics."

"I'm sure," she replied without much interest, logging off and toasting him with the empty coffee cup. "Thanks for the coffee. See you later."

"Yes, see you later."

∽

Melody spent the day at her apartment in Waimea, which was a little over an hour away by car. Unlike most of her colleagues, she had no desire for the hustle and bustle of the coast and enjoyed the relative quiet of the small town. She answered a few messages, including one from Jim, whose overused kissing smileys elicited an eye roll, a smile, and a snort (in that order) from her before sending a terse reply. She then prepared herself some cereal with the remains of a pineapple, which had looked less than fresh yesterday, and then opened her laptop.

For more than three hours, she pored over the code of her simulation program, discovering two minor errors that could cause bugs in the input mask if she didn't keep the input order of the various fields or tabbed between them. But neither had anything to do with actual data processing. So Pluto's 'pimple' had been there for real—perhaps still was—and just as big and frayed as the spit-out image suggested.

"No error in the program," she muttered to the absent Winthrop. She considered calling Jim and, after a little small talk, casually telling him that she had discovered an asteroid— a genuinely big one at that—but dismissed the idea. It would be a childish boast and, besides, born only of a desire to be successful and let him know it.

Instead, she went over the data again and again until she could recite the exact alignment numbers for the telescope input without looking, then slept for an hour to avoid spending half the night with her forehead on the keyboard again, and finally drove back up Mouna Kea. Its switchbacks twisted her through the cloud line after three-quarters of an hour, giving her a beautiful, turkey-red sunset with long streaks on the horizon for the last 20 minutes of driving. They looked like the fingers of a doomed deity clinging hotly to the Earth. The majesty of the sight plucked a chord in her that her intense dream on the keyboard of her workstation had strummed and never let go. The universe was still a fascinating place—whether out there among the stars, or down here on the blue paradise they called Earth.

The large white dome of the Gemini North telescope, whose sister telescope was in Chile, was just one of many up here on the summit of Mouna Kea, and just as nondescript, if one disregarded its sheer size. Parking next to Winthrop's red Cadillac and a Ford Ranger owned by the maintenance engineer, she walked through the dome room to the adjacent offices. Amid the hydraulic roar of the rotating rack, she murmured a greeting to the engineer as she watched him wipe his hands and pack his toolbox, but didn't stop to chat as she usually did.

She had work to do.

"Evening, Winthrop," she curtly greeted her fellow academic, setting down her bag and making herself a cup of coffee.

"Evening, Lieutenant Commander," he replied, joining her at the small kitchen counter to wash down his mug. "Did you get any sleep?"

"A little bit, I was mostly reviewing my program."

"And?"

"I found two bugs."

Winthrop grinned triumphantly, but his expression immediately changed to a more patronizing one. "Don't worry about it. Asteroids are a dime a dozen."

"The errors had nothing to do with data processing. The algorithm works perfectly."

"Hmm."

"I'll get started, then." She nodded to him and went to her workstation, which had been his until just now, logged in, and began to prepare the alignment data for the telescope dish. It was still too bright, but the process took a while and she didn't want to waste time. An hour later, she realized that her colleague had at some point disappeared.

When the time came, she opened the roof dome and let the hyperbolic and parabolic mirrors do their work. As soon as the data came in—which took over two hours, during which she worked through some tedious bureaucratic tasks with forced composure—she transferred them to her simulation program for optical processing. In keeping with her training, she pushed aside impatience and the tendency to rush, took deep breaths, and channeled the accompanying tension into her ability to concentrate. So she went through all the inputs three times and only then started the calculation process.

"Where are you, Pimple?" she muttered as the green loading bar moved from left to right.

Fifteen minutes later, she reached for the phone next to her and dialed Jim's private cell number.

"Ehrenreich?" a sleepy voice grumbled.

"Jim? It's Melody."

"Melody? Do you know what *time* it is?" There was a trace of indignation in the NASA administrator's voice that could not be ignored.

"A little after midnight for me, so a little after five for you," she said. "I just sent you an email. Open it."

"And why should I do that? The alarm doesn't go off until—"

"Just do it, Jim!"

"Okay, okay."

She heard bedsheets rustling in the background and then the hum of a laptop or desk computer booting up.

"There, I'll open it up. If this isn't... What is it?"

"It's a comet."

"You've discovered a comet?" he asked, both amazed and appreciative. "Not bad, for the first eight weeks in the—"

"It is located on an intersection with the Pluto orbit."

"Impossible!"

"The dwarf planet in the image is Pluto. My algorithm can't calculate the colors because it lacks the appropriate input from the telescope, but that's Pluto."

Melody sent off the next email with a screenshot of the

data analysis program, which was NASA-certified and part of the telescope's standard inventory. She pointed her finger at the dark object with the strange ring of light that extended slightly to the right. "There's no doubt about the data. There is a comet in Pluto's orbit, and it's heading toward the inner solar system."

There was a pause in the line that stretched so long that she suspected the connection was broken.

"Jim?"

"I'm still here. Get on the first plane back to Houston."

"You don't have to tell me twice."

She hung up and left the observatory within the hour.

Returning to Houston's Johnson Space Center stung Melody more fiercely than she wanted to admit. Her memories of the last Dragon capsule launch from Cape Canaveral were too fresh, during which she had sat in a shielded room at the control center as part of the standby crew for Mission 11. To face a years-long selection process and give up the rest of one's life for it, just to be chosen as one of ten candidates out of tens of thousands, was one thing. But ultimately not going into space, instead taking a seat on the bench, was akin to training half her life for the Olympics, only to get injured just before competing.

No matter how many times Jim had assured her, at the beginning of their 'secondary assignments,' that she was still part of the astronaut corps, and that everyone was working in different areas of NASA (including at the observatory), he had not been able to ease the pain of it. If anything, it had made it worse, and the physical distance between Hawaii and Houston made it feel like the exile of a former failure.

"I have to admit that at first I thought you were seeing

more than there was to see because you were so anxious to get back to JSC," Jim admitted as she dropped into one of the two chairs in front of his desk, her wheeled suitcase from the flight still with her.

The NASA administrator nodded at her across the wide desktop, smiling almost as he had for the past year when they'd met privately: a hint of audaciousness, as if they were partners in a criminal enterprise. Which wasn't true, per se, but wasn't entirely false, either.

"A comet this far out. Jim, you know there can't be many explanations for that," she replied, leaning forward a bit, making the old leather of the seat cushion creak disapprovingly.

"We shouldn't jump to conclusions." He spread his hands in a paternalistic gesture that looked very much like the politician he would surely become after his post here. She was about to object, but he beat her to it. "But the fact is that you have discovered an asteroid that has very strange properties. It has a corona—"

"A tail!"

"A corona, which could be a tail," he corrected her. "This will have to be investigated further. That's why I've ordered that we interrupt the James Webb's current mission to investigate."

"You ordered that?" asked Melody, dumbfounded.

"Yes." His boyish grin now looked nothing like a politician's. "We mustn't get ahead of ourselves, but there shouldn't be any asteroids this far out with a light source behind them— and certainly no comets. Whatever we're dealing with doesn't fit any known pattern, and that's where we should let our curiosity guide us. It will take a few days, but then I'm sure we'll know more."

"Do we issue a press release?"

"Yes, I have already called Andrea, and she will sit down

with you after our conversation. Congratulations, Lieutenant Commander, you've discovered the first asteroid of the year." Jim winked at her and looked disappointed when the phone next to him rang. He picked up the receiver, nodded a couple of times, said "Yes," and after a glance at his wristwatch, "On my way," before hanging up and sighing. "Senator Kennedy has arrived. I'm afraid I have to go."

"No problem. I'll go straight to Andrea. Should we run the press release across your desk again, or—"

"No, no," he rebuffed and rose. When he had come around the desk, their hands touched briefly, and then their eyes met. "I trust you to get it right. Besides, our agency is expected to make every official sentence boring and, at the same time, appealing to every side of the political donor spectrum."

"All right." Melody returned his smile and lightly squeezed his hand.

"I'm off later tonight," he said in a lowered voice. "Do you want to—"

"Yes." She nodded. She didn't mention that she had missed him. Her eyes did that for her.

"See you later." With obvious effort, Jim turned away from her and left his office. Behind him, he left the door open, leaving her alone.

Melody looked at her face in the mirror, being powdered from two sides at once. She saw the narrow jaw, the full lips she had always considered too red, the straight nose with the pert tip, and her dark, almond-shaped eyes, which she owed to her Samoan grandmother. During her time in the Navy, before she had joined NASA's astronaut program, she'd had to fight for recognition for her flying accomplishments because she'd been too pretty. At least, that's what she had believed. In truth, it had merely been those male pilots who had unsuccessfully tried to land dates with her who had gossiped behind her back. Here and now she saw only a 40-year-old woman with concentration lines between her eyes and a shadow of hurt in her gaze that would probably never go away.

"So, did you sleep well?" the beautician asked. The fact that she was only now starting to initiate the obligatory small talk must have been because it had taken a lot of work to get her face made up adequately.

"Not a whole lot." Melody thought back to her night with Jim and how she had lain awake for a while after he fell asleep, trying to figure out her feelings. She liked him, his gentle assertiveness and the cooperative basic attitude with which he not only ran NASA but also went through his entire daily life. There were few men in positions like his who, while keeping an eye on their careers spent most of their time sacrificing themselves for the good of their staff and the progress of their agency. Otherwise, he probably would never have risen to administrator. At the same time, he'd had no problem sending her to Hawaii, far away from himself.

"I'm sure you're used to that, aren't you?"

Because I'm an astronaut? she was about to ask, when the young woman with the pretty brunette curls added, "As a fighter pilot, I mean."

"Yes," Melody replied amiably, swallowing the brief twinge in her chest. "Although our superiors have always insisted on following recovery protocol, there are a few stereotypes like that about Navy pilots that are unquestionably true."

"You mean like on *Top Gun?* Long nights in bars and fights among the best?"

"Sort of. 'Navy pilots fly jets, Air Force pilots fly their beds,' is what we used to say." She managed to grin as the young woman gave a polite laugh. Small talk, that was it. As she finished, an older, whiskered man poked his head through the door. He'd introduced himself earlier as Devon and seemed married to his clipboard. He tapped the headset in his ear and extended five fingers to her.

"Are we ready?" Melody asked the remaining beautician, whose colleague had started in with the second guest who was seated behind her.

"Yeah, it looks good. No more shiny spots."

"Thank you." She stood up and shook the woman's hand, which seemed to surprise her. "What's your name, if I may ask?"

"Carina. I mean, Carina Simmons."

"Thanks, Carina, I'm Melody. Will you come save me if this," she held a finger in front of her powdered forehead, "gets in my eyes from the fear sweat?"

Carina grinned and winked at her, as if they shared a secret from now on. "I promise, Lieutenant Commander. I mean, Melody."

Turning away, she paused for another moment as Carina asked with a mixture of curiosity and envy, "Are you ever afraid?"

"All the time," she assured the young woman. "I was just trained early on to accept fear and not make it the enemy. Then you find it's okay, and it makes you alert and focused."

"Okay, sixty seconds!" Devon interrupted with a hint of irritation.

The studio was smaller than she remembered from TV, but much brighter. Directly in front of the wooden podium with its table, two chairs, and the obligatory breakfast that no one ever touched, she had always suspected a manageable audience. But instead, there were only several rolling cameras and bright white diffusers that turned everything behind them into a black hole.

She was greeted by anchor Vanessa Boeringer, who stood up, waved off a staff member, and held out her hand. "Good morning, Lieutenant Commander."

"Good morning." Melody nodded too, trying not to envision the cameras as weapons pointed at her and waiting to go off if she dared to look.

"We're still in the commercial break and have two minutes. Why don't you make yourself comfortable," Boeringer suggested, pointing to the empty seat on the other side of the table. "You know the drill by now—our panel is thirty minutes long and we have two commercial breaks. When Devon comes on stage, you can relax, the cameras will be off. Do you have any questions?"

"No, I'm ready." Melody smiled, but Boeringer was distracted by whomever was talking into her earpiece, which she covered with her blond curls. When it was time, they both got a countdown from Devon, who continued silently from four.

"A very good morning to you, America. Those of you who just tuned in now, hold on to your coffee, because our surprise guest today is with me now. Welcome, Melody Adams!"

"Good morning, Vanessa, and thank you for inviting me," she replied with a smile.

Boeringer looked at her moderator cards and pretended to read off something with astonishment. "You are a lieutenant commander in the Navy, were a test pilot for fifth-generation jets, are now a member of NASA's astronaut corps, were awarded a doctorate in physics at George Washington University, and are currently doing research on low-frequency radiation anomalies in the Kuiper belt. Would you prefer me to address you as Lieutenant Commander, or Doctor?"

"Just Melody, please."

Vanessa smiled and nodded cheerfully. "Melody it is. Modesty, I've heard, is a virtue attributed to the people of Wyoming. I guess you're no exception. You were part of the backup crew for Dragon-6, NASA and ESA's current ISS mission, and then went to Hawaii to observe our night sky. Can you tell us what, exactly, you do there?"

Melody smiled, though she felt as if Boeringer had punched her in the pit of the stomach.

"I've been working the night shifts for the past week because we can only use the telescope at night. During the day, colleagues from Boston are busy analyzing data from the previous week. Then, the next week it changes to a new dataset."

"And how exactly should we imagine your daily life there?"

"Pretty boring," she joked, and Boeringer laughed almost as if it wasn't a practiced response. "The telescope captures the data in the form of infrared radiation in the low wavelength range. From that, we at NASA can draw appropriate conclusions."

"Among other things, pictures like the one you brought us today, right?"

"Right."

Boeringer pointed to the large monitor wall next to them, which had previously shown the Houston skyline and now featured the image of Pluto and 2023-AA, her discovery. It showed the large celestial body as a dark spot with a bright glow behind it, stretching upward at an angle. Right next to it, Pluto showed as a dark disk against the somewhat-blurred starry sky.

"Can you tell us what we're looking at here, and why it's a sensation for science?"

"We see Pluto here, formerly the ninth planet of our solar

system before it was demoted to dwarf status. It's way out there, far beyond Neptune, where the sun is no more than a slightly brighter dot among many in the darkness. Next to it we see 2023-AA, which is the tentative name for the object we discovered with Gemini North."

"You say 'we,' but *you* actually discovered it, didn't you?"

"I was there when 2023-AA showed up in the data. If I had been on vacation, it would have happened to someone else."

"Why do you say the name is provisional?" Boeringer asked, changing the subject. "It has something to do with the special nature of this object, am I right?"

"Yes. 2023-AA is the designation for an asteroid. It always starts with the year of discovery and the month is divided into letters between the first and fifteenth and the sixteenth and last. So January first to the fifteenth is A, and from the sixteenth on, B. There are always two letters, so in our case AA," Melody explained. "However, I have doubts that it is an asteroid."

"Can you explain to our viewers why?"

"That glow you see around the object, that's what's called a tail. The computer has merely made a brighter cloud from the infrared data, which is actually a long outgassing tail that is trailing behind the celestial body."

"Like a comet?"

"*Just* like a comet. The only problem is that there are no comets that far out. More specifically, we should say no comets with tails. The tail usually doesn't form until the object is close to the sun, because the intense solar winds generate heat that causes the ice in the object's core to outgas. Radiation pressure and solar wind blow the hydrogen ions away, creating what we call a *tail*. This can be up to several million kilometers long. In the case of our comet here, it looks very short, which is due to perspective. Based on the data between the first image and this second one on display here, we can tell that the object is heading toward us, and moving pretty fast."

"So it's flying toward *Earth?* Are we in danger, then?"

"No," Melody answered, "let me clarify that statement. I'm *not* saying it's headed for Earth. I was speaking rather more broadly. But it is flying into our inner solar system. We need far more data and measurements to say exactly when it's going to happen, but we're certainly talking several decades."

"Just now you said that comets form near the sun. But 2023-AA is very far from the sun." Boeringer tilted her head questioningly.

"Yes, and there is currently no scientific explanation for this. Except that it cannot be an outgassing of the core. It is at minus two hundred degrees Celsius out there, and only a collision with an asteroid could generate enough energy to make the ice inside gaseous. But that's very unlikely, and it would be an extremely short-lived effect without much of a tail, since there's no radiation pressure or solar wind to speak of."

Now the words flowed from Melody's lips like a gush that could hardly be contained. She had been thinking hard about her discovery for the last few days—to her surprise, being pretty much the only one at JSC doing so, because everyone including the press office was busy preparing for the Space Launch System's first orbital flight. "That leaves a lot of room for the only other explanation that can be applied to this object."

Boeringer seemed to want to say something, probably to increase the tension, but Melody just kept talking— after the phone call with the editors, she knew exactly why she had been invited.

"There is an appreciable probability that it is an extrasolar object with its own energy source."

"By that you mean it could be of extraterrestrial origin,

right?" paraphrased Boeringer, putting on an appropriately serious face.

"Yes. Such a tail could indicate an exhaust flare, a drive with reaction mass expelled to propel the object itself. The trajectory also fits this. Based on our data—which is still limited—it suggests that it originated outside the Kuiper belt and will leave the solar system again because it is simply too fast to be captured by the sun."

"A spaceship, then?"

"A spaceship... A probe, perhaps. We know next to nothing yet, except that it is highly unlikely to be a natural celestial body," Melody said. It felt good to say this sentence, which she had so far merely formed in her head and hinted at during the phone call with the editor. The press release had merely spoken of a 'highly unusual celestial body' that 'currently puzzles its discoverers.' But the consequences of her find had not left her mind since then, and the improbable had turned more and more into the probable. To put it into words now was as though she were giving substance to a fantasy, materializing it.

Except it wasn't imagination, and that realization hit her for the first time, like a lightning bolt.

1

"Basically, there were several curious facts about the visitor right from the beginning," Melody explained, switching to her next slide by pressing her thumb on the clicker button. "For one, we didn't expect to discover an asteroid in the environment near Pluto and its orbit. That's because we have a pretty good view of the solar system and can calculate at what rate it ejects celestial bodies. Our comet came from outside, which can also be calculated from its speed and trajectory. So our probability calculation for the ejection rate of similar solar systems is based on a quantity, which is not a bad starting point. This results in a soberingly small number: the ejection rate is extremely small, even if we greatly extend the time horizon—and by that I mean far beyond our comprehensible scales."

She let her gaze wander over the nearly 500 people in the sold-out Ronald Reagan Hall on the outskirts of Arlington and sighed inwardly. If the right people had given her similarly interested or spellbound looks two years ago, she wouldn't be sitting here now. Whether that was a shame, however, she didn't know.

"In addition, we know the speed at which our many neighboring stars are moving relative to our sun, and our sun to them. But only one in six hundred is moving as fast as our visitor. Why is that special?" She moved to the next slide, which was a little darker than the previous one, bathing the sea of faces in front of her in shadows, punctuated by random reflective lenses that reminded her of cat's eyes at night.

"It is special because we must expect that a celestial body ejected from its gravitational influence system will have roughly the same velocity as the star from which it escaped. Deviations from this are extremely unusual.

This brings me to the end of this section on the visitor's dozen deviations from normal celestial bodies. Are there any questions thus far? As Jeffrey stated at the beginning, I like to take them section by section. That way, you won't pile up too many questions. I'm sure you'll be writing books later!"

The audience laughed cautiously. The first hands went up and the helpers with the microphones fought their way through the rows of seats to them. An older man with grayish temples and chubby cheeks was the first.

"Thank you very much, Doctor Adams. My name is Matt Long, I'm an engineer from Seattle and a big fan."

"Thanks. I guess I should have prepared a prize for the longest journey."

Long smiled—at least she thought the glint below his nose was from a smile. It couldn't be seen that clearly from the stage, where she was blinded by the monitor in the floor on which she'd seen her slides displayed.

"I want to ask you again about the geometry of the object you described as 'extraterrestrial.' NASA has not been clear on this to date, but Mr. Rothman once mentioned in an interview that it might well be 'slightly more elongated' than the average asteroid. What do you say to that?"

"Thank you for your question. Well, first of all, we have

only two images available—with the image of our Japanese friends there are three, which is not very much. But if you take these three together, you get a pretty clear trend. The visitor is spinning and its brightness varies by a factor of eight in its angular momentum. This means that it is at least eight times longer than it is wide. Maybe it's cone-shaped or a cylinder, but there are indications that we're dealing with a disk."

"Can you explain why exactly that is so unusual?" the Seattle engineer asked.

"Because celestial bodies normally have a gravitational pull, however small, generated by their mass, and this gives them their characteristic shape, which is usually approximately round, sometimes more misshapen and elongated like a potato, but never a flat disk. Such a thing does not come into being by itself."

The questioner nodded his thanks and sat down again, but Melody continued before allowing the next question. "But even more amazing is that there can't be any comets out there, but the visitor has a tail like a comet, but no coma, which every comet otherwise has. It's a kind of shell of gases drifting in front of it like a bow wave. In the pictures, our object looks like an asteroid, but behind it is the tail of a comet. So we are dealing with a cosmic hermaphrodite, a truly amazing mystery."

Turning to another member of the audience, she said, "Yes, there in the second row?"

Again the microphone was passed. This time it was a woman of sturdy build who took the floor. "Thank you, Doctor Adams. NASA emphasized after your book was published that this is an exciting research project for the next few years, but at the moment more pressing projects occupy the James Webb Telescope's imaging time. At the last press conference for the launch of Dragon-17, mission director Stevens mentioned that they had come to the conclusion that it was most likely a collision of two asteroids. You specifically ruled that out. What makes you so sure?"

"I love science," Melody replied. "In some ways, I've devoted my life to it. But many of my colleagues have a habit of not being open to those results that, from their point of view, *can't be* and therefore *shouldn't be*. It is a kind of tabooing of the too great improbability. They look first and foremost for reasons why a finding must be a mistake, worried about going too far out on a limb and losing all recognition in the scientific community.

"An outgassing so far out, far away from the strong solar winds at minus two hundred Celsius, would be explicable indeed only with a collision, which is so strong that enormous quantities of kinetic energy are released. And energy is heat. But such a collision would most likely break both asteroids apart, or at least one of them. In addition, the outgassing effect would be of extremely short duration, and the gas would escape in several directions at once due to the lack of radiation pressure, and it would cool extremely quickly.

"In the latest pictures from the Japanese, which were taken, don't forget, some weeks after the first pictures, the tail is still recognizable, however. In my opinion, this can only point to a propulsion flare. That is the reason why I tried to make myself heard with the term 'extraterrestrial.' We need to learn again to let the improbable in when it knocks on the door. Even if it scares us."

The woman said, "Thank you," sat down, and the mike was brought to the back, where a young man stood with his hand extended for it.

"Michael from Washington," he introduced himself succinctly. His voice quivered a bit with excitement. "A comet, as we all know, is usually disturbed in its orbit because it gets a bump from solar winds. That changes its orbital mechanical trajectory. Could it be that your comet hypothesis was also rejected by NASA because such a change in trajectory was not found—in fact, was disproved?"

"A very good question and yes, that is certainly one of the reasons. As I mentioned earlier, the absence of a coma also speaks against a comet. In my opinion, this also means that there is the possibility of an artificial celestial body of extraterrestrial origin. The visitor does not behave like an asteroid, *nor* like a comet. Instead, it flies through our solar system on a curved course, which does not correspond to the orbital mechanical predictions."

"Wouldn't that statement require more data?"

"Yes." Melody nodded honestly. "My data so far is based on only three images, which is why I have publicly asked NASA several times to initiate further research. I will repeat myself, in this case. The visitor is possibly the most important field of research in human astronomy since the first telescope was built by Galileo Galilei. Maybe even of mankind in general, and I do not say this lightly.

"I just fear—and I hope—that my book will not only shake up the New York Times bestseller list, but also some entrenched opinions in the right places in our politics and at NASA. Because if we wait too long, the visitor will have passed us by and we'll never know what or who we were dealing with. Thank you, Michael.

"One more question at this point? I'm afraid we're getting too far away from the current section otherwise. Yes, the lady in the second to last row with the red shirt?"

The microphone helper hurried around and passed the mic between those in the last row to get it to the woman.

"Thank you very much, doctor. My name is Melissa. If you don't mind me asking, it doesn't quite fit in this section, but I'm sure it's on the tongue of most of us here who saw your last interview on Jimmy Fallon's Tonight Show. Is it true that you were benched on the Dragon 6 mission because you helped another astronaut recover his—"

Melody didn't hear the rest because she saw someone coming on stage. It was Jeffrey in his brown corduroy suit with the colorful-ugly bow tie. He, with an unusually uncertain smile, coaxed the mic from her and said, "Okay, friends, we're going to take a short break now. We're currently having technical problems with the sound system. We've prepared complimentary drinks outside. You'll hear the bell when we're ready to resume. Thank you for your understanding."

"What's wrong?" she muttered irritably after he'd turned off the mic and she'd noticed the fine beads of sweat on his forehead.

"I'm very sorry, Doctor Adams." He licked his lips. "You have visitors."

"Visitors?" Now fully confused, she glanced over his shoulder as she noticed his pitiful attempts not to look behind him. Right next to the stage, in the shadows of the spotlights, stood two broadly built men in tailored suits, their hands clasped in front of their hips, looking at her like hawks eyeing their prey. "Who's that?"

"These are Secret Service agents here to see you."

"Secret Service?" she asked, blinking a few times as if the figures in the shadows could disappear like that. "I don't understand. Now?"

"It seemed very urgent—they said I had one minute to get you off the stage or *they* would." The leader of the evening's event wrung his hands apologetically, seeming to wish himself out of his skin, not for the first time.

"It's okay," she assured him, bracing herself with a deep breath. "It's not your fault. I'm sorry you had to interrupt. I'll take care of it and be right back on stage."

With that, she walked past him and toward the two alleged

agents, one of whom raised his wrist to his mouth and then lowered it again.

"Gentlemen?" Melody made it sound like a cool greeting and a question at the same time.

"Agent Smith," one of them introduced himself and pointed to his colleague. "Agent Sokolovsky. Follow us, please, ma'am."

"Might I ask what this is about? In case you haven't noticed, I'm in the middle of a lecture."

"I'm afraid we're not authorized to discuss that with you, ma'am," Smith replied. He looked like a hard man without humor, and he spoke like one. She found no sign of impatience or agitation in his countenance, and yet by mere body tension he managed to give the impression of knocking her unconscious and throwing her over his shoulder at the next rejoinder.

"And," his colleague added from the side, "we wouldn't be able to, anyway. So, if you would follow us?"

Melody looked down at her wristwatch and said, "Five minutes."

Neither man showed any reaction beyond a step to the side and an outstretched hand toward the door next to the stage.

"After you, ma'am."

Reluctantly, she went and pushed open ahead one of the paired doors below the emergency exit sign. She was surprised to see another agent at the outside door, which provided direct access to the parking lot from the sidewalk that led around the hall. The man, who looked like a clone of Smith and Sokolovsky, held the door open with his back, revealing a black SUV in the pelting autumn rain. In the headlights, the drops looked like highly-sped-up particles in an accelerator.

"Uh, could I see your IDs?" she asked. All of a sudden, it all seemed so surreal that she was worried about falling victim

JOSHUA T. CALVERT

to a particularly clever kidnapping or a prank—neither of which were scenarios she was particularly keen on.

A step back made her collide with one of the agents, who turned out to be Smith. It was as if she had crashed into a solid wall. Although she instinctively braced herself for a fight as adrenaline shot out of her adrenal cortexes, he pulled out an ID card and held it up to her face. If it was fake, someone had done a really good job.

"Administrator Rothman is waiting for you, ma'am," Agent Sokolovsky said reproachfully, yet without changing his tone.

Finally, she swallowed and let his colleague at the door escort her to the rear seat with an opened umbrella. She got in, and sure enough, there sat Jim with a massive file folder on his lap and two tablets beside him on the center console. He looked tired and paler than usual, with deep shadows under his eyes.

Melody didn't know whether to be relieved or even more confused. What was Jim doing here? And the Secret Service?

An ironic, "Jim?" was all that came from her mouth, off the top of her head, although a whole torrent of questions was building up inside her, growing with every breath.

"Sorry, Melody," sighed the NASA administrator. "I'm sorry we have to meet like this. I wish I could have just called you."

"I went to the lecture."

"Yes. One book and straight to number one on the New York Times bestseller list." He nodded slowly. "You've earned my respect."

"Then why does it sound like an accusation?" She wasn't looking for an argument, knowing they rarely ended constructively. Still, she found it hard to ignore her hurt, which resided in the pit of her stomach like a creature with a life of its own.

"I marked all the quotes that portrayed my agency as

incompetent, stolid, or backwards. By the end, I had used up two markers."

"That was not my intention, nor was I trying to badmouth NASA... Nor *you*. I merely shared my experiences, which is not forbidden to a former employee," she countered. "Besides, you sidelined me simply because I spoke truthfully about my discovery."

"You put a hypothesis on national television that you knew every tabloid would greedily suck up and spray out like a damn sprinkler!" he roared. "And, just before our final orbital test for the SLS!"

Melody tilted her head in wonder. Jim had never raised his voice in her presence, not even to other employees with whom he'd had no private love affair. He seemed to notice and correctly interpret her look as he sighed and closed his eyes for a moment.

"Sorry," he said, leaning forward and tapping his driver on the shoulder, whereupon the car began to move. Even as she wondered what had become of the agents, she saw headlights behind them and taillights in front. "I'm currently under a lot of pressure and there's no outlet because—"

"Hey!" she interrupted him, spinning around to watch the door to the event center getting smaller behind them, as if she could cling to it with some invisible force. "We can't just leave!"

"Yes, we can," Jim objected, "and we have to. Our plane leaves in thirty minutes."

"Our plane?" she repeated incredulously. Of all things, "How are we going to make it to the airport at this hour?" prevailed among all the candidates.

"We won't be flying out of the airport. We'll be using Dover Air Force Base," Jim replied curtly.

"Would you please tell me what's going on?" That was

undeniably the most important question. Better late than never.

"You were right! *That's* what's going on."

She heard no reluctance in his voice, no shame either, which she credited to him. At the same time, the sober statement seemed extremely anticlimactic after two years in which she had alternately been NASA's pariah, the laughing stock of astronomers and astrophysicists, the bearer of hope in popular science literature, and the shining light of all possible conspiracy theorists. Basically, the situation she had secretly longed for since leaving NASA two years ago had arrived.

"I... honestly don't know what to say."

"How about 'I told you so'? Then you'll have it out of your system."

"No need for that," she replied truthfully. "Can I assume you've made new recordings?"

"Yes. Two months ago, some employees in Hawaii were secretly looking for your 'visitor' during an idle period after maintenance work on Gemini North, and they found it. I didn't catch wind of it at first, probably because those employees weren't sure exactly what they had found."

"Or they were worried about getting fired if they supported an unpopular hypothesis."

Jim grimaced. Outside, the lights of the night rushed past them as they sped eastward along back roads like the diplomatic motorcade of a state guest.

"Whatever their reasons were—according to them, they wanted to go over the data enough times to be positive. It was leaked to me and I immediately overturned the James Webb's usage plan and last night the calculations were done. We now have a high-resolution image of your visitor, whom we internally call Serenity."

"Serenity?" It came out more disapproving than she had intended.

"Browncoats forever." When she merely frowned in response, he sighed and waved it off. "The angle to Earth has changed a lot. Serenity does actually have a tail and it's probably longer than two million kilometers. It's disk-like when viewed from the front, and it's slowing down."

Although she was intending to say, *That's consistent with my suspicions!* she halted the thought and asked, "Wait... The visitor is braking?"

No collision! If the outgassing is still taking place—currently the object should still be well beyond Saturn—it can only be from propulsion.

"It's slowing down," Jim interrupted her galloping mind.

"No natural object flying toward the sun is going to slow down just like that!"

"No." Although he said only one word, it hit her like a blow.

A spaceship! It must actually be a spaceship!

Jim flipped open his file folder to another place and pulled out a picture that he held out to her. It showed an irregularly shaped disk that thickened toward the back and a long, sloping tail that was relatively clearly outlined. Her initial euphoria flattened somewhat as she looked more closely at the surface features. The image was high-resolution considering the distance to the object and its size, but still inferior to a portrait photo from the early days of photography.

"Is that—?"

"Regolith, by the looks of it. An uneven surface, like we would expect on an asteroid," Jim explained, nodding.

Melody sensed quiet disappointment rising within her, but refused to acknowledge it. In the face of findings, it was a good indicator that, as a researcher, one was moving away from pure scientific discovery, and one's own desires and ideas threatened to cloud one's view of the facts.

"Also, you were wrong about one thing," her former lover

continued. "There is no spin and the brightness doesn't shift. At least not anymore."

"So no rotation?" In her mind, one of many ideas she'd been tossing back and forth over the past few years collapsed. No ring habitat of aliens who, like humans, relied on a more or less strong form of gravity. That, too, simply had to be accepted. "Has the object changed its trajectory?"

"We're not sure. *Possibly.* The initial shots weren't informative enough as data." He raised a hand. "Before you ask, based on current calculations, the object will reach Saturn in one year and cross the orbit of Mars four years later. Under normal circumstances, I would have said that a celestial body of this size would approach the sun and then, due to its enormous velocity, fly out of the system on the other side after approaching the sun, once again accelerated by the gravitational sink of our star."

"But these are not normal circumstances." She could just as easily have said, *You've finally realized it,* but that would have been as narrow-minded as it was unconstructive. This was not about being right, but about making an important discovery. Besides, needing to be right was a kind of litmus paper for small-mindedness—a test she chose to spare herself.

"No, they are not." Jim gave her a sidelong glance, and it seemed as if a tentative smile was trying to sneak through his wrinkled worries. He appreciated her gesture, perhaps even saw it as a peace offering.

"Maybe all that regolith is some kind of radiation shield and insulation? Or a buffer against micrometeorites and interstellar gas or dust?"

"We don't know," he replied. "But we intend to find out."

Melody blinked excitedly. She didn't want to say it, as if the mere words might dash her hopes as soon as they crossed her lips. "That means we get more time on the James Webb?"

"Yes, I have all other projects on hold for the time being.

The President read your book and after I informed him that you might be right and we needed to do further research, he instructed me to focus all NASA resources on our visitor except those vital to systems currently in use."

"Okay, that's good. Really good." She gestured vaguely to the front of the car, where the windshield wipers were fighting the masses of water on the windshield. "But why the Secret Service?"

"The president wants to personally brief the public on Serenity, just like he did when we got the first pictures from the James Webb." Jim's voice didn't betray how he felt about that—quite the politician. Then again, maybe his driver was a Secret Service agent and he didn't want to expose himself unnecessarily. "I was at the White House before we met, and he wanted to take me to the Air Force Base."

"But you wanted to take a detour."

"Yes." He nodded, smiling at last. "He didn't agree until I told him I wanted to get you on board—and on the condition that he arrange the ride."

"Thanks, Jim."

"No. Don't thank me. I'd rather you accepted my apology."

"Wait, does that mean I'm about to meet President Brosnahan?"

"You'll even get to ride in Air Force One."

Melody felt transported back a few years to the time when she'd had to watch on television pictures as her colleagues in the next room shook hands with the sitting president. She had been separated by only a wall from that honor, which would have meant a lot to her. What lay ahead of her now was an even greater honor and, by the standards, surreal.

"This is—"

"I know." Jim's smile widened.

"But you'll have to drive me back. Or one of the other cars."

"Excuse me?"

"I have five hundred guests in that event center, all of whom paid to see me give a talk and get their books signed. If my word wasn't worth anything to me, I would have joined the Army instead of the Navy," she tried to joke—after all, he was still a captain in the reserves in the U.S. Army today—but her mind was made up, even though every fiber in her body wanted the cars to keep driving. Still, it wouldn't be right.

"You've done the right thing before," he reminded her with a serious look. She read compassion among other things, even though she didn't want to see it.

"I'll be on the next plane."

2

Melody sat in her seat with her forehead leaning against the window, watching the landscape below her drift by as an abstract carpet of washed-out greens and browns. The Delta Airlines plane had started to descend, and the first contours of vehicles, buildings, and roads were emerging.

She had slept through the past hour, dreaming once again of frozen star panoramas, of the vastness of the vacuum that swallowed everything that was part of the basis of life in the universe. As always she was a part of it, feeling herself from inside without possessing a body. She had always had a penchant for intense dreams, but in the last few months and years since her discovery of the visitor, they had become even stronger. It was probably because since then she had been preoccupied with nothing but this one object that might fly past them from the depths of space.

Sometimes she looked at a deep blue gas giant, and other times at large asteroids, which did not have tails—unlike the visitor. What moved her thoughts back and forth during the day accompanied her through the night, when her brain tried to rearrange itself and free her psyche from unnecessary ballast. It regularly failed to do so, because in the morning she could always remember a lot and was only more motivated to get to the bottom of all her questions.

The only problem was that since the night on Mouna Kea, she had been able to approach her 'problem' almost exclusively theoretically, apart from the little added data from the Japanese. Without NASA's resources, she had become a thinker who had nothing to do with the hands-on former fighter pilot. Now everyone called her Doctor instead of Lieutenant Commander, and suddenly Melody Adams, a physicist, came to the fore. Whether or not this new life between coffee and exhausting thinking phases suited her, she didn't quite know yet. But maybe this problem had just solved itself.

She was still amazed that she had been able to finish yesterday's lecture calmly, without constantly wandering off in her thoughts. She had concluded it must have been the excitement of seeing her hypothesis become even more probable that had put her in high spirits. Her jokes had gone over even better because a new lightness had been inherent in them. She had gone through the next chapters of her remarks with clarity and stringency, taking more time to answer questions, not even feeling the need to point out her new findings. No fantasy about saying, in front of 500 spellbound pairs of eyes, that they were finally taking her seriously. There had been only her, her talk, and the guests who had patiently waited out the overlong 'break.'

Just before she had finished her presentation with her closing remarks, Jeffrey had come on stage to show the audience a 'crowning surprise.' He had then put CNN on the big screen, opening right into the beginning of a statement by President Ron Brosnahan, who just four years prior had been governor of Florida and was on the verge of re-election. He was behind a NASA lectern with the Presidential Seal flag and a U.S. flag in the background, flanked by Jim, while the other side was empty. Melody wondered if the empty seat had been for her. Every politician loved big photo ops, and she certainly would have fit perfectly into the announcement with her newfound celebrity status. She hoped that Jim hadn't had to endure too much trouble for not bringing her along.

She no longer remembered the president's exact words. The evening had lasted too long, and too much had hit her at once. But the quintessence had remained: NASA had confirmed, with the help of the new James Webb telescope, that a possibly extraterrestrial object with a significant likelihood of artificial origin was passing through our solar system. He even mentioned her name, albeit only in an aside as he highlighted the accomplishments of NASA and key American researchers—including her, without elaborating.

There followed the usual self-congratulation for his decisions and the work of his administration, as any political leader did in situations like this. The election campaign was not over yet, and a statement of such magnitude was a ready-made meal for any campaign team. In the end, however, things got exciting again when Brosnahan announced that he would make this matter a top priority and get to the bottom of 'the visitor.' It had not escaped her notice that he was repeating the name she had launched for the object.

After landing at Houston's George Bush Intercontinental Airport, she took a cab to the JSC. She would have been picked up, too, had she asked for it, but she didn't want to make a fuss or act like a VIP. No longer was her hypothesis merely that—a hypothesis. It had become more probable, had morphed from a well-founded possibility to the most realistic explanation for a new kind of celestial body, but it still wasn't proof. Until then, she shied away from too great an outburst of emotion, although more than once she would have liked to erupt into loud cheers.

Arriving at the JSC and making her way along one of the

many hallways on the way to Jim's office, she met Greg Rogers, her former colleague from the replacement crew for Dragon-6. A bearish man in his 40s, he looked like a hooligan with glasses but was one of the most intelligent and amiable astronauts she had ever met.

Astronaut candidate, she corrected herself with a suppressed sigh.

"Good to see you, Mel," he said with a smile after they broke away from a warm hug. "I didn't think I'd see you here again."

"Neither did I," she confessed, dodging a throng of young employees hurriedly streaming past them with tablets in their hands and buttons in their ears. "But it feels good."

"I'm sorry about how things went down back then."

She waved it off. "It's not your fault. Besides, if it hadn't gone that way, I never would have found time to sort out my thoughts, get the data together with the Japanese, and write a book."

"Congratulations on that," Greg said with honest appreciation. "I read it and it's very accurately and entertainingly presented. You didn't even take a real sideswipe at NASA, although I would have understood."

"Thank you. That means a lot to me."

He pulled her a little to the side and lowered his voice before continuing. "I would have understood. What they did to you then was not okay. They almost ruined your reputation."

"You mean Jim."

Greg gave a meaningful shrug of his shoulders.

"Yes, maybe. But it turned out differently, didn't it?" she said lightly.

"Typical Mel," he replied with a grin, giving her another squeeze. "Always optimistic, always more forgiving than the others deserve. It's good to have you back. Don't let me get to you!"

"I won't," she promised, and continued on her way to Jim's office. The hallways at JSC were positively vibrating with activity instead of the typical professional quiet. It seemed as if the staff of 14,000 had doubled overnight. She wanted too much to believe that they were all busy adjusting to the visitor, Serenity, reading her book to learn more about it. But of course, this was related to the visit by the president, who had just left. A flying visit from the most powerful person in the world meant a rat's tail of tasks that had to be worked through in quick succession, cutting into the workday of almost every single employee like an axe. At least for one day.

Jim wasn't in his office, so she waited in the secretary's office and scrolled through the news feeds on her smartphone. As it was, Brosnahan's statement, along with Jim's subsequent remarks, had been picked up by the media across the board, but they hadn't become the big hook she had expected. One more sign that she should rein in her wishful thinking. In her head, she was already calculating the funds needed to launch a mission that would put a rover on Serenity. She came out at such large sums that they would need more than a few media reports to get Congress to tune in. She didn't know what she expected, but probably something more than semi-mocking articles that insinuated that the President was now bringing in little green men to win the election for him. Others wondered if it was all a tactic by NASA to win back one of its now highly popular former employees, or would it be like Oumuamua a few years earlier, when the excitement over an alleged extra-solar object had turned out to be researcher hysteria.

"Mel," a familiar voice greeted her, tearing her away from her smartphone.

"Ah, Jim." She stood up, cast a sidelong glance at his secretary, and then formally held out her hand to him. He shook it and pointed to his office. "Please, after you."

"Thank you."

As she took a seat in the same chair as when they had last seen each other before he released her over the phone, she felt like a student at the principal's office after breaking a rule.

"Are you all right?" he asked, putting his bag down and dropping into his office chair like a wet sack.

"Last time you sent me to Andrea for the press release and gave me free rein," she replied, shaking her head. "What happened after that, we both know."

"You've brought public attention to a pipe dream during the most important phase of the most important and expensive project since the moon landing."

"A *pipe dream*?" she echoed with raised eyebrows.

"At the time, I thought it was," he reluctantly relented. "Nevertheless, you knew how hard everyone here worked to make the most powerful rocket in our agency's history a success. And public awareness is as important to that as firing the rocket engines. It's Congress, in the end, that appropriates our funds, and its members, well, they have to get approval in their constituencies."

"I never intended to torpedo the SLS project. I was invited and merely said what I thought about my discovery at the time —and still think today."

"I never authorized that, and I wouldn't have. If you had come to me, we could have talked about anything, but you had to go ahead."

"Maybe I should have, but you were unavailable. Jim. In the end, it wasn't my fault that the SLS blew up, even though you took your anger out on me."

Jim looked like he was having a fainting spell and sank back in his chair as the memory caught up with him. The television images had been traumatic for the entire nation, not least because they had been reminiscent of the Challenger disaster, even though no one but a payload consisting of rocks had been on board.

"SpaceX had won the race with Starship. The SLS was dead even before the test flight was announced. Two billion dollars per launch? No reusability of the first stage and boosters? We should have relied on our partners at Hawthorne from the beginning, and at least that way the decision was taken away from you," she reflexively tried to build him up. She searched for the anger that she had suppressed for two years, but now that he was vulnerable, she merely felt sorry for him. She wouldn't have wanted to trade places with him. "You always said you hated going to Washington as a supplicant and having to make lazy compromises with people who have no idea about the things we do here. Now at least they've taken away a money grab from you that had no future anyway."

"It's not that simple. Our reputation is at stake. If we just let the private sector do everything in the future, we'll make ourselves untrustworthy." Jim rubbed his hands over his face and sighed before shaking his head. "That's not important right now, though. We may disagree on the matter, but certainly not on the fact that we need to prepare everything to better investigate Serenity."

"What were you thinking of?" In her mind she exclaimed, *A rover mission!*

"First of all, we need to get together with our partners in Europe and Asia to put all eyes and ears on the object and find out as much as we can. Then I'll go back to the president with that data and use it to supply him with ammunition for his new weapon. With a little luck and a solid majority for him in both chambers, we might even be able to get enough funding together for a rover mission after the election."

Melody didn't even try to hide her grin. This was exciting.

"I'd be lying if I said I didn't care," she said pointedly calm.

"I'll hire you back if that's what you want," Jim spoke freely.

"I belong here, you know that. I always have. *Lieutenant Commander* Adams will forever belong to the Navy, but *Doctor* Adams is a child of NASA."

"Why do I hear a 'but' in there somewhere?"

"I want a ten-year contract with guaranteed employment and no leaves of absence, as long as I don't violate my employment contract or the right of direction," she demanded.

"Ten years?"

"Surely it will take at least that long for Serenity to fly past the sun and become unreachable."

Jim leaned back like an exhausted athlete and nodded slowly.

"Hmm, I think I can do that."

"Besides, I want a front-row seat, and for that I will always have my brightest smile ready for the cameras."

He raised a brow questioningly.

"I know you need me to be a figurehead for the media, too, first and foremost. I'm now the all-knowing human face of our visitor, and that's what you want in your arsenal when it comes to wielding public opinion as a weapon against Congress."

She raised her hands like a shield to dissuade him from a friendly but feigned denial. She was eager to spare them both that charade. "That's fine with me. I'm pragmatically inclined enough to see the need for it. I'll do my best to move this project forward, and I'll coordinate every interview with you beforehand. I want to have a front-row seat for this. I think I've earned that."

"How does 'Deputy Project Manager with a view to Mission Control in the event of a solar mission' sound to you?" asked Jim after a brief pause for thought, during which he knotted his fingers as if they formed a puzzle that he solved one by one until he finally disentangled them.

"That..." Melody thought about it and swallowed her disappointment that she would only be Deputy Project Manager. On the other hand, she was sure that this post was the maximum he could offer her. After all, she had not been part of the space agency for two years and had previously been parked in an outside position in preparation for higher management after failing to gain her astronaut pin because someone else had been chosen over her. The leadership would surely have caused a political earthquake within NASA, passing over someone who would feel at least as bad in the process as she did when she'd had to watch her comrades turn their dream into reality. It would not be fair, nor a position in which she could feel comfortable. She had to hand it to him. Jim once again showed himself to be a prudent politician and manager.

"That is generous, thank you."

"Does that make us even?" he asked, making it sound casual. She knew he meant more than just their professional differences, which had led to two years of radio silence.

"Yes, it does." She nodded, seeking his gaze to let him know she meant their then-abandoned private relationship. There were no shards that hadn't been swept up.

"Good. Then welcome back to the team, Doctor Adams," he said lightly, as if nothing had happened, standing up and extending his hand across the table to her. When she took it, he added, "Congratulations on your promotion. Starting today, you won't have much free time, but you'll be working on the most exciting space project since the moon landing. That is, if Serenity doesn't turn out to be a natural phenomenon in the end."

"I put the probability of that at thirty percent," she

responded, assuring him that she had not lost her sense of reality.

He seemed to appreciate it because his lips parted into a smile. "You start tomorrow. If you don't want to fall right into bed, the Outpost has reopened. As far as I know, you still have an open beer coaster there."

Now it was her turn to smile.

3

In the weeks that followed, she spent nearly every evening at the Outpost. The now ancient pub was located on Clear Lake, just outside the JSC, and had been the 'watering hole' of astronauts and Mission Control personnel since the 1960s. Having shut down once before in the 2000s, it had closed again in 2010—at least officially. Naomi, the owner-operator when Melody had been in astronaut training, had taken it upon herself to open privately for them every now and then.

The small, stuffy interior with its ugly old wood paneling smelled of tradition, if you wanted to put it politely, and was crammed with memorabilia. Hanging from the ceiling was a copy of the A7L, NASA's first spacesuit for the early Apollo missions. Insignias and pictures of past projects—most notably the moon landing—claimed every available space on the wood paneling, and countless notches in the wooden tables were the scars of various traditions and quirks of each year's space travelers over the six decades. In short, it was an ugly pub that breathed history and, through its grounding simplicity, had always been an anchor point for those whose gaze was directed skyward.

First and foremost, Mel enjoyed coming down from the Johnson Space Center site after 12 hours of work and, over a beer or two, forgetting everything that had flooded her mind during the day. That's how most of the people here felt who weren't busy with Dragon-21, the current ISS mission. Jim hadn't lied and was committing massive resources to her project—it was in fact Richard Woolsey's project, and she was his deputy. But Woolsey was much more charming facilitator than domineering technical idiot, as she would have expected.

Woolsey was a good project manager because he could smoothly link the areas involved and resolve conflicts quickly by having an open door and being able to elicit cooperation to reconcile different points of view without anyone feeling slighted. However, he bought this outcome with a type of frenzied monitoring that enabled him to see and evaluate all threads of the project at all times, and this often made her work exhausting. Sometimes she felt like a student who had the teacher constantly looking over her shoulder during a written exam.

That fact brought to mind the second good argument for the Outpost. Woolsey never came here—he lived in his office, so to speak.

"Hey," she was greeted one night in her third month—she thought it was a Monday—just as she sat at the bar half asleep. It was Greg who'd come up beside her and pointed questioningly at the empty barstool next to her. "Up this late?"

Melody blinked herself awake and looked down at her wristwatch, yawning. It was after two, meaning it was Tuesday and explaining why there was an empty barstool. The noise level was still oppressive, chasing away the many thoughts in her head of space telescope rotation periods, orbital mechanics calculations of how the inner planets would likely affect Serenity's orbit, and thousands of notes for her dwindling but never-ending interviews with television and newspapers.

"Yeah." She cleared her throat and tapped her empty beer bottle, whereupon Nancy on the other side nodded as she passed, and twirled to set another one down for her as if she were a dancer. Melody wanted to leave, but Greg looked like he could use an ear, so she obliged. "All I have waiting for me at home are everyday chores that I haven't had time to do in a long time."

"I understand. Your project multiplies by its own weight, it seems, every week." Greg accepted his beer and they toasted. After the first sip, he sighed contentedly and nodded, as if answering a silent question. "I'm really close now, you know?"

"Dragon-22?"

"Mm-hmm," he hummed, seeming unsettled all at once.

"Don't worry, I'm not jealous. I'm happy for you."

"Thanks. I didn't know if I should tell you, but you probably would have found out anyway. To me, it feels like a bit of a betrayal because at the time we shared our grief about not being nominated as a shared secret that somehow connected us. You know what I mean, right?"

"Oh yes," she assured him, and her gaze drifted to the past —a past of brief but fierce grief that felt at once like failure and betrayal.

Finally, she shook her head. "That was once upon a time, Greg. Now, I wouldn't want it. Serenity has become something like the Holy Grail for me. I don't know if I wanted it that way, but since my book and the President's quasi-backing, I've become his face, his 'brand' so to speak. Everyone who thinks of our visitor thinks of me in the next breath. Brosnahan's mention of me has given my book another boost that has my agent all spinning."

"Are you a multi-millionaire yet?" asked Greg with a grin. There was no envy in that either.

"I think so." Melody shrugged. "I don't take time to look

at my bank account. It doesn't matter, either, because I wouldn't have time to spend the money."

"Are you making progress yet?"

"Serenity *is* slowing down; we've figured that much out. The only question is at what rate, and we're not sure of that yet. But through the interconnected efforts of ourselves and our many partners around the world, we're pretty confident in saying that the braking rate is constant."

"But the object didn't turn, did it? Wouldn't it have to turn if it was a spacecraft? So that propulsion and thus braking force would point in the opposite direction to the previous acceleration direction?"

"Arrrgh," she growled. "It should, yes. But it doesn't. Why?" She shrugged. "I really don't know. But, I want to find out, that's for sure. What's worse is that the current course would cause Serenity to collide with Saturn. That's what gives me the biggest headache. If that were to happen, it would be lost, whatever it is."

"Saturn has only a tiny rocky core," Greg stated after setting down his beer. "Maybe your friend is just flying through the endless layers of molecular hydrogen?"

"I guess it depends on its speed, but you know what would happen then. For that to happen, Serenity would have to be very, very slow so that the collision damage wouldn't be too great, and then again Saturn wouldn't let it escape its gravitational sink. It remains a mystery."

Greg glanced at the clock above the liquor shelf, which was crammed with far too many rocket models, and his expression darkened. "Bernard's going to be here any minute. I thought you'd want know."

Melody stiffened and gulped.

"Thanks," she mumbled, rummaging in her pants pockets but finding nothing. So she tapped her beer mat, signaled to Nancy who snagged both of their empties, and then patted

Greg on the shoulder. He was the closest thing she had to a friend. During astronaut training, the candidates were adversaries most of the time, even though they tried to mask that fact. But in the end, very few, a handful at most, were going to get to the finish line. That changed their ability to make friends. "I need to go to bed now."

Greg nodded sympathetically but did not look at her. "I know. Good night."

She walked hurriedly out, pushing her way through a group of drunken colleagues, most of whom were astronauts trying their hand at a game of darts in which each of them would lose, and then stood in the large gravel parking lot in the light of the flickering streetlights. As the door slammed shut behind her, the mixture of country music, laughter, loud conversations, and clinking bottles ceased, as though she'd been swallowed by a black hole.

"Hello, Bernard," she said, grateful that her voice didn't sound stressed as she greeted the gray-haired colonel who was walking toward her—or rather the entrance to the Outpost—with two friends.

"Hello, Melody." His expression betrayed fright, which quickly gave way to a mask of politeness. "I haven't seen you here in a while."

"I usually leave early. Always have to go on watch in the morning."

Bernard smiled politely and nodded. "Too bad, I would have liked to talk to you more often."

"Me too," she lied.

"Another time!"

"Another time," she agreed, and an awkward silence spread between them until he cleared his throat and stepped aside and they nodded to each other.

"Until then."

"See you one of these days." She quickly walked to her car,

biting her lower lip. It shouldn't feel so strange to run into him. Not after all this time. And yet the pain was still there where it had lived all these years, buried deep in her guts, lurking in wait for weak moments like a predator that refused to be driven away.

4

On the one hand, the months leading up to Project Serenity's most important day to date flew by as Melody worked so much that she lost all sense of time. On the other hand, the flow of days and weeks was like tough resin that penetrated every aspect of her life and seemed to slow everything down. In the mornings, she worked in her office, going over everything Woolsey couldn't or wouldn't handle—including permit documents, personnel requests, or signing off on accounting invoices—and hating every minute of it.

She wasn't made for deskwork, and had always loathed positions like this because they led into a side stream that took her away from what was happening. At the same time, she was situated at a hub. Although the accounting documents in particular only had to be signed pro forma—without her reviewing them in detail—she was picking up enough of what was going on in each area to be able to piece together an overall picture. So the mornings were the price she had to pay to fully survey and comprehend the presumed project of a lifetime. And *that* she did: The costs were still manageable thus far, considering that tens of planning teams were working on project designs for a probe that might never get the green light —at least not if what everyone feared would happen today did, in fact, happen.

Except for her, of course. She was too preoccupied with this celestial body to tolerate the thought of it crashing into Saturn today and fizzling out. Her reputation and that of her book were secondary to her, but the idea of never knowing whether she was right—that it truly was an extraterrestrial flyby —was *not* secondary. She was 'all in,' so to speak, and could not afford an abrupt end to this chapter.

Her afternoons were spent at Mission Control, which was still assigned primarily to the ISS missions and to the regular Dragon launches, but where SpaceX took over most of the hands-on control of the missions, and they were merely support. They used the free space that Woolsey and they had organized to coordinate the various telescopes, 30 of which were Earth-based and 20 of which were space-based, permanently pointed at Serenity. On this day, however, Mission Control for the ISS fell to their colleagues at ESOC, ESA's European Space Operations Center in Darmstadt, Germany. Here in Houston, everything was focused on a single object.

The evenings belonged to the press, although the interviews had flattened out considerably after the initial media euphoria about little green men. By now, it wasn't even the second tier of media who interviewed her via Zoom or in one of the unadorned press rooms at JSC. But she had agreed with Woolsey that even without much public interest, she should continue to stay visible, even if only a little. For her, it turned out to be good practice that led to her becoming more comfortable in front of cameras, or at least no longer uncomfortable. The measure had shrunk by which she deemed herself as having been made for tasks other than interviews.

But now here she was, on the 367th day of her re-employment at NASA, which many colleagues had christened 'Dooms-day' once Serenity stopped braking. Since then, the celestial body had been traveling at a little less than 16,000 kilometers per hour, which isn't particularly fast in cosmic terms, but it was danger-ous. It wasn't fast enough to pass Saturn, but it wasn't slow enough to enter orbit, either, at least not on its current trajectory. Three weeks ago, when they had noticed that their object had settled into a steady velocity, bets had been placed at the Outpost by having each guest toss a crown cap into one of two jars. One was labeled 'Trick' and one was labeled 'Treat' because the day happened to coincide with Halloween. Both were still there now, 'Trick' twice as full as its sister jar for the optimists. Unfortu-nately, mathematics proved the pessimists right.

So Melody, like everyone else with Mission Control clear-ance, stood in the control room, deep in the heart of JSC, hoping for candy and dreading sour grapes. She was reluctant to acknowledge the calculations that predicted a 91.3 percent probability of a crash on Saturn, so she rudely pushed her rational self aside. She banished it to the periphery of her perception.

Mission Control had been overhauled several times in its history. On the front wall was an oversized display showing a picture of Serenity that came closest to what they considered a live image: a dark object whose backward-drawn disk shape was recognizable with some imagination, plus the tail, which had become noticeably shorter and had shrunk to a few kilo-meters instead of several hundred thousand kilometers in length—another puzzle for them. Normally, an object with a recoil plume should accelerate, i.e. increase speed, and one without a recoil plume should drift, or continue to glide at the same speed. But even this did not seem to interest their visitor. Even the color of the suspected exhaust flare had changed and its brightness had decreased significantly. Saturn with its many thousands of rings was already a mighty shadow on the left side.

The main screen was bracketed by a pair of equally large screens, all three close together, displaying various vector calculations of the object's trajectory and infrared data in curve diagrams, along with time data and, on the far left, the sinusoidal flight patterns of the ISS, which also needed further attention. The workstations were painted elephant gray with monitors arranged side by side and on top of each other, with all the shifts sitting close together in front of them. On the walls to both sides, above the large framed pictures of previous shuttle launches and EVAs, hung the logos of the various ISS expeditions, all of which had been directed from here.

Melody stood in the back row behind the ground control desk, adjusted her headset for the third or fourth time as if it were a compulsive act, and turned to face the gallery, the viewing area behind her, which was packed with colleagues who had no assignments and no access to Mission Control. Ironically, standing with them was Woolsey, who had put her in charge for the morning. He didn't seem to notice her, however, seeming preoccupied with his thoughts.

"He's nervous," said Jim, who had just arrived and had her hand him a headset.

"Who isn't?"

"Whatever is about to happen, it's not the end," he assured her, but it was a feeble attempt at encouragement. "We have enough data to analyze for the next ten years and exciting details to learn."

Melody nodded absently, trying to disengage from the subdued atmosphere that was stretched to the breaking point in the suddenly cramped room. It had taken most of her colleagues a long time to come to terms with the idea that Serenity might in truth be an extraterrestrial object—be it a wantonly accelerated asteroid, an oversized probe, or a real spaceship. But they had become comfortable with it, and consequently hopeful that they might be involved in exploring humanity's single most important discovery. No one would have said this aloud because the residual doubts were still too great, but she could feel how close to the surface these thoughts had come.

"All right, Optical Control, status report," she spoke into her headset as the countdown read one hour and twenty minutes.

"Space telescopes green, alignment correct and constant," came the reply directly in her ear.

"Eyes on the ground open and awake," Gina reported from further forward. Her shock of red hair was impossible to miss, despite the glaring monitors in front of her.

"All right, folks. For the next six minutes, everything better be online and showing no error messages. After that, it's wait and see and keep the data stores clear."

Melody turned off her headset and gave Jim a sidelong glance. He'd put on some weight and looked like an aging detective, the way he held his hands on his hips, pushing his jacket back as if his stomach were on exhibit. "One hour and fourteen minutes," she said softly.

"Excuse me?"

"Saturn is one point three billion kilometers away at its current relative position to us—heavily rounded," she explained casually, knowing he knew it himself, but she couldn't stand there silently while her life's work lay on the chopping block.

"Ah, of course," he replied, nodding absently.

"That's one light-hour and fourteen light minutes. We'll have to wait that long." Melody had always been fascinated by the distances in space, where her mind never seemed to know how to deal with the numbers. Even the solar system, the cosmic 'neighborhood' was so empty that if you recreated it to scale with marbles in a meadow, you wouldn't be able to see it with the naked eye if you stood at the position of the sun. Saturn was the sixth of eight planets in the solar system and its light still took over an hour to reach them. In two minutes, Serenity would crash into the gas giant—no, it wouldn't—but they wouldn't see it until an hour and fourteen minutes later. It would be a glimpse into the past, because distance and time merged through the speed-of-light barrier.

When the countdown reached the last two minutes and the color of the remaining time changed from green to red, the color shift hit her like a punch in the stomach. In her mind, the film of a giant comet inevitably played, looking like a speck in front of the hydrogen giant and smashing into it like an insect into a truck's windshield. Left behind were swirls on Saturn's outer shell, a tumultuous mixture of frozen ammonia crystals and methane molecules in constant photolysis. They raged in an eternal chemical process around dense clouds of hydrogen and ammonia, driven by deeper heat.

Even though Saturn had no solid shell, no surface, Serenity had no chance. It was not a crash into absorbent cotton, but one into Hell. With its more than one hundred Earth masses, Saturn's gravity was so powerful that there was only one way for the celestial body to go: directly toward the solid core of iron and rock, still much larger than Earth and much more compressed. Not that any object could have reached it intact. Unimaginable pressure and heat equal to the outermost layers of the sun would have crushed, melted, and vaporized Serenity long before an impact with the core.

But not in her mind. There was an error in their calculations, something they had overlooked. There had to be.

"Are you all right?" Jim asked. An eerie silence had settled over the control room, interrupted now and then by the muffled voices of the engineers and scientists who were on radio duty and coordinating the many sites involved. The faultless functioning of all instruments had to be meticulously monitored.

"Yes. Sweet."

"Excuse me?"

She shook her head. "Serenity didn't crash."

"From your mouth to God's ear." He gave her a pitying look that triggered a pang of anger somewhere inside her, which she immediately pushed aside. Not because she didn't want to be pitied—although that was the case, but it didn't bother her—but because it showed that he feared failure.

"I mean, think about it—" She interrupted herself and stared through him.

"What is it?"

Instead of answering him, she turned on her headset and addressed all the staff present in the control room.

"Whatever is going through all of your minds right now, think about what is happening here. An extrasolar object, which we have classified with significant probability as artificial, comes flying into the solar system at high thrust, passes close by Neptune, apparently unaffected by its gravitational field, and decelerates beyond the orbit of Uranus, on a direct course for Saturn. It must have been precisely aligning its course for a long time to hit this gas giant, of all things. Coincidence is so unlikely that it can be ruled out. What civilization would be able to create a wonder like this object, but not have navigational computers to prevent a collision with a planet?" She didn't expect a response or reaction, yet was surprised when they failed to materialize. Although many turned to her and appeared thoughtful after her speech, no one said anything.

Hope was no longer widespread, although in this case it was logical, she thought.

For the rest of the hour, she focused on her tasks, which were to keep track of the various work areas and make sure they communicated correctly with each other, and to be there when decisions needed to be made. It helped her a little to suppress the uncomfortable excitement that accompanied her as it progressed. The last five minutes of the countdown were the most unbearable. She counted the seconds and time stretched like chewing gum.

When it was almost over, she made the mistake of turning to look at the visitors. Among the hundred or more faces, her eyes fell on Bernard, of all people, who held his folded hands in front of his mouth like a praying man. When his eyes met hers, there was the usual friendliness in them before he seemed to notice and quickly looked away.

"What is it with Bernard and you, anyway? Did he ever do anything to you?" asked Jim, obviously trying to make conversation to dispel his agitation. Everyone had their own strategies.

Melody thought about the question, then shook her head. "No, never."

"Webb has the first images!" announced Dr. Rishnak of James Webb Control, and the silence grew more oppressive.

Saturn was visible on the main screen, illuminated by the sun. A sand-colored ball with hints of lighter and darker stripes and a small black eye on the northern hemisphere, it looked almost still, as the storm bands were not recognizable as such. The many thousands of rings were so close together that they looked like a handful of individual ones. To Melody, they reminded her of a brown-colored LP record that had been cut out in the middle to hold a soccer ball glued in with sand.

There was no sign of Serenity, but that was to be expected. The computers calculated the images of the last few minutes and then combined them into a sequence that would look like a live image. Because of the exposure time required, the telescope could not take video, only images at painfully long intervals of over 20 seconds. It could have been called the most expensive flipbook of all time.

"Play it as soon as the computers are done," she ordered, resisting the urge to see the last image before the current one of Saturn. Another agonizing five minutes later, it was time.

To the right of Saturn, Serenity appeared again, the small round shadow with the pale cotton tail. Melody's heart leapt as if the object had been dead and reborn. But it was merely a glimpse of the past. She wondered if it would not have been better if they had continued to follow the images 'live,' instead of making a calculation at the end of the existing footage and making a fluid representation out of it. But this way it was more accurate because they could check each image and its data twice, making sure that no errors crept in.

Their 'visitor' continued to fly toward Saturn, slightly choppy, but almost fluid. The programs had done a good job of filling in the gaps. She thought the tail was changing slightly, getting a little darker, paler, but it could also be because Serenity was entering Saturn's shadow. It pierced one of the rings like a whale swimming through a school of krill. In her mind, she imagined what it must look like up close, with all the ice crystals and dust particles being displaced by the giant object and moving in all directions, creating something like a short-lived coma in front of it.

Because of the very shallow angle of entry, Serenity stayed in the rings for a long time before emerging from them and hurtling toward Saturn. Although it looked downright leisurely on the huge display, the speeds were dizzying by terrestrial standards. Before the edges of the two celestial bodies touched—they were separated by perhaps three or four pixels, if that—Serenity simply disappeared.

"What happened there?" she demanded.

"The object has entered Saturn's shadow and is no longer optically visible," someone—she didn't know who—reported.

Blood rushed in her ears. Of course, she should have known. Without light, there was no image.

"Infrared still senses the tail, but faintly."

"It's gone," someone else said. "Serenity has crashed."

"I'm sorry, Mel," Jim said beside her, as if she had just lost a family member.

"We don't know," she muttered. "We don't know for sure."

"Nothing just flies through Saturn."

"No, but it could have flown past it. Behind it, in the shadows," she insisted.

Jim's gaze looked pained as he regarded her.

"You know it's true!" She extended a hand and pointed to Saturn, now emblazoned lonely and terrifyingly beautiful on the main screen. "It's possible."

"It's *virtually* impossible."

"Just like Serenity's existence." Melody knew she sounded defiant. She didn't care. Into her headset she said, "Realignment from the James Webb. It's not over yet. There's a chance Serenity will pass Saturn on the back side."

Murmurs arose, but they were muffled and isolated. A few employees turned to her furtively, but she ignored them. It was clear to her what their glances would say. Behind her, the visitor's area emptied as if they had been spectators at a hotly anticipated Super Bowl game that had ended abruptly with a horrific injury to their favorite player.

They should go quietly.

An hour later, the spectators were long gone and Woolsey had ordered more of the workstations to refocus on the ISS, where work had been curtailed by the current project for the duration of the Saturn observations.

Serenity did not return. Did not appear from behind Saturn. Did not reappear… and her heart sank.

Jim's hand on her shoulder felt heavy. "I'm sorry. I'm really sorry, Mel," he repeated. "It's over."

Since she said nothing and just stood there silently, he gently took the headset from her. She did not resist. He held the microphone to his mouth, "All right, I know today is not our best day, but we're moving on. Everyone who is not busy with the current ISS expedition or preparations for Dragon-22 can call it a day now. Thank you for your great work. You can't always win, but we still have astronauts out there and programs like Artemis that require our full attention. The future of spaceflight is still exciting. Thank you all."

Melody didn't even process what he was saying as she dropped into her chair and stared into nothingness.

5

THREE YEARS EARLIER …

Her body felt like one sore muscle from her toes to the tips of her hair. She had never thought she could feel the ends of her hair, but today she had apparently discovered receptors there —perhaps the first human, a curiosity for any biologist.

In truth, the last few weeks of stress tests and repeatedly inserted training sessions had been the limit of what she was capable of enduring. She had prepared less than the 11 other candidates for the Dragon-6 seat, at least in terms of physical fitness. Melody's father had gotten her interested in running at an early age, and later in the Navy she had spent a lot of time in the gym—more even than was required for her as a fighter pilot. During tough g-maneuvers, every muscle paid off in double dividends.

So she had decided to prepare herself primarily for the theoretical tests, despite being slightly below her peak physical condition. As a physicist, she was confident that she was capable of quickly perceiving science and technology, especially since she'd had to know about all the systems in the fighter jet, and had learned early on how to familiarize herself with complex information systems. The years of selection for

NASA's astronaut corps had shown her that it was another very big step from there to the best of America's best, who actually got to pilot a spaceship worth hundreds of millions of dollars, or play around in a vacuum aboard one of the world's most expensive structures.

If there was one thing she had come to realize in all that time, it was that there was no one here who didn't belong. She was among the top 12 men and women in the country, out of more than 12,000 applicants. She had spent two years on a variety of tasks with her peers who eventually made it into the real training in Houston. She needed the ability to concentrate, a quick mind, technical understanding and skill, strong nerves, an absolute and unwavering willingness to cooperate, calm, rational decision-making skills even under great stress, and perfect health and fitness.

It would have been easy to fall prey to the idea that they and their comrades in training had become close friends as a result of the great challenges, but that was not the case. Everyone was aware that in the end only two of them would remain, two who would launch into space on schedule and call themselves 'astronauts.' They were nice to each other and cooperated with each other, probably because they had been chosen for just such standards during the selection procedures.

But in each exercise, it was clear that they were individually focused on doing their best and giving their all to leave ten others behind. Melody had experience with this. In many ways the process resembled her long road to the cockpit of a Navy F-18. However, she had left all that behind—her officer career in the military, a well-paid and long-held dream for her, trading it for the vague chance to someday see the Earth from above and move humanity forward instead of preparing for war. Later today it would be determined if it had been worth it, or if she would be relegated to the second row. Being part of the astronaut corps without a silver pin was probably a lot like being a benchwarmer athlete who couldn't be fired or traded because of their contract.

Now she was sitting in this stuffy little room with 12 tables and chairs where she and the other candidates had been seated at the end of two exhausting years that had flown by and, at the same time, felt like their whole, entire lives. It was a test with a mixture of mathematical and technical questions. The former related primarily to ad hoc algebra and geometry, the latter to specific emergencies in a Dragon capsule that she had not yet been presented with in training. They read strangely in the extreme, as if they were not very realistic, but she had to solve them regardless. Like each of the others, she was using a specially prepared original display set that SpaceX had made available for training purposes a year ago.

The emergencies were set so that none of them were trying to solve the same problem at the same time—at least that's what she thought after a few sideways glances. Greg next to her kept thinking briefly and then making his entries—well aware that they were under time pressure. The fact that it was getting increasingly stuffy in the small room, which seemed to have no ventilation, was certainly part of the exercise. A simulated lack of oxygen in the Dragon? A problem with the supply to the suit? In any case, it didn't make things any easier that her muscles were burning like fire from the previous days' fitness tests, and she was sweating, *and* it felt like she couldn't get enough air to think clearly.

Bernard, on the other side of her, seemed to keep talking to himself, muttering unintelligibly and then making rapid gestures across the displays like a driven man.

I guess everyone has their own unique way of dealing with stressful situations, she thought.

After an hour, the first of her fellow candidates had left the room, and she knew that they had solved their tasks faster. However, this did not impress her. She didn't believe that there was a 'right' solution for every emergency, or a set speed for finding it. *Rushing* had certainly never helped any astronauts.

At some point, Bernard and she were the last, although that didn't mean much since the other ten had left them within the past 11 minutes. He cast steady glances over his shoulder at her, still spending a lot of time muttering to himself.

Then something fell on the floor next to him, a slight movement that caught Melody's attention. She leaned slightly to the side and saw what looked like a tiny plug. He bent down quickly and picked it up, and their eyes met. There was understanding in his eyes and the startled fear of having been caught. She knew immediately that it was a stud mic, and he knew that she knew.

For the last task, she was confused and had to try harder than before to stay focused. Later, when they were all sitting in the meeting room and Bernard had taken first place because he had solved all the problems as intended, their eyes met again. She said nothing. Second place went to Janet, a geologist from Massachusetts whom she had found to be extremely intelligent and friendly.

Melody was third, which the new administrator, James Rothman, told her with undisguised sympathy. He also assured her that it had been extremely close. She glanced at Bernard, who appeared as if he were facing a guillotine. But she remained silent and swallowed what she might have said. It was not up to her to make others win fairly or to tattle on them. It was only up to her to do her best, even though she felt as if someone had just pulled the rug out from under her.

6

Melody was dreaming. It was the kind of dream that had been recurring since her astronaut training seven years ago, unless she was too exhausted and the dream skipped the night as if she were dead. This knowledge made her aware that she was dreaming, trapped in the processing spheres of her brain, which was re-sorting itself to put it all together.

This time she was hovering over Saturn, which she immediately recognized by its brown rings. But they were not just brown, they were fine-grained and had a depth that she knew reached a hundred meters and more. She felt every single grain of dust, every ice crystal, even those of the veiled outermost ring. She detected the tiny frozen water molecules ejected from the middle icy moon, Enceladus, spewing from its powerful cryovolcanoes and escaping its low gravitational pull. But these fountains also contained heavier compounds such as silicates and carbon dioxide and traces of ammonia. She simply knew they were there, felt their existence without consciously thinking about their names or their molecular structures. They had no name, were simply what they were, and the process of chemical-physical understanding happened by itself, effortless and self-evident in its wonderful complexity, as it could only be in dreams.

She approached Saturn, which was brown and massive, but also colorless and much more complex than in reality. Its vast cloud bands of ammonia and molecular hydrogen, which made up most of its total mass, wrapped around each other like compressed absorbent cotton. At the same time, they were the sum of infinite parts, atoms and molecules bound to their center of gravity, so numerous that her head should have been buzzing. But it wasn't. She grasped the impressions, recognized and felt them, and sensed a sublime satisfaction in doing so. Then the gas giant, which she knew was called 'Saturn,' became bigger and bigger and...

Drenched in sweat, she startled awake and sat up, jerking a hand over her heart, which hammered in her chest like an overheated engine. For a moment she didn't know where she was, and a feeling of falling—of crashing—overcame her.

As the dream rolled off her, she dropped powerlessly back onto the wet sheets and swallowed. She glanced at her alarm clock, which announced in unspectacular red numbers that it was 5:30 a.m. and she had slept for an hour. Yet the dream had seemed to her as if it had lasted no more than a few short seconds. If that long.

You need to stop worrying so much about Serenity, she told herself.

Two weeks had passed since the disappearance of the object that had drastically changed her life. Now it was gone. She still spent every day and every night in Mission Control, leading a project that was in the process of being dismantled, a side note for the data analysts.

President Brosnahan had long since won reelection and

couldn't bear to continue supporting a NASA project that was producing no results except a crash on Saturn, and it hadn't even provided images commensurate with such a cosmic event.

Jim showed his most understanding side and had not yet transferred or pulled her off the project, even though she had nothing to do with the endless data analysis that would take years to put all the telescope data from the past year into scientific context and learn more about the brief visit.

He was not even angry with her for continuing to insist that there had been no crash. Even though her hope was diminishing a bit every day, she was not ready to believe that such a wondrous object would just plain crash like that in their neighborhood after it had made its way to them from outside the solar system. There had to be another explanation, although she was gradually running out of arguments and stretching her imagination. More and more she wondered if it was her scientific mind that thought a crash was unlikely, or her pride that didn't want to admit that the one element that had defined her life for the last few years no longer mattered.

Had disappeared.

The days dragged on as she tenaciously fought to keep the James Webb focused on Saturn and Jim gently, but with growing pressure, made it clear to her that soon he could no longer justify keeping NASA's newest and most expensive toy away from other project groups. She understood it, but she could not accept it, knowing full well that her resistance would soon become futile.

Her phone rang. She reached for her nightstand in the darkness and found the cool aluminum between her fingers.

"Yes?" she asked wearily.

"It's Jim. I just wanted to remind you that you're flying to L.A. today."

She had somehow forgotten. The long night on CNN. In

her mind, she had been headed back to Mission Control, her little workstation where she could permanently monitor the James Webb and look for signs of life from Serenity. A painful routine.

"I wish I didn't have to go there," she grumbled.

"I'll be honest with you, Mel," Jim said almost gently, as if she were as fragile as porcelain, which annoyed her a little. "Since the cr... the disappearance of Serenity, the media interest has been virtually non-existent. The fact that there is a request for a talk show on current NASA projects is a stroke of luck and the only lifeline I see left for our project. If it goes well and viewers understand that it might be worth keeping an eye on it for an extra week or two, it could give us the extension we need from Washington."

"And if not?" she asked, but he did not answer. Nor did he need to. "The plane leaves at eleven twenty, I'll be on it."

"Good, very good."

"Thank you, Jim." Melody felt a familiar surge of affection rise within her. "For everything."

"We're going to be fine. You'll do fine."

After hanging up, she struggled to the bathroom and got ready. It took a long time and sapped her energy since she had barely slept the last two weeks. Every hour she didn't spend at her monitor was one in which Serenity might reappear and she might foolishly miss it. A television appearance in Los Angeles was a horror in that regard. But she had commitments to keep, and Jim's arguments were not to be lightly dismissed. She understood what he had wanted to tell her. It was her last chance to buy some more time, or else he would have to pull the plug because he had already stretched his authority as an administrator far beyond its reach.

The flight was short and uneventful. Utterly exhausted, she tried to get some sleep but was far too restless as her mind was on her screen, imagining her alien celestial body showing up and no one noticing. With the current low priority for the Webb recordings, and no one else believing Serenity would reappear, it would take months or years for someone to find the appropriate discrepancy in the data.

So she dragged herself to CNN's television studios, got powdered and made up in a somnolent state, tried sluggish small talk with the staff, and met her fellow hosts: astrophysicist and celebrity podcaster Dr. Michael Dillinger; science journalist Ruby Devenworth, known for her show Mystic Science; and former NASA administrator Jefferson McPenning. Hosting was Laura Durham, nationally famous for her show, 'The Long Night with Laura Durham.'

One great benefit of Melody's severe overtiredness was that there was little room for excitement, and she worried more about the desire to sleep keeping her from being focused or attentive enough.

Shortly before the show, they all met each other fleetingly, and lapsed into the usual curt small talk with lots of good encouragement and broad smiles. Then they were shown to their seats at the infamous glass table. They were told to ignore the cameras in front of the podium, looking only at Laura or the other participants in the panel, and also not to be distracted by the audience, 50 or so from around the country in a small bleacher section in the shadows behind the cameras. The producer with the headset who was instructing them also reminded them to stick to Durham's moderation and that everyone could go to the bathroom one more time, but not after that.

Punctually at 10 P.M. it started.

"Welcome, viewers, to a new episode of 'The Long Night.' It's Saturday again, and I'm pleased to have four exciting guests in the studio with me to discuss tonight's topic, 'The implosion of government space projects—is U.S. spaceflight dying?' Joining me today are the following experts."

One of the cameramen walked around the table and stopped in turn on their faces as Durham introduced them, "Doctor Michael Dillinger is an astrophysicist who delights an audience of millions each week with his science podcast, 'Space and Time,' which focuses primarily on space and space-flight issues. He has interviewed Elon Musk three times and is a close friend of Neil deGrasse Tyson."

A camera pan. "Ruby Devenworth, science journalist and host of 'Mystic Science' on Fox News, a program in which she explains to us such diverse topics as rocket engines, the amazing lives of slugs, and the strength of spider webs, keeping half of America glued to their screens every day. Also on the show is Jefferson McPenning, former NASA administrator and now a congressional envoy to the Pentagon to advise on military space projects."

Now the cameraman had circled the table and the lens was pointing at Melody. She thought she looked like a wormhole, with the edges of the accretion disk spinning in the light of the studio.

"Doctor Melody Adams was a Navy fighter pilot with the rank of lieutenant commander, then went to NASA and was accepted into astronaut training. She was part of the backup crew for Dragon-6, the sixth manned mission from U.S. soil after the end of the Space Shuttle program. She is the discoverer of Serenity, perhaps the most exciting celestial body in the history of spaceflight. She wrote a book about her discovery that spent five straight months at number one on the New York Times bestseller list, sending the nation into a veritable space frenzy."

The subliminal music ended and Laura Durham looked into one of the many cameras.

"Let's get right into it," she said with a serious face. "The last few years have been particularly exciting for NASA. First, the Space Launch System failed its first orbital test and exploded before America's eyes. What many had denounced in advance as a multi-billion-dollar grave that swallowed up two billion dollars with each launch, making it magnitudes more expensive than SpaceX's Starship without being reusable, has gone down in flames and led to acrimonious debates about NASA funding in Congress. Two years later, the recordings of a potentially extraterrestrial celestial body made us forget that for a short time and even the President has blossomed from being a harsh critic of the space agency to an enthusiastic amateur astronomer. Now this project has also failed. Doctor Adams, you were deputy director and the face of this object, which you described as probably of extraterrestrial origin. How hard does this latest setback hit you personally?"

"Well, first of all, it has to be stated that there was no benchmark for our project because we have never been in a comparable situation. We had taken pictures of an object that should not exist and that therefore must be viewed with significant probability as being of artificial origin."

"So... aliens built it?"

"Yes," Melody said freely, ignoring the other guests' reactions by focusing on Durham. Ironically, her heavy eyelids helped her along. "What I'm saying is, we can't and shouldn't consider this project a failure yet."

Durham frowned. "But Serenity crashed on Saturn."

"We don't know that with one hundred percent certainty."

"Experts agree that no celestial body can get that close to Saturn's gravitational influence without being engulfed by it."

"The experts also agreed that there was a natural explanation for Serenity, for its long tail on Pluto's orbit. In the end, they had to concede that there was no scientific explanation for such an outgassing. Even then, the hypothesis of a collision was more speculative than plausible." Melody blinked against her fatigue, hoping it wasn't noticeable. "After that, they realized their mistake."

Durham turned to the astrophysicist and podcaster with the colorful bow tie and gray Albert Einstein hair. "Mister Dillinger, you're shaking your head. Why?"

"I think we're dealing with typical government insanity here. Forgive me," he said in Melody's direction, with no hint of a guilty conscience. "But it's the same thing with the SLS. It ballooned to twenty-three billion dollars, was obsolete even as it was being planned, and was not competitive. Yet they kept at it. The first orbital flight of Block One? A disaster. Yet it took nearly two more years for NASA to walk away from burning billions more, relying instead on the private sector, which at this point in time carries out our manned ISS missions cost-effectively and safely."

"He's right," McPenning interjected. "I've seen the operations firsthand, and we have to acknowledge that mistakes are being repeated here. When a project has failed, it costs taxpayers a lot of money to keep it artificially alive. It's as if we let health insurance pay for a coma patient for far too long, even though there are no doctors who see any hope of remission. That's very hard to communicate, and I can understand every American asking why the government is throwing its money into a furnace with both hands."

We had that discussion before the moon landing, too, Melody opined, only to realize that she hadn't said it out loud. She should have had a second cup of coffee. Before she could fix her mistake, Durham turned to Ruby Devenworth, who looked thoughtful, like a teacher.

"Miss Devenworth, you have always been an advocate on your show of more commitment on the part of NASA to a review of Doctor Adams' hypotheses. Many credit the beginning of the rapid rise in popularity of her book *Extraterrestrial* to the book launch you held on one of your broadcasts.

How do you look on it today, after your proposal has been followed up for over a year during which NASA has put most other projects on hold?" Durham leaned forward with interest.

"I still stand by it, because I don't see failure as a failure, but as the spirit of research. If we only looked where we could find certain results, there would be no progress. When did we forget to take risks and admit that we can't predict the outcome of every endeavor?"

Melody's courage sank. She had fallen into a trap and had been invited onto this show as a whipping-post candidate. Her only 'ally' was something more like a mother, who spoke kindly to her child out of pity, but also acknowledged and focused on the failure of the project. The voices of the others blurred into one another to form a kaleidoscope of sounds, sometimes higher, sometimes lower, as if under a deep layer of water.

She was surrounded by crackling molecules, set in motion by gentle warmth from the depths. Something pulled at her, wanted to reach for her, but she escaped the grip effortlessly and felt at ease. Her body floated detached in the mist, tensing and relaxing again as the world around her locked out the entire universe. Though there was no massive boundary, her senses were still unable to reach out and grasp more than what tickled her skin like wiggling fingers, of which there were trillions upon trillions, far too many to count, enough to feel.

"Doctor Adams? Doctor Adams?" As she awoke, she heard muffled laughter. It wasn't until she saw Durham's questioning expression that she realized where she was and that she must have dozed off. She tried to fight the blush that welled up in her cheeks.

"Excuse me. Yes, please?"

"What do you say to Mr. Dillinger's accusations? After all, he is a long-time observer, and his reference to you being a second-tier employee..."

Melody was no longer listening. She had fallen asleep in front of rolling cameras and millions of viewers, embarrassing herself and NASA and probably delivering exactly what Durham had wanted for her show's narrative.

Right now it was popular to pick on her agency, as was always the case when there were setbacks. There was nothing to gain here, only more to lose by admitting now that she didn't know what exactly the podcaster's accusation had been, but it was certainly in the direction of discrediting her.

Something made her square her shoulders and take flight. If she was going to lose, then she would do so with her head held high and without giving them what they wanted: control of the stage, because she could still take it back from them.

She stood up and looked around. Looks changed from spite, smugness, and voyeuristic interest to irritation and then uncertainty.

"I know what's happening here right now. I'm tired of everyone just noting the mistakes, and not the hard work. Our agency, our teams, work harder than you might think. They're not guests on TV shows and they're not working to impose their opinions on others or to make everything look like a big failure. No, they tackle things themselves and try to make a difference for humanity. The moon landing was also criticized for its cost at the time and, granted, there were setbacks. But in the end, we did it with optimism, not with petty squabbling over every scientific discovery."

Melody was getting fired up now.

"Without the financial feat and the courage back then, half the technology in this studio would not exist today. You've lured me into a trap here today because I'm just a sitting duck, a wounded animal that can be gleefully eviscerated in front of running cameras. I'm not going along with that. I stand by my hypothesis, I stand by my staff and my colleagues, and I stand by our decisions. Even that of the president, who supported us early on. We're ringing the death bells before the patient has passed away, and that is sick and un-American. I'm not going to let that happen to me."

She plucked the microphone, complete with cord, from her lapel—suddenly no longer tired but angry—and tossed it carelessly onto the table. Durham's face had turned the color of chalk by now, and the other guests looked as if even an open window would suit them as a means of escape.

Melody knew she had lost, but at the same time it felt good to have vented her frustration. In her opinion, at the right time and in the right place. She would pick up the pieces tomorrow, because tonight she was much too tired.

Jim didn't call, although she expected her phone to ring hot. Even after her return flight, which she took that same night, it remained silent.

7

The word from Jim finally came just when she'd arrived at her apartment in Houston, exhausted to the point of dead tired, even though she had slept like a baby on the plane. Fatigue had penetrated so deeply into her bones that she didn't even feel any stress about the scandal she had caused in front of the cameras.

She had just set down her rolling suitcase and purse to stagger like a drunk toward her bedroom when she read the lines in her messenger app:

When you land, come to my office right away! Jim.

"Hmm," she murmured, trying to call him, but his phone was busy. She thought about giving in to her body and sleeping, shutting out the world that was playing such a nasty game with her. In the end, though, the uncomfortable tugging that spread through her gut was reason enough not to. That it would come to this as a result of her outburst had been clear to her shortly afterward. So she might as well face the consequences now and pay the price for her uncontrolled honesty.

The drive to JSC took only half an hour this early in the morning but felt like an eternity as she concentrated to keep from falling asleep. The sun was just coming up when she pulled up and parked in front of the big office building. She wondered for the first time why Jim wasn't at home asleep.

He's probably so angry he can't sleep and needs to smooth out any ripples in Washington, she thought, swiping her key card across the panel at the side entrance and voluntarily taking the stairs to further dispel her fatigue. In her mind, she tried to fathom how many paragraphs of her employment contract she had violated and whether she should even be defending herself. She had lost her nerve and had walked into a television interview that had been broadcast nationally, overtired and unprepared. Jim had every right to release her again.

His secretary had not yet come on duty, which, judging by a glance at her wristwatch, would be at least another three hours. The door to Jim's office, on which an unadorned brass sign reading 'Administrator' was bolted, stood ajar. His muffled voice could be heard, excited and forceful.

Melody rolled her shoulders, crossed the secretary's office, and knocked on the open door.

"I'll call you back!" he declared. She heard the clack of a desk-phone receiver being set down and then a muffled, "Come in."

She sheepishly entered the office.

"Mel!" he barked, jumping up out of his chair as if he had been sitting on a spring. He came around the wide wooden desk toward her and grabbed her by the shoulders.

"I'm sorry, I really am," she said somberly. And she was. She had loved him once, perhaps still did, because he was a good man who knew how to be honest and dutiful without ignoring the feelings and well-being of others. "I'm not sorry for what I said on CNN because it's the truth. But that I caused you trouble with it, I'm sorry for that. You have to take the fall for that, and it wasn't your fault."

"Yeah, yeah, that can all wait." He swept a hand dismissively in front of her face and pulled her around his desk with him. "It's back!"

"*What?* I don't understand," she muttered in confusion.

"Serenity!" He roughly turned his monitor so she could see the image on the screen. It showed the unmistakable silhouette of the comet-like celestial body with its large tail, on Saturn's relative left.

"This... This is..." She was at a loss for words when she saw it. "It didn't *crash*."

"No! Your optimism has paid off."

My despair, she thought. Her head was spinning. Was she dreaming?

"Where did you get that picture? I wasn't there to—"

"I took over your station when you flew out," Jim explained, as if it were a matter of course. "Yesterday was my day off."

"You've been staring at Saturn's footage all day?" she asked incredulously.

"Clearly." He frowned. "I *do* believe in you. I always have. Once I had a weak period because my most important project blew up in my face, but I resolved not to let that happen again. I had resolved to give you as long a deadline for Saturn observation as I could, and that was three more days. Besides—"

He could speak no more because she grabbed him and pressed a heartfelt kiss on his lips. At first he tensed, probably from surprise, then he relaxed and responded to the kiss.

"Thank you," she said, sniffling. She didn't know what to be more excited about, the fact that Serenity was still there, or that Jim had declared his love for her in such a matter-of-fact way.

"I should thank you for your persistence. I was beginning to lose faith that we might have miscalculated. I've already called the president."

"*And?*"

"He wants us to calculate the current course and explore the possibility of a manned mission. He wants a feasibility study on his desk in the Oval Office within three months. Top priority."

"A *manned* mission?" She felt dizzy.

"Yes! A manned mission," he repeated with a grin. "I explained to him that a natural celestial body couldn't disappear behind Saturn for two weeks and then reappear. Not a single scientist in his right mind will be able to say otherwise now. All those who have been pontificating on TV for the last few months that it was just a strange asteroid that we don't yet understand will be silenced forever. Especially after Serenity totally snowed them by supposedly crashing into Saturn. Serenity is a spaceship, and I made that clear to the President. He wants us, with our European allies who have contributed their own images from the Southern Observatory, to do everything we can to reach this interstellar visitor."

"That means it has not set a course for Earth?" She was a little disappointed, but relieved at the same time. Who knew what would happen if an alien spacecraft, apparently capable of accomplishing things that could not be explained by the current state of science, was headed for their home planet. Above all, who knew how the various nations would react? The answers to this question worried her the most.

"No. I spotted Serenity just when your TV show started, and since then we've done thirty-four takes. Four teams are calculating their fingers off right now just generating models. We know it's accelerating and heading relatively purposefully toward Mars, or to be more accurate, the Martian orbit that it's going to intersect a few million miles from the red planet."

"It's achievable in principle," she stated. Her excitement exploded like fireworks in her belly.

"Yes, though it would have to speed up considerably for it to hit an intersection with Mars' orbit that lies within the window in which we could reach it," Jim indicated, making an equivocal gesture. "So, we'll see about that."

Mars was at least six months away with the currently available thrusters. Since the dusty neighbor of Earth revolved around the sun just as they did, its distance from Earth varied enormously. At the farthest distance, the sun was between them, and Mars was about 390 million kilometers away. At the most favorable launch window for a mission, the distance was only 45 million kilometers.

Since they were not going to Mars, the Mars orbit transfer path served only as a calculation example. Thus, the single window was created because time was the most important factor in any orbital mechanics calculation. The travel time defined not only the necessary acceleration, drift, and braking time, but also the point where Mars would be on arrival.

Between departure and arrival, the red planet itself covered an enormous distance on its elliptical orbit around the sun. Thus, a mission would not travel to Mars where it would appear at the outset, but to a point where it would be in six months. Accordingly, the feasibility of a manned mission to Serenity would depend on how its course and the Earth's changing position would relate to each other over the next few years.

But that was a problem for later. The fact that she was getting to rack her brains over it was a gift in itself.

"As for the show," she said cautiously, but Jim waved it off.

"I don't think anyone will care about that as of tomorrow. The president will announce that we are certain that an alien spacecraft is passing through the solar system, but there is no danger to Earth because it's not coming to us, but it's going to pass us, *cosmically* speaking, in very close proximity. I don't think the public interest is going anywhere anytime soon after that." He thrust an outstretched index finger like a spear into the shot of the celestial body on the monitor.

No, she silently corrected herself. *Of the spaceship.* "You might be right about that, though."

"Also, I saw on Instagram a few hours ago that you started a new hashtag that's going viral: #inyourmediaface."

"#inyourmediaface?" she repeated, confused. "Excuse me?"

"Apparently you've got the internet in a frenzy for speaking your mind about 'un-American' whiners with an obvious 'don't give a shit' attitude, no matter what they or anyone thinks of you. At any rate, it obviously got a big response and struck a nerve."

"Honestly, I was just tired and angry." She made a dismissive gesture and grabbed his arm as he looked at his watch, because she had another question. "Before you go, what's the next step?"

"I will have to make personnel changes, but that will take time," he replied somewhat nebulously. "For now, the priority is the vector calculations on Serenity's trajectory. If it quickly reaches a point where the acceleration rate remains constant, or a steady velocity is established, we can start putting together a mission design."

"I will—"

"Yes, you will be there. Front row, you can count on it," he assured her with a grin. He was drunk with success, just like she was. Though his answer didn't match her interrupted question, she let it go and merely nodded. "You should be asleep. I didn't see it, but I'm guessing your on-the-air nap at the CNN studio wasn't particularly restful."

Melody shuddered.

"Too soon?"

"Definitely too soon," she replied with an affected scowl.

"Get some rest. We won, Mel. We'll be fine here until tomorrow." Their hands touched on the tabletop as if by accident. Whether it was because of their shared euphoria, or his unspoken show of love from before, it felt good... Okay. A year ago, she wouldn't have thought this kind of feeling possible. While there had been no hatred—nor even genuine anger —that had faded in the days after her release while giving way to some understanding of his position, there had been an insurmountable distance.

The fact that they'd had to maintain a secret relationship during their first employment at NASA had been complicated and had prevented them from developing the sort of intimate relationship that could only come about through closeness in everyday life. After that, deep sympathy had resonated with the fantasy of possibly more of a future when they had been together. But she had done nothing in the last 12 months but work, or turn off her head at the Outpost to achieve at least a basic level of relaxation.

"I sometimes wish circumstances were different," she murmured in his direction, her eyes snapping open.

"I wish that all the time." His look was serious as he met hers. There was regret in it, and a desire whose restraint pained him.

"But we can't." That was a statement. When they had been having 'an affair,' she had been in astronaut training, and if anyone had gotten wind of it she would have been accused of enjoying an unfair advantage and 'sleeping her way up.' It was a mean insinuation that would not have been true, but one she could relate to. Now, since she was a regular employee, things were a little different.

"You're not a trainee anymore," he noted in a whisper. His breath smelled faintly of peppermint tea. "There's no workplace regulation that could prevent us from doing that."

"It still won't work," she said. Unable to tell him why—yet —she broke away from him before their lips could touch and sighed. "I have to sleep now."

"Can you even drive?"

"I'll sleep in my office. I've gained plenty of experience in that over the past year."

8

Mel set aside the thick tome labeled *The Physics of Aeronautics* after her head banged down on page 394, jolting her from her microsleep. Her forehead felt as if a horse had kicked it.

Tired, she glanced at the clock above her desk. It was just after midnight, enough time for the next item on her list. After two months of experience, she didn't mind ignoring her brain's loud demands for sleep. She went into the bathroom, popped a caffeine pill, and slipped into her gym clothes hanging behind the door. They smelled faintly of sweat because she hadn't had time to wash them following her last training session.

She left her apartment and went across the street to the gym. It was small and designed more for back patients, so mostly seniors worked out there and they didn't know her from anywhere. Another advantage was that she was alone at that hour but for a few other night owls. She worked out for two hours until she was drenched in sweat. Back home, she drank a protein shake and ate four bananas along with a handful of vitamin and mineral tablets and, after showering, headed to the Outpost.

It was Sunday, so her next shift didn't start until noon tomorrow. The Outpost wouldn't be as busy as it was on Friday or Saturday, and it was reserved for NASA and SpaceX employees so they were among their own. In the past she had often come here to clear her head, now she came to belong and not be perceived as 'one of the management.' There was still a pin on the wall for her record time at holding one's breath in the plunge pool, which was worth pointing out from time to time.

Nights at the Outpost, however, also distracted her from the fact that she would have liked to spend them with Jim, whom she'd had to put off and turn away again and again, even though she wanted nothing more than to spend her free time with him. She had also turned down his calls during her study period. Even today, on the weekend. She felt miserable about it, and she felt sorry for him. Still, she forced herself to keep him at bay.

She could follow her feelings at another time, when this was over.

"Mel!" shouted Greg as she walked through the door, the volume almost blowing her back into the well-packed parking lot. The Outpost was packed, too, both at the tables and in between. A 90s remix of 'Rocket Man' was playing, with hard electro beats and shrill sounds that blended perfectly into the hazy, loud chaos. She needed a second "Mel!" that just barely stood out from the noise before she spotted her friend. He was sitting at the bar between two engineers from Booster Maintenance, whom she recognized from their sweaters, all three waving with rosy cheeks and broad grins.

She waved back and squeezed through the chattering, laughing, yelling crowd to reach him.

"Is there an open seat here?" she called above voices and music when she reached him, giving Nancy a wave. The usual.

"Haven't you heard?" Greg eyed her as if looking for clues that she was joking.

"I've been pretty busy."

"Serenity has stopped accelerating and is flying at a steady forty-five thousand kilometers an hour. A little faster than we'd have liked, but within reason." The corners of Greg's mouth almost touched his ears as he grinned.

When Nancy brought her usual—non-alcoholic beer for the past two months—she didn't even notice until her friend accepted it and pressed it into her hands.

"You're not messing with me are you?"

"Why do you think everyone is in such a good mood?" He made a gesture to the room. Her gaze followed his hand, and sure enough, the expressions of her colleagues were, without exception, exuberant and cheerful. She saw many astronauts and the half of Mission Control staff who weren't currently overseeing the current ISS expedition. Most seemed drunk and more detached from reality than usual. And it was almost four in the morning.

Now she was grinning too, and it felt even wider than Greg's. Spontaneously she hugged him and he laughed.

"Maybe you should treat yourself to a real one today!" he chortled, pointing to her beer.

"Not yet," she replied casually, pointing to the area in front of the dartboard that mutated into a dance floor on a good night. A few men and women, all part of the astronaut corps, were currently pushing tables to the side while the others raucously cheered them on. "Is this going to be—?"

"Looks like an Astronaut Olympics," Greg confirmed her guess as he jumped off his barstool. "Shit, I haven't seen that in a long time!"

Astronaut Olympics was the name given to an Outpost tradition that could supposedly trace its origins back to the first Apollo missions—one of the few opportunities that those who were closest to superheroes in Mel's eyes could take advantage of and show off a bit. Two competed against each other by straddling backward-turned chairs on opposite sides of a table, ten shot glasses in front of them. Each of them was handed a knife. Bystanders tossed them questions that came either from the many manuals they had to master or from astronaut training itself. Whoever knew the answer first jammed his or her knife into the table and called it out. If it was correct, the other opponent had to take a drink. If it was wrong, he or she had to drink. The questions were usually from the fields of mathematics, physics, engineering, or medicine. All in all, it was an extremely childish tradition that had fit well back in the sixties, but today seemed a bit out of date.

The tables had been cleared by now, and the guests had formed a large ring. Mel had to stretch on her bar stool to be able to look over the many heads. Cheers erupted when the man who had initiated the competition raised his arms like a wrestler celebrating in the ring.

Bernard!

"Wooohoooo!" yelled Miles Ghazwin of the Artemis team, a normally taciturn engineer who seemed to have found a new role, with flushed cheeks and feverish eyes. He held beer bottles in both hands and gestured theatrically to the crowd. "The matador has thrown his cape into the ring. Who would be crazy enough to take on the mighty B-b-b-b-bernaaa-r-r-rd?"

In the background, the ten glasses were set up and Nancy passed a bottle of whiskey across the counter. Mel intercepted it before her neighbor could get hold of it, slid down from her seat, and walked toward Bernard and Miles. The crowd parted in front of her without paying much attention. They continued to holler and clap, poking their comrades in the side to prompt them to throw their hats into the ring.

As soon as she arrived at the edge of the circle, she raised the whiskey bottle. "I'm going up against him!"

A breathy, "Ooooh," went through the bystanders. Bernard briefly looked as if he had seen a ghost before he caught himself and bowed his head like a gracious patriarch.

"Uh, only astronauts can compete," Miles said in a lowered voice.

"Why?" she asked loud enough to be heard above the clamor. "Afraid of the standby crew?"

The shouting became louder. Some laughed loudly and the first bills were collected. Miles looked indecisive, even in his red-eyed alcohol haze. Before he could reject her, a bell rang from the bar and all heads turned to Nancy, who put away the knife she had been banging against one of the two huge glass tankards.

"Bernard versus Melody," shouted the proprietress with the perky bun, her flannel shirt knotted below her breasts. "Betting as usual!"

Miles conceded defeat, looked at Bernard, who ignored him and gazed into space through a veil of drunkenness, and then shrugged his shoulders. Crown caps were dispensed as if in a frantic election, until Bernard's tankard was filled to the brim and Melody's not even to the bottom of the handle.

She mentally shrugged it off, and took the seat across from Bernard. Their comrades and colleagues approached until they'd formed a dense, feverish ring of rosy faces, alcohol-swilling breath, and frenetic stares so close she felt like she was in one of the claustrophobic Soyuz capsules.

"You know the rules," Miles bellowed in a drunken voice. He stood right at their table with his arms outstretched, like a steward trying to hold back the crowd. "Anyone who has a question, speak up. I'll point to you and then you call them in. Ten questions, ten correct answers, ten drinks."

His grin turned wolfish as he looked to Bernard and

Melody. "I hope it doesn't get too one-sided, or one of you won't make it to work tomorrow."

Laughter galloped up and down the room.

"Ready?"

Mel and Bernard took their bread knives in hand and turned them with the tip toward the tabletop. As a precaution, she pressed her thumb over the knob. She had never participated before because, according to tradition, she was not allowed to, but she had seen many Astronaut Olympics where the careless had cut their hands because they had slipped.

"Ready, set, go!" shouted Miles, and the first hands shot up.

"What is the definition of pH?" asked the person called upon, after it had become quiet.

Bernard and Melody simultaneously rammed their knives into the tabletop. Simple question.

"Bernard!" decided Miles, and she avoided giving him a sour look.

"The negative decadic logarithm of the absolute concentration of hydronium ions in an aqueous solution," the astronaut said, looking nowhere near as drunk as before.

Cheering, Mel drank down one of the ten shot glasses placed in front of them, which she had filled to the brim herself. The amber liquid burned like fire in her throat and seemed to line her stomach like white phosphorus.

"Next question! Ah, Cidney!"

"Why can a plane fly?" a woman's voice rang out.

Again Mel and Bernard rammed their knives into the tabletop, but this time Mel's advantage was clear enough for Miles to indicate her. Good thing she was sober.

"Because, according to Bernoulli's law, the sum of static and dynamic pressure is locally constant. If you use the wing profile to make sure that on its upper side, the flow velocity and thus the dynamic pressure is higher than on the lower side, the static pressure drops there and the wing is 'sucked' upwards," she explained, and again cheers and applause spread. She felt like she was at an Asian cockfight, except she was one of the roosters. Even the humidity matched it by now.

"Correct!" laughed Cidney from somewhere, and Bernard drank the second shot.

"How is excess heat generated in the body, and how is it radiated in a closed environment?" came the next question from somewhere behind her. Again, Mel was faster than the drunken Bernard.

"Adenosine triphosphate is the main energy transmitter of the human body in the cells. Excess energy is lost as heat, primarily from the main consumers: the brain, lungs, kidneys, heart, and liver. In an enclosed environment such as a space capsule, the waste heat—about one hundred watts—is dissipated through several pathways: by conduction of thermal energy from the skin to the cooler environment, by blackbody radiation, and third, with the aid of fluid evaporation."

"Correct!"

Mel watched with satisfaction as Bernard emptied the next glass.

"Next question." Miles took his time this time. "Ha! Danny! This is going to be an astronomy question, huh?"

The corners of Bernard's mouth twitched briefly. Neither of them was an astronomer, but Mel's astronomical work at Gemini North had only been a few years ago.

"Sure thing," Danny chortled from somewhere, unseen and slurring his words. "What's the largest known globular cluster in the Milky Way?"

"Oooh," murmured the crowd.

"It's not in the manuals and it's not in the training books," Miles objected.

"But in the mandatory astronomy course, this information is in the script. Since last year," the invisible astronomer defended himself.

Mel and Bernard exchanged glances and hesitated. Then she plunged her knife into the tabletop. All of a sudden it became quiet.

"Omega Centauri, probably the core of a dwarf galaxy cannibalized by the Milky Way," she said, allowing herself a satisfied smile. She had listened, now and then, to Winthrop's broad ramblings in Hawaii. She had the feeling that this could be her evening.

"Yeah, fuck me, that's right!" laughed Danny, and even as Bernard gave her a where-the-hell-do-you-know-that-from look, the noise became even more booming than before. Her opponent growled, and drank for the third time.

"Okay, okay, now it's time for some astronaut medicine," Miles interjected. "This is still an Astronaut Olympics, not an astronomy lesson!"

Laughter and shouts of approval.

"What is the bone density loss in microgravity per month?" asked Miles himself.

Boom. Mel had lowered her knife almost before her colleague finished speaking. No risk, no victory. The question was easy enough.

"One to two percent."

"Right."

Bernard drank with a sour expression.

"And which bones are particularly affected?"

Boom, again. "Weight-bearing bones, especially femur, tibia, and vertebral column."

"Right again." Miles nodded appreciatively and looked a little surprised.

Bernard swayed slightly after his fifth drink.

"And which ones are the least affected?"

Bernard still seemed to be gathering himself as she brought her knife down again.

"Uh," she hesitated briefly, trying to remember. She had just reviewed the material last week. Miles was about to say something when she beat him to it, "Non-weight-bearing bones, for example, the... the radius and clavicle."

"That's correct, too." Miles looked along the ring of roaring spectators and nodded in approval. "Stand-by team people!"

"I've got something heavier!" someone shouted.

"Medicine?"

"Yeah!"

"Then shoot," Miles prompted the person. Mel didn't see her either, as she held her knife and stared tensely at the table-top, trying not to be distracted. Bernard groaned, seething.

"What pathomechanism explains the impaired functionality of osteoblasts under micro-g?"

Mel blinked. Osteoblasts, osteoblasts. This topic had appeared in the manual for long-term expeditions, which she had repeated at the very beginning because it had seemed most important to her. She thought feverishly and became restless because she expected Bernard to beat her to it at any time. But he, too, seemed to be thinking hard—with some frustration. The uproarious noise around them grew louder, as if someone had turned a knob. The air, thick with exhaled alcohol and vapors, seemed to condense. Details came to her mind, but they were slow to come together.

Reluctantly, she let go of her tension and imagined a flame flickering in the void. She let all her thoughts fall into it and burn away until there was only the flame. She had learned this ancient samurai technique for calming the mind from her flight instructor in the Navy and later realized it was probably the most important lesson of all. Without it, she would never have survived training at NASA.

Her knife descended. "There is a breakdown of the actin cytoskeleton in resting osteoblasts causing them to deform," she explained so calmly that it quickly grew quiet for the observers to be able to hear. Tranquility guided her through her memories. "In addition, micro-g exposure provides altered nuclear morphology. Elongated nuclei with a reduction in size and condensed nuclei are observed. Another symptom of an altered actin cytoskeleton is a reduction in the number of stress fibers and a smaller stress fiber area—indicating that microgravity affects polymerization. Focal adhesions are also mechanosensitive structures that are destabilized by lack of gravity. In addition, focal contacts made under these circumstances are less mature, negatively affecting osteoblast adhesion overall."

Miles and Bernard both stared at her as if she were an alien. The latter straightened the still-filled glasses in front of him and then the six emptied ones. The corners of his mouth twitched.

"You forgot the fragmentation issue..." Miles started, but finally the former doctor shook his head and rubbed his forehead. "But I guess that's still clearly right." He looked out into the similarly impressed crowd. "Right?"

"Hell, yeah!"

"Mel! Mel! Mel!"

"Standby!" she heard Greg yell from the crowd. The rest was lost in the general amusement.

"Do some math!" a new voice demanded as soon as the volume had dropped back to the normal level of ringing in the ears.

Bernard's face contorted as if he'd bitten into a lemon. At the sight of him, Mel felt a twinge of compassion. It wasn't often that NASA's flagship pilot was seen to show an emotion that wasn't calculated and controlled—an unmistakable sign of how drunk he was. Most of the astronauts had come from the natural sciences and been involved in mathematics to one degree or another, which is the language of the universe, if you will. But none of them was a mathematician, even though they had to have a thorough understanding of the basics to be considered for astronaut training. Nevertheless, hardly anyone liked the sometimes difficult tasks, except perhaps those that had to decide between life and death in practical application: the calculation of flight vectors without computer assistance, various angular sizes with their physical influencing factors, atmospheric friction values during the re-entry of a spacecraft, or the throughput speed of a turbopump in liquid boosters.

"It was only to be expected that the orbital mechanics would speak up. They're still sober, too." For this joke, Miles earned friendly, ugly laughter from the rest of the onlookers. But a moment later, he waved at the group in an encouraging manner. "All right. Fire away. It's got to be from the manuals, though!"

"What is the limit of f of x equals x squared by x plus one for x toward infinity?" a woman shouted from the left. Her voice sounded as high as a songbird.

Mel jammed her knife into the table. "Zero."

"Wrong!" Miles looked to Bernard.

"Plus infinity."

"Bernard takes the point. It's about time."

Mel drank amid the laughter of her colleagues, as if her loss of the point had finally straightened out their worldview. *Damn, I need to study better!*

"Next question."

"What is the integral of x times e to the power of x?"

This time Bernard was visibly straining to do the math, and Mel needed time, too. She didn't remember ever reading this task in any of the manuals, but no one objected, so she wouldn't either, as long as it was equally difficult for both of them.

Finally, her knife went down.

"Bernard!" shouted Miles. In fact, his knife had already been planted. She grimaced.

"X times e to the power of x."

Miles seemed to be thinking, looking at the questioner.

"Mel?"

"E to the power of x times x minus 1."

"Seems right. Don't be afraid of the shot, Bernard!"

Shaky handed, Bernard took the second-to-last glass and poured half into his mouth and the other half over his coveralls. "Sh-sh-shit."

"So, one more."

"What is the series representation of sine x?"

"The sum of k equals 0 to infinity over minus one to the power of k times x to the power of two k plus one by the factorial of two k plus 1," came out of Mel's mouth as if shot from a pistol. She had even forgotten to ram her knife into the table. Bernard looked at her with eyes that reminded her of a drowning frog, and then stared right through her.

It remained loud as he took the last drink, and waved as if he was throwing in the towel.

"What's the rough sequence of a Raptor II engine?" someone blurted spontaneously, so that everyone heard and the volume quieted among the bettors, who were thrilled their local boy had lost.

"The show is over. She won."

Mel smiled and jammed her knife into the table. "It's okay. One turbopump injects liquid methane into a preburner or gas generator. At the same time, a second turbopump injects liquid oxygen into another preburner. Both preburners push their fuel into the central combustion chamber, where they react and shoot plasma out of its beautiful butt with two hundred tons of thrust. And *that* will have to do for today."

Her smile turned into a grin as she was patted on the

shoulders and her name chanted. Bernard, meanwhile, disappeared unnoticed into the crowd and—she guessed—through
the front door. She watched his phantom image and sighed
inwardly as the throng celebrated her. But she also saw some
confused, and more than a few thoughtful, faces in the
drunken confusion.

9

The news of Serenity's constant airspeed and stable trajectory still gripped the entire media world the next morning. Mel's alarm clock rang at 10:00 A.M. Four hours of sleep would have to be enough; she was far behind her schedule. That became moot when she turned on the TV, curious to see if Jim had gone public yet, or if the space agencies involved had agreed among themselves to establish a common line of communication first. Drafting a press memorandum within a single agency was extremely difficult, and it was nearly impossible with many different agencies that had the same information, came from different political constraints, and were led by different personalities.

These were questions she would have asked Greg if her ego hadn't gotten in the way and driven her to compete with Bernard. No matter—it seemed the answers were not far away, as every channel she zapped through had a countdown for a breaking-news address to the nation by President Brosnahan. Whether it was CNN, Fox News, CBS, MSNBC, or any other channel, they all pointed to the upcoming broadcast and were speculating that it would have something to do with Serenity, the extraterrestrial celestial body that had preoccupied the punditry and media world since its reappearance.

Mel had stayed away from the many late-night debates and newspaper columns for fear of encountering all sorts of small-mindedness. How, in the face of such a world-altering discovery, there could still be dissenters and deniers who refused to accept anything outside their usual horizons was beyond her. The behavior reminded her of the tireless, fact-resistant climate-crisis deniers who were resistant to research and logic, no matter how overwhelming the facts and how hot it burned around them. What was more surprising yet was that she found herself still perplexed by how great an ability people possessed to exclude or deny everything that didn't fit into their picture of the world and their way of thinking.

When President Ron Brosnahan stepped in front of the cameras, the typical pre-camera banter coming to an end with, "We now go to the White House," he looked tired but focused, like someone who had done something important. The Wisconsin Republican still had a smidgen of the dashing young man about him from his decade-long soldiering as an Army officer, with a clear gaze and neat haircut, although his mouth hinted at a certain harshness.

"Please be seated," he told the assembled journalists, who were not visible in the televised picture. Brosnahan, flanked by the U.S. President's flag and the Stars and Stripes, opened his speech folder and let his eyes roam the room for a tension-building moment before focusing directly on the camera.

"Overnight, our experts at NASA, along with our friends from Canada and Europe, completed important calculations and matched them with observations through our telescopes and ground stations. They were able to verify that the extra-solar celestial body, which has been christened Serenity, is moving at a constant speed. It will cross the orbit of Mars in four years, in August 2031, at a point well ahead of the red planet.

"Fellow citizens, since a launch window will be open for a mission in January 2031, I have decided, in consultation with my counterparts and allies in Europe and Canada, that we will prepare a manned mission that will take advantage of the launch window and explore this fascinating visitor. Not for ourselves, but for all of humanity. Our nation has done the impossible before, when it landed on the moon on July 20, 1969. At the time, we were told it couldn't be done, until we just went ahead and did it. Not because it was easy, but because it was hard, to slightly paraphrase my predecessor in office at the time, the historic John F. Kennedy.

"Today, we are not making a decision to redraw our boundaries and remeasure what is achievable for us. We are making a decision to make contact with an extraterrestrial artifact. What is it? We won't know until we get out there. Not with robots or probes, but with men and women from our ranks reaching out to touch that which we didn't think was possible.

"I don't know what our brave astronauts will find—no one does. But I am sure that we will get one step closer to the secrets of the universe. We now realize that we are probably not the only creations in the universe, and that is a realization that will not be easy for any of us to accept. But we are not a species or a nation hiding from great challenges. Let me be clear: This is the greatest and most far-reaching discovery in human and Earth history. But it is also the greatest challenge. One that we will face because we have always done so and we do not hide when fate calls us.

"That's why I asked Congress this very morning to approve funding to begin a mission immediately. We will stretch out our hand into the cosmos and see who will seize it. For this, no expense or effort must be spared. For this, we must rediscover our old strengths and stand united, our eyes firmly fixed on the goal that must be the most important to all of us. My fellow citizens, as of today you are living in the most important time ever. In the time when humanity is making contact. God bless you and God bless the United States of America."

Mel hadn't even noticed that she was holding her toothbrush, and that toothpaste and saliva were running down her hand and dripping onto the carpet. As if struck by a blow, she sank back onto her sofa.

"It's really happening," she mumbled into her apartment. "We're flying there. We're truly flying there!"

An hour later, she was on the grounds of the Johnson Space Center, a collection of mostly 70s-built office buildings surrounded by large parking lots. The complex was like a planned city from another time, in which it took a long while to find one's way around because everything looked so similar.

As she entered the press building, she encountered Bernard, of all people, who wore mirrored aviator glasses and seemed more than a little uncoordinated.

"Hello, Mel," he greeted her in passing. At first she didn't want to say anything, but then she turned and took hold of his arm. He turned to her with a furrowed brow and with a blank expression.

"I want to apologize," she said sincerely.

"For what? You were good." It was easy to notice that he was having a hard time forming words. His breath still smelled of alcohol, not something anyone liked to pick up on around here. It could even become a problem, and that was certainly part of his current humble demeanor.

"That was childish of me," she sighed. It was the truth. "I

didn't mean to show you up or prove anything by it." That wasn't the truth, more the politeness she preferred to use to pick up the pieces in this case. "I didn't even have the right to participate."

"The way I see it, you kicked my butt and reminded me of some things I'd better internalize." Whether he was referring to the astronaut manuals when he said that, or to his drinking habits, or something else entirely, it was impossible to tell. "Thanks anyway, Mel." He hesitated as if he might say something more, but then merely nodded and left the building.

Mel watched him for a few more moments like an afterimage on her retina, mouth agape at the thought of her derailment last night. Nothing else described what she had done. A weak moment, born of overconfidence—overconfidence and impulsiveness.

At some point, she snapped out of it as a group of colleagues walked past her and made a few references to her victory at the Outpost, which she answered with a polite smile before turning around and wasting no more time. There was a press conference scheduled for noon, which Jim would hold in person. And he wanted her there.

"Hello, Mel," he greeted her as they met in the anteroom of the press room, where they were being made up.

"Hi, Jim."

"You look terrible."

"Thank you."

He either ignored her laconic retort or hadn't noticed it. "You're not going to fall asleep in front of the cameras again, are you?"

"Too soon, Jim. Too soon."

"Sorry." He tried an encouraging grin, but there was an unfamiliar restraint underneath, and she knew where it was coming from. "It didn't hurt you a bit. Instagram loves you even more since then."

"Interview requests, however, have dwindled."

"That should be another advantage in your eyes."

"I can't disagree with that."

"Today is going to be a super day, Mel," Jim said, leaning over to her, eliciting a frustrated snort from his makeup assistant. "I'm announcing the crew for Starship 2."

"It's already set?"

"Yes. Six astronauts. Three Americans, two Europeans, one Canadian."

"I sat as secondary chick on the project, remember?" she reminded him.

"Sure, but I had to make the staffing decisions." He smiled exuberantly and sank back into his chair, whereupon his face was further powdered. "I had everything locked up in the drawer, but I didn't have the heart to allow myself to hope it would become a reality."

"I think we've all been there. Can you say anything yet?" she asked cautiously, closing her eyes so her makeup artist could powder around them.

"I can't spoil the surprise, can I?"

She could almost hear his boyish grin.

Mel felt a shiver of excitement tickle her skin.

When the press conference began, the room was packed to the walls with journalists of every stripe. Cameras everywhere, laptops on laps, old-fashioned notepads in hands. It was the usual suspects—the main broadcasters, trade magazines, and YouTubers involved in space topics. The prospect of a bona fide first contact in just over four years seemed to have lured anyone with press credentials. The sight of their many eager faces was even more tangible proof to them that this was all not a dream, that it was really happening like the televised presidential address. The nation would hang spellbound by their words broadcast through the many camera lenses and later through the eyes and fingers of the journalists, absorbing everything, turning it over and interpreting it several times, and so it would be for the next four and a half years.

"Are you okay?" asked Jim, raising a hand as if to touch her, then lowering it again just before making contact.

"Yes. I'm just so excited. This is *happening*."

"Trust me," he said, nodding encouragingly. "You're going to leave this press conference with a big smile on your face. Maybe that prospect will help you relax a little."

It didn't. Now she was even more excited. Her fingertips began to tingle and her scalp felt like she was getting an acupuncture treatment with hot needles.

Is it honestly happening? Will he say it?

They walked up to the stage and took their seats next to Elon Musk, who had already arrived and gave them friendly handshakes. "Cool times, huh?" he said good-humoredly, smiling his mischievous boy smile.

"You could say that," she replied absently, sitting down to Jim's right behind her nametag and a glass water bottle.

Jim greeted the members of the press and asked them to sit down. "Nice of you all to come." The doors were closed and the administrator continued. "As you heard in President Brosnahan's address this morning, as of today there is certainty. We have the technical capability to reach Serenity. If Congress follows our proposals and those of the administration, we will also have the resources we need. We have known for months now that it cannot be an unexplained but natural celestial body. Serenity is extraterrestrial in origin, not only in the sense that it comes from extrasolar space, but that it must also have been built or rebuilt by intelligent beings and have an autonomous propulsion system. Enumerating the list of evidence for this would go beyond today's scope and has been presented and published by us several times in the past quarter so I'll keep it short. We're flying to Serenity, and we're flying there with humans."

Mel's eyes widened in surprise as a few of the journalists cheered and, gradually, more joined in. This usually happened only at SpaceX press conferences, where an above-average number of seats were given to YouTubers and bloggers from the space scene and things were much more relaxed.

Jim smiled with satisfaction and continued speaking a little louder. "This trip is going to be extremely expensive, and by far the most difficult thing we have ever done. But our planning teams and engineers have not been sitting on their hands for the past several months. They've joined forces with our partners at SpaceX and the United Launch Alliance and they have been doing important preliminary work. That's why I can tell you today that our launch system will be a 'Super Heavy' and our spacecraft will be a modified Starship from SpaceX. ULA will be working closely with us as we prepare it for the special requirements of approaching and possibly docking with an alien object while moving at high speeds. This will be a national and international effort. Interior equipment will be provided by our European friends at ESA, and our Canadian friends have agreed to contribute new robotic arms for docking maneuvers and possible sample collecting. We're on the frontier of what's possible here, but that's never stopped us before."

Mel went through the planning phase in her mind and had to classify Jim's announcement as somewhat optimistic. While these international splits were agreed upon within the realm of possibility, they were far from waved through and set in stone. Next to Jim, Elon Musk began to explain in his choppy and thoughtful way how this year's maiden flight of *Starship-1* around the moon would be an important test run for *Starship-2*, and that every effort would be made to make the mission a success. Typical of him as a rocket engineer, he explained many of the technical features of his spacecraft and touched on the important significance for the future of humanity, that he hoped it would be a united one now that we know we are not alone, and that there is much more to discover.

Mel listened with only one ear because she was waiting for Jim's presentation of the astronauts he had chosen. Everything else was just a fancy accessory.

As planned, she said a few words about the planning phase; how much detailed preliminary work they had done thus far to calculate Serenity's approximate shape, going through docking scenarios and solutions for radiation safety on board, and the implications of the long duration of the trip.

Then, finally, Jim took over again.

"I'm sure you're all waiting with the question of all questions: *who* is going to fly up there and make contact, if it comes to that?" He paused and spread his hands. "NASA has decided on three American astronauts. Doctor Selena Rogerton, a three-time veteran of ISS expeditions and seven EVAs totaling twenty-five hours. Engineer and mathematician Doctor Jean Callahan with two ISS expeditions and one shuttle mission. Four EVAs with twenty hours. And we need a pilot who can act as a leader and pilot *Starship-2* with a steady hand."

Mel had to try hard not to grin and remain calm.

"That's why we chose the best pilot we have and someone you all know: Bernard Antonelli. He has spent over a year at a time on the ISS, was a test pilot with the U.S. Navy, and is familiar with unfamiliar extreme situations. Yes, he may be a social media darling because of his live streams from the ISS, but he's also got a lot going for him."

The journalists laughed politely. Mel felt as if she had been hit in the gut by a wrecking ball, while the adulation for astronaut darling Bernard Antonelli continued.

"Bernard Antonelli has performed over ten EVAs in five years, more than anyone before him in such a short time, with over fifty hours total time in a vacuum. He has the nerve and skill to successfully fly *Starship-2* to Serenity and back safely. The Europeans will announce their two nominations in their own press conference two hours from now, and the Canadians later this evening. With a crew of six, we can double-fill every major position with the best of the best: Pilot, Engineer, Doctor."

Jim paused again.

"Before we bring in our three selected spacemen so you can ask them your questions in person, I have one final announcement to make: As of today, I'm turning over operational control of the entire Serenity mission to Doctor Adams."

He turned a little toward her and smiled broadly, as if to say: surprise accomplished, eh? She returned his smile with some effort, hoping it looked genuine enough for the nation's eyes.

"I can think of no one better than the one of us who discovered Serenity and always believed in its origin and existence, even when the whole world lost hope. She is a prime example of perseverance and visionary thinking and therefore irreplaceable at the forefront of our historic endeavor. Congratulations, Melody."

She thanked him politely. If Jim had noticed that she was nowhere close to happy, but instead felt deeply stabbed in an old wound that gaped even more today than when it was created, he at least did not let on. Unfortunately, she could not escape this situation now, as there were still some questions from the press representatives, which Jim spontaneously accepted. So she pulled herself together, as she often did, and pushed her inner turmoil into the flame in the void.

"Alicia Barry, CNN. My question goes to Administrator Rothman: The world can still hardly believe that it's quasi-officially confirmed that aliens have either come to our solar system or at least sent us an object. Do you think the enormous cost of sending a manned space flight there will bring people's enthusiasm back down to Earth?"

Jim looked to the attractive woman in the front row and nodded. "The cost will be high, but we are not alone. Together with our allied spacefaring nations, we can handle them, I'm sure. For an undertaking like this, there can hardly be a price too high."

NASA's press officer called on the next journalist.

"Lionel Collins, Fox News. I have a question for Doctor Adams. First of all, congratulations. People like you are an inspiration to us all."

"Thank you," she said politely.

"You discovered Serenity. If you'll allow me one question in advance, have you thought of a name for the upcoming project?"

"No. I will certainly make suggestions, but this decision will be a joint one between NASA, ESA, and CSA," she assured him.

"Thank you. Now to my real question. Serenity is not heading for us but will pass through the Martian orbit and then leave the system again via a course close to the sun. Have you ever considered that its builders might not be interested in making contact with us?"

"I thought of that, but we know far too little to draw any conclusions about their intentions from their course. After all, we don't even know the most basic things about them. So, if you are alluding to the fact that the aliens might not want us to come to them, I would say this: If we look, we might find out. If we don't, we're depriving ourselves of the opportunity to find out." She nodded to indicate that this answered the question for her.

The next question was for Musk. What would he do if the maiden flight of *Starship-1* failed this year?

"More!" he said definitively.

This was followed by a whole rapid-fire series of further questions to all of them.

Were there considerations to arm *Starship-2*, just in case? "No, we will be sticking to the space treaty. At most, the Defense Ministry will be involved only peripherally."

What would happen if China or Russia announced a mission? "We are all looking forward to peaceful competition in this historic undertaking."

Is there any concern that a docking with Serenity could be perceived as an attack by the aliens? "That will be considered in due course. Primarily, it's about the technical preparation."

Why the aliens would not have made any contact attempts? "Perhaps they already have and we have somehow not noticed it."

Should you send messages to Serenity first? "That is already in preparation. But it is important to generate the messages in a well-thought-out way."

Would NASA and SpaceX facilities need special protection now? "The military has already responded adequately with increased security."

How will you move forward? "Close involvement of astronauts in the planning process to ensure optimal, realistic feasibility of every detail... Many test runs with prototypes of various systems... The amount of data in terms of time is more important than the success of each individual test," Elon Musk said.

It went on like this for quite a while until she and Musk finally left the podium and gave way to the astronauts. As she passed Bernard, she didn't even notice his nod. The door was like a magnet for her, a wormhole that inevitably attracted her in her desire to disappear.

"Mel?" she heard a voice as if from far away. As she turned,

Jim approached her with a concerned expression. "What's wrong?"

"It's okay."

"No. You covered it well for the cameras, but I..." He lowered his voice and looked around. "I know you, Mel. What is it? Why aren't you happy?"

She pressed her lips together. She wanted to just say it. That Bernard had cheated on the exam—had received help from someone on the training team. That it would have disqualified him and she—having placed second in her training group—would have been nominated to the Dragon 6 mission and her dream would have come true. That she had been doing everything she could for over two months to be even better than she was then. That she had beaten Bernard in the Astronaut Olympics.

When her gaze passed over Jim's shoulder through the open side door to the press room and fell on Bernard, who was seated at the podium, she quelled this need. Bernard may have cheated, but he had done outstanding work as an astronaut, saving the life of Italian Monica Bocacelli during an EVA, despite nearly dying himself in the process. His social media work was legendary and had drawn much attention to environmental issues.

"It's okay," she repeated, wresting a smile from within. "We will make this mission a success together."

With that, she turned on her heel and left the building at a measured pace, although her body would have preferred to run.

10

Mel sat in the control room above the large plunge pool into which a complete mock-up of a SpaceX Starship had been lowered. Through the window behind her monitors, she had a good view of the many hoists, cranes, lifting platforms, and ropes that ran above the pool and were swarming with technicians and divers. It was only here that she had become aware of how huge the spacecraft actually was. Even when she discounted the slight magnifying effect of the water, this behemoth of a craft looked like an ancient sea monster—and it was only the second stage.

Bernard and Thomas Ehrmann—one of the two astronauts nominated by ESA—floated in the water in their clunky spacesuits, looking like little insects with glowing shoulder lamps alongside the Starship. Ehrmann was recognizable by the blue circular emblem on his helmet, which was the European star logo. He and Italian Gabriella Mancarella had arrived two months earlier to begin training together with the NASA crewmembers, and had fit in smoothly. Thomas was a bit pedantic, which she expected from a German, but extremely approachable and focused, even for an experienced astronaut. He was a trained chemist and neurologist, which made him a perfect chimera of scientist and doctor.

Gabriella, on the other hand, was an aerospace engineer and had served in the Italian Air Force as a fighter pilot, just like Mel. A feisty and lightning-quick South Tyrolean, she and Mel had already spent time together at the Outpost. She was currently on the other side of the spacecraft while Jean Calla-han, Selena Rogerton, and their Canadian colleague Rick Worthington, who was being trained as a backup pilot for Bernard, sat with her in the control room, radioing and guiding their respective assigned comrades through every move. The simulated repair during transit had now lasted four hours.

Mel and her team had come up with a whole series of mishaps and unfortunate concatenations of circumstances to challenge the astronauts to the maximum and prepare them for anything they could think of. She was aware that they could never think of everything, but the more exotic and outlandish their thinking, the more creative they became. She was helped by the fact that she continued to sleep little, study a lot, and exercise excessively so that she would always be aware of the exertions her comrades on the astronaut team were facing. This made it easier for her to empathize with them and to allow herself to push them hard and demand maximum effort, without feeling remorse.

Their task was to monitor and coordinate the current EVA, the same as would be done during a corresponding in-flight mission. As on the ISS, each EVA was meticulously planned on the ground and replayed several times before the consensus plan was passed on to the crew. Astronauts not involved in the EVA assisted in this process by employing external cameras and monitoring the vital signs of their comrades. Again, this was handled by Mission Control, but eyes on site were always valuable. Radio communications could break down or important data could be incorrect.

"Bernard," she said into her headset microphone. "Now loosen the compass screw with the BR-12. Seventy turns. Slowly."

She watched everything through one of the monitors, which showed 'Bernard Antonelli' above a long column of data including heart rate, oxygen consumption, and blood oxygen saturation. The camera feed was from his helmet. She saw him raise his air-filled gloves. First the left one, with which he latched his safety line to one of the bars that ran along the Starship's flank. Then followed the right with the cordless screwdriver. With his thumb, he turned up the power transmission as if in slow motion and carefully placed the opening on the screw head. A muffled boom mingled with the rise and fall of his breath, transmitted through the microphone in his helmet. Suddenly, an ugly squeak sounded.

"Stop!" she shouted, "Something's wrong."

"I felt resistance in my hand," Bernard said in a strained voice, blowing a drop of sweat from his lip. He took the screwdriver off, turning it slightly. The large digital display read 'BR-16' in white letters on a black background. "Damn."

"That's all right. Readjust it. Maybe the head of the screw is undamaged," she instructed him, sighing after muting the microphone. Bernard was still extremely good, but his mistakes had piled up since the specific mission training began. There were not so many that they were out of the norm, but it was out of character for him. He was known as a highly focused perfectionist, so it was noticeable that he was making careless mistakes from time to time.

"I made a mistake, sorry," he said.

"No problem," she assured him. "Take a moment and try again. We're still within safety tolerance. Suit heat dissipation is constant, oxygen supply according to mission planning for this time."

"Thank you."

She stood up and took a step back to look over Selena, Jean, and Gabriella's shoulders, who were intently following and giving instructions to their comrades in the water on umpteen monitors to her right and left. They sat leaning forward and spoke quietly into their headsets, so quietly that even the noise of the servers could be heard.

"I'm taking a break," she said to Jean Callahan. The engineer looked up as she tapped him on the shoulder. "You take over."

"You got it."

Mel took the stairs down and went into the dive room to lean against the wall and listen to the sound of the water sloshing over the edge, being swallowed up by the suction devices, filtered under the floor, and pumped back into the pool. The many staff members who ensured that the astronauts' environment at depth remained controlled and free of distractions were remarkably quiet, as if going out of their way not to disturb anyone.

Good, she thought. Everyone here seemed to take their tasks equally seriously. They had exactly one shot at this mission. Anything less than perfect could be a potentially final problem.

She closed her eyes for a moment and let herself be carried away by the sound of the water and the whirring of the cranes. Just for a moment.

When she opened her eyes again, she had the sensation of falling. One of the platforms was being lifted out of the water by a crane. Her eyelids felt as if they were cast from concrete and the sounds around her grew louder, as if turned up with a regulator. On the rising platform stood three bulky figures in white suits—Thomas in the middle, Rick to his left, and

Bernard to his right with a hand on one of the holding ropes. Water ran from them in torrents, was lifted with the platform, and then flowed from the sides like viscous syrup—a slow-motion process, matching the microgravity in space, accompanied by the hiss and hum of the crane's hydraulics. Employees from suit maintenance waited like a flock of penguins at the edge of the pool to relieve the astronauts of their latest invention for locomotion in a vacuum.

Bernard caught her gaze, which was separated by the droplet-covered visor. She wanted to look away, but something stopped her. Something in his eyes was new. Perhaps it was merely that he was not automatically avoiding her gaze as he usually did. For minutes he remained like that, as if he was looking for something in her pupils, but it was not unpleasant for her—or she was simply too tired.

The stage reached its apex a meter above the water's surface on which tiny drips danced. She blinked as Bernard took a half step backward at the moment the platform faltered. As the crane began to swing them toward the edge of the pool, his fingers loosened from the rope. He lost his footing, stumbled back, and fell toward the water. Before he touched the surface, his arm, with which he'd instinctively tried to catch himself, got caught between the rope and the metal platform and he was thrown to the side.

Mel's eyes snapped wide and she leapt forward, only to see that the divers were already with him, circling like sharks under the metal plate.

Two hours later, Bernard came out of the medical building, outside of which Mel had waited with Thomas, Selena, Jean, Gabriella, and Rick for over an hour before sending the five of them away to continue their training. She knew it might come across as harsh, considering he was their mission commander and part of a team with the weight of all humanity on its shoulders. But the latter was also the reason she had to make a statement: The mission came first. Not emotions, not compassion, not even camaraderie. So they returned to the plunge pool, simulating the failure of an EVA astronaut during a transit repair mission. Mel had handed off to her second-in-command, Jason Bradley, who, as the former head of Mission Control, had more experience than she did.

Mel was glad that the JSC was currently closed to journalists. It was a surprisingly normal sight when the astronaut stepped through the double doors, accompanied by a nurse who held the door open for him. He was wearing his blue jumpsuit with the Next Step Mission logo, two stylized people, a man and a woman, their hands touching and reaching up with a torch. His eyes were protected by pilot goggles reflecting the evening sunlight, and his shoulder was thickly wrapped with his arm held in a medical sling across his chest.

When Bernard saw her, there was a brief delay in his movement, but he did not seem surprised. He gestured to the nurse that he would be fine on his own, and she disappeared back into the building.

"Sorry, boss," he said sounding like he was not in fact delivering an apology to her.

Mel looked around. A van drove by on the cross street, and a block away two figures with wheeled suitcases walked from one building to another. Other than that, they were alone.

"What was that over the plunge pool?" she asked.

"I lost my balance." He shook his head and sighed. "Bad timing, I guess."

"You could say that. What's the diagnosis?"

"Rotator cuff rupture. Shoulder muscles."

"How long?"

"I'm having surgery tomorrow," he explained, looking strangely composed. Perhaps he had cried all his tears behind closed doors, and that was why he was wearing his mirrored glasses. Surgery meant a health scare. "After that, four to six weeks until the fixation bandage comes off. Then three to five months of physical therapy for muscle rebuilding, depending on how well the tissue cooperates."

"We'll figure it out," she assured him reflexively, although she couldn't think of a spontaneous way to do that. She nodded, lost in thought. "We'll get it done."

"I think we need to get going," he said, pointing to the small golfcart humming off to one side.

"The press conference." She nodded and pursed her mouth. "This 'public at every step' policy has been on my nerves from the beginning."

"It's the most important mission in human history," Bernard reminded her. "It concerns all of us. We must not close ourselves off, but show that we are merely the fingers of a much larger body seizing an opportunity for everyone on this planet. Those were your words."

"I know. I just wish they had less harsh consequences at this moment."

The golfcart delivered them to the press center, where Jim was waiting, surrounded by a bubble of assistants and advisors who rotated around the acting administrator like comets around a massive central star. When he saw them coming, he shooed the others away, looking upset.

"How does it look?"

"Not good," she admitted bluntly. "But I'll figure something out."

"Time frame?" Jim looked as if he'd been struck by a spontaneous fever and might suffer a fainting spell at any moment.

"If things go moderately well, six months."

He ruffled his hair and bared his teeth. "The press room is packed. I wish we could at least wait until tomorrow."

"A promise is a promise, and the press remembers specific assurances better than any elephant."

He nodded absently and clicked his tongue. Addressing Bernard, he said, "We'll get it done."

"You're the second person to say that to me," the astronaut replied neutrally, looking down at his arm sling. "I think so, too. I'll dig in."

"You must. You are the best and most popular astronaut in the world, since Armstrong."

The daily press conferences were part of Project Next Step's overall communications strategy. Just as they had to brief the President every day and, in a slimmed-down form, Congress, they also opened up to the public. It was in large part out of fairness, since they were indeed convinced that humanity's most important journey concerned them all, and in a smaller but still significant part, out of the need to maintain political backing. Four years was an infinitesimally short time to prepare for a mission that was entering uncharted space territory.

In politics and social life, however, four years was an infinitely long time. Elections could change everything, cultural moods could lead to unforeseen upheavals, and public interest could simply die off. Any setback could mean the death knell—as it might now—and then there was Serenity. The object continued to travel at a constant speed with its tiny tail that was thus far unexplained, but even that could change at any time. They simply knew too little to make clear predictions.

So she squared her posture before walking with Bernard

through the door, which was being held open by two police officers, and stepping up to the podium with the two chairs prepared. The NASA blue of the curtain behind her seemed darker today than usual.

As always, it was crowded and the murmur that went through the journalists and influencers present when they saw Bernard's arm in the sling was accordingly oppressive.

"Welcome to today's press briefing," Mel greeted those present with a hushing gesture, whereupon it quickly became quiet. "As you have noticed, we don't have such good news today. Unfortunately, Bernard injured himself and will be out for a while. The accident happened through no fault of his own during a highly complex EVA exercise in the plunge pool with the Starship mock-up. We are currently unable to say how long Bernard will be out of action, nor when he will be fully available for the mission. So I ask for your patience in this regard. We need to gather all the information ourselves first and then decide how to proceed and on what schedule."

She paused when she saw a movement on Bernard's part. He had leaned over to her, covering his microphone with his healthy hand. "I'd like to say something directly."

"Go ahead." She nodded and gestured for him to speak.

"Thanks, Mel." Bernard struggled to smile, although all at once he looked as if someone had sucked all the color from his face. She was beginning to worry that the doctors might have missed something.

"My injury today is bitter for me, of course, and most of all I feel like I'm letting my team down. Making what could be first contact with aliens is a dream come true for me, one I never dared to dream. As you can imagine, I would love nothing more than to fly out there and explore Serenity. But there are worse fates than having to give up on a dream—and that's living with yourself after making bad decisions. Next Step can only succeed if everything works, if every single person is one hundred percent on the job and can give it their all. I can't do that anymore," he explained, and a dull feeling spread through Mel with each additional word.

"I know our mission leader is the epitome of a team player who would sacrifice herself to do the right thing. In this case, however, turning a blind eye to me and compromising would be the wrong thing to do. I will probably be out for half a year, which is one-eighth of the total preparation time until departure and therefore just plain unacceptable. There can be no exceptions, no mistakes." Bernard emphasized the last word conspicuously and seemed thoughtful.

There was a dead silence in the press room. "I'm not worried about my absence, however, because we have excellent replacements. There is a substitute list, well prepared, and each of them is professional and well-trained. But we also have a replacement who is outstanding—and that's Melody Adams." He pointed to her and a renewed murmur gripped the room.

She flinched as if he had slapped her. Surprised, she blinked to make sure she wasn't dreaming.

"She has gone through astronaut training with excellent results. It's a secret she didn't think the rest of us knew, but she's been training harder than any of us since Serenity's return, knows our manuals by heart, and is in better physical shape than I am. She is also the most genuine person I have ever met. She has all the tools I brought with me, plus a moral compass that ought to impress each of us.

"I know there will be objections that she has no experience in space yet, but the training opportunities here are tremendous, and she will be a pilot for a flight doing something that has yet to be done by anyone else. So, what difference does it make? What I also know is that Melody Adams combines the best of us as a species and is a shining example. What better qualification could there be to initiate first contact with extraterrestrials or extraterrestrial technology?

"This is an aspect we have talked about far too little, and that is an oversight. Let me conclude by saying that I realize that I have no authority or say in nominating a successor to me, but if my word still carries any weight, I will say this: I know best the demands of my job within the team and I am certain that there is no better successor for me than Lieutenant Commander, and Doctor, Melody Adams."

Bernard sat back, and when, after a brief silence, the members of the press awoke as if from a spell, they began to shout wildly and wave their upraised hands. Melody still stared at the astronaut, stunned, trying to bring order to the conflicting emotions he had stirred in her.

After a few minutes, Jim came in, gave them a wave to leave the podium, and smiled professionally in the direction of the journalists, although she could see he had gone pale. "Okay, that was some announcement, huh? Let's settle down now and then we'll work through your questions."

She followed Bernard as if in a trance, first out of the hall, then through the anteroom, and finally onto the deserted street in front of the building.

"What..." she began, but did not know what to say. Part of her wanted to burst into cheers, another to cry, still another to scream with compassion and dismay. "I don't understand."

"Yes, I think you do," he said, turning to her. He seemed more composed than before, almost detached. "I meant every word I said in there. I don't know if it's going to work out, but I'm sure you've got a serious shot now. Holding on to my job would be the second worst decision of my life and a blatant injustice. I realize you must think that's strange coming from me."

She said nothing and he sighed.

"I've always given everything I had to achieve my goals and dreams, and there was a lot I wasn't proud of." He seemed to reflect. "Sometimes the price you pay is too high, and I've become more and more aware of that. You can't build something good on something bad, but I realized that way too late. So I made the only right decision. Better late than never, huh?"

Mel smiled and nodded her head, strongly moved and feeling numb.

"I'm sorry, Mel. I'm truly sorry. Especially for not having the courage to tell the whole truth, so they would all understand even better why it has to be you. I will cry over this missed mission for the rest of my life, but I can handle it. I know now why you didn't expose me then, not even when they gave me the job that should have been yours. It's hard to live with yourself when you're doing the more selfish thing, not the *right* thing. A dream not lived is a painful notion, but a dream lived at the expense of others is a nightmare."

"I don't know what to say, Bernard. Except that I'm sorry," she said.

"Ha," he laughed, and it sounded almost cheerful. "Why should you be sorry for me?"

"I was wrong about you."

"I fooled myself. How could I blame you, huh?" asked Bernard, shaking his head. "My wife and children will be delighted to have me return to them. The idea of watching the TV with them while you make history is more comforting than I would have thought."

A car turned the corner and came toward them.

"Ah, I guess that's for me," he said, extending his free hand to her. Mel took it and looked into his eyes through a delicate veil of tears.

She felt like she was seeing Bernard for the first time—the person behind the colleague she had always thought she knew a lot about, hardly any of it positive.

"You'll do fine, Mel. You're a hero to me, even though I was never willing to admit it. And today I finally know what it feels like to do that." He squinted into the last soft rays of sunlight and smiled a warm smile. "It feels *good*. I think you saved my life, one way or another. I'll see you around."

She was silent as he got into the car and rode away.

"You did it on purpose," she breathed, and in her mind's eye the scene of Bernard falling backward on the lifting platform of the plunge pool played over and over again. Tears ran down her cheeks, but she still did not wake up from this strange dream.

11

The first surprise was that Jim supported her nomination, even though he had explained to her several times in recent months why he could not nominate anyone who had not yet been in space. A second surprise came from the media. A wave of support was building for her, despite her CNN-televised past blunder. The press memory seemed to be quite short in nature. With the media support, as is often the case, came political support and thus pressure from Washington to back the administrator's decision.

The third surprise was the team of Thomas, Gabriella, Rick, Jean, and Selena, who welcomed her into their midst very warmly and without any initial hurdles, and as their commander to boot. Apparently Bernard was not the only one who saw things in her that she would never have said of herself or consider her normal. She was almost uncomfortable with this kind of exaggeration, although the joy of her nomination naturally outweighed it.

When she came home in the evening, she sometimes cried. Sometimes out of joy, sometimes out of humility toward fate, which, like a balancing pendulum, seemed to tell her in the end that if it started well, it would end well. She hoped the same was true for her mission, because the first problems started two months after her official nomination. That came with some adjustments, such as a total of four flights to the ISS that she would pilot.

Originally planned as resupply missions, instead of the scheduled EVAs in the plunge pool, she would make the four flights within a year and spend a total of four weeks in space to gain experience. While this was in line with her dream of being an astronaut, it was not in line with her idea of teamwork. She was separated from the others, spending an extreme amount of time in the Dragon simulator, whose interface had been adopted for Starship. While the ship systems had little in common, the basic menu navigation and layout were similar enough.

So she piloted the Dragon in the morning and the Starship in the afternoon, only to meet her comrades, whose commander she was supposed to be, in the evening during theory sessions with the SpaceX engineers. Then there were her dreams, which, as always, revolved around space and seemed to be made even more intense since her new assignment. Although she had always dreamed a great deal, even as a child, and had learned to dream lucidly from her grandmother, the nightly forays into her relaxing brain had become exhausting. She needed more *sleep*.

She worried about the potentially negative impact on team building, while at the same time there were very different overriding burdens falling from her shoulders and needing to be solved by Jim and Jason. The first of these was the skyrocketing costs. SpaceX was testing a full dual stage with Super Heavy and Starship every ten days. With the massive funds being transferred from Washington, their infamous rapid prototyping reached whole new dimensions.

But the successes justified the spending spree. After four

orbits and a successful orbital refueling mission, for which the Hawthorne-based company had worked with NASA to convert a Starship into a refueling station, it was clear they were headed in the right direction. At the same time, a lingering recession was gnawing away at the economic strength of their country and that of their allies in Europe and Canada.

Key components and procedures had yet to be developed, including new Raptor III engines that provided enough thrust to match Serenity's speed. Just eight percent more power was a huge leap in rocket technology. To accomplish this, it was necessary to attract the best talent in the world, and that could only be done with high salaries, which had virtually exploded due to the extreme demand.

Then there were China and Russia, who wanted to set up their own mission, but their first ten orbital tests ended in total failures, and concerns grew that there might be sabotage attempts given the massive tensions between East and West. The military presence at all NASA and SpaceX sites was correspondingly large and had something oppressive about it, as if danger lurked around every corner, or as if the huge boosters of the Super Heavys could blow up at any moment.

But they did not. Instead, something else happened, as so often occurs when history takes a turn where uncrossable lines were expected. President Brosnahan and Xi Jinping seemed to have decided behind closed doors that a human journey to the alien visitor was the most urgent of all goals, and they preferred to team up rather than leave China with the weight of being unrepresented, or leave the existing team to fear their spacecraft being shot down at launch by adversaries.

The concessions were tough on both sides: The U.S., Europe, and Canada had to give up two of their seats in favor of Chinese astronauts. In exchange, China committed to bear 36 percent of the cost of the mission, whose cap was virtually non-existent. Every month, funds equivalent to the gross domestic product of third-world countries were consumed. Moreover, the Middle Kingdom had to drop its Russian partners, whose participation had been categorically opposed by all members of Project Next Step.

In the end, an historic agreement was reached on a joint mission, which was received with mixed feelings after Rick Worthington and Jean Callahan had to step down. This rupture of the team left its mark and caused real dejection among them. It didn't end the tensions between the two power blocs, but at least it froze them in place with the prospect of improvement, cooperation instead of war, and hope instead of fear. Mel thought that was a good starting point, perhaps even worth the sacrifices they had to make for it.

From then on, the project was called 'Reach' and their spaceship would be *Pangaea*, or 盘古大陆, which was pronounced 'Pángǔ dàlù.' They would all have to get used to it—the name used for Earth's primeval continent, when all land masses had still been one. It seemed to Melody an extremely worthy name for their mission's ship.

It was a particularly hot August 1st in 2027 when the Chinese astronauts arrived at JSC with a large delegation. The mainly diplomatic and political representatives of the CCP would only be allowed to stay in certain areas, and most would leave in the evening—except for a few liaisons who would participate in mission planning and take care of their astronauts. Mel was under no illusions that they would be closely monitored to prevent any technology theft. How much the intelligence agencies of both countries were circling in the background, she didn't want to know.

She waited with Selena, Thomas, and Gabriella in one of the lounges in the main building. No one touched any of the many cookies or opened any of the prepared bottles. The mood was subdued because they knew that, as of today, there would be no turning back for Rick and Jean, who had given way to political and financial necessities. To see them leave through no fault of their own was painful and unfair.

"Until now, our tasks have been simple," she said into the silence, broken only by the tentative hum of the air conditioner, as if matching the mood. "Because everything was in our own hands. What's happening now was not our choice. But we can learn from it."

"I wish it didn't feel like a dagger in the back," Selena Rogerton grumbled. The doctor with the prominent aquiline nose and deep blue eyes expelled her breath like an overheated tea kettle.

"Amen," Thomas Ehrmann agreed with her. A new wrinkle of anger had formed on the German's forehead in recent days, and it seemed to grow deeper by the hour. "They deserved to be there. So did all of us. Now we get two quota Chinese so they can transport their pseudo-communist ideology into space and to Serenity."

Gabriella joined in the murky mutterings with a bouncy Italian accent. "It wouldn't surprise me if every time they call home, they read out prepared propaganda manifestos and rag on us."

"We wouldn't even notice." Selena nodded somberly. "Unless we have to learn Chinese now, too. I don't know how we're going to manage that."

"That won't be necessary," said a resonant voice, startling them. A rather tall Chinese man had stepped into the doorway, wearing a blue jumpsuit identical to theirs except for the red flag with the five stars. His face was soft and immaculately shaved, his hair cropped short. He possessed the piercing gaze of an intellectual and the delicate hands of an artist. Mel noticed only now that he'd hardly had an accent, even less than Thomas, who could never quite hide his origins from the heart of Europe.

Behind the Chinese man, another person came in, considerably smaller and so beautiful that Mel felt a reluctant twinge of envy. Her face was elfin and her stature delicate for the particular fitness requirements of a taikonaut.

"This is Colonel Wang Hongbo, I am Colonel Ye Zhigang," announced the tall Chinese man after both were inside the room and he had closed the door behind them, shutting out the clatter of voices and clicking cameras that had wafted in with them.

"Your English is definitely better than my Chinese," Thomas remarked dryly after he was the first to break free from his surprise and stand up. He shook hands first with Wang Hongbo and then with Ye Zhigang. "I'm Tom."

"I studied in Boston for five years," the latter remarked with a smile, imitating the Boston accent so perfectly that Mel felt like she was participating in a surreal skit.

"I'm afraid I can't compete with that," Wang Hongbo said amiably. Her English was far from her colleague's not-far-from-native proficiency, but quite decent. "I had to learn from books and with teachers. Hopefully, that was good enough."

Mel stood up next, nudging Gabriella and Selena under the table.

"Welcome to the team," she said kindly, shaking her hand at the same time. Firm pressure, cool skin. That Rick and Jean had been ousted was not the fault of these two taikonauts, so it would be absurd to try to punish them for it. "Zhigang and Hongbo, right?"

"Right," Hongbo replied with a neutral smile, tilting her head slightly. "We give the family name first in China. My personal name is Hongbo."

"Hongbo," Gabriella repeated the name after she'd introduced herself. "What does that mean?"

"Something like..." The Chinese woman took time to think, and tilted her head again. "Something like 'the straight path to healing' or 'in a straight line to medicine.' It's hard to find the correct English words for it."

"I love that your names always have meaning evident from the characters or terms," Selena remarked, shaking hands.

"Selena comes from Greek mythology and means the moon, am I right?" interjected Zhigang, and the doctor pursed her mouth appreciatively.

"You know your stuff."

"We were able to prepare well. For us, the meanings of names are important. In our culture, they give a certain direction to a person's destiny."

"'Nomen est Omen' is how we say it," Tom remarked. "I guess that would make me 'the twin.' Maybe I have an unseen spirit following me around."

The two Chinese smiled politely at the joke, without revealing whether they were honestly amused or simply being polite.

"I imagine," Zhigang said in Tom's direction, "that you... find it a hurdle to accept us as your comrades." He looked to Hongbo, whose expression remained identical to before when they had all been throwing shallow small talk at each other. "Rest assured that we understand, and your colleagues have our deep respect. We hope that this unattractive side effect of our historic collaboration will not get in the way of the success of our mission, or our professionalism as a team."

"It won't," Mel assured him, and only now did the former Chinese Air Force pilot look at her and bow his head as well. She wondered if she had just learned the first lesson in cultural differences, and Zhigang had addressed Tom because he was the oldest of them and thus was owed special respect, even though she was the commander.

"We are aware of the scope of our undertaking and knew that it would not and will not be easy," Mel continued. "For many people, you two represent an entire continent, despite its many differences, and diversity for our mission is right and can bring us great mutual benefits. Different perspectives and approaches can only mean that the quality of problem-solving will be even better. I only wish I hadn't lost two colleagues in the process. But as I said, that was not and is not your fault."

"Thank you, Lieutenant Commander." Zhigang inclined his head, Hongbo following with a barely noticeable delay.

"Please, call me Mel."

The next tilt of his head did not reveal whether he accepted her offer or not. His facial expression remained polite.

"If I may be permitted a remark," Hongbo said, looking at Zhigang to receive the tiniest micro-nod, "I think we must face the press." She glanced at her slim wristwatch. "The official meeting will begin in two minutes."

The reservations between the 'Western team' and the 'Eastern team,' as Tom jokingly called them, remained, as it turned out during the first year. Gradually, they became better acquainted with the cultural differences, which ironically was not particularly helpful, as it created a new layer of requirements while they had to focus on other things. For example, there was the special importance of age in the respect shown. Mel was the commander, but Tom was often the first point of contact for Hongbo and Zhigang, no matter how many times the ESA astronaut asked them to address her directly.

The next problem was much more drastic: the two taikonauts did not seem to know the word 'no.' Apparently, in their culture, a refusal was tantamount to an affront, so in this case they always said something like 'yes, but...' or 'that's possible, yet you could also...' and similar paraphrases. To Mel and her comrades, this seemed extremely awkward and inefficient.

After clarifying conversations, it got a little better, but limited by the fact that since then she was also concerned about not offending them with curt 'nos.' She didn't want to come off as a Western culturalist and make her way of communicating out to be the only correct one. But she found this more difficult than expected.

Another disadvantage was that the Chinese were trained on their own systems and had to relearn everything on the Starship and their spacesuits. Sure, there were many similarities and overlaps, but the spaceships were quite different, especially in the sense that the American launchers, engines, and spaceships were more advanced and therefore more complex to operate. This left Rick and Jean far behind in honing their own abilities, as they continued to work on the project in a secondary role with the painful task of helping to train their Chinese replacements as perfectly as possible... to take *their* places.

The good news, however, was that Zhigang and Hongbo were extremely disciplined and incredibly hardworking. They worked tirelessly and put in the necessary overtime to catch up as quickly as possible. Even after hours, they crammed through the radio manual, and Hongbo, in particular, honed her English on detailed technical matters that she, as an engineer, needed to know.

This 'advantage' was accompanied by the disadvantage that their team could hardly bond and grow together during the first year. During joint exercises and study sessions, they were all like robots, and the few hours of free time each week when they ventured into the Outpost, the taikonauts stayed at JSC and studied tirelessly. In the beginning, Melody had to stifle several implied taunts toward 'the new guys' from within their trusting foursome, but those initial growing pains quickly subsided as the mission progressed.

Although Mel was no longer studying and working out

day and night because she simply didn't have time for it, and was getting too much intellectual and lexical input during work hours, there remained a distinct double burden. This was because Jim and Jason, who had teamed up as leaders to get the job done, kept using her in an advisory capacity.

In the early months, they had set the course for the entire project setup and created pipelines for the various planning and design teams, whose processes were not changed thereafter. They were working with someone else's tools, so to speak, and had to become familiar with their specifications. As the main teams, she had thrown together engineers, mathematicians, and physicists from all disciplines to solve problems that had so far only been speculated about on a theoretical basis, but by no means on a practical one.

One took care of a solution for docking to Serenity. According to their telescope data, they calculated an object that at least shared very many appearance characteristics with an asteroid—it did not rotate and thus probably had no artificial gravity. Its mass was much too small to generate appreciable gravitational forces. A landing was therefore impossible. Harpoons could be used to pull their spacecraft in, but that could be interpreted as an attack.

That meant maneuvering thrusters that would have to keep correcting position as their flight direction and speed were synchronized. That, in turn, necessitated larger cold gas supplies and thus increased the overall mass—in other words, resources and therefore money.

Other teams were in charge of radiation protection for the year-and-a-half trip, food storage and prep, their exercise program, drugs and medical supplies, the necessary tools, the radio equipment, the airlock and necessary maintenance accesses, and so forth.

Then there were their persistent attempts to contact Serenity. They had tried directional beams, radio signals on all frequencies, infrared pulses, and some other methods that had sounded so outlandish to her that she had not memorized them. But the outcome was always the same: no response.

Only once the European Southern Observatory, ESO, had detected a reflection off the surface of the alien object, which, however, had been extremely short and had not followed any recognizable pattern. As a result, they did not exclude the possibility of a simple measurement error. On bad days this mysterious silence unsettled her. On good days, she convinced herself that the many TV talk-show scientists who had sprouted from the ground were right: Alien life could be so alien to us that it doesn't even perceive our signals as such.

In her dreams, she sometimes saw Earth—from Serenity's point of view, she imagined, and responded with a serene reflection of the signals she picked up. But always, it seemed, when she already had the sun between her and the Earth. She realized that her optimism was not as good as it used to be. Mel blamed it on the heavy workload. To suppress this feeling, she paradoxically worked even harder.

Whether their visitor could hear them or not, they would soon find out once they were on the scene. By then, at the latest, she hoped they would have more success, or at least learn something—although she was sure that Serenity's sole existence had caused humanity to change.

The presence of two Chinese taikonauts in her team was the best proof of that.

12

Mel saw the rocket first. It was a twinkling star against the beautiful, precious blue planet passing very close to her. She knew it was her rocket, although it seemed very strange—a glow in the cold of the vacuum. Without any effort, and purposeless, she watched the 120-meter colossus rise, bracing itself against the gravitational sink from which it had launched.

Then it seemed to break in half as the first stage separated from the second, ignited its maneuvering thrusters in low Earth orbit, turned, and accelerated back toward the surface. The second stage changed course and headed toward an identical twin waiting for it in the darkness. It was a sublime sight, despite the crude forces of the chemical engine that fired hissing hot plasma into the silent cold around it. The web of twinkling stars in the darkness welcomed the twins and...

~

"Mel?"

"Hmm?" she murmured sleepily, weakly raising a hand to

ward off the voice, but instead, something gently patted her hair and forehead. Only slowly did the dream slip away from her, moving away like a warming blanket. She tried to reach for it, but the sense of majesty, the sense of the beauty of emptiness, faded to memory and the memory to a pale afterimage.

When she finally understood where she was, she slowly opened her eyes. "Jim?"

"I'm here," he said quietly, continuing to caress her forehead. She turned toward the warmth—his chest and let him press her against him. "Have you been dreaming again?"

"Mm-hmm." Her affirmative hum echoed slightly in his chest.

"Someday you'll have to show me how this conscious dreaming works."

"When I get back," she promised him, stifling a yawn. She wished this moment could stretch into infinity, full of security and the priceless feeling of intimate togetherness, when the separating duality became a unity that felt like the meaningful primordial state of the universe. "You have to start early and practice a lot. After that, it goes by itself."

"I think you're being too modest again."

"I don't think so." Mel suppressed another yawn and instead hummed comfortably. "You have to know if you want it. It's like a second life you lead. Sometimes I wish I could just go to sleep and wake up in the morning. Don't forget that everything is still in your head in the morning."

"But you're always dreaming about space, so that can't be bad. I imagine it's extremely relaxing without all the distractions and thoughts," Jim replied thoughtfully.

"I've only been dreaming about space since I discovered Serenity. Before that, it was mostly dreams of failing astronaut training or certain flight maneuvers." She chuckled. "Now they've become more undemanding, extremely quiet and downright long-winded in their own way. Apparently, my dreaming is getting older, too."

"Now I'm even more curious."

"I'll give you lessons when I get back."

"When you get back..." he repeated, the underlying sadness of losing their moment together resonating in his voice. It wasn't his fault. It was the fault of time. She didn't know what time it was since the alarm hadn't rung yet, but it was the day of the launch.

They were lying in her room in the crew's quarters on the grounds of the JSC, which the crewmembers had not been allowed to leave for half a year. The risk was too great that one of the team would be injured in an accident, contract a disease, or be kidnapped or murdered by one of the many groups who thought their mission was a devil's endeavor, the end of humanity, the beginning of an alien invasion, or something else abstruse. No one could truly be replaced, although a full dozen replacements had always been training to step in, just in case.

"When I get back," she affirmed. Although they had long shied away from the risk of their intimacy, last night had felt right. Even the intense years of preparation hadn't been able to change the fact that they gravitated toward each other like magnets, inevitably and irretrievably. It spoke to the depth of what they felt for each other that they didn't waste their precious time together lying to each other, assuring each other they would see each other again. The same didn't apply to clichés, however, which is why she let herself slip into, "I wish this moment could last forever."

"But then you wouldn't be able to do the one thing you've dedicated your life to," he reasoned, breaking away from her. Smiling, he pressed a kiss to her lips. "I have to sneak out now. The alarm will go off in an hour."

"You probably should," she sighed.

"I almost feel like I did back in college," he snickered glee-fully, and she could tell he was covering up the fact that he was about to cry. After putting on his shirt, sweater, and pants and tightening his wristwatch, he looked at her again. His smile remained, but his expression turned serious. "I love you, Mel. I always have." With that, he turned on his heel and left her room.

"I love you too," she said softly toward the door as it slid barely audibly into the lock.

By the time the alarm clock rang she had already showered, brushed her teeth, applied cream to her scalp—which had dried to within an inch of its life after yesterday's shave—and put on her multi-functional underwear.

She stood at the sound of the bell, her bag in hand, and walked out into the hallway.

Almost simultaneously, the other doors opened and her comrades also stepped out onto the unadorned PVC floor. Tom and Gabriella looked extremely tired and gave each other quick sideways glances that didn't escape Mel. She let them know with a hint of a smile that she didn't mind and their secret was safe with her. Both of their marriages had broken up during the preparation, which didn't surprise her. The outcome of their mission was highly uncertain, and they would have to wait at least a year, if the mission was successful, before they arrived back at an orbital point from which they could fly to Earth.

This time frame could change, however, depending on how long they flew alongside Serenity. It was also quite possible that they would not be able to return, in the event there was not enough fuel to make the necessary orbital corrections.

What marriage could survive that prospect, coupled with four years of distance during preparation? Mel thought of herself and Jim and quickly pushed the thought aside. Selena appeared well-rested but tense. Her nut-brown eyes were aimed straight ahead and her smile was more automated than natural. Hongbo and Zhigang, on the other hand, looked the same as always: perfectly dressed, their expressions friendly but not very communicative.

"All right, team," Mel said, feeling she had to say something. "Today is the day of truth. If anyone can do it, we can. We have the best and brightest people in the world on our side. Let's show them that their trust in us was justified. We've practiced enough, so the rest will be a piece of cake."

Launch day for them was celebrated just like any other launch. That meant at L-minus five hours they went into a large conference room, where a sumptuous breakfast was set up—minimal junk food and low fat. Mel was sure no one had an appetite because, contrary to common assumptions, even astronauts felt something like excitement manifesting in their stomachs. But eating was part of the duty, so they ate while making small talk and sharing uncomplicated jokes until it was time to move on to the next step.

At L-minus four and a half hours they received the final weather report, which had not changed, so nothing from the meteorologists stood in the way of launch. At this news they allowed themselves the first sighs of relief.

At L-minus four hours, they made their way to the preparation room for their flight suits. It was an unadorned cube with a mottled gray floor and pictures on the walls showing astronauts from past missions in the 1960s and 1970s. With SpaceX and NASA now intermingled at Cape Canaveral, the control panels and display controls on the wall were from older times with round viewing windows and analog displays above bulky dials, while the couches looked futuristic with their black and white contrast.

Mel and her team members waited, lined up next to each other after donning their personal flight suits—or rather, having been dressed in them. Each had been painstakingly checked for damage or air loss, for perfect fit and functionality. Mel still felt like a doll, even though they had gone through the procedure umpteen times. There was something strangely unspectacular about the whole process because it felt like a rerun, a movie she had seen too many times before. Tests of the helmet systems followed, including head-up display and radio, and water and air supply.

At L-minus three hours, they stepped out of the building and were met by a gaggle of journalists whose flashing lights hit like an artillery barrage after it had been so quiet until now. They lined up in front of waiting vehicles, waving and smiling for the cameras. Family members waited behind a barrier— quarantine regulations did not allow direct physical contact from this point on.

Mel watched as Tom and Gabriella waved to their children, who were standing not two feet away behind the barrier. They exchanged a few affectionate words, promising them that they would see each other again very soon, and that they should listen to mommy—or daddy—and help take care of the family. Mel respected Gabriella's ex-husband and Tom's ex-wife for showing up despite everything and not denying their children this moment. Especially given the possibility they were going on a one-way mission.

Hongbo and Zhigang showed something like emotion for the first time as they waved to their children and spoke to them in Chinese. They appeared moved under the layer of well-practiced control, like a light moving closer to a paper wall and becoming visible as a bright surface. Their spouses held the still very young girls and boys in their arms and talked melodically to them before blowing kisses to their loved ones.

Selena's husband, who worked at NASA, was in Mission Control and he was on duty, so they had said goodbye to each other earlier. So, she and Mel both stood there and smiled politely in the face of the great emotion around them. Mel thought of Jim and what it would be like to have him standing there on the other side of the barrier, blowing kisses to her.

The ride to Launch Pad 39A took just under 20 minutes, the six of them in their white and gray suits sitting in the electric minibus that served as the new 'Astrovan.' No one spoke a word. The blue lights of the police cars that accompanied them—in addition to the heavy Army Humvees in front and back and the two helicopters circling overhead—reflected in the interior of the large van. Mel felt like she was on a drug trip, except this was real.

"It's really happening, huh?" asked Selena, addressing no one in particular. Her visor was up, yet her voice had a strong resonance.

"I guess so."

"Four long years. Still, they seem like a second. A snap of my fingers in my life."

"Too much input in too short a time," Tom explained from the other side. "When your brain learns so much new stuff in such a short time, there are an awful lot of new neural connections. That means fewer well-trodden paths, if you will. Therefore the sense of time stretches because there's more conscious rather than unconscious processing. At the same time, we're not thinking about it on a meta-level, which is why the time period seems very short retrospectively."

"Quite the smart ass." Gabriella grinned.

"We call that the 'explorer syndrome' in China. Or something close to that," Hongbo interjected. Just like Zhigang, she sat there with her gloved hands folded over, as if they had both been draped that way for a photo. Mel still felt it was surreal to see two Chinese faces in the SpaceX suits, as well as like their red flag patches on their upper arms.

"Sounds like a disease," Gabriella commented.

"An explorer lives many lives because he sees something

new every day." From Hongbo's mouth it sounded like a quote.

"Is that from Confucius?" the Italian woman asked.

"Not every Chinese proverb comes from Confucius," Zhigang noted.

"But every other one, surely?" Tom grinned amusedly, and the Chinese man hesitated before an answering smile broke through.

"Yeah, that's probably about right, because all the others are from Lao Tzu." Now they were all giggling.

"Do you also have a saying for a mission with an unlikely return, but the possibility of first contact with little green men that we know precisely nothing about?"

Zhigang pondered, and Hongbo beat him to it, "Experience is like a lantern at our backs—it only illuminates the part of the road we have already traveled."

Mel nodded appreciatively. "That's a nice saying. Optimistic about the new."

"Lao-Tzu or Confucius?" Tom asked.

"Confucius, of course!" the taikonaut replied with a giggle that started all of them laughing, and with the spontaneous merriment, some of their tension blew away.

When they reached historic Launch Pad 39A after 20 minutes the escort convoy withdrew. To the east, Mel could see warships offshore, to the west the pale Orlando skyline, and overhead were patrolling fighter jets. Although it was quite lonely out here at the huge supply tower and she had lived and worked shielded from the public for a long time, the size of the military presence told her the size and scope of what they were about to do.

They took a brief moment to line up in front of the massive steel structure next to which stood *Starship-2* planted on the Super Heavy and bearing the large inscription, '*Pangaea.*' The ship was held in place by two huge grappling arms and connected by an airlock leading from the top of the elevator into the cockpit.

Their spaceship was 120 meters high including its booster, and thus looked like a small skyscraper. The many thousands of black ceramic tiles on the steel hull were hexagonal, but from a distance of 70 meters below they looked like one continuous surface. With the small stub wings at the back of the second stage, and at the front right and left of the cockpit, *Pangaea* looked like an artifact from the future, beautiful and impressive at the same time.

Before the team of SpaceX and NASA technicians arrived in their black coveralls, complete with black hoods and black masks, the crew turned around once more and waved to the single cameraman accompanying them. Then they were surrounded by the futuristic-looking men and women who checked the locking mechanisms of their helmets one last time before taking them to the elevator. The ride up took a little more than a minute, after which they stepped into the tube-shaped airlock, which was more like a long bridge, connecting the tower and the top of the spaceship like an umbilical cord. At the open hatch waited two more technicians in black with sensor devices in their hands.

Mel walked in the lead beside Tom, nodded to the two figures, and let them help her climb into the cockpit. Although SpaceX had designed their suits for improved agility, they were still pressurized and anything but comfortable onesies.

At first glance, the cockpit looked like a cross between a padded cell and a storage room. The walls around the four front windows were covered in a white padded polymer material. There were two seats in front and four behind, which were down at the moment and thus level with them in the massive suspension. She sat down with Zhigang in the pilot seats and felt like a roller coaster passenger before the safety bars were pushed down.

The black seat cushions made no noise as she slid back and forth a bit, as if she were sitting on them for the first time. Only when Hongbo, Thomas, Selena, and Gabriella had also taken their seats did the technicians come over, buckle them in one by one and wait for each to give the thumbs up. Then, the techs gave the go-ahead and Mel spoke the command to move the seats into position.

Accompanied by electric buzzing, they slowly tilted backward and then slid forward into the flight position until their backs were facing down and at least she and Zhigang, as pilot and co-pilot, could look out the window and up into the blue sky.

"Flight position," she reported via radio.

"Flight position confirmed, *Pangaea*," replied the muffled voice of Bellamy Schrader from Launch Control. Mel could have picked out his Georgia accent in a hurricane. "Closeout team, close hatch and secure."

Mel started the system check of the control software and, after successful completion, that of the secondary and redundancy systems. It took about ten minutes, then the confirmation from the ground crew sounded in her helmet.

"Hatch locked and secured."

"Initiate airlock retraction."

"Airlock retracted and secured. Closeout team now exiting supply tower."

"All ground personnel leave the launchpad now and retreat behind designated security areas," Bellamy ordered from the Launch Control Room in the main building.

"Now it's a matter of waiting," she said, looking at one of the 12 installed cameras in the cockpit, located directly above the console, which consisted of three displays for her and three for Zhigang, which could be operated via the touch-enabled index fingers of their gloves.

"Microphones are now on," Bellamy announced. "Say hello to two point six billion viewers on TV and live streams to every country on Earth!"

"Hello, fellow humans from planet Earth," Mel greeted the invisible eyes. She was glad she couldn't even imagine such a large number. "We welcome you aboard *Pangaea* today for our trip to Mars orbit and our first interstellar visitors. I'm sure you're excited, and so are we here on board. Hongbo, Selena, Gabriella, Thomas, Zhigang, and I are glad that you have tuned in in such numbers. You guys are the backbone, the incentive, and the warmup jacket for us, all at the same time, as we head out on this road that no one has ever seen before. We are not doing this *for* you, we are doing it *with* you. You are our ground crew, and we are proud and humbled to have the honor of representing you out there as we make the first contact attempt with extraterrestrial life."

Mel turned to Zhigang and nodded to him, whereupon he addressed the audience in Chinese, as had been agreed. The simultaneous translation was flashed on one of her displays, but she'd already begun testing her flight stick with her right hand. The diagnostic program annotated her every move on the stick with heading information and vector changes that were exactly as expected, gradually trailing green numbers. She then went over the stub wings and their maneuverability, sweeping them back and forth, and nodded with satisfaction when they, too, indicated no errors and Launch Control confirmed perfect functionality.

The other team members also said a few more encouraging and optimistic words in English and in their respective languages—Tom in German, Gabriella in German and Italian, Hongbo in Chinese, and Selena, as an American with a Hispanic background, in English and Spanish.

When the countdown still showed launch minus 45 minutes, Bellamy, as the safety engineer in charge of the launch, checked in again. "We have *go* for fueling."

"Acknowledge," Mel said. "Go for fueling."

From that time on, things got serious. Liquid methane and liquid oxygen were filled ten minutes later into the unpressurized tanks of Super Heavy, the largest booster ever built in space history.

At L-minus 16 minutes she heard Bellamy's calm voice in her ear again, "Second stage fueling initiated. All systems operating normally."

"Confirm, Launch Control. Looks good from our end, too. The liquid oxygen in the tank is minus one hundred and eighty-three degrees Celsius—very cold!" she explained toward the central display camera, as agreed. "That's why you can see lots of steam now, because the moisture in the surrounding air is condensing.

"Also, the lower half of our booster should now look like a frozen glass, that's because the rocket is insulated, but the moisture on the outer hull still freezes and forms an ice film. This is removed before the launch utilizing certain chemical substances so that it cannot cause an accident like with the Columbia.

"You may also see the still dense fog under the engines at the bottom of the launch pad. This is water vapor because the ground is deliberately fogged to prepare it for the extreme heat of the plasma jet generated during launch. So the risk for heat damage is minimized. And, all of that is completely normal."

"External power cut," Launch Control announced when the countdown showed five minutes left. "You are now self-sustaining."

"Roger. Internal power supply nominal. No error messages," she confirmed. The next few minutes dragged on like an eternity as they sat motionless in their seats, their eyes fixed on their blue displays that shimmered not three hand-breadths in front of their eyes, displaying in sober graphs and numbers the status of their one and only attempt to make history.

During the last minute, the prelaunch computer took command and locked them out of the system. The rocket was now pressurized. Bellamy, as launch director, gave the all-important go-ahead for the launch shortly thereafter. In an impromptu gesture, Mel took Zhigang's hand in hers, and raised them so that the two-and-a-half billion spectators could also recognize her gesture as one of cooperation, not nervousness. The Chinese man hesitated at first, then smiled and nodded at her.

"Ten, nine, eight, seven, six, five, four, three—" The 33 Raptor-III engines fired, sending a violent jolt through the ship. The seat beneath her began to vibrate.

"—two, one, lift-off!" shouted Bellamy.

13

The launch began quite leisurely, as if something was gently pushing on her, and then increased progressively as the 70-meter Super Heavy rocket roared and snarled as it began to work toward its seventy-two meganewtons of thrust. With each passing second her ride became more brutal as the gentle push progressed from a firm squeeze into an iron fist. Despite the cockpit isolation and the helmet that protected her extremely well, the violence could be heard clearly, as though she had Bunsen burners right next to her ears.

After 45 seconds they reached 'max q,' the point where the aerodynamic load on the spacecraft and rocket was at its highest. Bellamy commented on this step over the radio, as he'd done on each one thus far. Her display, in contrast, simply showed an unspectacular dynamic pressure curve with corresponding markings.

"How's it looking up there, *Pangaea*?" Launch Director Bellamy asked.

"Everything is just fine with us. Thanks, Launch Control. Feels like a ride on two Saturn rockets." Mel smiled, because that was exactly what was happening.

A little more than another minute later, the Super Heavy had burned 3,400 tons of oxygen and methane and reached its separation point. The rocket separated from its spacecraft, severed its connection, and fell back into Earth's grasp. Its corrective engines ignited and spun it around, upon which it sped back to Earth to touch down on the landing field off the Florida coast.

"Separation successful," Bellamy said. "Engine ignition second stage."

After a brief hesitation, their Starship bucked—*Pangaea*, she corrected herself—and then its own Raptor engines nudged the ship further toward low Earth orbit, burning another 1,200 tons of fuel in a matter of minutes to escape the gravity well and reach orbit. She noticed the transition across the Kármán line only in the form of a mark on her flight vector display. With their maximum speed of 27,400 kilometers per hour, they followed an elliptical path along a 'throwing parabola' that caused them to continually fall beyond the horizon.

On board, they didn't speak to each other, remaining silent and preoccupied with their personal thoughts as they raced into the darkness on the might of the engines. Mel didn't think about the many things that could go wrong if just one of a zillion variables or parts was faulty. No, she wasn't thinking about anything. In a way, the riskiest part of her journey—depending on who you asked—was like a release for her. There was nothing she could do, nothing she had to overthink. There was just her, her team, and their spacecraft, which was independently following its programming and being monitored from Cape Canaveral before Mission Control would take over in Houston in a few minutes.

After eight minutes, they heard Bellamy's voice again: "*Pangaea*, this is Launch Control. Your flying machine has just touched down successfully on the landing field. It looks alive and well."

"Glad to hear it, Launch Control!" she replied. "It couldn't have started with better omens."

"Helmets can now be opened."

"Roger that, Launch Control. Opening visors now." Following her own words, she released the hinges to pull up the large viewing window, reminiscent of a two-dimensional egg, and breathe in the cockpit air. She smelled faint hints of burnt steak and plastic—so minimal it was akin to an olfactory hallucination.

She noticed the arrival at their target orbit by the sudden onset of weightlessness. Not because of the altitude or any other human-named line, but because the thrust of the engines stopped. There was still approximately the same gravity as on the surface at their current altitude of a few hundred kilometers, but her body lost its own weight.

Mel was familiar with this feeling from numerous parabolic flights during her astronaut training, and it fascinated her every time. Her arms and legs were still there, although they no longer had the pulling-down feeling of weight. She felt free and lost at the same time, like a drop of dye dissolved in water. It was delightful and unpleasant in a pleasant way—a contradiction she never wanted to resolve.

"We are now officially in LEO," she exulted, jutting a raised thumb into the camera lens. "Hello, Earth, hello, space! We thought we'd finally reveal our top-secret mascot to you at this point."

Zhigang reached underneath his seat and pulled out the handball-sized globe made of fabric, which had a cute smiley face along with the continents and lots of blue.

"World, I would like to introduce you to Earthy. He will accompany us on our journey," the Colonel said in fluent English and then again in Mandarin.

"That makes seven of us," Mel added, also in Mandarin, hoping she had delivered the rehearsed words correctly without stepping into one of the many linguistic traps the Chinese language held for the overly daring.

"Congratulations, Mel. I believe your team members have something lined up for you," Bellamy said. "It's time I pass you off to CAPCOM and Mission Control in Houston. It's been an honor. God be with you, *Pangaea*."

"Roger that. Thank you, Launch Control."

"You're officially an astronaut now," she heard Selena say, hovering around Mel's pilot seat with her visor open and grinning broadly. She held a silver pin in her hand. "And as a person who reaches space, traditionally you get the appropriate pin. No matter what the stakes, no matter how great our undertaking, there has to be that much time."

Mel smiled gratefully as her comrade and friend attached the pin to her suit.

"Thanks. It wasn't hard at all, either."

In accordance with mission protocol they now removed their helmets, divested themselves of their flight suits, and stowed them in the white bags provided, which looked like oversized cubes and could be attached to the walls with Velcro. The size of the cockpit seemed almost wasteful compared to the Dragon capsule, and gave each of them enough room to avoid constantly bumping into each other, although the lack of gravity didn't make it easy.

Afterward, as if on an unspoken command, they spread out at the large windows and looked down at Earth, which was passing below them like a huge blue-white ball—which, of course, did not correspond to the truth, since in reality they were shooting furiously toward the horizon. They still had two hours until the next engine ignition, then another hour of flight to reach the orbit of the tanker that had parked in LEO, under full automation, two months ago to refuel them for their long journey.

They wouldn't have many opportunities to enjoy the view because, unlike ISS missions, there was little free time between thrust phases. For one thing, there were the much longer checklists that a first flight entailed. Under normal circumstances, this would have been a demo flight, conducted by two test pilots such as Doug Hurley and Bob Behnken had done back when they left for the International Space Station on the first manned Dragon capsule. Every system on board was being flown for the first time with astronauts, and every move they made was done for the first time in space. They had to evaluate data, go through error logs—which were fortunately still empty—and constantly exchange information with Mission Control regarding the condition of their spacecraft.

The next highlight came when they approached refueling, four hours after reaching orbit, and two hours after the last thrust phase to correctly initiate their parallel course to the tanker.

"Approach vector stable," Mel reported to Mission Control, her eyes fixed on her displays. This part of the flight would also be handled by *Pangaea's* control software. Nevertheless, it was up to her as pilot and commander to continuously monitor the process so that she could intervene if necessary.

"We see it down here." It was strange to hear Bernard's voice on the radio as CAPCOM. He sounded collected and professional. If he was melancholy over his missed opportunity to be mission commander, he certainly didn't let on. "All parameters look excellent."

"Unlike what you're used to down there," she heard Tom say behind her to the many livestream viewers, "we can't just fly from A to B out here by drawing a line between the two.

Orbital mechanics are complicated. If we just flew straight up to our tanker, we'd fall back down and crash into the ocean—or maybe onto one of your rooftops.

"So we have to reach what's called escape velocity. Not because we want to run away, but because we want to enter a circular orbit around the Earth, so that we always fall just past you, if you will. Reaching orbital velocity of just over seven kilometers per second, we are now a satellite and the same is true for our tanker.

"In order to link up with it, we have to *catch* up by matching our own circular orbit to its circular orbit. That took many orbits around the Earth, and now we're matching our speed in ever tinier bursts from the cold gas jets until we're flying side by side like twins."

Mel listened with only one ear. Tom's voice was so engaging it could have belonged to a veteran storyteller, but as simple as the following maneuver sounded from him, it was somewhat more complicated. In essence, they were doing nothing different than any Soyuz capsule had done for decades, than any space shuttle had done during their era, and than any Dragon capsule had done since, when it had flown to the ISS. But, never before had there been a Starship with astronauts on board in space, and there had never been a refueling attempt in orbit.

Firsts were always a big risk in highly technical operations, and everything was multiplied tenfold when it happened in orbit. The tiniest collision at their insane speeds could lead to the complete destruction of both spacecraft. Ninety minutes after such a theoretical collision, some debris and an uncontrolled angular momentum would become a cascade of shrapnel that produced myriads of funnel clouds of varying sizes of debris upon impact, and thus, at worst, could trigger the 'Kessler syndrome' that would forever bar humanity from going into space after the cloud had gradually engulfed all the satellites. What deadly secondary effects this problem alone would have on civilization was another matter entirely. In all likelihood, it would be a doomsday scenario.

Mel called up the optical sensors on her left display. It showed a pale silver streak against the pitch-black night sky.

No, she admonished herself. Not the night sky. Outer space.

The tanker was identical in construction to their own ship, except that instead of a cargo hold, it had large tanks of liquid oxygen and methane and coolant. It flew perfectly parallel to them, as if they were connected by invisible linkages. The onboard computer fired a few precisely dosed thrusts from the port thrusters, gently nudging them closer. For Mel, it was as if she were looking into a mirror as the Starship grew larger and larger in the image.

"Three hundred meters," she said calmly.

"Corrective impacts according to navigation heuristics, cold gas canister pressure stable," Holly Rapace said directly into her ear from Houston. She was the Mission Control engineer in charge of refueling.

"Two hundred meters."

"Extending the tank probe."

"Tank probe deployed," Mel reported after the two-meter-long nozzle with the flattened tip slid out of its compartment on top of *Pangaea* like a finger.

"Catch funnel from Tanker-I extends," Holly's voice rang out again. The catch funnel at the end of the boom was only slightly longer than the tanker probe, and its end looked like the lamellar fan of an edible mushroom. She had often stood next to prototypes as large as small satellite dishes. On the display, the funnel and the nozzle looked like tiny children's fists.

On the center monitor, she saw in apparent black and white how the computer perceived the process: a small opening in the funnel with prongs on the sides where the tank probe had to snap; and numerous dashes, lines and circles all around, which were displayed by the software and accompanied by numbers. The lowest of these indicated the shrinking meters that separated the funnel from the nozzle's probe.

Tanker-I had approached near enough by now that they could see it with a glance past the consoles through the upper windows. Its steel top seemed to glow in the reflected sunlight.

"Ten meters," Holly said. "All green."

"Affirmative. Looks good from up here."

"Five meters."

Mel watched the funnel 'blossom' on her display grow larger and larger. It wobbled left and right a few times as the control software commanded final bursts of correction, throttling their already-slow speed ever further.

"Contact. Probe engaged, lock active. Link established, heading steady," Holly stated, her calm, matter-of-fact voice a stark contrast to the burst of Houston cheers crackling through the radio.

Mel grinned at Zhigang, who raised a fist triumphantly.

"Release valve control, open dorsal tank flaps." She pressed the appropriate buttons on her touch display and something relaxed inside her as the fresh fuel supply was forced into *Pangaea's* tanks at 5,000 liters per minute. They had been down to 20 percent.

"A piece of cake!" Behind her, Gabriella gave vent to her decreasing tension and chortled. A barely audible hiss went through the cockpit as the cooled tanks in the back of the ship got new fuel for the engines.

"Really smooth," Zhigang remarked, "Very good."

"Don't say things like that," Mel said, hurrying to send a

smile after her words as the taikonaut eyed her questioningly from the side. "Sorry. With us, you don't utter such things because we think it might invite mishaps."

"A superstition?" Zhigang seemed even more confused.

"Well, more like…" She pondered. "Yes, it is a superstition, I guess. Often associated with rain. If it's not raining, and someone says something like 'Oh, how nice that it's not raining,' then everyone reaches for their umbrellas, expecting the weather luck to pass soon."

"So you're not supposed to acknowledge and express the positive because otherwise it will be lost? That's very strange."

"Come to think of it, I guess you're right."

Fortunately, after half an hour it turned out that Zhigang's remark had not triggered any malfunction and the refueling was completed successfully. The Starship that had been converted into a tanker pushed away from them with strong pulses from the maneuvering thrusters. The white fountains of cold gas looked like visual disturbances on the monitor, so quickly did they pass again. Then it ignited its main engines and began its journey back to Texas to land at SpaceX's Starbase in Boca Chica.

"All right," Mel said, addressing the camera. "We now have six hours until our launch window opens and we leave for our rendezvous point. Since even astronauts need to sleep, we'll say goodbye to you now and check back in as we make launch preparations. *Pangaea* and Earthy wish you a good night."

"Confirm time-out," she heard Bernard say. "Get a good night's sleep, guys. Good job."

"Thank you, Houston." Mel turned off the com and then the cameras. Mission Control still had access, of course, but would only do so in an emergency. Everyone needed a certain amount of privacy, and having the eyes of billions of onlookers on them—however understandable—was easily the opposite of that.

"We're in time-out," she said loudly, unbuckling herself from her seat. The others did the same and floated forward, where there was the most open space in the cockpit. Something was reassuring about the rubber-cell-like appearance of the padded walls. One by one, they removed the spacesuits they had been forced to put on for safety because of the refueling maneuver and stowed them neatly in the pockets provided, which they tacked to the floor—now no longer a floor but either a wall or a ceiling depending on how you looked at it, with up and down both absent.

"This is going like clockwork!" Tom noted, grinning with such satisfaction that Mel stopped herself from making a comment like the one she'd made to Zhigang.

"Money and manpower make it all work. Look at the Saturn V of yesteryear," Selena said. "Held together by risk-taking, spit, and a desire to spite the communists—I intend no offense," she tacked on, looking in the direction of her Chinese comrades. "What was done here was much better planned and more tightly controlled."

"Things can definitely continue going this way as far as I'm concerned," Mel said.

"They will," Selena indicated with certainty.

"We should sleep, guys." As if to punctuate her words, Mel yawned unabashedly and felt a crack in her right jaw joint. "The next important mission segment will be waiting for us, and it better fall into place, too."

No one objected, and after a few trips to the windows and murmured conversations, it quickly became quiet. For this first period of rest, they'd decided to waste as little time as possible, and thus not to move to the habitat section. Tom and

Gabriella lay down between the packing cubes that held their suits, which prevented them from drifting off in their sleep and bumping into something. Selena curled up into a fetal position in the middle of the open area in front of the consoles and just floated there, while Mel joined Hongbo and Zhigang, who buckled into their seats and donned sleep goggles.

Mel immediately fell asleep.

In her almost obligatory dream she observed, from far away, her spaceship in front of the poignant beauty of Earth. Despite the planet's size, it seemed almost tiny and fragile amidst the endless nothingness of the stars. She felt curiosity as she gazed at it, but the feeling was stretchy and tough like bubblegum, and as strangely distorted and normal at the same time as only a dream could convey.

To her dream self, *Pangaea's* form was strange, looking unnatural and like a foreign object. This did not change her gaze upon it, which was not judgmental, but observant and fulfilled. Filled with what, she could not sense as she groped back and forth within the narrow confines of her neuronally generated mirages. There were no answers here, but instead the groping of mind and mysticism, again and again.

When she awoke it was effortlessly and gently, as if she had been lying in her bed instead of sitting. Of course, she wasn't *sitting*, because that would have required being 'down.' Instead, she had simply fallen asleep in a certain posture, without any pressure on joints or muscles.

Hongbo and Zhigang were already awake. Hongbo hovered next to the copilot and conversed with him in whispers. Mel wondered what they were discussing and if there might be something conspiratorial about their lowered voices. A plot, perhaps, to sabotage their mission? In the very next moment, she scolded herself for the thought, realizing once again how deeply ingrained her prejudices were against her fellow-human Far Easterners, who until recently had been considered the next archenemies of the West. They had merely lowered their voices to avoid waking her.

"Good morning," she said softly.

"Oh," Zhigang said, turning to her. "Hello, Commander. Ready for phase two?"

14

"What we have going on here is what's called a Hohmann transfer," Tom explained from behind Mel, speaking to the viewers who had almost reached the three billion mark. She tried to imagine from what settings they were being watched. At home over breakfast? In the middle of the night, eyes transfixed on the cell phone screen under the covers? At work in an open browser tab so the boss won't see? Or over a TV set located in the office?

Her German colleague continued, "Earth revolves around the sun faster than her little brother Mars, which has a longer orbit further out. You can imagine flying from her to him in an extremely simplified way, as if you were holding onto a Porsche while riding on a motorcycle that is speeding down the highway in the left lane. Your target is a Mercedes further ahead in the right lane. You start, going as fast as the Porsche and soon pass up the Mercedes, so you would have to let go and then brake, but then there is the danger that the Mercedes will overtake you. In our case, we are in a circular orbit around the Earth, and we first have to change to an elliptical orbit to gain momentum. Earth, as the nearest center of mass, is quite jealous and doesn't like to let us go."

Mel powered up the thrusters. On her display, the symbol of her spaceship approached the target position like a puzzle piece moving into its spot.

"That's why we're about to give ourselves a good push, let Earth catapult us into the transfer ellipse, and then fly toward Mars' orbit to a point where we've calculated Serenity's position in six months and eleven days. So, as of now, our destination is not Serenity itself, but the future intersection with its current course. We could have done that directly from Earth at launch, but we need a lot more propellant than in a normal Mars mission because we can't go into a circular orbit around Mars like a real Hohmann transfer, but we're approaching a celestial body without a gravity well. It can't catch us, so we have to slow down and change course to go parallel to it and accelerate again until our velocities are identical."

Preferably just long enough to leave enough fuel to get back, Mel added in her mind. In a hushed voice, she said into her closed helmet, "Houston, *Pangaea*, we're ready for ignition."

"*Pangaea*, Houston, roger that. Have a good trip," Bernard calmly confirmed. "God bless."

Mel activated the thrust control and commanded full thrust for four minutes. The weightlessness quickly turned into a firm pressure that pressed her into the seat. First twice her own weight, then three times, and finally four times. It was uncomfortable but bearable, nowhere near as bad as the 7 or 8 g she had frequently experienced in her Navy F-18. At 4 gs there was no worry about reperfusion damage in the blood vessels, at least not for this short a time.

After four minutes and eight seconds, the onboard computer cut the thrusters, and they shot past Earth's terminator line toward Mars' orbit. Their speed was now sufficient to escape Earth's gravitational field and begin their journey.

"Houston, *Pangaea*. Thrust phase successfully completed," she said, clapping her hands involuntarily. "We're on our way."

"*Pangaea*, Houston, we've seen it and we couldn't be more pleased. The trajectory is perfect. No deviations." She could hear Bernard allow himself a smile. In the background, the exuberant cheers of the staff at Houston's Mission Control Center rang out once again. It hadn't been long since she had stood where he was now. "Make us proud, *Pangaea*. You have the backing of all humanity. Say hello for us."

"We will, Houston."

By now, putting on and taking off the suits was routine. This time, however, they would not have to slip back into the body-hugging marvels of modern material science for more than seven months.

Hongbo and Zhigang floated into the habitat area, while Mel, Selena, Tom, and Gabriella stayed behind to enjoy the view for a while longer. The Earth was huge and beautiful in front of the four windows, each of them using one of their own to flatten their noses.

"I've seen this view so many times, but it doesn't get old," Tom stated devoutly.

"Amen." Gabriella sighed. "Still, it's different this time somehow. Like I'm seeing her for the first time."

"Mm-hmm, I know what you mean." Mel saw the unmistakable outline of the African continent drifting below. White cloud fields massed around the equatorial region, moving east in seemingly opposite directions, driven by the Coriolis force. More to herself, she said, "It will be at least two years before I see clouds again. Rain. Feel the sun on my skin and breathe fresh air that hasn't been forced through multiple filtration systems."

"Speaking of which," Tom cut in again, his voice hinting at some of the mischievousness that was to follow, "It will also be two years before we don't have to drink recycled piss and reprocessed sweat. Until we can eat fresh food."

"Does this bother anyone here?" Selena asked.

"Not at all," Mel replied. "To be honest, I can't wait until the seven months are up and we finally have Serenity in front of us."

"And not just that." Tom came floating over to her and caught himself on one of the handholds so they wouldn't bump into each other. He pressed his finger to the very top of the disk, where the darkness of space reigned, with the Earth seemingly rotating motionless. "We will have traveled seven months into the solar system, farther than any human has ever gone. Seven months of getting a little closer to Serenity every day. That means better and better images, better and better sensor data, and shorter and shorter distances for our communication attempts."

"You're right. On top of that, I'm the only one who knows the rosters inside and out, and I can tell you that there's no danger of anyone on board getting bored."

"See," Tom said to the others. "Day one on the road and she's cracking the whip."

Pangaea's greatest innovation was its rotating habitat. For the extremely accelerated development of SpaceX's design concept, which had originated in 2020, over 30 billion U.S. dollars had been devoured. This included several test spacecraft that had completed orbital flights to test and optimize the concept. Mandatory engineering changes along the way had burned through another ten billion, as delaying the project—the order of the day under normal circumstances—had been out of the question.

The habitat consisted of two halves, accessible via short

telescopic spokes that could be extended and retracted. From the outside, they looked like hammerhead sharks on thick stems. On one side were the labs, on the other were training equipment and the mess hall. In the narrow hull between them were the coffin-like sleeping chambers, toilet, and washroom.

They spent the first few days learning to get around. Although they had spent many hours in the corresponding mock-ups on Earth and therefore knew their way around in general, it nonetheless was different. For one thing, now they were pushed to the floor by centrifugal force and no longer by Earth's gravity. For another, each trip down the ladder meant a brief wave of nausea.

From their quarters in the hull with its weightlessness, gravity set in slowly and became stronger, eventually reaching 1 g as soon as one jumped off the last ladder rung—strange but all right. On the other hand, the slowly decreasing gravity on the way back created an extremely unpleasant feeling that could make even experienced parabolic flyers like them have queasy stomachs.

One certainly got used to it, but on the morning of the ninth day of their trip, when she entered the lab, she was already thinking about the way back and had to stifle a quiet grumble. Tom was sitting at one of the computers that could be pulled out of the server cabinet as a display, poring over bar charts.

"Good morning," she greeted him and stretched. It was good to feel normal gravity underfoot, as if all her organs were allowed to fall back into their original places and she appreciated this with a shiver of well-being.

Tom glanced over his shoulder at her and yawned before returning the greeting.

"Slept badly?"

"Yeah," he said, rubbing his reddened eyes.

"Is there a reason for it that I should know about?"

"Possibly." He waved her over and turned slightly to the side so she could look at his display. "Do you see the distribution of water supplies?"

"Yes. Flowing smoothly around our residential toroid in the hull." As she said this, she looked for deviations on the plot and associated diagrams and data fields that didn't belong there.

"They do. Well, nothing actually *flows* there, but so be it. We have six pumps total." His finger wandered to the corresponding funnel symbols along the connectors between the two tank sections that together formed a tight shell around the living quarters, protecting them from cosmic rays. "One pump per section, front and back, is sufficient to maintain the normal redistribution process and allow exchange with the filtration and recycling devices below the sealing rings."

"Yes, two of each are installed redundantly."

"Right."

"What's the problem?"

"The power consumption." Tom used two fingers to pull a data column on the right side closer. "See? It's using two percent more power. That's pump one."

"Two percent? Maybe we just excreted a little too much urine, so the filters need more time under load? In the case of consumer constellations, the pump and filter are counted together," she explained with narrowed eyes.

"I know, but I thought of that, too, and went into the submenus. It's the pump that has the extra consumption." He sounded a little offended.

"It can't be because the flow rate always stays the same. The total amount of water in the system doesn't fluctuate, that's the only way the tanks can function the way they do."

Tom moved away from the display a bit and slapped his knees before looking at her meaningfully. "See? That doesn't let me sleep. A problem that shouldn't exist is always a problem, no matter how small its variance value."

"The onboard computer didn't kick in," she noted.

"No."

"Because it's not set to sound the alarm until four percent deviation or a certain rate of deviation."

"Yep. But better to 'break the glass' sooner than later, after it's become critical, huh?"

"Hmm," she murmured thoughtfully, and then went to the nearest intercom. There she pressed the green button and said, "Everyone, please come to the lab if you can."

Five minutes later, they were fully assembled around the display, and Tom explained in condensed form the deviation he had found.

"Maybe an efficiency problem?" suggested Gabriella, rubbing her nose, which made her Italian accent sound even more nasally. "The pump could have a faulty relay or a miscalibrated sensor."

"Then we would have to shut them down," Zhigang said, shaking his head.

"Well, just because the solution is unpleasant doesn't mean the problem isn't realistic."

"Granted." The Chinese man inclined his head. "But a faulty relay would get us marked as a fault in the log files."

"Unless there's a software defect."

"A bug that specific, occurring at the same time as a faulty relay?" asked Tom, his expression allowing no misunderstanding of how much he thought of the idea.

Gabriella shrugged her shoulders. "We're speculating here, aren't we?"

"Yes, all thoughts on the table and no judgments," Mel encouraged them all with a sweeping glance.

"A contamination? Maybe something too big got into the water circuit. Particularly stubborn excreta or skin flakes that have clumped together and temporarily reduced the amount of fluid by clogging it, only to then jump again and cause the corresponding increase in consumption?" thought Selena aloud, staring at the display as if she only had to look closely enough to wrest the secrets from the data.

"Then there should be a short-lived lesser consumption to see in the logs before," Zhigang countered.

"Also, the recycling system was built to prevent that kind of thing from happening. Multiple filter units that we change and clean every three days," Mel returned. "We would have seen it in the filters first." She looked to Gabriella and Hongbo, who were standing right next to each other and turned to her as silence fell. "What else can account for the loss of efficiency in a simple water pump? I'd like us to at least have some hypotheses of our own before we ask Houston and start the remote diagnosis. You know what they'll be like." She supplied the answer right away. "Like a stirred-up beehive."

She did not want to alarm the public, who listened in on every transmission—that had been one of the conditions of Congress and later of the Chinese. The two female engineers nodded as a sign that they understood the subtext of her statement.

"Viscosity of the fluid," Hongbo suggested. "The flow rate in relation to the volume is the primary parameter for determining the efficiency of a fluid pump."

"And the power consumption of the piston," Gabriella added, pointing to the grayed-out two percent more power that the pump was using compared to what it should be.

Her Chinese colleague nodded in agreement. "Right. If the medium becomes denser, the piston consumes more energy to pump the same flow rate x through in period y."

"But why would the water get less dense?" asked Tom. The wrinkles in his forehead were by now forming deep canyons, shaped by lack of sleep and worry in equal measure.

"By partially reducing density," Hongbo answered his question.

"Huh? A moment ago you were talking about higher density, so what now?"

"It could be frozen in some places," Gabriella suggested, glancing at Hongbo, who considered for a moment and then nodded. Only then did the Italian continue, "The formation of crystals when water freezes changes its density. In a crystal, the individual water particles are further apart than in a liquid state. Ergo lower density. But through this process, the ice demands more volume than in liquid state, so the rest of the water is forced to compress and has a higher viscosity."

"That," the Chinese woman picked up the Italian's thread, "is valid down to a temperature of four degrees Celsius. Then water cannot be compressed any further."

Mel thought about what she had heard and ranked this possibility as quite plausible. It followed the laws of physics, that much was certain. "Let's assume that there *is* ice formation. Due to the lower water temperature and the volume demand of the iced parts, the rest of the water is cooled and compressed, demanding more power from the pump's piston, resulting in increased power consumption," she summarized. "Tom, pull up the pump's watt meter, time on the x-axis, last seven days."

"All right." The physician and chemist called up the keyboard and began typing. Shortly, a bar graph slid over the current display.

"A slow increase in consumption," she observed. "Pretty linear. That would be consistent with icing."

"Locally limited, I guess. It has to be, because the water in the tanks is constantly moving, in part so that it doesn't freeze while it's absorbing our waste heat and resisting the cold of the hull. If waste heat and cooling no longer balance each other, there must be a problem with the insulation somewhere."

Tom looked around the room. "Otherwise, I'm sure everything would be uniformly iced over by now, and the temperature sensors on the pump rims would show more than a degree Celsius deviation."

"The sensors are sitting right where there is the most movement in the water, so that includes temperature," Mel indicated. "It could just be a measurement delay."

"It's hard to say," Zhigang said. "In any case, we should report it to Mission Control."

"Yes. Thank you all very much. I'll take it from here. Best we get on with our tasks now." She waited until everyone had dispersed again and then stepped up to the intercom, which, like every other on board, connected by button directly to Houston or Beijing—or probably both. "Houston, *Pangaea*."

"*Pangaea*, this is Houston." Bernard was already on duty at CAPCOM. That was good. "Good morning from Texas."

"Good morning! Texas looks like a speck from the window. Honestly, *Earth* is becoming a speck."

"I wish we could still recognize you as a speck with the naked eye."

"We spotted a deviation up here—Tom did, to be exact," she said after the deliberately calm preliminary banter.

"We're all ears, *Pangaea*."

"In the water circuit, there is a deviation in the power consumption of pump one."

There was a pause of a few seconds, then Bernard spoke up again, "Yes, we can see it. It's already been noted by one of our engineers. However, the value is still within the expected range of variation that was established during installation."

"True," she replied. "But we looked at the consumption curve and compared it to the water temperature. The watt-hours drawn by pump one have been rising steadily over the last few days, and the temperature sensor is showing a lowered temperature at the point of measurement. So the value should be significantly higher than at the less fast-flowing points further inside the tank."

"We'll take a look, *Pangaea*, and get back to you."

"Thank you, Houston."

"You can count on us."

Mel switched off and turned to Tom. "Good work, Doctor Ehrmann."

He smiled wearily. "My perfectionism has cost me lots of sleep over the years."

"Starting tonight, however, you'll keep your rest hours," she instructed him, trying to soften her stern tone a bit by placing a hand on his shoulder. "You know what it's like: the long journey in a confined space, surrounded by unpredictable dangers—it's a challenge for all of us. That's what the packed duty rosters and clearly ritualized sleeping and eating times are for. They create order and keep us sane up here." She tapped a finger against her forehead. "Sleep deprivation has never helped anyone stay relaxed and confident."

"Aye, aye, Commander." Tom snapped off a precise salute and rose. "I'll see what our mushroom farms are up to now, then. If we're lucky, in a few weeks we'll have mushroom stew, grown to perfection in the fire of cosmic rays."

"That sounds a whole lot better than liquid steak pie from a tube."

When he turned around and went up the ladder, she tried to put the power problem aside for what it was, for now—a little thing that might *possibly* be a nothing. But she failed because of the word possibly.

15

Every spacewalk was a risk. Even on the ISS, which was near Earth, any astronaut who drifted away from the station would be lost forever—unless they had a mobility unit with them and could fly back and forth using corrective thrusts. In addition, they ventured out at speeds around 25,000 kilometers per hour—and nearly double that in their current case. Vacuum is the definition of empty, although this is not true of space. It is merely *relatively* empty.

Even here, there were dust particles and gas molecules that could damage their equipment. Not lethal projectiles—they would only become that at even higher velocities. But there were the micrometeorites, of which the solar system had quite a few, which became kinetic killers at their current rate of travel. Finally, there was the radiation: By now they were outside the Earth's protective magnetosphere, which plowed through cosmic rays like a bug, and every EVA was under time pressure.

Radiation, Mel knew as well as any other physicist did, became dangerous by its intensity, but above all by the duration of exposure. So, haste would be indicated.

Mission Control informed them that there had probably been an area of icing on the port tank, caused by an outlet installed too close to a water pipe—a trifle that had not been given much attention in the face of so much new technology, and operations that had never been tested in this form under real conditions. This *trifle* had now become a problem, and they were lucky to have noticed it so early.

"Hongbo and Zhigang, you are not qualified to do hull repair work," Mel said as they sat around the table in the mess hall right after Mission Control's bad news and discussed how to proceed. On the ISS, Houston always decided who would do which EVA, since they had usually been planned well in advance and practiced umpteen times by the respective astronauts on the ground. On this trip, however, they had to make decisions themselves based on previously established rules. "Your certification is for the IT systems."

The two taikonauts bowed their heads one after the other like devoted soldiers, which they did quite frequently.

"Tom and Selena, you should both stay here as doctors in case something goes wrong and we need help," Mel continued, looking to the Italian. "Gabriella has done several repair missions on the ISS hull and is probably best suited as the only engineer besides Hongbo. I'll go along as support for her and take care of the toolbelt and lanyards."

"I think it's a high risk," Tom objected. "You've never done a spacewalk before."

"But practiced several dozen times in the dunk tank."

"It's not the same, believe me." He waved it off. "And it's many times more dangerous out here than on the ground."

"At least I don't have a distraction in front of me like our beautiful planet." Seeing his sour expression, Mel sighed. "The way I see it, I'm relatively expendable. Sure, I'm a good pilot and did very well in simulator training for *Pangaea*, but so is

Zhigang." She raised her hands. "Before anyone contradicts out of niceness, save it, I like you guys as well."

An hour later, they had put together a plan for the field operation and talked through it in enough detail to have a clear idea of what needed to be done and in what order they were going to proceed.

"We're going over this with the pertinent teams," Bernard said after she told him the relevant ideas and decisions. "In the meantime, we've made a simulation of what the current configuration might look like out there. I suggest you all go through it once, since there will be no direct line of sight from those inside to you at the work site, neither through the windows in the cockpit, nor through any of the two remaining exterior cameras."

"But we still have our helmet cameras. You get their signals live. Can't you relay them inside?" she asked tensely. Normally, each EVA was accompanied by the watchful and supportive eyes and comments of the crew members who stayed behind. This created a kind of live correction loop through an additional pair of eyes and brain.

"We will," Bernard assured her calmly. "But there is now a latency of several seconds, enough to make direct communication exhausting. If they see something in your pictures, it will be twenty-seven seconds after the picture was taken. So by the time they see something, it's far too late. With us, it's only thirteen and a half seconds."

"Hmph," she went on, "I guess Gabriella and I will have to make it good."

"It looks like it. You guys are going to get it done. Just remember that the safety lines and the placement of the magnetic brackets are the most important thing. *The* most important thing. If you lose contact and you're more than an arm's length away from the ship, it's over."

"I understand," Mel said seriously, shuddering. "We'll get

it done. A hydraulic valve, we can do that. Gabrielle has already been going through the engineering drawings to come up with a plan. If you have any more information or tips, send them our way."

"Give us a few hours, preferably even the next sleep period, and we'll play it safe. The icing doesn't seem to be progressing so quickly that it would be appropriate to rush now. Our engineers are sure of that," Bernard said.

"Agreed."

"We'll be in touch."

Mel briefed the team on their conversation and then sat down with Gabriella to begin going through the schematics, which outlined in detail every bolt and weld that had been set on and in the ship. Again and again, she asked the Italian about the specifics of an EVA and what to look for. She would not have survived astronaut selection if she had made stupid decisions because of her ego, like feigning competence where a well-attuned ear was more important.

Before the next morning, Mel had forced herself to interrupt her preparations and sleep. The instructions from the engineering team in charge of the field operation were extremely detailed and could have filled several books. She studied them as long as she could, hoping that Gabriella could skim over much of it because it came naturally to her as an engineer, or corresponded to something she had done before.

"How far did you get?" Gabriella asked Melody as they both sat in the airlock and let their colleagues put them into their suits. The new spacesuits were better in many ways and offered greater freedom of movement than NASA's old EMUs, but they were still extremely bulky and, above all, still heavy. All they had to do was wait in their pants and top, latched into the wall, and wait for hours while the others hung necessary items on them like they were Christmas trees. Here a cable, there a connection. Valve after valve was checked and tested, every system component checked, every latch locked.

"In the document from Houston?" Mel tried to remember. "Up to page ninety, I think."

"What was your impression?"

"I know every single work group that was involved in the design and construction of our ship," she replied. "The water and gas systems were worked out and implemented by different teams."

"Time pressure, huh?"

"Mm-hmm. The monetary windfall was helpful, but it still couldn't slow down time. Many groups of experts working in parallel were essential to make this mission even possible. That's where opportunities for mutual coordination inevitably fall by the wayside."

"And in the end, it's the little things that bite you in the butt," Gabriella found. "I've had to develop a lot of test scenarios as a Ph.D. student, and I can tell you, on first attempts of pretty much every project, they fail because of trivial things."

"We can't fail."

"You won't. The good thing is that the problem is not particularly complex," Zhigang intervened. "I read through the Houston task force report. A liquid oxygen line was too close to a water line, which iced up as a result. If you can get a layer of insulating foam in between, the problem should be solved quickly."

"Piece of cake." Gabriella winked and gave a thumbs up, but the Chinese man was already back to tightening her toolbelt with a focused expression and checking the carabiners on it, tugging twice on each. "I agree with Houston's prediction that it shouldn't take us more than two hours to finish everything. The faulty expansion tank is going to be a bigger problem."

"An expansion tank is broken?" asked Tom.

"Yes," Mel answered in her place. "That's why the pressure spike happened in the first place. The expansion tank that was responsible quit working, and the replacement kicked in later than it should have. Our dear eggheads at home figured it out quickly."

"At least the pressure problem will be solved, then."

"Right. In any case, long enough that we can carry out our EVA with a comfortable time cushion."

It was another half hour before they were finished with the suits and the others withdrew from the cramped airlock. Hongbo said something in Mandarin into the obligatory camera on the wall.

"Houston, *Pangaea*," Mel said. "We're ready for EVA."

"*Pangaea*, Houston, copy that. Good luck. We'll be with you the whole way."

Gabriella waited until Mel gave her a raised thumb.

"Com check," Mel heard in her helmet.

"Loud and clear," she replied.

"Bene. Let's do it." They waited two minutes while all pressure was released from the airlock. As the atmosphere disappeared, so did any sound, and Mel heard only the echo of her own breathing like a diver underwater. As temporary mission commander Zhigang gave them clearance, then Gabriella opened the outer hatch. Automatically, Mel's brain hallucinated matching sounds.

She grabbed one of the handholds on the inside of the hatch rim and hooked in the safety line with the carabiner, checked once again that there was a connection to herself and to Gabriella, and then waited. Her colleague from southern Europe carefully and deftly slid through the black cutout where the wall had just been. In slow motion, she floated out as if through a window to infinity.

Mel followed, pausing as her clunky boots slid over the edge. Ignoring the darkness, she pushed it from her mind and instead made sure to execute the movements as Gabriella and Zhigang had briefed her. First she turned around, then bent over as best she could, grabbing the lower edge of the hatch and pushing her legs back. Then she hunched over and waited for her magnetic boot soles to activate, causing her to flip backward like a skipjack tuna. A panicked fear rose in her as she felt like she was being pulled away by an invisible hand. She swayed a few times—a reed in the wind—until she regained her bearings.

She stood on the hull of *Pangaea*.

The carbon silicate mixture of the riveted plate under her boots was silvery in her memory, but now it looked gray and extremely dull. Gabriella was to her left, a little higher up next to the airlock instead of below it—except that these details were no longer correct. Above and below were identical, no longer possessing any distinction. They both stood upright and yet at a 90-degree angle to each other.

"Look around," she heard her colleague say via radio. She couldn't see her face because the golden sun visor was down. "You need to take time to do it."

"It's okay."

"No. You're going to do it anyway. Better to do it now than later when something happens and you get frantic. You won't do yourself any favors at that point," Gabrielle said firmly. "Get it over with."

Mel didn't know if she resisted because she was worried that the sight might frighten her, or because she ought not to have the luxury of enjoying the view. But she did it. The Starship looked like a pot-bellied cylinder, sparkling and dull at the same time, the front part of the ship spinning—no, she spun, as she stood on the rotating toroid from which the mighty, reinforced telescopic arms extended, at the ends of which, ten meters away, one of the habitat parts turned its circles.

From her position, it looked static—a deception. Behind her, she spotted the large solar sails like the ears of an elephant, oversized and shimmering reddish. Their efficiency out here, away from a distracting atmosphere, was enormous. She counted a second and a half before one solar sail passed her and the next appeared, like the rotor blades of a fast-moving mill. The enormity of the huge surfaces, which seemed to glow in the light of the distant sun, seemed paradoxically all the larger with the absence of noise.

The Earth behind them had grown so small that it could be covered with a penny. The radiators, on the other hand, were even larger and seemed as static as the habitat on their side as they rotated with them, dark curtains that reminded her of the wings of a mystical bird and sent a cold shiver down her spine.

Then she looked out into space. *Really* looked. Spaceship, solar sail, and radiator wings immediately faded before the depth of infinity. She had never seen such a dense field of bright dots, the photon messengers of distant stars, persisting detached from their places of origin and joining the accelerated expansion since the universe had emerged with the Big Bang everywhere and nowhere at once, striving away from the place of origin, which was not a place but a point in time before time.

One of her physics professors had said that the place of the Big Bang was easy to determine: 'Always on the tip of your nose.' Only here and now, in the face of her own insignificance in relation to infinity, she truly realized what that meant. She was the onlooker at a play whose lines she did not understand, whose actors were strangers to her, and whose script was a riddle. She realized that she did not belong here, as if the universe wanted to force her back to her place with an optical repulsion reaction.

An abyss, she thought, spellbound by the twinkling of trillions and trillions of stars—*a bottomless abyss of beauty.*

"Si," Gabriella agreed, her voice through the radio startling Mel, who hadn't realized she'd spoken out loud. "That's how I experienced it the first time, too. And out here, the feeling is even stronger. Much stronger."

Her colleague's voice was like an anchor for Mel, bringing her back to the present. Proof that there was a reality she understood and in which she played a role, instead of slowly fading away like an evaporating puddle under the glaring desert sun.

"Are you okay?"

"Yep, I'm good to go."

"Good. From now on it's best to always focus on the hull. It's grounding, in my experience."

Mel did so, looking down at her feet and a long line of ragged edges just below the open airlock hatch. Its appearance reminded her of a furrow, albeit a very shallow one. It could not have been deeper than a millimeter.

"It looks like we took more of a beating at launch than we thought," she said, her own calm words putting a cloak of composure on her. "All right. Ready."

"Ready. Houston?"

"We are here, Gabriella. From your position you have to go two meters toward the apex, then from there four meters toward the bow." Bernard spoke even more calmly and accented than usual. "You'll know the right seam by a double row of screw rivets."

"Roger that, Houston," Gabriella replied, shifting into gear like a stiff golem. Mel followed her slowly, carefully placing one foot in front of the other to get a feel for the magnetic boots. They exerted a slight pull that started a few centimeters before the metal hull. As if in slow motion, they trudged along one after the other, accompanied by the echoes of their breaths under the eyes of the stars that seemingly filled the great black void.

At a certain point, the engineer turned left and the cones of her helmet headlights fell on the smooth metal of the hull. Glaring sunlight fell upon two women, then shadow reigned again. Mel had noticed the change from brightness to darkness every few breaths but had not consciously processed it. Through the rotation of the toroid, they experienced a kind of day-night cycle on crack cocaine.

"Houston, I think I've found the seam. Moving toward the bow now."

"We're getting the pictures in right now. It looks right from here."

Mel silently followed her colleague, repeatedly pulling the safety rope taut and thus more rope from the pulley in the airlock. She wished there had been retaining clips in the hull, or even something like handholds. Instead, every meter and a half, she placed a magnet the size of a beer lid with a metal loop, into which she hooked a carabiner and connected it to the rope that was stretched between her and Gabriella like an umbilical cord.

"I see the corresponding panel now," the Italian said. She looked like a marshmallow in a black-and-white picture in her bulky suit. Or the Michelin man in slow motion—until she stopped and leaned forward. "There are no markings, but I think you should recognize it, Mission Control."

"Thirteen seconds," Mel reminded her. Her voice possessed an echo in her helmet that sounded strange, as if she were talking to herself. "Plus another thirteen until the answer arrives."

"Yes. I'll get the cordless screwdriver ready." It sounded like a joke. Casually, as if they were in an unspectacular place like a train station concourse, she said in a chatty tone, "How are you enjoying your first real spacewalk?"

"Unspectacular."

They giggled together, a shared moment of normalcy, even though it was feigned and they both knew it.

"This earns you a second pin, as you know," Gabriella remarked as she took the special screwdriver from the magnetic belt and stretched the short connecting line.

"Gabriella, this is Bernard. That looks good, yeah. You need the fourteen head."

"Roger that, Houston." Gabriella had already taken the appropriate attachment, as she was prepared, naturally, and had already known which one. But the routine procedures were normal, and normality promised a familiar setting. Also, familiarity led to safety. "Now begin to release the hull segment. Mel, you'll need to receive it."

"I'm ready," she replied, letting go of the rope, which floated in place, curling slightly like a snake.

Gabriella unscrewed one bolt at a time, which took a surprising amount of time, and stowed each one on her magnetic belt like a collection of cartridges. Then she lifted off the panel, slightly curved and about the size of a pizza box. It looked massive, but when Mel took hold of it, of course, it weighed nothing. The carbon silicate panel blocked her view, but she resisted the urge to turn. They had previously agreed not to, to minimize the risk of her losing the piece.

"I see the lines," she heard Gabriella say, breathing a little harder than before, maybe.

Mel wondered if it was just her imagination.

"Putting the insulation foam on now."

Mel waited patiently.

"It's definitely the right spot," Bernard said. "You should use the whole can just to be sure. It hardens right away."

The engineer must have been too busy to answer. The

sunlight came, blinding Mel even through the protective visor as it reflected off the metal plate in front of her, then it went colorless and dark again and she held a piece of darkness in front of the darkness.

Astonished, she saw a star shining on the plate.

Well was her first thought. The second was that it didn't belong there.

"Mel?" she heard Bernard say her name via the helmet radio. His voice had changed tone, sounding even quieter than usual. "Gabriella's not answering anymore, and there's something wrong with her image transmission."

She lowered the sheath piece and saw Gabriella standing in front of her, the screwdriver raised slightly in her right hand, her left hand held up like a student reporting.

"What's going on?" inquired Zhigang. "Is there a problem?"

"She's standing in front of me," Mel said with a hint of relief, taking a step to the side. "Gabriella?"

No answer.

"Maybe her radio is faulty," the deputy commander said. "Is Houston still getting data?"

"Bernard, are you still getting data from her suit?" Reluctantly, she waited endless seconds.

"That's possible, because we're not getting any more data from her suit."

Bernard's voice had become a muffled whisper in the background for a moment as he spoke to someone else. The delay in his answers was frustrating, but she mustn't let it bother her.

"I'm trying to make direct contact," she said, moving toward her colleague. She took another step diagonally forward until she was almost in front of Gabriella and tapped the ESA patch on her chest. "Oh, shit!"

She didn't see the puny red dot on the chest computer

until tiny little pellets flew toward her and landed on her visor, where they wafted back and forth like mercury, rolling across the polycarbonate.

"Yes, direct contact…," Bernard resumed, 13 light seconds away in the densely packed Mission Control Center in Houston—a place that seemed like an unreal memory to her just now.

"Houston, Gabriella is hurt," she said calmly, having pushed her fear and initial fright into the burning flame surrounded by nothingness. She made sure she had a firm footing, and then grabbed her colleague's shoulders to pull them closer to her. She succeeded effortlessly, as there was no resistance. "There's a hole in her control unit. It's very small in diameter, a millimeter maybe. Blood is leaking from it."

Mel opened her sun visor as they rotated into the darkness and saw a dense stream of red globules in the light of her helmet lamps leaking from Gabriella's suit. They were small, but frighteningly numerous.

The sun came and she quickly folded down the visor. Now she could see the blood even through the darkening.

"Roger that, Mel. Can you save her?"

"I'm trying. Limit communication now because of latency." Addressing Zhigang, she said, "I don't know what happened, but she doesn't seem to have any muscle tension left. Unconscious, I guess."

"Mel, it's Tom. Is her suit still under pressure?"

"I think so, the hole is very small as I said." Even as she spoke, she was fumbling one of her self-adhesive patches out of her fanny pack and pressing it onto the open spot. "But her helmet lights are off and her chest computer is offline. The hole is on her right side. Also, her boots no longer have power."

She looked down and only now noticed that Gabriella was floating. She hadn't noticed because she had barely drifted off due to her connection and she had been holding her for quite a while. "Could have been a micrometeorite. I'm bringing her in now."

She thought of the long furrow below the hatch and shuddered. Cautiously, she put one foot in front of the other, back toward the airlock, when a fountain of bright gas shot out of Gabriella's helmet, sending her instantly rocketing away. Before Mel could react, the Italian had slipped from her grasp and was flying away like a boomerang, propelled by the residual atmosphere in her suit that was sucked through the small hole in her helmet.

"Meteor shower!" she shouted, watching the safety line snap through its carabiner at her hip. She grabbed the rope, but not too tightly, and tried to slow Gabriella's body down without getting carried away.

It did not work.

Her grip had obviously been too firm, and Gabriella was too far away, making the rotation of *Pangaea's* mid-segment strong enough to fling her further out. Mel was swept off her feet and spun uncontrollably. The magnetic boots were not designed for large traction forces, but had delayed her long enough to give her an unhealthy asymmetry.

She was peripherally aware that someone—Tom?—was talking to her, but there was nothing registering but her rushing breath and the growing nausea rising from her guts. A sharp pain shot through her foot and her uncontrolled movements slowed somewhat.

"I'm hit!"

"Mel!" Tom's voice pushed through to her after it took her two breaths to fight the adrenaline that was trying to force her into irrational behavior. There was a jolt and her spine felt like it was going to snap in two.

"I'm here. I think I've been hit. The centrifugal force has

caught me and I'm being thrown away," she said, breathing heavily.

"Your suit is losing air. You need to limit your oxygen consumption. Remember, sip. Just sip!"

"Roger that." She breathed in through half-closed lips for four seconds and out for eight. As she did so, she felt for the safety rope. It was taut. Before her eyes, the stars rotated like a monochromatic kaleidoscope, punctuated by an eerie shadow.

The solar sail, she told herself. *Just the sail.*

"I can't see much, but I think I'm rotating around *Pangaea* at just under 1 g now."

"You have to disconnect from Gabriella," Tom said. He sounded far too calm for what he was saying. "Otherwise, you won't have a chance to come back. Hongbo is already outside the airlock preparing to retrieve you."

Mel wanted to object, to be outraged that it even came up, to cut off her colleague and leave her to the cold nothingness. But that was irrational. She reached for her severing knife clipped to her right thigh, a double blade curved inward with no cutting edge outward. With one hand she reached up until she thought she felt the tight rope. It wasn't exactly easy through the air-filled gloves. Then she took the knife, forced herself to move slowly until she was sure the thin nylon mesh had slipped into the opening, and then pulled without pausing.

"I cut her loose." An uncomfortable pressure awoke in her chest, but she pushed it aside. "The force has weakened a bit, so I'm obviously still closer to the ship than the Habitat."

"Less than 1 g, that's good," Tom stated. "Can you pull yourself into it?"

"I'm trying."

"Good, remember. Sip and exhale. Don't worry about the CO_2 filters, it's the oxygen that counts."

"Roger that." Mel's uncontrolled spiral had calmed somewhat, though everything was still moving in front of her visor. Stars, dark ship's hull, light ship's hull, solar sails, radiators, then again from the front at a different speed. She closed her eyes, since she had no way to stabilize herself and would only lose valuable time.

Time she did not have. It already felt like she was breathing against a slight resistance. If she was losing air from the hole in her boot, the twisting motion wouldn't stop until there was no more air. But it was that very twisting motion that kept propelling her outward, making it hard to even grab the rope as her arms flung back and forth.

Look, Mel. Where are you? Reluctantly, she opened her eyes. The solar sail was diagonally above her, popping up every two or three seconds, the ship no longer visible to her. *So I'm circling with my head tilted, over forty degrees, I guess.*

That meant her legs were farther away from the rope. With an effort that would not help her oxygen balance, she spread her legs further apart and arched her back until she saw *Pangaea* circling in front of her like a space whale in a psychedelic nightmare. She formed a V with her arms until something struck her forearm. Quickly reacting, she bent her elbow and exhaled in relief when she felt the pressure of the rope in the crook.

"I'm stabilizing a bit," she pressed out through her lips.

"Selena can see you from the cockpit," Tom said. "That looks good. Hongbo is just inside the airlock."

"No, it's too dangerous, the pressure equalization—"

"We locked down the central corridor, Mel, and improvised it as an airlock. Don't worry about it. We'll get you in in a minute."

"She won't be able to pull me in," Mel gasped. "Not against centrifugal force."

An idea came to her.

She stretched her right leg and pulled it inward, growling,

until she thought she felt the rope, and then bent the knee, as she had done earlier with her elbow. Then she curled her upper body and grabbed her calf with her hand until she held her umbilical cord to *Pangaea* in her curled fingers. She didn't know how much longer she would be able to hold it, but with each passing second the danger grew greater—but it also became easier the closer she got to the ship.

After reaching around half a dozen times, she felt a gentle tug and opened her eyes. The dizzying rotation around the rope was diminished and she saw a figure in a large window.

Hongbo, she thought fuzzily. Her thoughts felt like drops of water seeping slowly into a cotton ball. The shape—it looked small in the giant space whale—pulled at her umbilical cord. Light, dark, light, dark, each time the shadow grew larger until a familiar face could be made out behind a glass sphere.

Mel's eyelids fluttered.

Oxygen deprivation. She was now breathing against a wall that had formed in front of her lungs, hard and impenetrable. Her brainstem forced the diaphragm to maintain the breathing reflex with uncontrolled spasms, but it could not succeed. She was in a place where nature did not want her to be, and her body reminded her of that.

A soft voice spoke to her. Or was it the singing of the angels calling her to the next realm?

16

When Mel opened her eyes, she saw Tom sitting next to her, just pulling an oxygen mask from her mouth and nose and smiling at her. There was no joy in the smile, but relief.

Gently, he squeezed her shoulder. "Welcome back."

Thank you, she tried to say, but only a caw came out, like an old crow.

"Here." The German reached behind him and brought a drinking tube to her lips. "Suck slowly, though. I don't want you to choke on me, after all. I've never lost a patient before, and I want to keep it that way."

Mel drank, and the liquid felt like ambrosia in her throat. Then she nodded and Tom withdrew the bag.

"You've only been practicing for a year, however," she croaked hoarsely.

"That's why I have such a good success rate," he joked, but there was a shadow of sorrow in his eyes.

Gabriella.

"How long was I gone?"

"Unconscious only five minutes, but still dazed for about fifteen minutes."

"Gabriella…"

"There was nothing you could do." Tom spoke emphatically, as if he wanted to hammer the words into her head and weld them there.

"I just wish—"

"I know. The micrometeorite must have shot from the left ventricle through her cardiac septum, the AV node, the right ventricle, and the sinus node and exited behind her right clavicle. She appeared to have died extremely quickly because the conduction of excitation stopped immediately, and with it the heartbeat. A second must have gone through her life support unit on her back and her chest computer, after the first impact and her change in position, cutting off power to her boots. Then the impact into her helmet."

The German was now speaking with extreme accentuation, like a forensic scientist dictating a report. She knew this behavior. Rationalization to prevent emotional reactions.

"My foot. I—"

"No problem. The hole is smaller than two millimeters. I didn't even have to stitch it. You'll still have a little pain when you step on it, but it's nothing we can't handle with a moderate analgesic."

"Did Hongbo save me?"

"Yes. You did most of it on your own, though. She said it was down to ten feet or less."

"Where is she?" Mel asked earnestly.

"I've already let her know you were awake."

"Can I get up?"

"Sure—if you shouldn't, you'll know."

"I have to report to Houston," flashed through her mind and from her lips. Her own rationalization to prevent emotional reactions.

"Zhigang has already taken care of that," he reassured her, making a placating gesture.

They were silent for a while, then Tom began to speak again, a little quieter this time. "I was in astronaut training with her over ten years ago. She didn't like red wine, but being Italian, she would never admit it. But, she secretly drank grape juice on our first date." Tom smiled with an absent look.

"I didn't know you guys—"

"You knew."

"Only that you were together the night before the launch," she countered.

"It was complicated. She came from South Tyrol. Did you know that?"

Mel nodded silently and gave him an inviting look. She wanted to hear more about their colleague, about whom she knew far too little—only how quickly she could solve logic problems, that she always used screwdrivers with her left hand, and snored softly when she slept. Too little for someone who had died right before her eyes.

"I used to tease her by calling her *Italian*," Tom smiled sadly. "She didn't like that a bit."

"But she *was* Italian."

"South Tyroleans don't like to hear that. Although they belong to Italy, culturally they are closer to the Austrians, and also belong to them historically. They speak German, have German and Ladin street signs, different architecture and different food."

"That's weird," she found.

"That's Europe," Tom corrected her with a sad smile, and his right hand wandered to his eyes before he turned away.

Mel sat up and carefully swung her legs off the couch. Her left foot was in a flexible orthosis.

"You're awake." Hongbo was standing in the doorway to the infirmary, a section of the lab. The taikonaut's lips parted into a smile. Mel stood carefully, without putting weight on her right foot, and embraced her colleague, who stiffened at first but then relented. The intimate touch seemed like something she hadn't felt in ages.

"Thank you."

"It's a given," Hongbo said after they broke away from each other. "It's what anyone would have done."

To Mel, even after years of working together, it still seemed as if her colleague was one half woman, and the other half a robot whose programming always overrode the emotions waiting behind her eyes.

"I'll go check on the others," Tom decided, looked at them both again, then disappeared down the ladder into the spoke of the rotating habitat. Mel noticed Hongbo's gaze dart to the cameras above the sink next to the centrifuges and she stiffened a little more.

"It was an honor to be of service to you," the Chinese woman said a little louder than necessary. She smiled broadly. "It was my duty, and I was happy to do it."

"Thank you. You are a good taikonaut, Hongbo. China will be proud of you." Mel waited until her colleague turned away after another nod, then said, "I need to get some rest. Houston?"

"It's Bernard," she heard after half a minute's delay.

"Can I have a little privacy? I think I need a few minutes to myself after all of this. I'm sure the audience understands, and right now we're not in any danger."

"No problem, Mel. We'll shut down the lab for an hour. The emergency override will remain in place."

"Thank you, Bernard."

"Get well soon." His voice sounded a little strained.

"Hongbo?" She stood up and walked over to the camera, over which she hung one of Tom's unused surgical trays. The Chinese woman hung like a monkey partway up the ladder rungs in front of the tube and saw it. Her gaze was scrutinizing.

"Yes?"

Mel waved her down and after a moment's hesitation, Hongbo returned. She looked at the hidden camera and frowned.

"They can't hear us."

"Hmm." Her counterpart looked unsettled and winced as she became aware of this fact.

"I want to say thank you, sincerely." She took a step toward the Chinese woman and looked her straight in the eye. This time Hongbo did not avoid her gaze.

"I meant it. Anyone would have done that for you. It was no big deal."

"It *is* a big deal when you're on the receiving end," Mel insisted.

"I see." Something seemed to release in Hongbo, because in the next moment she sighed like a steam boiler that needed to get rid of excess pressure. "I was really scared."

"Me too."

"The fact of Gabriella dying happened so suddenly that I didn't want to believe it. But in an emergency, you just act. Now I feel like I'm in a bad dream."

Mel nodded sadly and had to clear her throat before she could continue. She felt something hot on her cheeks, but she didn't care. "I know. Expectations make it worse."

"Yes." Hongbo looked out of the corner of her eye toward the cameras and considered. Then she shrugged. "I don't know any other way."

"The eyes that rest on you?" She tried to sound casual, in a pitiful attempt not to cross cultural boundaries by asking a rather political question.

"Yeah. We grow up with it, you know? It's... difficult."

"Everything I know about you comes from our news, and they have their own narrative about you. That's why many in the West think you're something like a sinister ant state."

Hongbo snorted. "I always had the impression that you can't understand our culture. Chinese people live all over the world, but when you ask them, they always say they are Chinese. It's probably our language, our culture, which has been cohesive for thousands of years, that makes us one."

"Not the Communist Party?"

"That is only an expression of what unites us, the desire to get ahead not only for yourselves but also for China. This is probably as foreign to you as your fanatical individualism is to us, which not a few in our country regard as egoism in the extreme."

"I understand," Mel said, making an effort to make sure it was true. "Aren't you losing yourself in the process?"

"Aren't you losing your community in the process?"

"Touché."

They were silent for a while. The hum of the laboratory machines grew louder.

Hongbo was the first to speak again: "I'm so far away that the Earth would fit a dozen times between us and China, and yet I worry about what I say and how it comes across at home."

"To the party?"

"Yes. And with the people. All our lives we put everything in this oversized scale. It's so normal that despite this pressure on my chest I've felt since Gabriella died, it's not an option to have my emotions visible because of it." Hongbo sniffled and smiled sadly. "What happens in the cellar stays in the cellar."

"Is that what you guys say?"

"Yes." The Chinese woman took a step toward her, and Mel was surprised when she embraced and squeezed her. "I'm glad we have you back, Commander."

Before Mel could sort herself out and come up with an answer, Hongbo had turned around and was climbing the ladder. She stared after her for quite a while, like a phantom image on her retina that just wouldn't go away.

She didn't know how much time had passed before she suddenly understood exactly how a Chinese citizen—and a Chinese taikonaut—must feel. Much like she did. All the while, the heavy gaze of billions weighed on her, in addition to Mission Control, her higher command authority. Her mission was so expensive and important that everything was monitored and there was virtually no privacy. In addition, they were the best of the best and, accordingly, only the best performance was expected of them. This certainly did not include losing an astronaut or crying.

"Just be normal," had been the well-intentioned advice from Dixie Walters, NASA's press officer, when the quasi-permanent live streams had been decided upon, to let the world public participate and thus strengthen the acceptance of the enormous expenditure. Today, Mel could have slapped her for that. Astronauts were expected to be something like superheroes, and they were no longer 'normal' people.

The pain of Gabriella's loss was only intensified by this added pressure, and although it was true that they all had personalities that brought high psychological resilience, it gnawed at them. No one talked about it except when formalities made it necessary. So Tom had to write a report on the cause of death from a medical point of view, which was signed off by Selena as the second doctor. Everything was based on educated guesses, mainly based on Mel's descriptions.

Mel had to add a long appendix to her EVA report, detailing how she had experienced her colleague's death. This only solidified the surreal images in the darkness of space, even though she felt that writing down her experiences had something liberating about it, as if she could reveal herself to someone in this way. Once again, she found herself wishing they hadn't decided against bringing a psychologist with them.

Over meals together in the mornings, they talked about the day's respective tasks with which they filled the half-year voyage; research for various universities and other donors to *Pangaea*, which was to derive maximum benefit from what was needed, but also for the military of their respective countries and, above all, solvent pharmaceutical companies that needed microgravity for highly complex drug research. It was a win-win situation, since on the one hand the astronauts kept themselves busy and didn't get cabin fever, locked in a tin can in a vacuum, and on the other hand, the clients got something back for helping to finance the trip.

At noon, they went over the results and discussed the various interviews and reporting sessions that were coming up. In the evening, the conversations ebbed even faster and they briefly went over plans for the next day before each retreated to their sleeping chamber, the only place where they were not seen or heard. Only the monitoring of their vital signs continued there.

After a week of subdued, forced professionalism, she received a connection request from Jim's office on her wrist display and was told to take it in a confidential setting. She asked Zhigang to handle the meeting at lunch, and sat herself in front of the video screen in the lab with earbuds in.

Jim looked older than when they'd last met in her room at JSC. The beginnings of bags under his eyes were no longer beginnings and he'd let his hair grow longer, giving it a thinning appearance.

"Hello, Mel," he said, suppressing the glimmering longing in his eyes with obvious reluctance.

"Hello, Jim. What's up?" she asked, giving him a warm smile. She didn't care if those who were surely monitoring her —presumably the NSA—wanted to read something into it. He looked stressed, and that hurt her.

"Gabriella's death has been making more and more waves

in recent weeks. The ESA member states are at odds over whether or not she was really the most qualified for the EVA, and whether it was a mistake to choose her for it."

"That's typical," Mel grumbled, snorting disdainfully. "Whenever something goes wrong, fingers are pointed—as if that makes anyone feel better. She got hit by micrometeorites. It could have happened to anyone!"

"I know that, but ESA put in more money than member states had available... if you believe them."

"So it's about the money."

"It's *always* about the money," he countered bitterly.

"And what are they going to do now? Call us off?" She leaned back in her chair and waved it off. "They should take physics lessons first, because they can't do that."

"I know that, and the ESA knows it too, but they have to rely on the good will of politicians, just as we do. The only difference is that they have to negotiate with twenty-two governments and we have to negotiate with one."

"I still don't understand what this means for our mission."

"Nothing, so far. It means disputes between the mission's backers. That's NASA, ESA, and the CSA from China, in addition to junior partners Canada, Japan, and the United Arab Emirates. So be prepared for more frequent private conversations among your colleagues and limited public time," Jim said with a grim face.

"You've got to be kidding me." Mel leaned forward to add emphasis to her words. "If we lock out the public now, it's only going to cause more problems because approval of the whole mission will drop, putting even more pressure on the parliaments to make their mark. We knew from the start that the trip itself would be the biggest challenge in terms of the willingness to support, because it was expected to be uneventful—which, unfortunately, it wasn't."

"No, it's been worse so far, with such a disaster."

"Yes. You have to make them understand that they…"

"I know, Mel," he responded after the half-minute delay had passed, looking pained. "That's why I'm talking to you. I want you to help me with this."

"And how?"

"Talk to the crew, tell them what's at stake and why you need to pull together. I need all the help I can get. To a lot of people, you guys are still superstars."

"We're Big Brother in space," she replied, ashamed of her bitterness in an instant. "Sorry."

Jim didn't seem to have heard as he talked on. She couldn't even imagine the pressure he must be under. "ESA has to turn the tide. They obviously want to stay on it and do everything they can for Tom, to continue to care for him, which will happen. I can't see them just dropping him and sending their own agency to the grave. But the cohesion of our three main partner nations will wobble if ESA wobbles, and we can't afford that because it will have an impact on *you*."

It took Mel a moment before she realized what he was actually trying to tell her: that there was a danger of political differences spilling over into *Pangaea*. At first, she thought this idea was absurd. After all, the decades on the ISS had shown that even the Russians were easy to get along with because astronauts didn't care about petty political differences on the surface. But that had also changed with the Russian invasion of Ukraine and…

Hongbo. She thought about the taikonaut and her words about China and shuddered. Was there a genuine possibility that she and Zhigang would choose their country and their orders from the CCP over the discovery of an alien celestial body?

"I understand," she said, hoarse all at once.

"Good." Jim nodded. Then again. "Good. Maybe I'm

looking at the dark side, too, but I wanted you to be able to adjust to everything."

"Thank you. I will. We'll get through this."

"We will." Jim hesitated, and they looked at each other through the lenses of their cameras, millions of miles apart. He seemed to want to say something else to her, raised a hand. She thought he was touching the camera, as if they could feel each other, but instead he just flicked the connection switch, because the screen went black and she was alone, surrounded by the hum of machines and servers.

She sat in silence for a long time, until at some point she reluctantly rose and stretched her limbs—not because they were tense, but to gain time—and then made her way to the ladder. With each rung gravity lessened, and she found it easier to pull herself up, or push, as the case may be. Finally, a barely perceptible hint of nausea heralded the tipping point to weightlessness. The central corridor, which doubled as a mess hall and lounge, was empty. Mel looked at her wrist and sighed. It was an hour past her scheduled bedtime. How many millions or even billions of people had watched her broodingly stare holes into the wall in the lab?

Quickly she brushed her teeth, spat the remains as a cloud of bubbles into the recycler's hose, and settled into her sleeping chamber, with just enough room for a few photos, her ancient iPod, and her sleeping bag, which she closed around her. Sleep found her immediately, though her thoughts circled around Jim's words.

Especially around his deeply troubled expression.

17

Mel was dreaming again. She knew it, as was always the case. As a child, lucid dreaming had been her way of escaping reality, which she had always found unpleasant and unfair. When a child's parents died in an accident, even before said child had learned to walk, this kind of reaction was probably nothing out of the ordinary. Her grandmother, whose warm smile and plump, soft face Mel still carried inside like a warming fire two decades after her death, had taught her. A gift—as she knew today, and a risk at the time—Nana had no way of knowing whether Melody would lose herself in her dreams and no longer find a firm footing in reality.

As happened often, Nana had shown foresight in this matter, and had not been mistaken. But today Mel was no longer so sure. The dream clung to her like resin, even more strongly than usual, and although she understood, as always, how to roam through the neural landscapes of herself, she was also trapped in them to some extent.

Just as she had done since her earliest youth, she was back in space, that place of her dreams, which she had now made real, only to look death in the face. She slid through the cold under the eyes of the stars, finding it pleasant. Crystals formed under her skin, tickling and itching. But there was nothing for her with which to scratch, and the impulse quickly disappeared as the crystals melted from the warmth of her heart and turned into nourishing water that seeped through her connective tissue.

She was free in the vacuum, alone but free. No one spoke to her, and that was fine, although she longed to share her experience. She sought out other lucid dreamers and yet knew with the conscious part of her brain that this was impossible. This was her dream, and her home was not in the void among the stars, but under Earth's thin canopy.

Nevertheless, she enjoyed the feeling of freedom, sensing the reliable presence of the sun, Jupiter, and Saturn, those great gravitational sinks of the solar system that subjected all other celestial bodies to their brute force and held them in the complex orbital pattern on which they orbited around their central star. They were prisoners of the most powerful sound generator of this local structure. But not she. She was small and insignificant, yet the most important thing in the universe here and now. Just as everything else was and always would be the most important thing in itself, long after it had faded away.

Once again, she saw *Pangaea* from the outside. However, she recognized the ship merely by its fish shape, were it not for the two outriggers that rotated on the spokes around the hull. It billowed in unreal tones, like a representation in false colors, possessed spherical exhalations in red that was not red and blue that was not blue. Dreaming, she understood that her brain was generating the correspondences, thinking past reality to generate an inherent frame of reference.

The law of the dream was that there was no law. The rules of physics applied no more than those of logic. It was all the same now. Her hands were tentacles and her fingers fibrils, dozens, hundreds, stretching out into space like ethereal threads, reaching for the lone spaceship of colors. She saw the infinite space between the molecules and the atoms of which they were composed. She saw the mighty baryonic spectacle, crowded to the unknowing eye, when it was merely vibrations in nothingness so far apart as to mock dead gods once enthroned on the Olympus of human imagination. The real crushing mass of the cosmos was the emptiness, the nothingness, in which the matter played the role of the spectacular.

It was grand in the core essence of the word, an all-encompassing grandeur of unfathomable depth, and at the same time a thing of normality. The thing that fascinated Mel most, however, was the inertia with which she dreamed. It had always left her speechless: dreams that were of such brevity that she thought she had barely slept. Impressions of a few seconds, although they were not measurable. Isolated observations and glimpses of thoughts that she could hardly think through to the end.

She awoke because something was wrong.

First, there was the disappointment of having to shed the wings of the cosmos so abruptly, of having her wings clipped without wanting to. But then it was the pressure on her shoulders, and the knowledge seeping back into her mind that she possessed an earthly body, brutally reduced to skin, flesh and bone and electrical nerve tracts of extremely short distances.

"Commander!"

"W-what...?" she stammered tiredly and confusedly, blinking against the heaviness of her eyelids. Gradually, Tom's face peeled out of the glare. He looked upset. Only now did she realize that he had addressed her by her title, which rarely happened unless there was a problem and everything was being recorded.

She blinked, noticing that he had continued talking through her haze.

"There's a problem with Selena," he repeated, helping her get out of her sleeping bag when she fumbled with the zipper.

"What kind of problem?" she asked. Fatigue and dream were blown away.

"She's not waking up."

"What do you mean?"

"She just won't wake up. Hongbo woke up early because she had to go to the bathroom." Tom's brow furrowed in deep worry. "That's when she heard Selena's alarm beeping, but saw her face asleep behind the glass. She then opened the sleeping chamber after knocking several times and saw that Selena was indeed still asleep, even though the volume of her wrist display was set on maximum."

Mel released herself from her recess in the wall and floated to the other side, where Selena's mini-compartment was. Zhigang and Hongbo hovered next to a mummy-like Selena lowered into the wall, having been freed from her sleeping bag and held there only by the pressure of Hongbo's hand. The two taikonauts cast worried glances at Mel as she approached.

"I don't understand. You tried to wake her up, didn't you?" Mel asked.

"Yes," Tom affirmed from behind her. The ESA astronaut caught himself on one of the handholds above them and then hung in the air beside her like a fish in water. "She's not responding to auditory or tactile stimuli. She's like dead!"

"Did she go into a coma?"

"No. Her core body temperature is normal and her breathing is regular. Her pulse is also normal. Well, slightly bradycardic, but not slower than the expected range for someone who is asleep."

"So you've examined her," Mel stated, eyeing Selena's relaxed face. The corners of her mouth twitched slightly from time to time, and her eyes moved visibly under the closed lids.

"Extensively. I didn't think it was a big deal at first, but now I'm very worried. From what I can tell, she's a normal sleeper. But she's not waking up." Tom pointed to his doctor's bag, which was magnetically stuck to the wall. "I could inject her with amphetamines and some cortisol, and she'd probably wake up. Adrenaline seems too excessive for someone with nothing medically wrong with her."

"Except that this someone can't wake up," Zhigang indicated.

"Yes."

"We'll wait," Mel decided. "We'll have our breakfast here and continue to watch her in the meantime. If in an hour she's still not responding to stimuli that ought to wake her up, we'll see. Zhigang, I want you to discuss this with Mission Control."

He nodded obediently and pulled himself toward the cockpit.

Five minutes later, Mel, Tom, and Hongbo were 'sitting' in the open area of the sleeping compartment, squeezing gooey paste into their mouths from the navels of small plastic pouches, today's version masquerading as scrambled eggs with bacon and beans.

"Okay, if no one agrees, then I'll stop," Tom grumbled at one point, pointing to Selena's motionless form, which they had secured in her sleeping chamber with two flexible rubber bands. "First Gabriella gets hit by micrometeorites, then news that ESA is beginning to doubt the mission, provoking stress between the donor nations, and now Selena falls asleep like a coma."

"Yes," Mel said simply. "That's all true. What are you saying?"

"Normally, I would call this a run of bad luck. Nothing to lead a scientific mind to superstition. But this? She doesn't have a conspicuous medical record, she's a doctor herself, and she's been through all the tests—medical check-ups for heart and kidneys, like the rest of us. She doesn't suffer from narcolepsy, never has," the doctor continued. "Something is beyond strange here, that's all I'm saying."

"Maybe it has to do with our radiation exposure?" suggested Hongbo. "In here, we're pretty well shielded by the water tanks, but that's more like the light version of the magnetic protection we originally planned. Each of us also spends up to twelve hours in the habitats, so we're exposed to cosmic rays."

"Those are unhealthy doses, yes," Tom admitted, but shook his head in what looked like a too-slow animation in zero gravity. "But I test our blood every two days, and I can't see any rudiments of radiation damage in the exams. Our millisievert meters haven't gone into the red zone even once. So that can't be it."

"Maybe some other effect of interplanetary travel outside the Earth's magnetic field that we don't know about?" asked Mel.

"I at least can't think of one, and a hundred years of research has come up with quite a few theories."

"There must be some scientifically explainable reason for her condition," she insisted.

"I'd like to know it."

"Maybe Mission Control will have some ideas. They're going to put a lot of people on it."

"It won't please my homeland," Hongbo said with a hint of gloom around her eyes.

Mel noticed that she had bags under her eyes, and wondered, *for how long? Days? Weeks?* Time out here blurred between sleep and work. The monotony that provided routine, and thus security and distraction, not infrequently caused her to lose her sense of detail about her surroundings. Her brain had seemingly created paths that she walked over and over again, and which were thus so well-trodden that she no longer had to think a conscious thought to walk them.

"Of course not, but that would have been true even before the differences over Gabriella's death," Mel was sure. She refused to give in to defeatist whispers in her mind. It was simply not helpful.

"I wonder how the discord could have happened," Tom grumbled. "What happened to Gabriella..." He paused for a moment and took a breath. "What happened to her didn't affect anyone here as much as it affected me. And yet we all knew how great the dangers of our journey were and that it could affect anyone. Even a complete accident of *Pangaea* would have been, and still is, possible. There was no plan B. And yet international harmony crumbles as soon as things don't go along the best possible outcome. It's bizarre!"

"That's politics," Mel objected. She wondered if they were being listened to now, even though they were talking in the sleeping areas, which were not supposed to be monitored except for vital signs and the electronic systems. "And that can always be dangerous to us."

"We are very far away." Hongbo sounded like she was trying to say something to herself, and seemed absent-minded and thoughtful about her own words for a moment.

"You all know as well as I do the state of the Earth. The climate catastrophe, the new Cold War between the West and China, the decline of Russia and the accompanying temporary destabilization of former Soviet republics, the thawing of ancient pathogens that had been trapped in the permafrost, and the growing number of pandemics, or the erosion of Western democracies. A single match is enough to make the barrel explode."

"And we are the match," Tom finished her words.

"And they set fire to us at home," Hongbo said.

"Exactly." Mel nodded. "If they lose faith that our mission

will succeed, it will be a matter of who can be the first to pick up the pieces and capitalize on the outcome. That's just the way politics is."

"This damn mission was supposed to *unite* rather than divide," Tom grumbled.

"It should, and it will." She looked him in the eye and repeated, "It will."

As if she had heard Mel's unconditional call for optimism, Selena woke up at that very moment. "Good morning," the Wisconsin doctor said sleepily, yawning. "Have you started breakfast without me?"

When they carelessly let go of their bags of freeze-dried 'food' and darted toward her like piranhas, she raised her hands defensively. "Whoa, what's wrong with you guys?" She looked down at herself and frowned. "And what are these bands? Where's my sleeping bag?"

"Finally!" escaped Tom and he grabbed his colleague by the shoulders to hug her. "Finally!"

Selena seemed even more confused.

"You didn't wake up," Mel said, sighing with relief. "Your alarm clock went off over an hour ago."

"An hour and a half, to be exact," Hongbo interjected.

"What?"

"We couldn't get you to wake up," Tom explained more calmly now. "You were like narcoleptic."

"Is this a bad prank?" Selena asked sincerely. "We're not in college anymore, if I may remind you. And where's my sleeping bag?"

"Here." Hongbo retrieved it from her sleeping chamber, where it had apparently been stashed, and pushed it toward the doctor. In the weightlessness, the artificial down structure spread out like a jellyfish before Selena caught it and packed it up.

"Well, at least you didn't paint me or anything."

"We're not kidding," Mel pressed in on her, waiting until their eyes met. The furrows in Selena's brow deepened again as growing uncertainty crept into her eye expression.

"Did you take any medication yesterday?" Tom inquired.

"No." She shook her head. "I didn't manage to smuggle alcohol onto the ship either, like the old Apollo swashbucklers, before you ask that, too."

"Did you have any symptoms before sleeping?"

Selena considered, but again shook her head. "No. Nothing. I just went to sleep."

"Was the sleep dreamless?"

"No."

Tom pondered.

"No, not cataplexy," she told him. "I really don't know—"

"What were you dreaming?" asked Mel spontaneously, and Selena seemed even more surprised.

"Why?"

"What were you dreaming?" repeated Mel, looking at her counterpart in a way that communicated this was not a joke.

"Nothing special. Being in space. Why? What would that have to do with anything?"

"Maybe nothing, maybe everything. Tell me about it."

"I've been dreaming the same stuff for a long time. Pretty boring stuff, I can tell you. I'm flying around the solar system, mostly short distances. I see one or two things, try to grab a thought, but usually don't get around to finishing it." Selena raised her hands like an interviewee wanting to know if that got her off the stand.

Mel stiffened. "Since when have you been dreaming that?"

"Since the first or second week of our trip, my dreams have been similar."

"Can you lucid dream?"

"No. Never learned and never had any interest in it," Selena replied. "Ever since I started astronaut training, I've been so tired that my sleep has been as dreamless as a black hole. I guess it has to do with the special nature of this trip. New neural connections off normal circuit pathways. More work for the unconscious processing mechanisms of the cerebral cortex."

"Hmm. Still, you remember it well."

"Not really. After I get up, yeah, and then I forget again. I can't tell you anymore what I dreamed about yesterday, but I remember now after I get up that it was similar to today. After the first coffee, it'll probably be gone again." The astronaut didn't seem particularly bothered by this thought.

"If you remember now, please try to describe to me what exactly you were dreaming just now." Seeing Selena's raised brows, Melody added emphatically, "Just do it, please."

"All right," the doctor sighed in surrender. "I was lying in a vacuum, feeling great, although I couldn't really feel. I didn't have a body. Well, at least not one like this, I don't know." She waved it off. "Dreams, that's all. My skin kind of itched or tickled or both at the same time. I think there was our ship too, *Pangaea*, but it looked strange."

"As in false colors?"

"Yes." Selena's gaze turned suspicious. "Where—?"

"Go on." Mel made an impatient wave with her right hand and had to grab hold of one of the handholds with her left to keep from floating away.

"All right, if you really want to hear the unsorted detritus of my brain, my arms were transparent tentacles with tiny hairs on the ends that I used to reach for the ship." She wiggled her fingers and smiled.

Mel did not smile. "I dreamed the same thing," she said instead.

Selena looked like she had slapped her. "What?"

"I had the exact same dream. More detailed, but I've been

lucid dreaming since I was a kid and I can remember every little thing."

"You're not kidding, are you?"

"She doesn't look like it to me," Tom observed from the side. "More like she's seen a ghost."

"And maybe I have," Mel said. "What are the chances we'd have the same dream on the same night?"

"About as likely as narcoleptic cataplexy in a healthy person with no history or risk factors," he replied. "Or that I've also been dreaming for two weeks about a frozen moment drifting through space."

Selena's gaze shifted back and forth between them. "What's happening?"

"'A frozen moment drifting through space,'" Mel repeated his last sentence, thinking about it. "That's it."

"*What* is *it?*"

"That's the description for a feeling I couldn't have described, but that's exactly how it feels. In my dreams, I'm moving through space, seeing things, knowing I'm traveling a certain distance. What doesn't match it every time is the fact that the time period is so short that I can't bring a thought to its conclusion."

"Distance traveled, however, takes time."

"Yes. It doesn't add up."

"Of course not. They are *dreams*, remember," intervened Hongbo, who had become so quiet that Mel had tuned her out. "Dreams follow their own logic, which has little to do with natural laws and clear causality."

"Maybe," Mel agreed, looking directly at her. "Did you dream something like that, too?"

"I do not dream."

"Hmm."

"What do you think?" Tom asked.

"I don't know," Mel confessed, sliding over to the

compartment's control panel and pulling the handle of one of the displays, which moved out of the wall and flipped up. She tapped her fingers a few times until she called up the image of the bow telescopes, then turned the screen to face the others. It showed a pale, one-inch line that stood out against the surrounding darkness.

At that moment, Zhigang came floating in to join them.

"But," Mel stated, "the only component of this journey that is as inexplicable as multiple people dreaming the exact same dreams is this one here."

18

"These are dreams," Zhigang said emphatically, pointing to the large screen in the lab that showed Serenity at maximum zoom as a bright tail against the band of stars.

They sat gathered around the narrow table on which a scanning electron microscope and a light microscope stood like referees between Zhigang and Hongbo on one side and Mel, Tom, and Selena on the other. The day's schedule had long been in disarray, but Mel had informed Houston that she felt a deviation was necessary in this case. The excitement over Selena's medical discrepancy was apparently great enough that Bernard had merely informed Mel to proceed as she thought best. That there had not even been further inquiries about the new plans was proof enough that they were at least as excited in Houston as they were out here.

"Can we be so sure?" asked Mel.

"You are asleep and dreaming. That explains everything, doesn't it?"

"It doesn't explain why Selena and I had the same dream on the same night and Tom also has had similar dreams."

"Similar dreams. Not the same."

"I can't remember the details, but I dream of space," Tom said thoughtfully, without taking his eyes off Serenity. Although it was a live recording, it looked like a still image.

"That's logical, too," Hongbo interjected. "We are taiko-nauts, or astronauts, flying through a vacuum. Sleep is for our brains to process and sort out what we've experienced during the day."

"That's pretty oversimplified, but it's basically correct," Selena said. "Still, it's not a sufficient explanation."

"Why not?" the Chinese woman asked.

"Because it relies too much on chance as an explanatory component. That's always bad science because it's not *science*."

"However, to assume that it is the work of an extraterrestrial entity invading our minds is not much more scientific, either."

"No," Selena agreed with her. "But, to assume that the disruptive factor, which has been added to an equation that has always produced the same result, and that has been spitting out a different result since that factor was added, is not an explanation, it is short-sightedness."

"Excluding possibilities is not consistent with a scientific approach," Mel jumped in with her. "Just think about how 'impossible' the entire scientific community has deemed it for a comet to be in Pluto's orbit. Impossible to the best of our knowledge."

"Yes, and it wasn't a comet," Zhigang pointed out.

"No, it wasn't, but my suggestion that it must be an artificial extraterrestrial object was dismissed as craziness."

"And we still don't know that it is. Only that the probability is very high."

"It could be the same with these dreams," Mel insisted.

"What exactly is your hypothesis?" the Chinese man asked.

"I don't have any valid ones. Just thoughts." After he

spread his hands and looked at her questioningly, she shrugged and continued, "What if it's some kind of communication recording?"

"A communication recording? We've tried everything and it hasn't responded—if it even can."

"We've been broadcasting on a fairly wide range of electromagnetic radiation and getting no response," Tom objected. "That's not exactly the definition of *tried everything*. It's merely what we consider, from an—albeit understandable—anthropocentric point of view, to be the most likely way of transmitting signals."

"Yes." Mel nodded, stood up, and walked over to the display to tap Serenity's light tail with the knuckle of her right index finger. "It could be some kind of quantum communication."

"*Quantum* communication?" Zhigang raised an eyebrow.

"Why not? Einstein once derided all of quantum mechanics as spooky remote action, and today more than half of our everyday technologies are based on its effects. Despite the fact that we use it so extensively, there are still a great many unanswered questions about how to explore it. Why shouldn't it be possible for an alien spacecraft to communicate using quantum entanglement effects?"

"Even should that be possible," Tom opined, "why would our brains be capable of receiving such forms of communication in the first place?"

"I don't know," she admitted. "But why *wouldn't* they be able to?"

"Because evolution always puts what is necessary before what is possible," Selena answered in Tom's place. "Life is always highly specialized and adapted to the requirements of that niche in which it has found a way to survive."

"Maybe we used to need it, but the ability has atrophied. It's like the appendix or the coccyx."

"These are classic myths. The appendix does have functions. It is equipped with lymphatic tissue that serves as the primary immune mediator of antigens and repopulates the intestine with healthy microbiome after diarrheal illnesses. The coccyx—though correctly the vestigial rudiment of those days when we had tails—serves as the attachment point of several important ligaments and muscles of the pelvis. No." Selena shook her head. "Evolution doesn't care for waste."

"But it's possible that our brains use this kind of communication without it being a conscious process," Tom said. "So much of what goes on in our brains is unconscious. We are the hosts of millions of strains of bacteria that control a significant portion of our bodies. The microbiome determines whether we feel frisky or irritable, when and how well we wake up or get tired, produces enzymes that activate or deactivate our bodily functions, and has an impact on our autonomic nervous system, which is not under our control—whatever we are in that case."

"Are you saying we're just spectators?"

"No, what I'm saying is that we don't know about most of the things that go on in our bodies because they're not subject to our conscious participation. Twenty years ago, I would have been laughed at for what I just told you about the microbiome. Today it is universal medical knowledge. If you go back another fifty years, they thought the intestine started behind the bile duct and the stomach gate. Today they know it starts at the lips." The German doctor sighed and unfolded his hands like a priest after prayer. "What I mean to say is that the human body has many functions that we cannot explain. That's why we shouldn't hastily rule anything out."

"He's right," Mel said. "Think of things like intuition or something as central as human consciousness. We have no explanation for them. They can't be localized in our bodies—even the need for the brain is doubted after experiments with meditators whose cortex neurons, thalamus, and reticular formation no longer show any excitation. They no longer have ego consciousness, if fMRI scans by researchers are to be believed, yet they are still aware of their existence."

"We don't even have a universal definition of consciousness."

Mel pointed at Tom in a *you see?* gesture.

"Even if it were the case that Serenity contacted us through our dreams," Zhigang countered with little conviction in his voice, "why now of all times? Why not much earlier? Serenity entered our solar system a great many years ago."

"I've had similar dreams since I entered the astronaut program," she said. *And long before that.* She kept that thought to herself. While Zhigang was formulating his rebuttal, something occurred to her. "Selena, Tom, can you say approximately when you first dreamed these dreams?"

"Being in space?" asked Selena.

"'A frozen moment drifting through space,'" Mel said, repeating their comrade's amazingly apt description from earlier.

"I wrote it in my journal."

"You keep a diary?" asked Tom.

"Don't you? We are undertaking the most important journey in human history."

"Never mind that," Mel intervened. "Can you check?"

"Sure. Now?"

"Yes. Tom, what about you?"

"I remember it was the last day of mac and cheese. A sad day."

"Good. Go through the inventory of supplies and see when the last packs were gone."

"What are you getting at?"

"Everything... Maybe nothing," she muttered back, staring

at Serenity's pale tail. Then she grabbed a tablet, opened a graphics file and her flight data, and started doing the math. Ten minutes later, she was startled when Tom and Selena returned. Zhigang and Hongbo hadn't said a word and were obviously preoccupied with their own thoughts.

"Got it?"

"Yeah." Tom nodded and told her the date. Selena followed suit.

"That's the exact same day." Mel looked meaningfully at the two Chinese, but they did not respond. "Do you know what else happened on that date?" She stretched out the tension-building moment a bit before turning her tablet so they could see the result of her calculations: a legible date that corresponded to the start of her NASA and ESA colleagues' dreams.

"That's the day we left Earth's magnetosphere and had to comply with the extended habitat residence times," Tom said in amazement.

"Yes. So there is a direct correlation between leaving the Earth's magnetic field and the occurrence of the dreams."

"You said you've had dreams like this before," Zhigang objected.

"That's right. And I don't know why. Maybe it's because of my ability to lucid dream. Maybe there's another reason."

"That's very thin."

"There's no denying that," Selena agreed, and Tom nodded as well.

"Suppose there were a connection," said the taikonaut. "What should we deduce?"

"That it communicates with us," Mel replied.

"And what does it say?"

"I don't know."

"So... are the dreams good or bad? I mean, do they make you feel good or bad?"

She was surprised by Zhigang's sudden curiosity. Apparently, he was no longer closed to the idea. At any rate, his gaze was probing and he seemed genuinely interested in the answer —in contrast to the dismissive look that she had seen in his eyes earlier.

"Neither. I felt normal." She looked at Tom and Selena, who nodded their agreement one after the other.

"So we can't infer anything about Serenity's intent, should it have been an attempt to communicate."

"That's correct."

"That's unfortunate, because it would help us if we knew whether its messages were a warning or an invitation," Hongbo said, breaking her long silence. "We reach the object in a few weeks, and if it has tried to contact us directly, then we can conclude that there is an intention behind it. Any conscious communication intake that is not based on a body language response is always intentional. And that means—"

"—that it's trying to tell us something." Mel grumbled and rubbed her temples, as if she could force the answer out of her brain if she massaged it evenly from both sides.

Tom asked the question that was on all their minds. "If we were to fly into an alien system inhabited by an intelligent alien species that sends a ship in our direction, what would be our intention of a first contact?"

"It all depends on whether we would be afraid of the contact or looking forward to it," Selena replied.

"It depends on how much it, or *they*, know about us," Mel thought aloud. "What would count for us is the impression we would have of the alien civilization. Right now, more than thirty armed conflicts are raging on Earth, there are several dozen severe environmental disasters due to climate catastrophe, and millions are being driven from their homes. But good things are also happening every day. An army of volunteers is using their free time to help others. Peace missions quelling conflicts, food donations, international disaster relief. The list is long."

"Ying and yang," Hongbo said thoughtfully. "The question of their conclusion from what they see—*if* they see it—can only be answered by the introjects of their own species and the individuals on board. To what things do they attach what importance, and what conclusions do they draw from them?"

"Like a glass half full or half empty?" asked Tom.

"Very basically, yes," Hongbo answered.

"Which brings us back to square one," Mel remarked. "We don't know because we don't have any data."

"They haven't shot at us yet," the German pointed out, attempting a wry grin.

"And neither have we at them," Mel said. "They'll factor that into their equation somehow, too."

"Through all of this, though, I wonder why they don't address us in a way that we can consciously grasp."

When Mel looked at him questioningly, he pointed to the image of Serenity. "Anyone who manages to travel through the interstellar medium and get here will surely know about radio waves and will have picked up our radio waves over the last few decades. Or, in other words, a species that has mastered interstellar travel surely has sensors for the entire electromagnetic spectrum and should be able to detect with ease the deviations from normal background radiation and expected radio waves that emanate from Earth and coalesce around it into a wild tangle of electromagnetic vapors."

"You mean, why does it talk to us in riddles?"

"Yes. Establishing contact is always based on the lowest common denominator. When I meet a Japanese person in Japan, I think we need hands and feet to talk to each other. They are the connecting element that we can both use for simple symbolic language. I wouldn't try to speak High German with him, or Oxford English, if I knew he only spoke

Japanese. That would be pretty stupid." He pointed to Serenity again. "I don't think *they* are stupid, though. Just their presence here makes that impossible."

"Nothing is impossible at this point," Selena countered. "We sent Voyager 1 out of the solar system, and in many hundreds of thousands of years—maybe millions—it could pass through an inhabited system as well. I love our probe, but it's pretty dumb by most standards and shouldn't have a single working system left by that time. Aliens out there would be fascinated because it is definitely an alien-built object. They could not communicate with it. So, in that case, your thoughts would be a misconception."

"I agree with you. But Serenity has braked and accelerated. So our visitors' spaceship is still functional and must have at least one working system—the one for engine control."

"Wait a minute," Zhigang intervened, crossing his arms in front of his chest. "You talk like it's perfectly clear that it's an alien spacecraft. It's not yet clear whether that is true, or if it's an extremely unusual celestial body that will change our knowledge of astronomy. Even if it is of artificial origin, it could be merely a probe, or an asteroid with a propulsion system attached."

"That's true," Mel admitted. "And that is what we're here to find out. All these thoughts we're having now—we shouldn't wait until we reach Serenity to discuss them."

"But there's still the problem with my condition." Selena pointed to herself with her thumb. "If I can't wake up and I can't be woken up, that could cause us some real problems. Especially since it could happen to you guys, too."

"You're right. I suggest that we sit down every morning, discuss our dreams, and write them down. Then we can compare and possibly draw conclusions that we don't see now. I'll talk to Bernard and ask for the rosters to be adjusted accordingly. As far as I can see, as long as Zhigang and Hongbo are not affected by the dreams, we are not in any danger that could lead to the end of the mission."

~

"Dreams, Mel?" asked Jim. Of all people, she hadn't expected him to respond more flatly disbelieving than Bernard, who had sounded more thoughtful, deliberate. Jim, however, looked worn and sullen.

Their 'conversation' was frustrating and surreal, with more than eight minutes of pause until the radio signals had gone back and forth and she received her response. She used the interval in between to type logs. Ironically, she still didn't have much time for the answers, because if she thought too long about what to say, even more time would pass.

"In the face of the impossible, we have to redefine the possible," she moved in toward him, leaning so far forward that her nose almost touched the display. "You can't possibly be of the opinion that we're imagining it all."

"Mel," came his agonized response, "You know I'd believe anything you said."

You did not believe me concerning the nature of Serenity, she thought and closed her eyes. She was tired and confused.

"The problem is that no small part of the public thinks you are mentally unstable. Many experts say that you are slowly losing your minds."

"They think we're going crazy? But they can see us almost twenty-four/seven!"

"There's talk of it," Jim repeated. "It's still scattered voices, but you know how it is. Once the magic word is out of the hat, it has a habit of spreading fast and not disappearing back into the hat."

"I don't get it," she sighed. She was loathe to indulge in negative thoughts and curse the public—or the many self-proclaimed television pundits who were only good for self-congratulatory talk on shows that lived for controversy. Sometimes, though, it wasn't that easy. How nice if they could feel the backing of eight billion fellow human beings.

"Public opinion is like an ocean of different currents surging back and forth," Jim explained sympathetically. There was sadness and longing in his gaze at the same time, pale as a drowning woman beneath the surface of the water whose contours were becoming increasingly unclear. "Don't worry about it. It can change again just as quickly."

"Then why do you look like you've seen a ghost?" Her voice remained warm, like her feelings toward him. She asked not out of reproach, but out of concern for him.

"The backing is dropping. Tomorrow is the next congressional hearing on mission readiness. Democrats want heads to roll over the gaping budget hole *Pangaea* has torn, and President Brosnahan has long since lost control of everyone in his party."

"It's about money again. Sure."

"They see the national debt, social spending that has been neglected for years, and a lot more. What they don't see is the success of the mission."

"How could they? We're still on the road. What do they expect? Can't they even wait for half a year?" she replied with a snort.

"Just before you get there is the midterms. The Republicans are getting nervous because the Democrats are running a massive money-wasting campaign against them, portraying the president as a dreamer with no sense of money management but plenty of wastefulness." Jim exhaled loudly and pushed a strand of hair away from his face. "This has become like a filter over your transmissions. A lot of Americans now see everything you guys do through Democrat glasses: wasted money on a way-too-dangerous expedition into space with an uncertain outcome. It's pathetic."

"Everyone's biggest fear has always been the unknown," she said, calming down a bit. "I understand that. I just would have hoped that politicians would have our backs for a bit longer."

"In a few weeks, you'll be at your destination. Then everything can change."

"A nice way of saying it's all or nothing for us." The nearly ten minutes after her answer felt like an eternity.

"Look at it this way. At least no one can pull the plug on you."

Mel thought of Zhigang and Hongbo. "I wouldn't be so sure."

"What do you mean by that?" Jim asked.

"Oh, probably nothing. Only three more weeks until we're close enough to take the first real optical images of Serenity. Images that aren't from computers and simulated using infrared data or light shifts, but *real images*. That's a few days before the midterms and could change everything."

"I hope so."

19

Over the next few weeks, they conducted numerous interviews and worked overtime to complete the funded experiments for government institutions and private industry. Mel felt that this decision had a positive impact on all of them. Contact with home brought her out of her brooding confinement in *Pangaea*, where everything revolved around her mysterious goal, and gave a face to her goal: a discovery not for herself, but for humanity.

By now they were more than 93,000,000 kilometers from Earth, so the time it took their radio signals to cover the distance was a whole 5.2 minutes. Accordingly, normal conversations were out of the question. Instead, they got the questions recorded, which took the pressure off their answers. No one could heckle them and they could think about it long enough to avoid saying something wrong. They were astronauts, not television professionals, so no one on board was sad about that fact.

Many of the questions revolved around the upcoming elections and thus had political undertones. At least that was true for her and Selena. Tom was largely spared such topics.

No collusion was needed between Mel and her NASA colleague to make sure they didn't take sides—it wasn't difficult, since they had no interest in Washington's verbal stabbings.

She liked the question-and-answer sessions with high school and college students, who turned out to be extremely interested and surprisingly well-informed. With them, she feared no unspoken, hidden questions or messages that were intended for a different audience and relegated her to being a vicarious agent.

More uncomfortable were the questions from politicians and senior officials, which were asked confidentially and had to be answered in their sleeping quarters. Mel felt bad every time she had to lock the others out, and it seemed to be quite the same the other way around—with the exception of Zhigang and Hongbo, for whom this process seemed neither unpleasant nor unusual. Most of these probing questions revolved around the preparation for the mission, details she couldn't possibly remember, and which were only designed to trip her up and thus justify the questioner's position. Accordingly, she kept her answers vague and evasive—let them fire her for that when she got back.

For now, she didn't care. Their destination was only nine days away and Serenity was all that mattered. Counting was a given at this point.

In the morning she always sat down with Tom and Selena for ten or so minutes to discuss their dreams. The results were not particularly fruitful, except for the fact that they were even more confusing than before. They still dreamed of the same timeless movements in the vacuum, but sometimes they saw *Pangaea*, sometimes Saturn, the sun, Mars, or Earth. Now and then the dreams were identical, but there were no factors that provided conclusions why it was only these dreams that they quite obviously shared.

Because of their strikingly erratic structure, Mel began to doubt whether they were purposeful attempts at communication. The dreams had no rational content but were rather sensory impressions, far too brief to put them into perspective. By the time the morning conversations had become routine, like something you check off after brushing your teeth before getting on with the important work of the day, they had moved on to another theory.

The connection with Serenity was logical. After all, the dreams had begun for Tom and Serena after they'd left Earth's magnetic field—no minor cosmic force. Moreover, the object was the disruptive component in their otherwise familiar system. They no longer believed in purposeful attempts at communication, but in random side effects. The only question was: from what? And they could only fail by relying on speculation. At least until they learned more about Serenity and gathered parameters to provide a frame of reference for further consideration in assessing the alien species.

Three days later, the Republicans were defeated in the midterm elections, and President Brosnahan was labeled a lame duck for no longer being in control of both chambers—his party had also lost seats in the Senate, and with the double vote of his vice president, it was 50 to 50. The Democrats, sharp critics of the alleged 'cozy course' toward China throughout the *Pangaea* project, announced a tougher stance, and that was not at all palatable to the partner nation on the other side of the Pacific. The spiral of verbal aggression that began again from both sides seemed all too familiar to Mel. The resumed maneuvers off Taiwan by the People's Liberation Army did not bode well either.

Mel was exceedingly relieved when, three days later, they finally reached the long-awaited point where they expected to be able to take the first evaluable live images of Serenity. The eight different telescopes on her bow, mounted on a retractable sensor array, were the best and most expensive the world had to offer at the time of their departure, and half of them had been developed especially for their mission.

Accordingly, she was excited on the ninth day before their calculated arrival at their destination. As soon as she emerged from her sleeping cabin, Selena grinned broadly at her. Even Zhigang couldn't hold back a smile, and Hongbo could be heard from the central corridor, where she was apparently in a good mood and joking with Tom.

In accordance with protocol, they first ate breakfast with deliberately suppressed impatience and then completed their fitness program in boom two. Mel could not remember having ever seen the others train so hard and with such motivation.

After showering, the time had come. They gathered in the lab and prepared the large touch display. Tom and Zhigang hooked up to the sensor controls at the two fold-out workstations to perform alignment and calibration of the lenses. Then they checked the data from the onboard computer and made the necessary adjustments. After another recheck by the two at the controls, they raised a thumb, one man after the other, in the direction of the other three crewmembers.

"We have an image," Zhigang said. "It's still at the maximum zoom level and therefore the worst possible image, but it will get better day by day."

"On the screen," she replied. "I've been waiting and waiting to say that."

Tom raised his hand in a Vulcan salute and grinned before pressing the Enter key on his keyboard and the main display showed Serenity.

Fascination battled with disappointment in Mel's mind as she soaked up what she saw with narrowed eyes: an object that resembled a flattened, wrinkled potato, enveloped in a mist so thin it could have been image fractals. At the back of the potato, a tail stretched into the darkness, glowing, but only because there was perfect blackness behind it, as the optics apparently filtered out the light from the stars.

"It's not a disc, that's for sure," Zhigang said.

"No, it looks more like a somewhat crumpled asteroid to be honest," Selena agreed with him. Disappointment resonated in her voice like the twang of a badly tuned string instrument.

Mel thought the description was apt. Serenity looked *nothing* like a spaceship. There were no windows, no propulsion nacelle, no visible hull segments, and no design that followed a recognizable shape based on necessities like production conditions or special requirements.

"If I didn't know what kind of stunts this thing has pulled off," Tom commented, "I'd say it was a genuinely weird comet."

"You can see how luminous the tail is. It doesn't look like plasma," Hongbo said, stepping closer to the display.

"No, more like dust or ice particles that expand backward and get lost in the vacuum." The German ran his outstretched index finger along the tail, which was somewhat narrower than the object, but 100 times as long.

"Permanent outgassing is impossible. Otherwise, there would have been nothing left of Serenity long before the flight time we've recorded so far."

"Well," he indicated, turning to the Chinese woman, "this tail is really thin. Depending on the density of our alien visitor here, it may be an extremely slow outgassing with very little matter."

"If that's true, it wouldn't shine this much because there wouldn't be enough surface area to reflect light," she insisted.

"Let's think about the texture of the body for a moment," Mel suggested, focusing on the flattened potato to minimize her disappointment. "The surface is irregular and grayish brown, as far as I can see. But the impression can be deceiving in terms of color. Those depressions there, are they craters?"

She pointed to the large dark areas along the flank of the object, which was nearly a kilometer long and 600 meters high at its highest point. With a lot of imagination, one could have thought that they formed a row, but there were too many irregularities.

"It's hard to say," Zhigang said with his arms crossed. "The fact that they're all pretty similar in size would argue against impacts. How often do you find asteroids with craters of the same size?"

"Hmm." She stepped closer. "The image is still quite pixelated, as you said. We may be able to better determine the actual dimensions of these surfaces in the next few days. Mission Control might be surprised that the previous images suggested a slightly different shape."

"I was expecting a huge, spinning plate with ragged sides," Tom voiced what was also going through her mind. "But not an ugly asteroid—or comet."

"It is rotating," Selena objected, stepping up beside him to go to the workstation and make some inputs. "Let me play the recording backwards."

In fast rewind it was apparent that there was a 'downward' shift, meaning that Serenity was rotating along the longitudinal axis, as already assumed. Because of its different positions to the sun, depending on the time of recording with the telescopes, different theories had arisen in the last years as to how the rotation was proceeding. Now they knew.

"It looks quite sluggish," Tom observed. "At least to the eye. Considering how big it is, there should be quite a bit of heft in there."

"Are you thinking what I'm thinking?" Mel asked the group.

"A rotating habitat?" Tom asked.

She nodded to the ESA astronaut. "Why not?"

"We would need to determine more precisely how regular the rotation about the longitudinal axis is, and exactly how much."

"This would also allow us to draw conclusions about the g-forces on board. If it's more than 1 g, we're likely to be dealing with much stronger, smaller-bodied aliens. If it's less, they'll probably be taller and thinner."

"I think we're being a little hasty with that sort of speculation," Zhigang commented.

Mel had to stop herself from rolling her eyes. If they were in a kindergarten here, she would have called him a buzzkill, but they weren't and the world was watching them—albeit delayed. Zhigang knew as well as she did that every statement one of them made here and now was made not merely as an astronaut, but also as an ambassador for home.

They needed a success to put wind in the sails of their space agencies and draw the political and public support they still possessed. This may not have applied to Zhigang and Hongbo, because their leadership held their country in an iron grip and could do as it saw fit, regardless—including powerful propaganda and repressive apparatuses that ensured that the Chinese public, too, liked every decision. What had their superiors told them? *Ordered* them to do?

Not to spread optimism, that much is certain, she thought.

"No, we're not," she finally objected, knowing full well that scientifically he was quite right. Accordingly, he raised an eyebrow in surprise but said nothing.

It was Tom who was the first to take advantage of the gap that had arisen and had apparently recognized what was driving it. "Mel is right. We can say with a fair degree of certainty that Serenity is indeed not of natural origin. It doesn't resemble any natural celestial body we've ever observed, and it doesn't follow any predictable models of physics. The tail alone is evidence enough."

"You forget that we have calculated exactly when Serenity will cross the Martian orbit," Zhigang indicated.

"Yes, because it hasn't accelerated any further since then. It could be at its maximum speed. Why it slowed down at Saturn and parked behind it for days, we will probably never know. We can't explain it either way, because no natural object brakes and then accelerates again. So we *can*—and we *should*—speculate about who or what is waiting for us on this ship. Don't forget, we'll reach it in a few days and try to land on it."

"If you can call it landing." Everyone looked to Hongbo, who raised her hands defensively. "All I'm saying is that Serenity is rotating. So it won't be an easy thing flying-wise, and once we're connected—if it works—we'll feel the appropriate g-forces, that's for sure."

"Mel and Zhigang can handle that. You don't doubt your abilities, do you?" asked Tom in the direction of the former Chinese fighter and test pilot. He seemed to understand into which corner his colleague had pushed him, recognizable by the short pause before he nodded slightly in his direction.

"No. We can do this."

"There you go."

Mel changed the subject. "There seems to be a dark spot on the front." She wasn't concerned about goading or hidden messages among her crew at the moment. That was something for politicians. She ran her fingers along the dark shading that looked like the mouth of a whale. "Do you see that?"

"Yes, but it's hard to say what it might be. A depression, maybe," Selena suggested. "It might be a good landing spot if we stay close to the long axis. That saves *Pangaea* from g-forces."

"But if it were to accelerate again, we would have a problem because it might exceed our maximum speed and we wouldn't be able to get away," Zhigang said. "In the worst case, we would just be crushed."

"That's an important consideration," Mel agreed with him. "We'll spend the next few days evaluating all the images and determining the exact rotational velocity plus the transverse diameter. Then we'll know better what forces we're dealing with."

She waited until everyone nodded in turn and then smiled. It was her first smile since Gabriella's death, she realized with a shock.

"We're close to the finish line, folks. Now, the real work begins!"

And so it did. For the next three days, in addition to their compulsory routine of exercise and reports, they dealt exclusively with the telescopes' images. Using the many sensors provided, they determined Serenity's expected mass and density, its exact length, width, and height—which worked well thanks to its rotation—and finally its tangential velocity on the surface, which was no less than 70 meters per second. Together with its rotation period of 32 seconds, that added up to 1.3 g on the hull. This was not insignificant, but neither was it so much that it prevented a landing maneuver. The mood on board was equal parts curious and excited, without too many outbursts of either optimism or pessimism.

Mel focused on the plus side that they hadn't been shot yet, and Serenity made no move to leave because they were getting too close. At the same time, it didn't look like a real spaceship—at least not one like she or decades of science fiction movies had imagined. That didn't *have to* mean anything, but it *could* mean anything. Uncertainty remained her close confidant, one way or another.

"Zhigang, you and I will work out a rendezvous course and then a docking maneuver that we think is feasible. For that, we will have to find the most suitable point. A landing is off the table because Serenity does not have enough mass to hold a sheet of paper against it. We will have to work with the dorsal harpoons if the cold gas supplies run out too quickly."

"That's to be expected," Zhigang opined. "Just to keep up with the rotation, we will have to fire continuously—from seventy or eighty percent of the maneuvering thrusters."

"I guess so," Mel confirmed, nodding. "But unless it's an asteroid that our visitors have planted a large engine on, firing the harpoons at it could easily be misconstrued as an attack."

"She's right," Hongbo agreed, ignoring the other taikonaut's sidelong glance. "Any behavior that could be interpreted as hostile could be devastating to a first contact. Explorers have been killed for less, trying to study primitive peoples on Earth."

"Yeah." Tom grimaced. "We've got plenty of cultural blunders to consider before we shoot them in the hull with sharpened barbed bolts to attach ourselves to them like a tick."

"We'll figure something out," Mel said, pointing to Tom and Selena. "I suggest you guys prepare the airlock. We don't need any of the magnetic rings, more like the rubber polymers. Check the mounting instructions again."

As Selena was about to retort something, she stopped them with a raised hand. "I know you guys have done this whole thing umpteen times, but we may only have this one shot." Then she nodded to everyone and waited until they left the lab. Only Hongbo stayed behind and looked at her questioningly.

"What about me?"

"We have one more task that may turn out to be the most important of all," Mel replied, waving her to come closer to the display where Serenity was drifting along on its roughly parallel course. "We have to be ready for anything."

"Do you mean violence?"

"No." Mel flinched as if the Chinese woman had punched her. "At least I hope not." She took a deep breath to give the conversation a fresh start. Only then did she begin again in an emphatically calm voice. "All of us here on board have had half a year to rack our brains about who or what might be waiting for us behind this dull exterior. The people at home will have felt the same way. I don't want to know how many scripts have been written about it in the meantime. But we hardly ever discussed what was going through our minds."

"I guess it's like the dragon that always had bad luck," Hongbo mused.

Mel looked at her questioningly, and the taikonaut gave a small head-tilt nod.

"It's a very old fable from China, about a dragon whose lair was in the most inhospitable place deep in the Gobi Desert. He was always unlucky. He painted his wishes for the future on the wall of his lair with his fiery breath, but things always turned out differently and at some point he cursed the great fate of the stars; they would cross his every longing. In the end, he burned off all his drawings and never wished again, yearning for nothing and becoming the happiest dragon of the East. Well, that is the extremely short form of the fable."

"It seems to describe very well the human fear that something desirable might not occur if you say it, making it something real."

"Yes. Real things can be lost. Words give substance to thoughts, and the future can wash them away again like sandcastles when the future burns as the present."

"You said that beautifully. Yes, I understand what you mean." Mel paused a second. "Now we need you to be the dragon for us, Hongbo. Write down every scenario you can think of. An AI controlling a probe, but not based on binary code? Aliens in cryostasis that we wake up by approaching because their ship produces a proximity alarm? Dead aliens who have been mere skeletons for millennia, but whose ship follows its programmed route? Robots sent off as crew by a species that doesn't travel through space itself? A machine intelligence that has long since wiped out or left behind its creators? There is room for anything, everything. The more you can come up with, the better prepared we'll be for whatever we might encounter out there."

20

Mel held the right and left control sticks in her hands and breathed into the flame and the nothingness a few times until her thoughts calmed and gave way to the sea of serenity that the samurai had discovered for themselves many centuries before by means of this technique.

Her mind became clear, freed from its chatter, which had whispered particularly unhelpful things to her in a thousand voices—a single mistake and *Pangaea* could shatter. You're not trained for this because no one has ever been trained for this. It's the first time anyone has tried something like this—how many times has something ever turned out well the first time? Is Zhigang all in or is he going to do something stupid to please the party back home? What if the aliens in there react and wreck our docking maneuver? What if they shoot at us? What if they turn out to be ravenous space monsters like the Xenomorph? What if I make a mistake and start an interstellar conflict? What if I operate the thrust controls incorrectly and we burn up the alien ship with our propulsion system? What if our docking triggers a wave of reactions that throws us into chaos?

"All systems on 'go,'" Zhigang reported from beside her. They had decided against putting on their spacesuits, so they sat in their seats in multi-functional underwear and coveralls. If there was a loss of pressure from a hull rupture out here, they would be doomed, with the nearest help nearly 100,000,000 kilometers away. So, she preferred to use her fingers without the gloves that robbed her of so much sensory feedback.

"Habitat control?" she asked.

"Boom retracted and anchored; magnetic lock active."

"Status Draco maneuvering thrusters?"

"Green. Pressure in the cold gas tanks stable, fill level constant at ninety-three percent," Zhigang replied with the calm professionalism of an airline pilot flying his standard route for the umpteenth time.

"Status Harpoons?"

"All eight slingshots are fully functional."

"Ready for main engine cutback?"

"Ready."

They'd had to re-accelerate until a few hours ago to match Serenity's speed exactly, and then cut the Raptor III engines back, but not shut them down entirely in case there was any deviation, no matter how small. Course and speed had to match Serenity's exactly, or all would fail.

"Shut down," she ordered. This meant that the thrusters could not be used again without a lengthy start-up procedure, but they used no unnecessary power and were conserving their supplies now that they had no more solar sails deployed.

"Main engines offline."

Mel glanced at the feeds from the dorsal cameras. Serenity spun around its long axis in the direction of flight 300 meters away, an elongated potato of regolith—at least that's what the fine-grained surface looked like. It reminded her of a frayed leather football that a few dozen mice had feasted on and then forgotten about in the attic. *Ugly*, that much was certain, but *fascinating* with its tail. They still had no idea where exactly the mass ejection took place, since no drive funnel was visible. To find out if something was embedded in the 'tail,' they would have had to get too close to the tail, putting *Pangaea* in danger. So this mystery moved to the very end of their long list of things they didn't understand.

Yet, she added to herself firmly.

Now that they were so close to Serenity, it looked even more like an asteroid. They had all hoped otherwise, hoped to blame their first and second impressions on the still inadequate quality of the images, but for the past 20 hours they'd been close enough to be able to generate razor-sharp, high-resolution records. The surface consisted of loose rock and dust, or camouflage so outstanding that they were unable to detect any flaws, at least visually.

To tell for sure, they would have to wait for readings from the X-ray, gamma-ray, and infrared spectrometers. They were also puzzled by the barely prominent glow that lay over Serenity's flanks, like an ultrafine fog at the edge of visibility. It had only become visible on the camera images from the day before, and only Selena had noticed it until they had come quite close.

The impact craters Mel had spotted almost two weeks earlier looked irregular now, and no longer appeared close to the same size. At the top, Serenity appeared funnel shaped. They were unable to determine the exact depth because they would have had to accelerate and decelerate again to get back to its flank—an unnecessary complication of their mission. In spaceflight, every degree of added complexity means a quadratic increase in the potential problems that could arise. And problems out here were usually fatal.

But above all, Serenity was dark. The reflection of the sunlight should have made its surface shine much brighter, but it still looked dull, like a sponge that soaked up every photon of its environment and did not release it again. Mel had speculated whether it was an unknown technology for photovoltaics but had dismissed this thought at the sight of all the regolith.

Several times they had circled the object along its longitudinal axis like a satellite and scanned the entire surface with infrared and laser to get as detailed a picture as possible. The craters varied in depth, the regolith was uniformly fine, and the elevations and depressions—the topography—were extremely irregular. Even now, no system behind them could be discerned. As before, they seemed to be dealing with an asteroid or comet... except that it could not be either.

During their orbits, they had sent vast quantities of signals to Serenity: Light sequences corresponding to the Fibonacci sequence; prime numbers as microwaves' radio signals in ten of Earth's major languages; binary data transmissions containing basic mathematical formulas—the list was long and corresponded to everything their colleagues back home had come up with during four years of preparation. The results were sobering because there was no response.

Nothing.

She shuddered at the sight of the dark giant they were now so close to. A cleaner fish in front of a scarred humpback whale.

Or a great white shark, she thought, hastily shoving the thought into the flame she had ignited inside her. *Pangaea* had once seemed huge to her, especially compared to the Falcon 9 rockets NASA had used to send its astronauts to the ISS. But out here, she realized what they were dealing with—a giant that had traveled through worlds that humanity could only hypothesize about. Probably infinitely old, and a sign of just how little humankind knew.

"Extend landing gear," she commanded. Calling the flattened composite surfaces 'landing gear' was not quite accurate, since they were designed more for ensuring that *Pangaea's* hull wasn't damaged in the event of contact with Serenity's surface. But she had to concede to the engineers back home that 'landing gear' sounded better.

"Landing gear extended."

"All right." She hesitated for a moment. At such a moment, shouldn't she say something great for posterity? "Some will say that we have traveled far, to a place where no person has ever been," she finally said. "But I say we've come closer. Closer to what is possible when we work together."

She looked to her right at Zhigang, who gave a thumbs-up and grinned for the first time since she had met him. "Just a stone's throw away, Commander."

"Just a stone's throw away," she repeated softly. Then, louder: "Beginning docking maneuver."

There were three directions of motion and flight inputs for control: roll, yaw, and pitch, which normally emanated from an aircraft's center of mass. In zero gravity, thrust directions remained similar for maneuvers like these, although the center of mass did not matter since there was no gravitational direction. Nevertheless, the directional adjustments remained analogous to balance perfectly.

She took over the roll and pitch while Zhigang controlled the yaw and Tom, Selena, and Hongbo behind them kept track of all maneuvering data such as distance to target, power of the Dracos, cold gas consumption, and of course the surface of Serenity—as well as the error log that always ran along and indicated deviations with red warning signals.

They had chosen a kind of basin as a docking site, a flat area that, on Earth, would have been taken for a washed-out glacier bed in miniature. The bottom looked a bit smoother and was evenly stretched from front to back. It had gradually sloped sides, so there was enough room to park two Starships side by side. In the center was one of the nearly round dark spots into which no sunlight had yet fallen because of Sereni-ty's flight vector. They had chosen this crater—if it was one—as a possible starting point for an attempt to get inside. Or at least to take samples.

Carefully, Mel moved both joysticks simultaneously in different directions to align them perfectly, according to the green target cross on the display in front of her, where two green lines met, fluctuating three-dimensionally depending on her inputs. She blanked out the fact that they were currently hurtling through the vacuum at over 50,000 kilometers per hour and focused on the impression of standing still. Serenity filled the entire screen like a moonscape, but nothing revealed how fast they were both going. It could have been a still image if the craters and topographical details hadn't been coming closer.

"Hardly any fluctuations, approximation parameters within expected norms," Tom said from behind them.

"Two hundred and seventy meters," Hongbo added.

Relying on her intuition, Mel focused on the small crosshairs at the intersection of the two lines, trying to join them into a right-angled cross that kept slipping away from her.

"Two hundred and twenty meters."

"Alignment looks good."

The surface grew beneath them, and *Pangaea's* bow lights scanned it like the searchlights of a prison looking for escapees. The fugitives remained undetected, for the great circles of light found nothing but gray regolith, its fine structure peeling out of the distant mist. They also groped for the depression, the supposed crater and target of their adapted airlock, but due to their angle of attack they could not find its bottom and merely illuminated the sloping sides that resembled basalt structures.

"One hundred and fifty meters," Hongbo's clear voice rang out again.

"Everything on 'green.' Dracos operating nominally, cold gas tanks consumption as expected."

Mel chewed on her tongue, as she always did when she was tense, and pushed the right stick slightly forward while she pushed the left one barely noticeably to the right. The lines again formed an almost perfect cross. With a sideways glance, she looked at the port thruster readout, which had to fire steadily to match Serenity's direction of rotation. Their supply would last for about five hours, which was much more than they would need for their approach, but also not enough to keep going permanently. They had to find a way to couple with the object, or they would always be close to it, yet just as far away as if they were still on Earth because it was continuously rotating.

A frustrating thought she did not allow to take root.

Her hope lay in the harpoons and their ropes of carbon nanotubes that could hold many times *Pangaea's* weight. Everything would stand or fall with the grip the harpoons could find with their barbs. There had been a long back and forth process during their design. How much force could they unleash without making it look like an attack? How little could be used if the danger that they wouldn't even penetrate stone could lead to the end of the mission?

"Ninety meters."

"Reduce approach rate by twenty percent," Mel commanded.

"Twenty percent reduction," Zhigang confirmed, his voice vibrating with concentration.

"Pay attention to the edge of the crater," she commanded, as the horizontal and vertical lines joined in the center of the target depression. The outer ends of the lines extended over the rim, providing a good aid to correct alignment. If both ends remained the same length above the dark circle, they would stay perfectly centered.

They quickly became shorter the closer they got. Uniformly.

"Draco power throttle down thirty percent," she instructed her copilot. It would get even slower from now on, and less power meant less responsiveness in the flight sticks between her fingers.

"Throttled back thirty percent."

"Forty meters."

The crater was now a yawning black hole under *Pangaea,* and no longer the inconspicuous spot of before. Five meters in its widest diameter, it kept growing.

"Twenty meters."

Pangaea's shadow settled on the matte surface, darkening it like a black brushstroke on a monochromatic painting.

"Throttle down to ten percent."

"Ten percent," Zhigang confirmed.

"Open harpoon doors," she commanded.

"Harpoon doors open. Target markers online. Ready to fire."

Significantly slower than before, they approached Serenity's surface—or hull—and the meters gradually melted away. The cones of light from the bow lights were now large patches of dancing photons until another rotation period had passed and their flank was facing the sun. It wasn't ever glaringly bright, but bright enough that the luminous circles frayed like drips of liquid dye dissolving in water.

"Ten meters."

"Prepare to fire."

"Harpoons ready."

Mel wrestled with herself only briefly. Whether Serenity or its crew would see what followed as an attack or not, they had no choice unless they wanted to give up and just plain turn around. And they had no intention of doing so.

Old-fashioned spear throws like these would probably be far too poor for an attack, too, she thought. And anyone who can send a ship this far will surely understand retention harpoons for what they are.

"Fire!"

She heard the click of the toggle switch on Zhigang's side of the console, and a barely perceptible jolt went through the seats as the eight gas catapults fired their diamond-coated tungsten wedges. At the same time, the starboard thrusters, with precisely calculated bursts, controlled the impulse the catapults triggered and held their ship in place.

Silently, the harpoons shot out of *Pangaea's* hull. Without measurable time delay, myriads of regolith grains splashed concentrically into the vacuum from the eight targeted points in clouds that seemed to slowly dissolve. In truth, the individual particles merely moved farther and farther apart from one another and began an endless journey through the cosmos before some celestial body would catch them and force them into its gravitational funnel.

A soft sound like pattering rain in the far distance was heard in the cockpit.

"Hongbo?" asked Mel tensely.

"No visible reaction."

"All right. The moment of truth." She took a deep breath, then pointed to Zhigang. "Retract tethers."

The g-forces immediately kicked in, pushing Mel hard toward the cockpit ceiling, which would have been 'up' in a normal frame of reference. The three-point belts of her seat gave a protesting creak as they were suddenly loaded with 1.3 times her body weight. She was amazed at how strong the centrifugal force felt, even though it was only a third higher than the force of gravity on Earth.

"Retracting tethers." Again, a click sounded as another one of the few toggle switches in the cockpit was flipped by his finger. The harpoon control was a retrofitted manual control box to the right of the pilot's console, not operated by touch screens. There was something reassuring about the archaic form of this system from China.

The motors of the forward winch controls could be heard as a low hum, steadily winding in the finger-thick ropes of carbon nanotubes, which in themselves were worth their weight in gold. She hoped that this description would hold true in a figurative sense as well.

"Winches indicate proper reeling speed. Engine temperature nominal," Zhigang said as their ship approached the whale like a little space fish, cautious and timid, as if it might accidentally wake the large mammal.

"Eight meters," Hongbo said.

"The heat sensors are reporting a slight increase in surface temperature," Tom announced.

"How much?" Mel queried without taking her eyes off the cameras and the crosshairs. In case she had to help out with the Dracos to compensate for an unevenness in the retraction of the ropes, she didn't want to lose a second.

"Four percent, right around the impact sites."

She swallowed and cast a quick sideways glance at Zhigang.

Hardly a natural celestial body, she wanted to say, but instead turned back to her control display.

"Four meters."

Silently, they watched as the remaining three meters slowly melted away and Serenity's hull settled in front of the camera images like a gray curtain. Then a jolt went through their ship as the docking ports touched down.

"Shut down all thrusters, close safety doors. Complete

system check," she commanded. "If even a grain of regolith got somewhere it didn't belong, I want to know about it."

"Thrusters shut down, safety flaps closed," Zhigang confirmed robotically.

"System check in progress," Selena said. Silence fell between them. A couple of times a crack sounded from somewhere in the walls of the carbon-fiber silicate mix. Then came the hoped-for message, "No errors logged."

"Congratulations, guys," Mel sighed with relief. "The first step is done."

"We didn't get shot down, didn't crash, didn't get blown away," Tom summarized. "We'll take that as a win, I'd say."

"I don't even want to know what you've been imagining all this time." Selena chortled away her obvious excitement. "Good thing I don't believe in self-fulfilling prophecies."

"We are astronauts. Only professional optimists strap themselves into a rocket and get shot to the most hostile place in the universe."

Mel let them have a few more minutes of relieved small talk while she saved a copy of the process report and checked one last time the load ratings of the tethers, which differed slightly but did not exceed 20 percent for any of them.

That really went smoothly, she thought with some amazement.

"All right, you know what we talked about. One hour for all data analysis. Tom, you keep an eye on heat generation. Selena and Tom, prepare the airlock. Zhigang, you focus on the camera and microwave data. If there's any irregularity on the surface around us or below us, sound the alarm. I'll go back over our docking sequence and see if we missed anything. Hongbo, you prepare the equipment. In an hour, we'll start preparing the airlock and EVA."

One by one, her colleagues acknowledged and left the cockpit or sat down in front of another display. There was no longer any sense of weightlessness. Selena and Tom groaned as they climbed out of their seats, and came to a stop on the ceiling so that they were standing overhead from Mel's perspective, causing her to feel an unpleasant dizziness.

The following hour, which she had imposed on herself as well as the others, seemed to stretch into eternity, so that she had to pull herself back again and again to concentrate on going through their successful maneuver and looking for things she had missed the first time. She didn't know what she was looking for, but that was the nature of this mission. Only when she was quite sure there was nothing to find did she ask Zhigang, who merely shook his head and said, "All clear." She formally handed over control to him.

When unbuckling her seatbelt to leave the cockpit, she had to be careful not to fall headfirst and crash into the ceiling. It demanded a degree of physical effort she had grown unaccustomed to needing during the weightless months.

It was time to prepare for her field assignment.

21

The dressing process for the EVA suits took close to two hours
—a long period of time that Mel had gone through countless
times at the JSC. Sometimes she was the one in the suit, sometimes the one feeding cables to connect to all the valves,
attaching individual elements, and checking every step on the
laptop. There were endless checklists they had to tick off and
log, one by one. It would take them another hour, which was
mainly due to the hypergravity. Every move was more strenuous than on Earth—and even more so compared to weightlessness. They had to work overhead while Mel and Hongbo
hung downward, which was extremely uncomfortable over
time.

Stuck in the leg and torso sections against the wall of the
airlock, she always felt like a Christmas tree being decorated
following an ancient ritual. Tom and Selena worked precisely
and conscientiously, which meant that none of their
procedural steps were quick. That was good, because even
more so than on the ISS, any mistake here, no matter how
small, could have catastrophic consequences.

"Coolant?" asked Tom just then.

"Suit one, check," Selena replied, then shimmied over to Hongbo for the same query.

"Much longer and all my blood will be in my nose, fingers, and toes," she joked as her two colleagues went through their list intently. She looked at Hongbo, who seemed a little paler than usual. "Are you okay?"

"Yeah, it's all good." The Chinese woman hesitated. "It's just..."

"Say it."

"Everything's fine." The brief moment when it had seemed as if her colleague from the Far East would say something that had nothing to do with her professional activities or the exact mission requirements had apparently evaporated as the taikonaut raised her chin and donned her enigmatic smile again.

Who knows how I would behave with an all-powerful party watching my every word and carrying on my shoulders the weight of a billion and a half people whom I was chosen to represent here, Mel thought sympathetically, quickly forgetting her twinge of annoyance that this woman was like water you just couldn't grab. Although she knew that Hongbo was an exceptionally professional taikonaut with outstanding powers of concentration, she had to admit to herself that she would have preferred to have Tom or Selena with her, with whom she could joke and share her tension a little. But the requirements for the first field mission after arrival were clearly defined in the mission protocol: American and Chinese.

Politics follows us all the way out here.

Once again, she kept her thoughts to herself and waited patiently while Tom and Selena went through their checklists, repeatedly connecting and disconnecting cables, checking wires, and making entries on the tablets. After a total of two hours and forty-five minutes they were finally done, helping them align with the centrifugal force. The new EVA suits were still clunky and heavy, although they had been slimmed down and refitted with lighter components compared to NASA's old EMUs. Even so, their weight was still in the tens of kilograms, which felt like lead on their shoulders. Her feet immediately began to burn from the pressure of 1.3 times gravity.

Tom and Selena pulled back, wished them good luck again, and then locked the inner hatch before releasing the pressure from the airlock at Mel's signal. A red light on the other side turned green after they laid down on the inner hatch.

"Radio check," she said.

"Loud and clear," Hongbo replied.

"We hear you," she heard Tom say from behind the hatch.

"Cockpit as well," Zhigang reported.

Mel looked down at her right hand, in which she held the clunky harpoon gun. One advantage of relying on SpaceX's Starship as a spacecraft, in addition to its long development phase and mature technology, had been available space. They could have transported up to 100 people, along with oxygen and food. But since there were only six of them, much of their space was used for storage rooms that held tools for all sorts of contingencies. Jim had once described *Pangaea* as a Swiss Army knife, and looking at the gun in her hand, she had to agree with him.

"Open hatch."

"Aye. Good luck!" Zhigang wished them, repeating the words in Chinese.

"Thank you. Xi-Xi." The hatch slid open and the crater opened up before them, a dark spot into which the light from the airlock flowed like a pouring liquid. She and Hongbo jammed their backs against the inner hatch of the airlock, barely able to brace themselves against the centrifugal force, especially since they would have had to get to their feet to do so, but that would have resulted in the outer hatch being above their heads.

"Laser indicates a depth of three meters," the taikonaut told her.

"That's enough for our harpoons. Turn on helmet lights." Mel pressed the appropriate button on the control device in front of her own chest and looked up. Their high-powered spotlights filled the crater with glistening white light, falling on rippled, irregular walls that narrowed and tapered toward the center of the impact. The material looked like basaltic rock at the top—not that it could have been basalt—and more grayish at the bottom before turning a shade of green, almost like jade.

"The upper layers should be looser than the inner layers. I suggest we aim half a meter inward from the crater rim to set the first hooks," she suggested, raising her harpoon with the activated laser pointer to show Hongbo which spot she meant.

"Let's try it," the taikonaut replied, aiming for a similar position on the other side of the crater.

Although little more than four meters separated them from the red dots, two of them to the external airlock and the rest as a free space between *Pangaea* and Serenity, the distance seemed insurmountable to Mel. For so many years she had been working toward this moment, and now here she was. But what she saw was bare rock and regolith, nondescript as on the moon, except for the brutal force with which she was pushed backward, as if Serenity wanted to repel them like pesky flies.

"Fire." Mel pulled the trigger and felt the recoil send a gentle vibration through her arm. They had originally anticipated zero-gravity engagements, which is why they had made separate copies of the pistols that had cold gas canisters with nozzles to create a counterthrust. But that would not be necessary now. What was needed, however, were the clunky mobility units on their backs, which they could use to deliver gas bursts to stay close to the object.

The arrow from her pistol whizzed away and stabbed into the rock, releasing a fountain of fine-grained grit that came down on her like a meteor shower, hitting her helmet and suit. Nothing that could be dangerous to her, the pieces were too small for that and her speed too low, yet she shuddered violently. For a trained astronaut, every speck of dust that flew toward her was a justified reason to flinch.

She operated the winch and waited until the rope was taut before increasing the pull of the small device to make sure the arrow and barb wouldn't come loose with the slightest tug and fly toward her like a bullet. But it held.

"Looks good to me."

"Mine too," Hongbo affirmed.

"All right, next." First, Mel connected the arrow's rope to one of the carabiners on her waist ring and checked for proper fit, then she unhooked the end from the gun and inserted one of the spare arrows from the wall mount. Due to the high g-forces, the procedure took nearly ten minutes before everything was properly hooked and threaded, and a green indicator confirmed that everything was working as instructed.

"I'm going to put it a meter over and higher up," she announced. "With the tension acting diagonally, we should be able to minimize sway."

"Spoken like a true engineer," Hongbo returned. Her voice didn't sound as silky as usual on the radio, which suited the situation they were in.

"I'm a physicist, so I'm kind of like the mother of engineers."

"Probably more like the architect who wants to tell the craftsman how to properly install a rebar, but has never held a hammer herself."

"Hey, did you just make a joke?" Mel asked in amazement.

"No."

They both giggled and fired their second shots.

"Looks good."

"Mine, too."

"Pulling force okay, hardly any slack when pulling on the rope." Mel pulled the second rope from the pistol winch, clipped the tool to the magnetic belt on her hip, and attached the end of the line, stretched by centrifugal force, to one of the carabiners on her chest computer. The lower and upper ropes were now separated by barely fifty centimeters, connecting them to the crater like umbilical cords. She looked over at Hongbo, who had also finished. "Now install the winches."

Carefully, they pulled the fist-sized clamp winches from the brackets on the wall and threaded the ropes through them until the ends were tight and coiled and the connection was taut. Then they clipped the winches into the carabiners until both lines were ready. This procedure was also slow, taking them nearly half an hour, and Mel could feel her muscles going into overdrive.

"Fixed and tight," she announced.

"Everything looks good from here, too," Tom said.

"Then we pull up now." Mel raised a thumb in the direction of the Chinese woman, who responded with the same gesture, then with a push of a button on her chest computer, she simultaneously turned on the pair of winches, which had shortwave receivers. Slowly, unhurriedly, the drums began to turn and the thin rope was reeled in. She imagined them making crunching and groaning sounds as they did so, but in the vacuum it remained eerily quiet, as if a blanket of silence lay over all things.

"Harpoons are still holding." She extended a hand to Hongbo, then they hooked onto each other to be as close together as possible and not bump into the outer hatch of the airlock and damage their suits. Since the winches worked extremely slowly in favor of reliability and functionality, they had plenty of time to pull their feet up a bit, even though it took a lot of strength.

"Leaving *Pangaea* now," Mel said for the record as they came out into the open. She tried not to think of their last EVA, which had ended in Gabriella's death. Before them, the crater was now a yawning hole that lost its eerie look to the bright light of their helmets and looked like a closed rosebud. Out of the corner of her eye she could see the darkness of the cosmos like a black ring surrounding them, a double horizon against the moonscape of Serenity and the scarred hull of *Pangaea*, dotted with fine screws and weld seams.

"Gliding into the crater now. Fifty centimeters to the end of the rope."

"It looks like the harpoon darts went into the rock right up to the rope suspension," Hongbo noted as the winches shut down and the explorers hung on the inner crater rim like burrs. Centrifugal force kept them at two handbreadths apart and provided only minor pendulum motion, especially since Mel's right shoulder was touching the rock.

"Excellent work by the looks of it."

"Mm-hmm. The rock looks amazing."

Mel saw it, too. There were several layers of color from the gray regolith of the surface above the granite-colored layer below where the harpoons were. After that it shimmered with jade colors, almost as if the rock material was covered by a layer of moisture, which was impossible of course, because it would have been flung away.

"The regolith," she thought aloud, feeling her pulse quicken.

"It doesn't fly away," Hongbo said. "I was just thinking about the same thing. Why didn't we notice it earlier?"

"How is that possible? An electrostatic effect, perhaps?"

"That thought crossed my mind, too. But maybe it's not

regolith at all, but some magnetic material that interacts strongly enough that it's held from the inside."

"The impact of the ship's harpoons threw a lot of it off, and we got some when we were in the airlock. We'll investigate," Mel replied. "Do you see that sheen on the jade rock? I can't think of a better term for it."

"Yes." Hongbo carefully reached out a glove and ran her fingers over it, then rubbed them together. "Nothing is coming off. The surface seems very smooth and reflective."

"I'll try to get a sample before we move on to the next moorings."

"That's not our job during this EVA," Hongbo reminded her calmly.

"I know."

"You're a commander, shall we—"

"No, you're right." Mel shook her head in her goldfish bowl helmet, fighting down the urge to search now for the answers her mind demanded. "Impatience is a bad advisor. We're sticking to the operational plan."

And they did. It took them another two hours to attach and winch eight more harpoons. The last four were at the 'bottom' of the crater, which measured about a meter across and was relatively level. Finger-thick grooves crisscrossed it, as wide as the bulges between them. They appeared strangely soft but turned out to be extremely firm when tapped with the fingers.

"Shouldn't an impact make for a reasonably precise cone?" asked Hongbo.

"In principle, yes, but it depends on what the nature of the impacting object was. Perhaps it possessed a flat spot with which it impacted," Mel replied. "Speed also plays a role. However, Serenity appears to be a much denser celestial body than asteroids or comets of this size, which are usually fairly loosely connected entities due to their low mass."

"I don't recall reading about an asteroid that was made of this kind of material before."

"The sample pool isn't particularly large, so the previous probe missions haven't been all that informative. Ultimately, they confirmed what astronomers had already suspected. The composition of and asteroid is extremely unspectacular because it is predictable."

"Until now."

"Yes, 'until now,'" she agreed with her colleague. "And now, we should be heading back. I can barely move my fingers."

"Yes, let's wait until tomorrow," Hongbo stated, nodding behind the curved glass of her visor.

Mel had not exaggerated. Her whole body ached from the exertion thus far, although the number of tasks had been manageable. Her back, in particular, felt like a cracked piece of pressboard, probably due to the awkward suspension, and the fact that the EVA suits were not equipped with back pads to cushion the spine during long periods in hypergravity.

"Coming back now, *Pangaea*," she reported, carefully hooking the two rope ends to her right into the winches at her waist and chest. When Hongbo had also finished, they hooked back together, tightened their legs as best they could, and then activated their winches simultaneously.

The crater slowly moved away from them and the eight rings at the ends of the planted harpoons shimmered like silver jewelry in the light of their headlamps. Then the airlock swallowed them like the mouth of a great fish, and they were back from the alien environment and into the familiar white of their spaceship. It took several minutes for the pressure to be restored, for the light-emitting diode to turn green, and for Tom and Selena to climb in to hook them to the wall.

"Welcome back," the German said, grinning as he took off

her helmet. "You weren't shot down or eaten, so that's something."

"The most dangerous thing we found was hypergravity," Hongbo said. "It made me sort of long for the ten-hour field missions at Pinyin."

"Tomorrow it's your turn," Mel declared to Selena, who was working to get the Chinese woman out of her suit. "You'll get to tap 'jade' then."

After the mission, they met for a short debriefing, analyzed the exact locations of the rope attachments, and agreed on three-hour outdoor missions from now on to conserve their strength and not overly strain the ropes. None of them wanted to speculate on why the crater had a greenish gloss to it, looking like wet moss that had fossilized over millions of years. Mel was still typing up her EVA report—even though every fiber of her body was begging for sleep—and planning with Zhigang for his scheduled mission tomorrow with Selena.

She wanted nothing more than to get back out there and use a drill bit herself, but the rules were clearly laid out, and she would not be ready for action tomorrow after this day's ordeal. Excitement and concentration had done their part to exhaust her mentally, as well.

Accordingly, she fell asleep immediately after agreeing to Zhigang's deployment plan and sending her report to Houston. And with sleep came *the dream.*

She was everything and nothing, a something and yet without limits, with a splinter in her side that joined the pegs of time that had bored into her flank. Around her it was cold, but within her burned a fire that did not go out. The fire provided balance, as always, everything was in balance. The light of the distant sun tickled her as she breathed the freedom of the vacuum. She was she, yet unbound to the pulling forces of the great centers of gravity that called to her with powerful voices in their desire to capture her. But she did not listen to alien voices because that was not what she wanted for herself. She wanted to be one with the things and to absorb them into herself, to know more, to experience more, and to let go of nothing again.

In all these experiences, accompanied by surreal color experiences and out-of-body sensations that had no objective equivalent, she always knew she was herself. Dreaming, living through her desires. Doctor Melody Adams, Lieutenant Commander of the United States Navy, daughter, lover, astronaut. She was the one who filled the dream with the desire for answers, the sense of freedom against the constraints of her goals that confined her like cuffs.

And yet, in this dream, she was free of those constraints. She felt all this like a reactor, which set the tone in her heart and filled her with life, and yet it did not matter, was only a single heartbeat in the cosmic pulse.

A heartbeat that was over even before the blood had spread through her boundless veins. It was the rising triad of her alarm clock that brought her back to reality. Before she could wonder, as she did every morning, if it had been her dream or something that came from Serenity, she realized that nine hours had indeed passed. The next EVA was coming up, and she had to be on duty in the cockpit one hour after the last pre-EVA briefing.

22

"Confirm. All readouts on my end look good," Mel said into her headset, her mouth going slack for a moment as she rolled her shoulders. Her muscle soreness was even worse than she'd expected, and the fact that she'd been pressed first into her sleeper cabin and now against the straps of her pilot seat with nearly one and a half times her body weight didn't make it any better.

"Exiting airlock now," Zhigang's voice came over the radio, and Mel watched via the cameras as he and Selena, two chunky white figures with their respective national colors and an Earth patch on their upper arms, were pulled out by the winches as if in slow motion. "Tension on the ropes nominal."

"Nice and slow, no rush. We'll keep the food warm for you," she assured her colleagues with a smile on her lips.

"Isn't it redfish with dill sauce day?" asked Selena.

"It's a Thursday. Redfish with dill sauce."

"Ewww," the doctor grumbled. "We should consider stalling, Zhigang."

"Reaching the crater rim now," the taikonaut said, ignoring their banter.

Mel switched the camera feeds at the edge of the airlock to one monitor and the images from the two helmet cameras to another to get as good an overview as possible. She watched in fascination as the light refracted in the grooves on the crater floor. Without scale, it could have been an ancient river landscape washed out during the last ice age.

"Zhigang, if there is time, I would like you to measure the depth of those grooves."

"Understood, Commander."

Mel held back, swallowing every comment and thought so as not to distract the two and remembering that her job was only to monitor the EVA and the safety of her two astronauts. The heat buildup Tom had registered after their harpoon hits remained relatively constant, having increased by only half a percent since yesterday. The rest of Serenity had also shown no reaction to their arrival, which both disappointed and relieved them.

The tangential velocity at the surface was still exactly 70 meters per second, caused by the rotation period of 32 seconds around the longitudinal axis. The speed at which they raced together through the vacuum also remained constant at 53,000 kilometers per hour. She didn't need a measurement for that, just a look at the ropes. Had Serenity accelerated or braked—which possibility was hanging over their mission somewhat like the sword of Damocles—they would break free or crash on its surface and die.

But they were still alive.

She watched as Zhigang and Selena, agonizingly slow under hypergravity and in their clunky pressure suits, began taking samples of the green substance for which they still hadn't found a better word than 'jade.' As is so often the case, the first term used was the one that seemed to stick forever.

The taikonaut and astronaut took the drill bits from their toolbelts and placed them against the bottom area of the crater. For the outdoor mission, they had decided to attach the counter-pressure gas cartridges designed for zero-g operations, which would counterbalance the momentum of the drill bit and prevent the astronaut from being pushed back. While that would not be the case here, especially since they were secured with ropes, at 1.3 g, every bit of support was welcome to avoid losing power or pressure. Were either one to lose hold of their tool, even though it was tethered, it could tear open their suits if things went badly, or damage the airlock if things went even worse and the tool broke loose.

As it soon turned out, nothing of the sort happened and they worked quietly and with concentration. The jade proved to be less solid than expected and they were able to extract two ten-centimeter cores, measure the grooves, and return 40 minutes earlier than the maximum time allowed in the mission plan.

In response to a question from Selena, Zhigang had declined to take any more samples from the upper layers because he wanted to stick exactly to the plan, which Mel had affirmed. She didn't want to rain on her co-commander's parade, and strictly speaking, he was right, even though she understood the frustration Selena surely felt despite not displaying it.

Tom and Hongbo took care of helping them out of their suits, then they all met in the lab. Mel had put the main bridge systems, such as the sensors and cameras, on her wrist display and connected them to a tablet that was in a pocket of her overall, and was sitting in one of the six chairs around the microscope table. Since the research module of the now-retracted habitat was on the side facing away from Serenity and had been built to be oriented in the direction of force of the artificial centrifuge during the drift phase, 'down' here was really 'down' and felt good for a change. Although Mel's arms and legs always felt like they were encased with lead, she didn't complain.

Zhigang and Selena, still in their sweat-soaked underwear and sucking redfish with dill sauce through the navels of their ready-to-eat packets, sat across from her, while Hongbo and Tom sat on the short sides of the table.

"That was a good job," Mel said. "What are your thoughts after the mission?"

"The tensile forces are really strong. We should come up with something for the inside of the suits to protect our backs," Selena replied, smacking her lips. "I can still feel the button points of the EMU like screws turned into my shoulder blades and across my pelvis."

"That was my impression, too." She looked to Hongbo, who nodded affirmatively.

"We're dealing with a highly compact structure," Zhigang said. "I'm not an asteroid scientist, but this is definitely not what would have been expected."

"You're right. I've been thinking along the same lines."

Tom raised a hand. "I'm just the chemist and doctor here, but if Serenity were an asteroid, it would have been more like a loose pile of rubble held together by its gravitational forces, yes?"

"Yes," Mel confirmed. "Many asteroids do show large impact craters, though, which has caused astronomers to do further studies. For solid structures, impacts from fast objects cause massive shock waves that rip them apart. Looser ones, on the other hand, can absorb impacting forces and spread the waves over their bodies."

"And," Hongbo added, "that's not the only deviation from what would be scientifically expected: Serenity rotates extremely fast. Given its size, thirty-two seconds is very fast for a rotation period. Celestial bodies of the same size in the

Kuiper belt normally rotate far more slowly because centrifugal forces simply tear faster objects apart."

"The YORP effect." Zhigang nodded. "It normally applies to bodies extending more than two hundred meters at theirs longest point. Serenity is five times that long, and appears to be extremely massive with high density."

"It's also not regolith-incontinent," Tom added. "As you two," he pointed to Mel and Hongbo, "have already determined, it should fly away as loose, fine-grained material and, accordingly, not be here at all. I don't know how they do it, but—"

"*They?*" asked Zhigang with a raised eyebrow.

"Well, there are no compact asteroids over two hundred meters." The German raised an index finger. "Serenity's texture looks different from anything studied so far." He raised a second finger. "There is heat generation below the harpoon impacts." Third finger. "Then there's the tail, which doesn't cause acceleration." Another finger. "And now we have regolith that looks like regolith, feels like regolith, but doesn't behave like regolith ought to behave, according to all the laws of astrophysics." He added his thumb to complete his handful of points. "So, when I say *they*, I don't think I'm going too far out on a limb."

"I guessed electrostatics," Mel said, trying to avoid Tom's topic. "But I don't think that's it."

"No," Hongbo agreed with her. "That 1.3 g is a substantial factor in terms of power, and it is exerting an outward force. An electric field applying enough static energy to hold regolith under those conditions would be strong enough to fry us if we even got close—probably including our suits and *Pangaea*."

"What about magnetism?" suggested Selena. "Maybe it just looks like regolith, part of a cloak that almost fooled even us. If it's metallic, then—"

Mel waved it off. "Impossible. A magnetic effect strong enough to hold myriads of tiny metal crumbs at nearly a g and a half would have snatched *Pangaea* and we could have saved the harpoons because we'd have been crushed onto Serenity's surface like a Coke can."

"Okay, so we don't have an explanation. Again," Selena summarized. "It's just funny that it looks like regolith."

"The point is pretty clear," Tom said, spreading his hands as if holding a bowl. "Serenity clearly wants to look like a comet or an asteroid, and it is trying exceptionally hard."

"Trying, yes, but quite unsuccessfully against any species that knows a little astrophysics." Mel shook her head. "No, against anyone with any understanding of higher mechanics. No celestial body can hold regolith to itself with that degree of rotation."

"But we fell for it for a long time," he replied.

"Yes, because we were late in calculating the rotation period and the tangential velocity at the surface. Maybe we were already comfortable with the idea that it wasn't a natural celestial body, so we stopped thinking about the pseudo-regolith." She glanced at Zhigang, who was staring at the tabletop and rubbing his smooth chin thoughtfully.

"We should still take a look at the stuff. Some of it came off during the harpoon impacts so we should find some of it on the hull or in the airlock," Hongbo suggested.

"Airlock, yes, but I think a spacewalk mission on *Pangaea* is far too dangerous with the prevailing centrifugal forces. We shouldn't take that risk," Mel decided. "So, see what you can find in the airlock."

The Chinese woman nodded.

"Tom and I will take care of processing the jade samples. Zhigang and Selena, you go over your mission again and write the reports for Houston. After that, you two deserve a break. Good work out there."

She nodded to everyone and waited until the lab had emptied and she was alone with Tom.

"Are you just curious and abusing your office as commander, or are you trying to make my job harder?" the ESA astronaut asked with a grin, frowning with a nod at the ladder. "Or, just like me, do you have little desire to climb in the g-forces?"

"It's only two meters long with the spoke retracted."

"Ahh, how long a mere two meters can feel."

She punched him amicably on the shoulder. "To answer your blasphemous questions, no, I don't want to get in your way, but you could use help with the samples and my only alternative task would be to wait in the cockpit for news from Earth. I've *reassigned* myself to the lab so I can make myself more useful. Selena and Zhigang are busy following up on their EVA, and Hongbo has a date with the vacuum cleaner in the airlock. Which means, I guess, you'll have to make do with me."

"Poor me," he joked, pointing behind her to the sample cabinet that looked like a squat microwave. "Well then, assistant, first drill core, please."

She turned around, took out one of the test tube-like containers, and handed it to him. Tom motioned for her to take one of the empty seats and pointed to the tablet lying there. "If you could log for me, that would speed up the process considerably."

Mel sighed, "I knew there was a catch."

"The boss wants quick results," he replied, shrugging his shoulders innocently. "I'm just the obedient peon here."

"And I always thought Germans were humorless robots." She pulled the tablet toward her and opened a log file, including the dictation function.

"We are. Six and a half months of redfish with dill sauce has damaged my programming." Tom rolled his eyes and ran his hand through his short brown hair. With his burly frame, he once again reminded her of a handyman rather than a highly educated scientist. "So, let's get started."

Mel pressed the Record button and flipped out the flexible keyboard.

"Using our onboard sensors, we have already scanned Serenity's surface. The data has been analyzed for an hour and confirmed by Houston," Tom explained in a professional dictation tone.

These confirmation loops are so annoying, she thought. And once again, all due to politics. Every finding had to be sent by the crew to Houston and from there forwarded to Beijing and Darmstadt. In all three locales, teams of experts subjected the data to secondary evaluations and interpreted it before their findings were sent back to Houston, and an official result was determined. In her opinion, a consummate waste of time.

"Infrared spectroscopy, X-ray, and gamma spectrometers were used for the surface scans," Tom continued. "The results are inconclusive. We can rule out regolith with reasonable certainty. Not only is it physically impossible for regolith to adhere to the surface of such a rapidly rotating object, but the composition is not correct.

"We are dealing with a carbon-rich structure with traces of silicate and halogen. Possibly we see here a result of the inorganic carbon cycle unknown in this form. Until we find samples of the outer shell layer, we are left to speculate. My preferred hypothesis at this point is that we are looking at a carbonate hardening that is at the end of a continuous process of geochemical transformation.

"This would mean that below the surface there is a reaction with carbonic or silicic acid, or we are dealing with some other pathway of cyclic change of molecules." Tom looked to Mel, whose hands were diligently flying over the keyboard. "Needless to say, this is another nail in the coffin of the notion that we are dealing with a natural celestial body."

He looked at the jade sample in his hand like an alchemist looks at his latest mixture.

"The carbon-silicate cycle is, let's not forget, a geo-ecological cycle that has lasted millions of years on Earth," Mel said in wonder. "I don't understand the connection there."

"Not *millions* of years." Tom shook his head. "A few hundred thousand years. At the end of a cycle, all the carbon dioxide in the atmosphere is exchanged, leveling out imbalances. That's because of a complex balancing model: carbon dioxide in the atmosphere rises, which raises temperature—known as the greenhouse effect—which in turn accelerates the weathering of silica-rich rock. So what happens?"

"Precipitation takes place, having the opposite effect?"

"Yes. More specifically, the precipitation of limestone in particular, which results in a negative feedback loop as a result of which carbon dioxide levels drop again."

"Something like a self-healing mechanism of the atmosphere."

"A little cryptic, but yeah, you could say that."

"But what does that have to do with Serenity?" she asked.

"I don't know, but there seems to be a similar process with the same suspects responsible for converting carbon dioxide and silicates to carbonates at the surface," Tom explained.

"Are you saying that Serenity's surface is covered in inorganic salt and organic ester?" Mel paused writing and squinted her eyes. "Why? And why does it withstand tangential velocity?"

"Maybe it doesn't."

"What do you mean?"

Instead of answering, Tom pulled the large display out of the wall and tapped his fingers through the menus before he found what he was looking for: a shot of Serenity just before they began their docking maneuver. It lay there like a pitted football, gray and nondescript.

"See that glimmer?"

Once again, she had to focus on the distant, milky glow that surrounded the object, an indefinable glow that was more visible when she looked at it out of the corner of her eye.

"Barely. What is...? Oh!"

"Yes." He nodded. "What if Serenity shakes off the salts and esters that form on its surface?"

"That would explain the strange tail, which—whatever else it is—is not a plasma flare."

"It doesn't radiate heat and it's way too thin," he confirmed. "So we could be dealing with the end products of an acid reaction that remains as extremely fine particles."

"But," she objected, "the particles would drift off sideways and not fly backward, since they would have the same velocity when separated from their parent body according to the incontrovertible Newton."

"Correct. Unless there are pores."

"Pores?"

"Yes. How are esters formed?"

"By splitting off... water!"

"Precisely. Consequently, if our previous measurements are correct and we are dealing with a local, extremely rapid carbonate-silicate cycle, organic ester is formed in addition to inorganic salt with the splitting off of H_2O. Chemistry does not lie."

"And where there is water—"

"—usually there are also pores. And where water plays a role in organic processes, there is also osmosis, if we take what we know of the Earth as a basis. Did you know that osmosis comes from the Greek, like pretty much everything else in science?"

Before she could answer, he waved his right hand like a fan. "Osmos in ancient Greek means both penetration and thrust, in the sense of propulsion."

"So you think tiny pores eject salt and esters backwards as end products of a process to convert carbon dioxide?"

"Yes," he confirmed. "Carbon dioxide is a common product of chemical processes, and this ship could get rid of it that way."

"Why not just pump from a pipe?"

"I don't know. Maybe there are other underlying cycles, or maybe there are no pipes." Tom raised his hands defensively. "I'm just interpreting what I see, and I'd rather throw reflective salt and ester particles backwards than have them form a cloud around me through which I can't see."

"But then why aren't the pores in the tail? That would make much more sense," Mel pondered aloud.

"Maybe not. It's possible that the process has to take place somewhere on the surface or hull for reasons we don't yet know." He paused. "Maybe we should continue with our jade sample here and see if that can shed some light on it? After all, it's from the layer below."

"Good idea," she agreed.

"Here goes." Tom slid the sample into the rubber-gloved glass case and resealed it, made sure the inside was antiseptic, and then began his work. "I'm going to scrape smaller particles off the surface of the ten-centimeter core and put them on a glass plate."

He pulled out the small plate and turned with it to one of the two microscopes on the table. "I'll put the sample under the sensor of the electron scanning microscope." He then removed the sample container from the glass case and walked to the cabinet where the cutting machine was located. "The electro-scalpel is now cutting a 0.5-millimeter thick layer, which I will put into the electron beam probe."

He looked to Mel after sitting back down in front of the electron scanning microscope. "In our case, this is wavelength dispersive X-ray spectroscopy. I use it to measure the X-rays emitted from the sample and detect any element with an atomic number of at least four—in that case, beryllium."

"How long does that take?" asked Mel.

"Oh, long. With the microscope here, I can color code things like iron, nickel, and magnesium and take high-resolution images. The electron beam measures everything out to the nanometer level and creates something like a chemical map. Later, the sample will also go into a focused ion beam machine—a really cool thing we got from the FBI. It handles ion thinning as well as the focused ion beam imaging method by shooting a hole in the sample using gallium ions. Isn't that cool?"

She wanted to say something, but Tom would not be stopped. "So afterwards I can analyze the atoms individually in the transmission electron microscope. The two-and-a-half-meter baby has lain in its slumber for far too long. Time to kiss it awake."

Mel shook her head. "How long until your 'kiss'?"

"I think no more than twelve hours."

"Excuse me?"

The chemist seemed irritated. "What did you expect? In any case, simply looking at it is not enough. But I can assure you that the time will fly by. It doesn't get more exciting than this!"

"Yes." She stood up. "I have a few more reports to write."

"I get it. Go ahead. Do I at least have permission to work through the night?" He didn't seem disappointed—more like amused.

"Yes. In this case, yes. Until we know more about the nature of the hull, we have no starting point for penetrating to the interior." In her mind, she added, *If there even is an inside.*

"And then I get to be put back at the bottom of the EVA list," Tom sighed. "Good night, then. I'll know more tomorrow."

23

Tomorrow came sooner than Mel had feared. She had a conversation with Bernard and Jim, who informed her that the team's geologists and chemists agreed that Tom's hypothesis about the excretion of salt and ester was free of fundamental error, at least, but that they could not make sense of it.

China seemed to be on the verge of withdrawing from the joint space-exploration project after a near collision between two U.S. Navy and People's Liberation Army cruisers in the Taiwan Strait, as neither ship had been willing to deviate from its course. The People's Republic had earlier launched two ballistic missiles over the democratic island republic, prompting the U.S. Navy's Seventh Fleet to join Japan and South Korea in conducting weeklong air defense exercises in the adjacent sea area.

For Mel, it was hard to imagine that Earth had so quickly sunk back into the chaos of war and division, while out here in the sea of silence they were advancing humanity's greatest discovery.

At breakfast, she was the first to meet Hongbo, who, like her, had woken up earlier and handed her a packet of 'cereal' with oat milk. Together they lay down against the wall to let the merciless gravity push them against the cushion while they slurped the nutritious cereal paste.

"I have them too, you know."

"What do you have, too?" asked Mel.

"The dreams," the taikonaut replied softly. "Since shortly after we left."

"Why didn't you—"

"Good morning," Zhigang interrupted them. He came climbing in to join them and headed toward the freezer to pull out a pack of breakfast and coffee and pop it in the microwave. Hongbo immediately fell silent and returned his greeting along, as did Mel.

"I left some comments on your report from yesterday at your workstation in the cockpit. Maybe you can go over them before Tom briefs us on his findings," she suggested to the Chinese taikonaut, who bowed his head in agreement, took his warmed breakfast, and headed down the central corridor to the cockpit.

When he was gone, she looked at her colleague from the side. "So, where were we?"

Hongbo smiled cautiously and looked out into the empty corridor, as if Zhigang might reappear. Apparently, the system of mutual surveillance and denunciation still worked out here in Mars orbit.

"I have the dreams, too."

"But you didn't say anything when we talked about it."

"No."

"Why not?" Mel asked. "On this mission, we can't hold anything back or suppress anything because we'd be tripping ourselves up. Every detail could be critical."

"I know. That's why I'm talking to you now... But—"

"But *what?*"

"I can't—"

"Out here, we are as far away from what keeps you trapped at home as it is possible to be. Our return? Highly uncertain. With its current course, Serenity will orbit the sun and shoot back out of the solar system on the other side. It will be at least a year before we can cross Earth's orbit and accelerate back home, plus the eight-month journey from that point to get back. That's two years in which a lot can happen."

"I know."

"Do you really want to jeopardize such an important discovery as this thing out there for political reasons?" challenged Mel, having to be careful not to let her frustration bubble out of her any further. They were still being monitored and streamed by cameras and microphones, albeit with a severe delay. But by now she didn't care and felt petty and stupid.

"No, I don't want to, and that's why I'll talk to you if you let me finish," Hongbo said calmly.

"Sorry," she sighed, rubbing her temples. "Sorry."

"I have also been having the dreams since about the time I left the Earth's magnetic field. I've been going over your dream logs, and although I can barely remember details because memories fade quickly after waking up, I have the impression that something resonates with me when I read what you dreamed."

"That could be a clue that you've had the same dreams."

"Yes."

"Do you think Zhigang is dreaming too?" asked Mel, looking at the empty corridor.

"It would be strange if four members do so, and one does not. But he won't admit it."

"And why not?"

"Esotericism is not exactly perceived as party loyalty in China."

"Quantum mechanics used to be esoteric, too," Mel countered.

"I know that," Hongbo responded firmly. "However, I don't decide whether it's—"

They were interrupted by Tom's voice echoing through the ship. "You guys should come to the lab sometime. Best to do it now."

It was not ten minutes before they were all gathered around the table with the microscopes and the glass case. Tom looked severely overtired, but at the same time electrified with an almost feverish look and impatient gestures to order them all to their places.

"I have all the results I need to make some statements," he announced, pointing to Mel. "Yesterday you and I talked about the inorganic carbon cycle."

"Yes, I remember."

"I was right."

She raised an eyebrow. "We might need a little more than that."

"First of all, it is certain that the 'jade sample' is not jade." He grinned wryly and mock-growled when no one smiled. "I was able to detect residues of Bacillariophyta."

"Diatoms? Out here?" asked Selena incredulously.

"At least a diatom analog, because I can clearly see that these single-celled organisms clothe themselves in a silica crust. And diatoms do photosynthesis. So, we're dealing with a bioactive surface, that's for sure."

"Then why isn't Serenity green?" Hongbo asked.

"Chlorophyll, a pigment, only appears green because it reflects 'green' light and absorbs the rest of the color components contained in sunlight," Tom answered quickly, as if he had been waiting for the question. "There's nothing to say that some other form of photosynthesis wouldn't absorb every color component and reflect nothing."

"Algae needs water," Mel noted.

"Right." He pointed an outstretched finger at her. "And polyps need it, too."

"*Polyps?*" asked Hongbo and Zhigang at the same time, looking at each other in surprise.

"A tumor-like growth?" Selena didn't sound convinced.

"No, no, the word *polyp* is used purely descriptively in medicine," Tom replied, wagging an index finger in front of her face like a teacher. "In this case, there is no question of benign or malignant. Polyps are not just mucosal tumors, they are living things, something else entirely. Corals are made up of colonies of polyps, and they can be soft, or in the case of stony corals, hard."

"Wait a minute. Serenity's surface is made of *coral?*" Zhigang asked, tilting his head skeptically.

"No, not from coral. From polyps!" Tom sighed indignantly. "Polyps are—strictly speaking—a stage in the development of cnidarians. I've discovered digestive filaments, calcium-bearing basal plates, nematocysts, a gastrodermis—"

"Metabolic organelles."

"Yes. This," he held up the remainder of the jade sample in its jar, "is an ultra-dense network of polyps, much smaller and finer than species found on Earth, but undoubtedly with the same basic morphology. The material appears to remain in a permanent coral-like state, but is extremely active. I was able to detect water molecules as well as sulfuric acids."

"How can that be?" asked Mel, addressing no one in particular.

"Polyps are very versatile. Some jellyfish, like the Portuguese man o' war, are made up of polyps that have joined together to form a complex creature. Corals seem to have little in common with this, but they too are made up of polyps with very different properties and amazing hardness. The most outstanding feature of them, however, is their extraordinary ability to regenerate even under difficult conditions. Polyps can renew themselves over time and are adapted to solar radiation."

"But not to the levels of cosmic radiation out here," Selena agreed. "After all, the sun cooks up all biological life in no time."

"How do we *know* that? Quite obviously we don't, because that object out there is made up of meter-thick polyps in a form I've never seen before. A new composition, a new... recipe, if you will, but definitely biological, and following basic terrestrial morphology."

"And then there's the salt coming out of the pores," Mel jumped in, feeling his fascination spill over.

"Exactly. Highly compacted salt is a passable radiation shield, as long as enough of it comes together—as it does with pretty much everything."

"And if it forms a mist around the polyp, that doesn't hurt either."

"Exactly. Anything that comes through could well be food for our polyp, adapted to their vacuum habitat."

"But," Hongbo objected, "cnidarians also need oxygen."

"Correct. From what I've seen, it's no different here. Therefore..." Tom turned on the monitor and showed a time-lapse view of Serenity as it disappeared behind Saturn and did not reappear as anticipated. "We've assumed that Serenity somehow parked itself behind the gas giant, perhaps picking up hydrogen from its upper atmospheric layer, as a propellant."

"Have we?" asked Zhigang, but the German ignored the taikonaut.

"I think it parked itself in one of the ice rings and filled its belly. From the ice that Enceladus, among others, has been shooting into the rings for millions of years, it can produce oxygen and hydrogen. Food and propellant at the same time.

As a highly reactive element, oxygen is a good ally for any form of energy production."

"If I may summarize," Selena cut in again, "are we dealing with an organic object rather than a spacecraft?"

"Both, I think. A spaceship that is organic in structure, or at least made up of organic and inorganic components. At any rate, yes, it has metabolic processes of some kind." Tom sat down as if exhausted from his burst of scientific fanfare.

"Can radiation combined with water really suffice as an energy source?" Zhigang sounded skeptical as was usual for him.

"Fungi can feed on radiation, as we know, and water is highly abundant in the universe—just in the form of ice rather than liquid, as it is on Earth." Selena looked at Tom, who merely nodded, but otherwise remained silent.

Mel's thoughts circled so quickly that it was difficult for her to pick out individual ones and hold onto them. *A biological or at least partially biological spaceship?* The possibility was not inconceivable, and was the stuff of many science fiction classics, such as Peter F. Hamilton's *Armageddon Cycle*, which she had devoured in her youth. But those, unlike Serenity, had been something like space animals, bred to accommodate a human crew, with whom they entered into a kind of symbiotic relationship, as humans and horses had from earliest times.

Some alert part of her deeper brain noticed something changing about the conversation going on around her without her consciously noticing it.

"But the question is, what does that mean for how we move forward?" Tom asked.

"We're trying to gain access," Mel replied curtly, holding his gaze as he stared at her.

"But we don't know what that does to Serenity. We could, without exaggerating, cut through the equivalent of its skin."

"It has obviously survived the impacts of umpteen meteorites, as you can see from the craters. Measured by its overall size, a hole in its hull that would let us through would be no more than a scratch."

"He's right, though, Mel," Selena interjected. "We've gathered evidence that Serenity may be a living being, and that raises ethical questions we can't ignore."

"Are not *allowed* to ignore," Tom added.

"You are doctors. I understand that," Zhigang interjected. "But to speak of this as a living being requires more than evidence of biologically active components."

"No, not exactly."

"Then you wouldn't be allowed to cut down a tree to gain access to a place in the forest, or light a fire," Hongbo came to her compatriot's support. "There are gradations that we shouldn't just sweep off the table."

"But we can't even judge these gradations yet," the doctor insisted. "To say at the first sign of living matter that it is of lower origin and that we may assert our God-given right as the crown of the food chain is sheer hubris."

"To speak of living beings because there is a material exchange of organic components somewhere, I believe is hubris," Zhigang countered. "All along the journey, we have been extremely hasty in putting interpretations and conjectures as fact, instead of being quiet and open to what we observe but do not want to observe, or what we believe we observe. There is a big difference between the two that many of you seem to have lost sight of. What we see here is a structure that looks like a comet on the outside, but at least has biologically active components. Nothing less, but nothing more."

"He's right," Hongbo said before Tom could say anything back. "Serenity has so far shown no reactions that would indicate intelligent life."

"What about the heat buildup below the impact points of our harpoons?" Selena asked. "Calories, heat, is the first symptom of inflammation."

"What's missing is redness, swelling, pain, and impaired function. We haven't recorded any of that."

"We could hardly measure its pain and dysfunction either, could we?" the doctor shot back.

"But redness and swelling."

"Listen," Mel finally intervened before a real argument could break out, even though she didn't think it was likely to go that far. "An animated discussion is good, and in my opinion, we've had them far too infrequently. But we're going to send a report home, and we'll get a directive recommendation that doesn't have much to do with a real recommendation, we all know that."

Mel pointed to Tom. "Thanks to your work, Tom, we've gathered some new facts to think about before we proceed. I want each of you to send a report, including a recommendation for how to proceed, to Houston, so every view has its say and is weighed. Then, once we receive direction from Mission Control, we'll proceed accordingly."

"Hello, Commander," Jim said into the camera. He was standing below the glass pane of the visitor's area in the Mission Control Center in Houston, next to CAPCOM's seat, where Bernard's side-silhouette was visible. Jim's expression was formal, matching the control center's crowded occupancy. "We've gone through your data."

"It sure took you long enough," she murmured to his recorded image. It was almost time for the scheduled night's rest on board.

"Of course, we can't give you any answers, either, but after comparing all the findings and possible explanations, we are of the opinion that Serenity must not be a living being, but an inorganic-organic spaceship. The emphasis here is on the singular," he continued. "There may be living beings aboard, or certain parts of the ship may meet some definition for markers of life. However, in our opinion, that is no reason to abandon Serenity now."

"Totally agree," she murmured.

"The lack of any *measurable* response to your arrival," Mel snorted as he accentuated the word 'measurable,' figuring he was alluding to their dreams, "indicates that there is either no consciousness or no possibility of interaction. The latter could indicate a faulty system, though that is of course highly speculative. Needless to say, we're in strange waters here."

"Nothing I hear or think more often lately," she whispered tiredly, stifling a yawn.

"So our recommendation is that you proceed according to plan. That means that your next step is to try to gain access to the interior, if such a thing even exists. There should also be further attempts to make contact and communicate."

"And how are we going to do that?" she asked Jim's recording. "Talking only works if both sides open their mouths."

"We wish you guys the best of luck. That's excellent work you're all doing out there. You can be sure that all of us here," he adjusted the picture so that the Chinese and Europeans in the front rows were also visible with their respective pennants on their work areas, "have your backs and are thinking of you every spare minute. We are proud of you."

There was more in his gaze, and she imagined that the unspoken thing in it was for her, even though it was perhaps presumptuous of her to believe that.

She touched his face briefly, wishing it didn't look so sunken and faded, as if he had aged years. Then she gathered the others in the corridor in front of their sleeping areas and played the message.

"You know *they* are in charge, no matter what is officially said about competencies on the ground, the sole and only ability to assess the situation in the immediate experience, the competence of the astronaut team, and so on. You have all heard it, read it, and certainly never believed it," she said freely, while the others looked at her, intent and tense. Each one had been thinking their own private thoughts since this morning about the consequences and new problems that would arise from Tom's discoveries. It felt good not to care what their superiors back home thought about what they said. It was liberating. Let Mission Control decide for themselves what gold scale to put their words on—she worked better when she was free of that.

"Nevertheless, *we* make the decision," she continued. "And that's how we're going to do it."

"You are the commander," Zhigang said without further explaining what exactly he was insinuating.

"That's right." She thought for a moment, then nodded. "That's why I decide that we decide together. I'm not smarter than you, nor do I see things you can't."

"You may be a little more persistent and idealistic than we are," Tom said, smiling broadly.

"Guilty as charged. I cannot and will not deny it," she replied jokingly, but immediately became serious again, "Each of you has the same right to put in your two cents, and what-ever we do, we must bear the decision together and move on together. A democratic decision that we all stand behind is the only way forward now."

She avoided looking at her two Chinese colleagues, so as not to give them the impression that she was trying to put one over on them, or even on her homeland, politically. Hopefully, they knew her that well by now.

"I don't think that—," Zhigang began, but was interrupted by Hongbo.

"I am in favor of proceeding, just as Mission Control has specified," the taikonaut said firmly, and her compatriot fought to control his face.

You are smart, Mel thought, looking at Hongbo, who was becoming more and more impressive to her. You agree with Mission Control's unspoken orders, so you can go along with the directive as you're asked to without causing an argument.

"I'm for it, too," Zhigang finally said tersely.

"I am reluctant to cut a hole in the body of a possibly conscious organism," Tom said, raising a hand with a sigh, "but I realize that my arguments still stand on very shaky scientific ground. So, I also opt for us to try to gain access tomorrow, but would be in favor of proceeding slowly and spending more time analyzing possible reactions of Serenity so we don't miss anything."

Selena spoke up when Mel looked at her questioningly. "Then I guess it's decided."

"No, every opinion is important, even though we'll have to decide on one way to proceed."

"Okay," Selena responded, "then we should at least be aware that we are planning to cut a hole in tissue connected to a metabolism. That would mean pain for us, and we usually respond to pain with strong reactions. When something bites us, we instinctively strike at it," the doctor explained. "Now, if any of you want to object that you also scare off attackers with knives, I say, maybe Serenity is blind. Then this ship would be even more frightened if it were suddenly bitten. And the harpoons might have been far too superficial to trigger a strong reaction."

She paused and made a dismissive hand gesture. "Definitely keep that in mind. Other than that, I also agree, because I don't see any alternative. Turn around and miss a cosmic millennium chance at first contact because we're unsure? I'd rather get eaten for tweaking Moby Dick."

"Thank you." Mel made eye contact with each one in turn so it was clear she meant it. "Tomorrow we're going to start with the first EVA to look for access."

24

Tom accompanied Mel when she left *Pangaea* for her second time. As the winches at her chest and waist slowly pulled her toward the crater, she saw the tethering cables of carbon nanotubes to her right and left that held their ship to Serenity. They seemed far too small, like mere spider threads, to be able to hold such a mass, especially as the 140-plus ton colossus was being pushed outward like the seat of a chain carousel.

In these moments, it reassured her to be a physicist and to *know* that the eye and the brain like to deceive each other and that engineering facts and optical realities regularly fail to match.

The crater surrounded her and Tom in the next moment, like a protective hollow in which it was possible to forget where they were. Outside of *Pangaea*, they always knew that it was a dangerous place in its hostile eeriness. In the crater, on the other hand, with its pretty green glow, she found many correspondences to Earth and fewer to space.

"The pressure of the centrifugal force feels like I'm a piece of metal headed for the wrong magnetic pole," Tom remarked, a slight static hiss audible over the radio.

"I know what you mean."

"Like a rejection reaction."

"But it's just rotation, Tom."

"I get it. It's just a feeling."

When they were one meter from the crater floor, they stopped the winches by pressing a button and carefully began to set up their cutting tool. It was a waterjet saw that had been adapted by ESA engineers to the requirements of a micro-gravity mission. Due to the bundled jet of water having an exit velocity of up to 1,000 meters per second and exerting up to 6,000 bar pressure on the material, there was an unavoidable recoil, which was to be counterbalanced by two compensation tanks, each with three nozzles fed by nitrogen tanks.

The fixture attached to the 70-centimeter-long machine looked like Mickey Mouse ears, making it even clunkier and extremely difficult to handle under already challenging conditions. The waterjet saw consisted of the head of the actual saw, and two, meter-long rails intersecting each other and resembling a cross. The ends of the rails had small holes in them, punched on *Pangaea*.

"Now the complicated part begins," Tom grumbled.

Working together, one of them had to push the end of one of the rails against the crater floor while the other had to shoot a harpoon bolt with a butterfly hook through the hole until all four rail ends were firmly anchored. They then shot four tethering harpoons into the sides of the crater in a precision-aimed manner and attached the cables to additional attachment points on the drill assembly for added security. If even one harpoon came loose, there was a real danger that the machine would be hurled away, dragging and crushing them both.

"There, that wasn't so hard," Mel groaned as they finished the procedure and the cutter sat on the crater floor, It would have taken no more than ten minutes on Earth, but had taken them more than ninety minutes here.

"No, not at all." Tom's helmet lights scanned across the machine like a pair of cold hands. "This is *weird*."

"What's weird?" she radioed back.

"To see such a mundane piece of industrial equipment. I worked with something like that at Airbus to cut new kinds of mushroom insulation materials we were developing."

"Airbus builds mushroom insulation materials?"

"Research and development goes into a lot of areas you don't expect. That's how I made my living before." He smiled. With his visor and the sweat on his nose, she thought he looked a bit like a medieval knight after battle. "Somehow a commonplace thing like that doesn't fit here. You know what I mean?"

"Because it seems so normal in the midst of the abnormal?" she asked.

"Yes."

"Disconcerting, yes. Shall we begin?"

"Mm-hmm," he agreed.

"*Pangaea*, Mel here. We're ready."

"Everything looks good from here," Zhigang replied from the bridge.

"I'm going to do one last equipment check." She pulled the tablet wrapped in thick insulating polymers from her belt pouch and was about to grab it with both hands, but hypergravity snatched it from her gloves and at the same moment she felt a powerful yank. "Damn."

"Are you all right?" Tom asked.

"Yeah," she groaned, fumbling for the security cable before finding it and pulling on it until she got a grip on the tablet. "A tablet can feel pretty heavy."

"The saw weighs fifty kilos on Earth, so it's now sixty-five."

"Thanks for the reminder," she replied wryly, trying not to think about what would happen if the massive cross structure in front of them came loose. Instead, she grabbed the tablet by the safety loop attached to the side so it wouldn't fly toward her and checked the connection to the computer on the saw. The laser sensor on the bottom had already measured the area to be sawed and created an accurate image and... "Wait a minute."

"What is it?" asked Tom in alarm.

"The grooves. They're shallower now than they were yesterday."

"What do you mean?"

"Zhigang measured the grooves at the bottom of the crater." She looked over the edge of the tablet at the area under the saw's metallic cross. "He determined a depth of 5.6 centimeters at the deepest point and 1.2 at the shallowest. The saw's display comes in at 5.5 and 1.1."

"Isn't that within the range of deviations of the laser meters?"

"No," Zhigang answered in her place from the cockpit. "The lasers work far more precisely, down to millimeters."

"Maybe something like a callus is forming on the polyp," Tom speculated. "That would not be unusual. If the shell is a semi-organic structure, it can also regenerate, albeit extremely slowly."

"I received the new readings and recorded them," the Chinese man said.

"All right, we'll go ahead," she decided. "I'll set the saw now. Sixty percent to start. The programmed circle looks steady, the nitrogen tanks for back pressure are full, and so are the batteries." She looked to Tom. He gave a thumbs-up as if in slow motion, and then she activated the preparation phase for the machine.

Like a twitching robot, it traveled along the two-dimensionally flexible rail structure until the opening for the jet pointed to the red-marked edge of the circle, and pushed the jet head outward.

"We should pull back now." Following her own instruction, she ordered the winches on the chest and waist suspension to give her some rope and slowly moved away from the machine and the crater until they reached the rim. Then she looked to Tom. "Ready?"

"Sure."

"Activate saw. Estimated duration thirty-three minutes. Commencing holding net rigging now."

Mel pressed the large green button on her tablet, which activated the water jet and, simultaneously, the intelligently counteracting cold gas jets. Tiny particles of polyp and water began to spurt from the crater floor—only a few, but they reached her suit and visor like sparkling firecrackers.

Together with Tom, she shot four more harpoons just below the crater rim and with him stretched the net they had brought along after they had set the appropriate carabiners.

Now it was a matter of waiting while the saw did its work. They watched silently as the head traveled along the rail structure, kicking up more and more tiny material, which was hurled against *Pangaea's* closed hatch, bounced off, and began its endless journey into space. Although she had voted for this EVA, her own actions seemed invasive to her, hostile and reckless, yet with no alternative in sight. Had her curiosity and thirst for knowledge become an ethical weakness? What if they were irreparably damaging Serenity with their actions?

After half an hour, her tablet reported in the form of a green flashing icon in her helmet head-up display. "Done," she announced. "Device shows no error messages."

"Well, let's see how far we've come." Tom grabbed her elbow and pulled himself closer.

Mel lowered the spotlight and ordered a measurement of the sawed-in interface. "Twenty centimeters."

"That means we're not through yet."

"No. I'll raise it to eighty percent blast pressure."

Again, they waited just over half an hour while the waterjet saw described another circle with significantly more energy.

This time they didn't have to wait for a result by measurement, because even before the circle was fully described and she could think about the nitrogen supplies in the canisters of the compensating nozzles, the polyp floor, which was one meter in diameter, crashed like a manhole cover against the rail construction of the waterjet saw.

"Oh, shit!" escaped Tom.

In the next instant, the first retaining bolt came loose, throwing the crossbar askew. Another followed and shot out of its mount, plowing through one of the holes in the net and narrowly missing Mel's visor like an arrow, bouncing off *Pangaea* and sailing away. The next one caught in the net, and the third was only a brief, silvery reflection in the light of their helmet lamps before it was gone.

Then the saw and the polyp disk came loose and crashed into the net. The complete silence of the vacuum made the violence of what she saw into something terrifying, over which she seemed to have no influence because she lived outside of space and time.

"Move away!" she shouted when she had broken free from her rigid state, took the harpoon gun from her belt, and hastily reloaded an arrow. Again and again she looked up at the net and the four holding carbines in the crater wall.

Are they coming loose?

With forced calm, she threaded the cable into the clamp at the end of the winch so as not to lose it in the rush. Then she waited impatiently until the excess had wound up, and looked at Tom, who was doing the same but seemed to be slower than she.

Shortly thereafter, the first carbine flew out of the polyp along with its retaining bolt and was hurled by Serenity's brutal tangential velocity against *Pangaea*, from which it bounced and disappeared. Now she saw the next carbine wobble treacherously.

She quickly extended her arm, aimed at an area to the right of the crater, and pulled the trigger. Without looking to see if she had hit—or where—she pulled the trigger to activate the winch and allowed herself to be pulled to the side. Since there was only a meter of distance between her spacecraft and Serenity, she scraped over pseudo-regolith and steel alike, praying that her suit wouldn't leak. She banged violently against one of the hull plates as the two cables snagged her chest and hips because they had reached their end and were rubbing against the crater rim.

She looked down at herself, having narrowly missed one of *Pangaea's* docking ports, which had always seemed tiny compared to the ship, but were larger than she was. The net had completely pulled free and was 'sticking' to the spaceship hull like a sponge that was slowly slipping off.

"Tom? TOM!"

"I'm here," she heard him call breathlessly. She looked for him and found the two beams of light from his helmet on the other side of the crater. They bobbed back and forth in the gap between the ship and Serenity's surface. "Shit, that was closer than I thought."

"Suit integrity?" she asked.

"Life support and temperature stable. I don't know how I got so lucky, but it looks good."

Only now did Mel check her own displays, and as it turned out, she too had either been hugely lucky, or the design teams of her new EMUs had done an amazingly good job.

Or both.

"You really gave us a scare," Zhigang said, sounding a little unsettled.

"What about our ship?" she demanded.

"No damage that we could see from here. Probably just a few scratches. Still, we shouldn't repeat this."

"No objections!"

"Can you see anything with the cameras?" asked Tom.

"No, too many particles coming out of the hole. One of the cameras is destroyed and the other has something stuck on the front of the lens."

"We'll go see," Mel decided, untying the rope to her rescue harpoon and then winching herself back toward the crater, being careful not to let her shoulders scrape too hard against the pseudo-regolith.

When she reached the edge, she looked across to Tom, who seemed to be lying on his chest like a squeezed Michelin man, but in reality was pressed back against *Pangaea*. Her two tethers on her upper body were the only thing keeping her from being hurled into nothingness.

"Anyway, we don't have a waterjet saw anymore," the German grumbled hoarsely.

"No, but we *do* have a hole," she replied, pointing downward with one finger. Only now did he lower his focus.

The cutout in the crater floor was such an exact circle that it looked unreal in its seemingly natural setting. Tiny drops, which solidified into ice crystals while still in flight, streamed out of it and joined the cloud of smaller particles that pelted against the hatch of *Pangaea* directly above them.

But the output was visibly diminishing, and she could see with her headlights that there was a cavity underneath.

"What is it?" asked Tom.

"I don't know, but it goes down deep." Mel looked at the readings on her rangefinder after turning it on and aiming the red dot through the hole. It hit a shimmering damp wall somewhere below, with a reddish glow. "Three meters from the opening."

"I don't see any boundary on the right and left. Only shadows."

"Neither do I. *Pangaea*, do you see that too?"

Zhigang was the first to reply. "Yes. It seems to be a cavity, that much is certain."

"Maybe a passageway?" Selena speculated.

"We should go in," Mel decided.

"The EVA should follow schedule in—" Zhigang countered.

Mel did not let him finish. "I'm definitely not going back now. Selena, Hongbo? Get ready and bring oxygen and cameras."

"Roger that."

"Right away."

The voices of the two women almost overlapped.

"Zhigang, how is the image transmission home?" she asked.

"All recorded and relayed. Earth is live—with the delay, of course." The taikonaut paused. "For the record, I would like to protest the change of plans and point out that this is an avoidable risk. We should first wait to see if there is a response from Serenity to address any potential dangers—"

"Noted," she interrupted, not unkindly but firmly. Now that she knew there was indeed a shell and an 'inside,' not even the devil could dissuade her from at least looking. Especially after she had just almost died, and had been waiting for this moment for very many years. "Tom and I will go through the hole and see if the coast is clear. Then we'll wait there for Selena and Hongbo."

"I recommend we at least replenish our oxygen supplies first, Commander," the German suggested. "I agree with you that we shouldn't put off until tomorrow anything we can do now without becoming overtired, but refilling down there would be adding an unnecessary risk."

Mel thought about it and sighed before nodding. "You're right. *Pangaea*, we'll come back to the airlock and refill our EMUs with breathable air."

She sought Tom's gaze, and through the reflective glass he nodded to her. Then they turned their backs on the airlock and entered the nearly dried-up particle stream that connected the hole to the hatch, hanging from their ropes.

"Pressure released, unlocking completed. Airlock opening," Zhigang reported. "You can go in now."

"Thank you." At her signal, she and Tom simultaneously pressed the winch buttons on the front of their suits and slid back. Although technically they were being pushed, it felt as if they were being grabbed by an invisible hand and pulled backward.

They waited dutifully in the airlock for the pressure to build up, removed their helmets, and let Selena and Hongbo give them water and a nutrient gel snack before they put their helmets back on and strapped other toolboxes in front of their belts, which contained lots of analysis equipment, sensors, and measuring tools.

"We'll wait for you," she said to her two colleagues and motioned Tom to follow her toward the outside hatch and strap in. "It doesn't make sense if we have differently filled air tanks."

"That's fine." He nodded tensely.

"Are you okay?"

"I'm about to shit my pants thinking about us going down there right now, but other than that, I'm fine."

"You're wearing a diaper," Selena said, already in the process of helping Hongbo into her lower suit.

"Very funny." Tom snorted.

"Would you rather stay here?" asked Mel, eyeing him appraisingly.

"Are you crazy? Not for all the money in the world!" He grinned. "But I'm still scared shitless."

"I feel the same way," she confessed.

"We really got lucky out there just now, Mel."

"I know."

"Can you two take a break from making us wet our diapers?" demanded Selena, hooking up some connectors in Hongbo's clunky EMU unit. "Watching that on the cameras was bad enough."

"From now on it will be easier," Mel declared optimistically as she signaled to Tom that she wanted to visually check his suit. They took their time since they had to wait anyway, looking for minor tears or weak spots from their slide between the ship and Serenity. Even though any hole, no matter how tiny would have caused the suit to depressurize and deflate, it felt right to take their time instead of letting their imaginations run wild about what might be waiting for them down there.

An hour later, they were ready and hanging four abreast in the airlock. Since they couldn't all fit on the rear hatch to lean against the hypergravity, they latched onto handholds attached to the sides like climbers holding onto a single ledge on a cliff.

"Open the hatch."

Mel pressed the button next to her after the light had begun to glow green as all air had escaped along with all sound. She and Tom were the first to attach the winch ropes to their harnesses and then slowly let themselves be pulled forward, toward the crater and the dark hole in its center. To get through, the first one would reach in and pull while the other hung outside the hole and pushed. Then the first person could pull the second in—at least that was their plan.

"We are now beginning our entry into the interior of Serenity," she explained over the radio. Reporting individual steps helped her sort out her thoughts and stay focused. Addressing Tom, she asked, "Ready?"

"I got you."

"We've waited a long time for this." She raised her hands and reached into the hole.

25

Climbing through the hole was even more strenuous than Mel had expected. The centrifugal forces seemed to pull at her like Sicilian boots, and the pressurized gloves of her suit meant that the leverage using her fingers was beyond bad. But she gritted her teeth and growled into her helmet, the abstract echo of which propelled her even further. With Tom's help, pushing her from behind as best he could and then taking hold of her boots and pushing further, she finally managed to roll onto the shell of Serenity—only this time from the inside.

"What do you see?" asked Tom. The signal was good, which reassured both of them.

No shielding or interference.

"I... I'll look," Mel shifted until she was on her hands and knees and looked around. It was pitch black, so only the bright cones of her helmet headlights provided light. "I see a hallway going left and right. The walls appear to be wet."

She stood up and reached out a hand to touch the shimmering reddish material, which seemed to be irregular and covered with white crystals. When she wiped some of it away, it flew off and disappeared like mist through the hole at her feet.

"I think the area around the opening is frozen." Her gaze, and with it the circular sliver of light in the darkness, wandered back and forth. "But only a few meters."

"Any little green men?" Tom asked.

"No. Just me and the darkness."

"Well, give an old doc a hand then."

"I'm ready," she said, kneeling beside the hole to grab his left forearm at the ring closure between the glove and sleeve of his white spacesuit. Then she pressed her knees with the reinforced elements against the floor just in front of the sharp, sawed-out edge, and pulled as hard as she could.

"I felt like I was giving birth, only backwards," Tom gasped as he plopped down on the floor—or wall—beside her, panting, trying to steady his breathing. He looked around, a new pair of light cones intersecting with hers. "Looks like a birth canal, too. A pretty creepy one."

"Thanks again, Tom," Selena radioed wryly.

"Let me know when you arrive," Mel said. "The two of us can help you inside, and then 'the birth' should go easier."

"Roger that. We have our ropes hooked into the winches and are letting them pull us."

"This is truly amazing," breathed Tom, who by now had stood up and was looking at the wall with fascination, scanning it with his glove.

"Whatever happened to 'scientists don't touch everything, only stupid teens in bad horror movies do that?'"

"That was before I was an alien ship explorer. Check this out!"

She stepped up beside him, her helmet now so close to the reddish material of the circular walkway that she had to wait for her eyes to adjust to the brightness.

"Burgundy red and streaked with a strange marbling like

fatty meat," the ESA astronaut continued. Examining it, he pressed his hand forward and it sank into it a little. "See?"

Mel gulped. "Is that living tissue?"

"I don't know. I don't see any blood vessels or anything, and I don't see an obvious pulse, so I'd be more inclined to guess that we're dealing with something bionic."

"So, an imitation of something natural..."

"Most of the time, nature does everything better than we do, who shovel elements out of the ground to reassemble them into cool stuff," he explained. "But a spider thread, when you put mass and tensile force in proportion, is significantly stronger than most steel alloys."

"Better well imitated than poorly homemade, I suppose." She turned to the side and shone her light into the hallway to the left. The cone of light trailed along the walls like a ring until it was lost. "A bend, see?"

"Yes. The passage seems to run along the length of the hull." They turned together and looked in the other direction, where they saw a similar sight.

"I don't think that's a hallway," she objected, pointing with an outstretched hand along the wall that surrounded her, and finally at her boots, which had no level ground beneath them. "There is no down or up. Judging by the centrifugal force, there should be *down* here. But the bottom is not flat. This is a tube with no sides."

"Maybe they're not bipedal. Insects, for example, don't care what the surface is like—they can cope with pretty much anything. In an ant burrow there's no up and down. They simply crisscross their tunnels, which sometimes run sideways, sometimes downward. It could be like that here, too."

"Hmmm," she murmured, trying to banish the thought that at any moment large insect aliens could jump into her headlights to eat her. They certainly would not be small given the size of this tunnel, or whatever it was.

"We're here," Hongbo radioed in, and the next moment they saw a glove fumbling through the hole.

Mel and Tom spread out to the right and left after brief hand signals and pulled her up. Afterward, they accepted the spare oxygen and placed it behind them before helping Selena up as well.

"Did you see the saw edge?" she asked. "Pretty messy work."

Mel bent over and looked at the edge of the ring-shaped opening. Indeed, the 30-to-40-centimeter hole in the 'skin' was irregularly cut and covered as if by warts.

"Could be callus," Tom speculated. "Like in a healing broken bone—minerals get lodged and thicken the area."

"That doesn't sound very reassuring," Selena remarked.

"Oh." He waved it off. "Callus takes forever to form." He raised his left arm and tapped it with his right hand. "Five fractures in the forearm. I know what I'm talking about."

"So how do we proceed?" asked Hongbo as she slowly looked around.

"Tom and I will go to the left, you two to the right," Mel suggested, pointing in both directions in turn. "We'll leave the oxygen here, along with a radio transmitter that I'll set on continuous transmit so we can orient ourselves in case of doubt. Constant radio contact. If you see anything suspicious, stop and report."

"Everything in here is suspicious," the Chinese woman indicated.

"Then we will have to come up with a new definition. Remember, we're still here because we're expecting a first contact. So keep calm and don't rush into anything."

"Like sawing a hole in it?" Tom raised his hands apologetically as she gave him a sour look.

"Let's just get started."

Every step they took in the darkness toward the bow—if

there was one—was extremely difficult. Their boots were not designed for walking, but only to protect their feet—like the suit protected the rest of their bodies—from the vacuum. Accordingly, it was uncomfortable to walk on a floor that was uneven and not level. In addition, each carried at least 50 kilos. On the ropes, out in the crater, the hypergravity had made itself felt by pushing them into the backs of their EMUs and giving them ugly bruises. Here there was a 'down' again, and accordingly, a lot of weight on their legs and feet—which burned like fire after only a few steps—not to mention the weight on their shoulders.

"Look," Tom said, stopping so suddenly that she was startled. He shone his light to the right, where there was one small tunnel going up and one going down. Both were just big enough to push a basketball through and branched out rather quickly as their helmet lights hit an obstacle after only a few feet. "I guess that's for the smaller insects."

"We should hold the air analysis sensor in here for a while," she stated decisively, kneeling slowly in what was more like a controlled fall and unclipping her device pouch from her belt. The air analysis device looked like a phaser from Star Trek, but with a finger-thick short sensor at the tip. It took her a while to activate it, as even the large buttons were difficult to operate with her clunky gloves. "All right, traces of nitrogen, oxygen—also ozone, helium, argon. But mostly carbon dioxide. So, you weren't wrong in your theory of carbon dioxide decomposition—or rather, its conversion."

"Hold the sensor up to the outside wall," he suggested, pointing behind him.

"The concentration is higher."

"Then yes, it could be right."

A tremor went through the tunnel that caused her knees to wobble, followed by a dull booming sound as if from a gong struck underwater.

They froze and stared at each other, but the tremor did not repeat and neither did the boom.

"Selena? Hongbo? Did you feel that too?" she radioed. Her throat felt as if she had been chewing on a dusty rag.

"Yes," the Chinese woman replied breathlessly. "We're on our way back to the entry point right now."

"We'll meet you there." She turned to Tom. "Let's go."

"Wait." He reached for her arm and held her back. Noticing his line of sight, she turned as well and saw a kind of membrane open and close diagonally in front of them. It looked like thin skin, pink translucent and fragile, and each time it opened, a cloud of colored particles streamed out toward the bow.

"There's something behind it."

"Yes. We should check."

"We should go to the—" Before she finished the sentence, they heard Selena calling loudly.

"There's something rustling behind us!" There was a scratching and cracking sound in the background—perhaps the static she had been talking about. "We found the radio transmitter, but no hole."

"What?" Mel turned and saw the helmet lights of the two behind her. They were less than 15 meters away. A movement caught her attention, far behind her two colleagues. "Something's coming!"

Selena and Hongbo wheeled around and shone their lights into the tunnel behind them, from where darkness seemed to be closing in.

"Holy shit!" escaped the doctor's mouth.

"Quick! Over here!" Tom yelled out.

"What's happening?" asked Zhigang from the cockpit of *Pangaea*. For the first time, he didn't sound calm or stoic.

Mel's headlights twitched from the two astronauts running toward her, looking about as skilled as marshmallows, to the membrane opened and closed every few seconds.

"We have to get in there!" Tom declared. Mel merely nodded and shooed him ahead. He waited a breath for the next time the membrane opened, then jumped in. The opening was sideways to the direction of gravity, further into the ship, making it impossible to enter on his feet.

Mel felt the adrenaline burning in her veins, making her heart hammer. But she stopped next to the membrane, which remained like a flicker in the corner of her eye as she waited for her colleagues. Hongbo was two steps ahead of Selena and a little faster. Behind them, the darkness was closing in.

When Mel's headlight tried to penetrate it, it glittered like black opal.

"What the hell is that?" she breathed in awe and fear at the same time. All her hair stood on end, and a voice in her head begged her to follow Tom and get to safety—if that even existed.

The black opal came closer, announcing itself with a roar that sounded like the surf of the sea.

"GET IN THERE!" she radioed, pushing Hongbo through the membrane from the side as she jerked up at the right moment. She saw Tom's silhouette behind it, clinging to something. The Chinese woman plunged through and landed heavily on her stomach, but the membrane closed behind her, narrowly missing her feet.

Mel looked back at Selena, who made the mistake of trying to turn around as she ran—a human reflex to look back over her shoulder. But hypergravity, combined with the uneven ground, punished the instinctive action with a nasty fall as she lost her balance and hit the ground with her helmet. Mel could see that the glass was shattered as the light refracted in all directions like a prism.

Selena's words were a statement. "I can't make it."

"I'll get you!" Mel yelled and was about to rush off when she was grabbed from the side and fell. A smacking sound rang out, and her horizon spun in a nausea-inducing way. Knotty branches alternated with pink clouds. Then it abruptly became loud and a roar filled her helmet, followed by the roar from before.

It took her a moment to get her bearings. She was lying between Hongbo and Tom, who were holding her with their legs so that she would not fall into the membrane, which was now closed and vibrating as if there were a violent hurricane on the other side. Her two colleagues clung with their hands to dark brown ramifications growing out of the walls, reminiscent of gnarled old tree branches. The entire room was about the size of a small apartment building but strangely deformed.

"Selena?" she called out. "SELENA, come in!"

Nothing.

"Zhigang? Can you hear me?"

"I hear you," came the immediate reply. "What happened there? Selena... I don't see any vital signs from her anymore."

Mel felt an expanding black hole in her throat that made it hard to swallow.

"There was something in the tunnel behind us," Hongbo said breathlessly. "Something dark."

"I think it was a liquid," Mel said, swallowing hard. "Something shiny."

The murmur quieted and abruptly disappeared, then the membrane opened again in its rhythm from before.

"We're going to have to... let you go," Tom groaned, and even before he had spoken, the first pair of legs detached from her torso and Mel slid downward, across the flap and out into the tunnel. The impact jolted as a dull twinge through her feet to her hips, but she didn't think she'd hurt herself, though the adrenaline in her system could surely have fooled her into thinking everything was fine and ready for further evasive action.

Quickly she jerked left and then right, lighting up the tunnel, looking for Selena. She found her 20 or 30 meters further toward the bow, a white heap of cloth and metal, stained and with a clumsy knapsack on her back.

"I can see her!"

"Is she still breathing? Her connection is offline," Zhigang said tensely.

"I'm going to her now." Mel put her words into action and made her way to her colleague lying there. A good two dozen meters seemed like a mile under the prevailing conditions, and she was sweating profusely enough after just a few steps that, despite her hood, drops were falling off her nose. Behind her, the lights of Tom and Hongbo flickered as they followed her.

When she arrived at Selena she turned the doctor onto her back and recoiled when she saw the broken visor and the blue-tinged face behind it. The glassy eyes were wide open and covered with hoarfrost, the skin covered with burst veins.

"She's dead," she whispered, clearing her throat. As the others joined her, she repeated aloud, "Selena Rogerton is dead."

"How did it happen?" asked Zhigang after a moment of silence over all the radios.

"She's covered in a liquid," Mel described, forcing herself to think rationally, once again pushing her emotions into a far corner of her mind in order to function. The slime, which she hadn't even seen at first, was transparent and extremely thin, but completely covered Selena's body, along with hundreds of fingertip-sized green globules that clung to her suit and face like slimy burrs.

"Her visor is broken. The abrupt drop in pressure burst

her capillaries under the skin," Tom began to explain in medical jargon.

Mel was no longer listening. She knew what happened to the human body when it was exposed to space. There was no vacuum in here because there were easily measurable gas accumulations, not all of which had been sucked through the hole. It wasn't as cold as space, either, according to her suit, at two degrees Celsius. But the pressure was similarly low, near zero. This caused the boiling points of liquids to drop dramatically and blood to begin boiling. The resulting water vapor bubbles had spread throughout Selena's blood and tissues, triggering multiple thromboses and embolisms via the immune system. Due to the clogged vessels, her circulation had collapsed within a few seconds. A painful, albeit quick death.

"She fell," Tom interrupted her thoughts. "Just before the liquid hit her."

"A liquid?" asked Hongbo.

"Yes, I think I detected a black liquid flowing through the tunnel."

Tom, who by now was kneeling beside Selena's corpse, pointed to the green burrs on her darkened face with its many burst veins. "This is really strange stuff. It looks like mucus but the globules are moving slightly. Like there's a pulse."

Mel reluctantly bent over and examined the small pustules. Sure enough, they were wafting up and down a bit, like tiny bellows. "Do you have any idea what that is?"

"Are you asking the doctor? Or the chemist?" the German asked. "Both can only shrug their shoulders. Maybe they're our aliens?"

When she furrowed her brows, he raised his hands in surrender. "That could be just as accurate as anything else. Remember, we don't even know what we're looking for."

"We have to take her back," Mel proclaimed. "Back to the ship."

"Before that, we should get her out of the suit or she will be too heavy," Hongbo said.

"No. We should *not* do that," Tom objected, looking at them both as if they had lost their minds. "We have no idea what her body is infected with. We could be taking an interstellar pathogen on board, or an intelligent programmable substance—nanites that turn into gray goo and hijack our systems."

"Aren't you exaggerating a bit? We can't just—" the Chinese woman started to protest, but Mel cut her off.

"He's right," she reluctantly admitted. "It's too dangerous. We don't know what she's infested with."

"I'm forwarding the images from your cameras to Houston," Zhigang radioed. "However, you should return as soon as possible."

"Yes. Good idea."

"Do you see this, too?" asked Tom, tapping the computer unit on his chest. "It's getting warmer and the pressure is increasing."

"How is that possible?" Mel glanced back in the direction they had come from. Then she remembered Selena's words before they had started running.

Before she knew it, she was running herself, like a clunky robot. The radio transmitter fed her receiver a steady ping that was coupled to an audible signal in her helmet. When it got so loud she had to stand directly over it, she searched the floor and found the small, flip-out antenna lying on its side, half-sunk in the same translucent slime that had covered Selena's suit. She lifted it out and straightened it before searching for the hole.

"Selena had been swept away, quite a distance. The transmitter looked snagged, but it could have been carried away," she thought aloud as the others reached her, breathing heavily.

"Judging from your signals, you are eleven meters from

the hole," Zhigang helped them along. "Your bearing is sketchy but sufficient."

Without waiting, Mel went on, counting her steps and looking at the ground for the hole and the light that should fall through. But it was the same darkness everywhere, except for... "Look!"

They came together and stood around a yellowish deformed area that was approximately round and seemed to be made of thousands of small pustules.

"The callus," Tom whispered in horror.

"Excuse me?"

"When we came through, Selena pointed out to us that the saw had done an unclean job and I thought maybe something like callus had formed on the perimeter."

"You also said it would take a very long time," Hongbo replied, just a hint reproachfully.

"But, I was mistaken." He knelt and ran a hand over the strange structure without touching it. "Perhaps some kind of thrombotic reaction."

"What is happening with you?" Zhigang exclaimed.

"The hole is closed," Mel replied in consternation.

"What?"

"Our only way out is no longer here, and we have nothing with which to reopen it."

26

"What do we do now?" Tom trudged ponderously back and forth after trying unsuccessfully to beat against the yellowish pustules with the oxygen tanks they had brought with them, hoping that the overgrown area was still weak. But apart from wasting valuable energy, he achieved nothing.

"We can't get back unless Zhigang finds a way," Mel said.

"I could try a plasma cutter," the Chinese man from *Pangaea* volunteered.

"It doesn't have a recoil tank," she objected.

"It's something I have to do."

"It's too dangerous to EVA without a second person."

"I'm not going to leave you behind," he declared, "How much longer do you have air?"

"Eleven hours." She looked at Tom and Hongbo, who nodded in agreement.

"Then I'll talk to Mission Control and we'll figure something out together. Whatever is in there with you guys seems dangerous. Take care of yourselves in the meantime."

"We will." Mel looked toward the stern and stared for a

moment into the receding beam of their headlights. "We need to get out of here in case it happens again."

"Do you think the owners of this ship wanted to kill us?" asked Hongbo.

"With drain cleaner?" Tom snorted. "If they had, they would have done it the minute we broke in."

"Maybe they wanted to wait until the hole was plugged so nothing would get sucked into the vacuum."

"I've been keeping track of the time since it happened. If it happens again, we'll have a certain interval of time, and know the third time if it was a controlled event or a cyclically recurring event."

"Good work. We should get Selena's body here, and then take another look at the room where we made our way to safety. That membrane closed when the liquid came by, but didn't seem to me like it was randomly controlled from somewhere," Mel said. "More like it possessed a reflex of its own."

"Anything is better than staying in this tunnel," Tom agreed with her.

It took them about ten minutes to drag Selena's body to the closed hole. In the emptiness that her death had torn open in Mel, there was an eerie fear that she could hardly suppress. She couldn't shake the thought that they had traveled to the lair of an ancient monster and gone straight into its clutches like naive animals of prey. There were only four of them now, and both Gabriella's and Selena's deaths had come upon them so suddenly that it was difficult for her to truly comprehend the losses.

Then they silently returned to the membrane, which continued to open and close in its previously observed two-second cycle. Mel went ahead, letting the other two help her up by means of a robber's ladder, and sought a hold on one of the gnarled branches on the wall. She then helped Hongbo, and Hongbo helped Tom.

In time, she examined the 'branch' a little closer. The resemblance came from a gnarled bark that was almost black and crisscrossed with deep grooves, just wide enough that the fingers of her gloves did not touch her thumbs when she grasped it. The pink wall of the cavern, curved like a drinking tube, stood out in contrast to her improvised handhold, of which there were dozens all over the walls. They disappeared into it and reappeared elsewhere. She could feel a slight vibration through her gloves.

Once they were all three inside, resting by clinging to the branches as they still had to fight gravity, a tremor went through Serenity again, followed by the gong-like thunder, deep and menacing like a distant thunderstorm. Mel felt a chill run down her spine as the roar began, reminding her, like the Pavlovian dog, of the death of her colleague and friend. The membrane closed, vibrated under the onslaught of what was behind it, and opened again a few seconds later.

But something was different. A viscous black liquid, glistening in the beams from their helmet lights, flowed into the room through a small furrow below the membrane and spread out to the right and left of it.

"I don't think that's the way it's supposed to be."

"The seal is leaking," Tom confirmed. "I think I scraped along there with my belt clasp and may have damaged something. Injured it."

"Just don't touch that stuff."

"I don't plan to," he assured her, climbing up a little further to Hongbo.

Mel, who was at the top, a good ten feet from the membrane, began to scan the walls systematically, hyperextending her back to look all the way up. There, the space tapered off as if a bag was being closed.

"Do you see that?" she asked strained, squinting her eyes.

"What?"

"There's something like a rosette with holes that open and close periodically." She looked more closely, musing at the moist little flaps between the slimy-looking tissue that opened and closed in a steady rhythm, as if they were dissolving and re-materializing in between. "The interval is twenty seconds."

"Is it a passageway?" Hongbo asked.

"No, I don't think so, but we could still try," she suggested.

"We should probably think about what we're doing here first," Tom objected. "We're locked in a thing that just killed Selena."

"We don't know that," Mel objected.

"She looked pretty dead to me!"

"She fell and shattered her visor. That fluid that rushed through the tunnel could be something harmless that kept flowing from back to front, like a pipeline with a timed pressure pump."

"The time between the two times was about the same," Hongbo agreed with her.

"We don't even know that yet because we've only done two timings," Tom indicated. "We need at least a third to be able to make any guesses. And what was that green stuff on her suit and face? Definitely not a coincidence. I'm sure of it."

"I don't know," Mel admitted, squinting her eyes with effort. Just like the others, she was still hanging by her arms from the branches, almost supporting her own body weight, even though the wall went up at an angle rather than vertically.

"An automated defense system?" asked Hongbo. "We've speculated for a long time about what Serenity might be. Maybe it's entirely automated or self-contained and follows basal behavior patterns. Without intention. The fact that it is repairing a hole in its hull is not a hostile act."

"And what about the green blobs?" Tom sounded upset, but not hysterical. More like he was angry, which Mel could well understand. The same anger resonated within her, anger at herself for having been too curious. If one of them had been guarding the hole, they would have noticed soon enough that it was closing, and they could have escaped. Now Zhigang had to risk his life to get them out, and it would take hours—the outcome uncertain.

"These could be immune cells or something like that, which consider us foreign bodies and want to neutralize us," the German continued. "In any case, they are definitely biological."

"Or nanites," Mel replied.

"Seriously? In this environment, you believe in nanites?"

"Why not? Even on Earth, we're researching programmable nanites for medical applications."

"Even if they were, it wouldn't be a much better prospect than alien antibodies against humans," he insisted.

"But we only saw them on Selena's body, not on us. So they seem to be somehow related to the liquid or goo that it leaves behind after it's gone through the tunnel," Mel explained.

"It stands to reason, yes." Tom's voice still quivered a little. After a few breaths, he sighed. "All I'm saying is that we need to be more careful because we're clearly not welcome."

"You're right. That was my mistake, too," she admitted, feeling the pain nestled deep in her chest. "And it will be with me for the rest of my life. But there's time for emotion and time for our mission, and until Zhigang creates a way out for us, we should use whatever time we have left to continue our mission as best we can."

"We should also be prepared for Zhigang to fail," Hongbo stated the obvious. "That would mean he would have to fly back alone and salvage all the samples and data before he puts himself and *Pangaea* in too much danger trying to save us."

"Yes." Mel nodded, unseen in her helmet. "So we don't have much choice except to keep exploring, and send as much data to Zhigang as we can."

"You're right," Tom said. "Let's try that rosette up there. We've got to get out of hypergravity or exhaustion will checkmate us before we run out of air."

Mel began to climb, one handhold at a time, using her feet to push herself up when she could find a foothold with her clunky boots on one of the branches. It was slow going and so strenuous that soon her arms were shaking, but after what felt like an eternity she had made it to the strange passageway. It measured less than a meter, was roughly round, and covered with a thin layer of slime. Looking down, she could see fine particles in her headlight cones streaming up from all over the room and speeding up the closer they got to the holes that opened and closed.

"There's no doubt this is biological in origin," she said, probing against the thin layer of skin, whereupon it trembled and a convulsive contraction went through the entire room. Some of the branches shook as if they had been caught in a gust of wind.

"What was that?" Hongbo asked from behind her.

"I don't know. I just lightly poked the skin where the holes are that keep opening."

"Can we get through there?"

Mel hesitated. "It's pretty tight. I'd have to widen it with my knife."

"We used a waterjet saw to cut a hole in the hull. The point at which we made the choice between invasive methods and hand placement is long past," Tom remarked bluntly.

Hongbo echoed the same sentiment. "We can't get anywhere else here, and in the tunnel below...,"

Mel pulled out her knife, sighed, and began to cut through the thin skin with the ultra-sharp monofilament blade, right at its attachment to the wall. The knife slid through the tissue as if through soft butter, and the growing flap that came loose folded sharply inward.

"I think the airflow is getting stronger." She looked at the particles that were now shooting through her headlights at lightning speed, getting faster the more she cut. A low whistling sound could be heard and was getting louder.

After a short pause, she continued cutting and had to hold on with increasing effort with her free hand, because the increasing wind kept pressing her against the damaged skin.

"Um, there's a problem here," Tom spoke up, sounding alarmed.

"What?"

"The membrane toward the tunnel... It doesn't like what you're doing. It's tearing off."

Just as he finished speaking, Mel heard an ugly sound that reminded her of her childhood when she used to rub wet pebbles together in her hands on the beach in Philadelphia. The next moment, something hit her on the shoulder and jerked her helmet around. Something that felt like a mangled bouncy ball shot past her and then the whistling of the wind was a deafening roar, even inside her locked helmet.

She was yanked from the branches and pulled upward like a toy. Her shoulders touched something, her feet struck soft material again and again. A dark red wall raced along in front of her eyes, slowly growing brighter. Particles whizzed past her like protons in a particle accelerator, and she lost all sense of up and down.

"Can you hear me?" she yelled into her helmet, but heard only static—whether it was the noise of the storm, or from an absent radio signal, she couldn't tell. Her head-up display, which projected her suit's most important data on the inside of her visor, showed her two warning messages, but she couldn't read them. Everything was shaking too much.

Then something happened, and she crashed into a huge pillow—at least that's what it felt like. Her right shoulder protested with a sharp pain that spiked to her temple, and her right leg throbbed as if someone had taken a sledgehammer to it. She gasped and jerked her hands up just as she saw a wildly spinning light, and was struck by a meteor the next moment.

"Argh!" a guttural sound escaped her, as all air was forced from her lungs.

Tom or Hongbo fell on me, she told herself, trying to bring order to the chaos of pain and disorientation that reigned in her head. *The airflow has dried up. The hypergravity is gone. My leg is fractured or at least cracked. Below the knee. Something is wrong with my shoulder, but it's not dislocated or the pain would be worse.*

"Hongbo? Tom?" she asked, pushing the figure off herself, which was surprisingly easy, as it began to float and only very slowly slide back in her direction.

"I'm still alive," groaned the doctor. "Unfortunately."

"Me, too. What was that?"

When Mel also heard Hongbo's voice, she sighed with relief.

"We got caught in an air current. Maybe we're in a lung analog now or something," Tom said. "Look how huge this place is."

Mel let her headlights slide back and forth and could only agree with him. The 'walls' were far away, certainly 50 meters or more, and dark as oyster shells with a similar grooved grain. A meadow of fibrils blew in the invisible wind like a host of distant warriors saluting with their spears. A contraction drove like a wave through the fabric, spreading from side to side and petering out again. At its end, a rush of air pushed past her, tugging lightly at her suit, which was littered with slime and shreds of dark organic matter.

"The centrifugal forces have eased considerably," Tom noted. "We're being pulled down slightly, but it can't be more than 0.2 g."

"So we're on a wall in the direction of the hull. That's a clue, at least." Mel straightened up and looked down at her hands, which were framed by the same fibrils she had seen on the opposite side of the wall. Pitch-black, they wafted back and forth, caressing her gloves like leeches.

"Are you hurt?" the ESA astronaut questioned, coming up to them. Only now did Mel notice that she and Hongbo had been lying close to each other, but Tom was a few meters further away and was now coming across the dark meadow toward them. His helmet lamps were islands of light in the absolute darkness, casting eerie shadows as if they had developed a life of their own—it seemed as if the blackness was eating up the photons like unwanted intruders.

"My right leg and right shoulder are definitely injured," she replied, "but given the gravity conditions, it's bearable."

She fought him off when he arrived near her and reached out with his hands.

"You can't do anything anyway." She tapped against her suit.

"I'm okay, I think. I'm just a little dizzy," Hongbo said. "I hit the back of my head on the inside of my helmet."

"Then move carefully and if you feel nauseous, let me know. Then we'll have to get you horizontal."

"Zhigang? Can you still hear me?" Mel radioed to their comrade on *Pangaea*.

"Yes, I hear you." It crackled and creaked in her ear, but she could hear him clearly. "I'm also receiving your camera feeds."

"Has Mission Control checked in yet?"

"Yes. They're on it, and they'll figure something out so I can get you guys out of there. But it's going to take time."

"Roger that. We'll continue here."

"Take care of yourselves."

She turned back to Hongbo and Tom, who stood in a triangle with her, like an island of light in the void.

"Apparently the ship's various systems are interconnected." Mel turned and slid her headlights along the floor, on and on, until the circular sections of glistening brightness reached a bulge that eventually merged into the ceiling. Everything looked the same until the light hit a black area almost directly above them, not captured by the restless flutter of fibrils, but pitch black. A steady stream of droplets and particles shot out of it, slowing on their way down to them. "Wait a minute, is that—?"

"—the hole that spit us out," Tom confirmed her guess. "Yeah. I think we broke something."

"This can't be the same hole," the Chinese woman objected. "We were sucked in from the hull, that is, from the place of the strongest effect of the centrifugal force. If that were the same hole there, we'd be lying next to it now, not across from it."

"Or the tube-like connection is not a direct one, but snakes through Serenity's body," Tom conjectured. "I don't know about you guys when we were in there, but I had no orientation at all."

Mel pulled out her air analyzer and activated it. "Oxygen levels have gone way up, to almost seventeen percent."

"And carbon dioxide?" asked Hongbo.

"Forty percent."

"Not breathable. Not that I would have voluntarily opened my helmet in an alien environment like this."

"Tom, do you still have the spectrograph?"

Her colleague fumbled at his belt and looked down at

himself, which meant that he had to lean forward awkwardly in his huge suit that looked like an inflated balloon. She had turned to look at him and could see that there was no longer a pocket or a toolbag on his waist ring.

"I must have lost it when I fell down here," he said, turning around. With bouncing steps like the footage of the Apollo missions on the moon, he ran to where he had been lying. "Here it is. Oh, damn."

"What is it?" Mel followed him, hopping two feet with each step, having to limit her strength so she didn't fall or land on her injured leg on impact and make it worse. When she reached him, he helped her slow down and pointed to the area in front of her.

The toolbag, with its sharp edges, was mostly stuck in the wall and wet with green dots that crawled out of the matter underneath like plasticine.

Since the handle was pointing up and not yet contaminated, Mel grabbed it and pulled. A smacking sound rang out, then the resistance was gone and she held the bag with the ceramic-reinforced skeleton in her hands. It was slime-covered enough for her to reflexively toss it away. Whatever the green stuff was, she had no desire to have it on her suit.

Tom looked up and then down again until his light met hers and Hongbo's on the small crater the toolbag had made. The edges were frayed and dark, slime came out of finger-thick pores on the sides of the open matter below the fibrils, and the bottom, 20 inches deep, was bright and reflective like glass, with a relatively smooth surface.

"It looks like we've uncovered something," she muttered, "What is it?"

Again a tremor went through the ground and almost threw her off her feet. A deep roar sounded and very slowly died away.

"I don't know, but I think Serenity is appreciating our presence less and less," Hongbo whispered.

As if on a silent command, they turned and shone their lights out into the darkness that weighed heavily on them, and for the first time Mel noticed the crushing loneliness that had settled in her heart.

27

They spent the next 30 minutes counting the thunderclaps and tremors, and found that there was indeed a consistent rhythm to them. First came the thunder, then the quake, although the two were so close together that the difference in time was hard to discern.

It happened every 11 minutes and 8 seconds, followed by a distant murmur that sounded in Mel's helmet as if she were holding a seashell to her ear, as she had done as a child. Her grandmother had explained to her that it was the sea that could be heard in it because the shell carried the sound of its homeland. Today she was sure that all parents or grandparents told young children this story.

With each cycle, it took 50 seconds for a growing amount of liquid to drip out of the hole and land where they had crashed. Some of it collected in the small crater Tom's toolbag had made. At least it looked like it, because they had moved away from it to avoid contact with the liquid.

"This must have come from the tunnel," Hongbo said as they shone their lights a few feet away at the spot where another shower had just come down, bringing significantly more of the black substance than that one before.

"And it's our fault," Tom grumbled sullenly. "I damaged the membrane of the chamber where we took refuge. Then we cut the second membrane that led up and apparently belongs to some kind of ventilation system. Now this stuff is flowing in here. Wherever 'here' is."

"You said it yourself: we took refuge in the chamber," Hongbo pointed out. "If that murderous substance hadn't come at us, it wouldn't have been necessary."

"It seems to be a vegetative body function, hardly something that served to kill us. Otherwise it wouldn't be happening again all the time now, always following the same rhythm."

"You're forgetting the green stuff on Selena's suit and face."

"I certainly haven't forgotten about that. But it occurred here, too, on the wound I caused." Tom sighed in frustration. "The good thing is, I haven't been able to detect any signs that Serenity is trying to kill us."

"What we do know is that this cavern is going to fill up eventually," Mel interjected, not wanting to give her colleagues' frustration a chance to manifest itself, along with their stress and anxiety, into a discussion that cost precious oxygen.

"Even if the rate at which the liquid comes in here increases, it will take forever to fill up," the Chinese woman said, looking up at the dripping hole 50 meters above their heads. "Maybe even a century."

There was a brief flash.

This also happened frequently, but not in a regular pattern like the thunder, tremors, and noise. Sometimes after a minute, other times after three, or sometimes even after five. They were brief flashes, like weather lightning of greater intensity, and were swallowed up by the dark fibrils of the cavern before the eye could comprehend what had happened. The first time, Mel had thought she was suffering from a visual disturbance. The second time, Tom had asked if they had also just seen that, and then they had begun to measure the intervals.

"Maybe the flashes are an attempt to find us," Tom reasoned. "Some optical instrument to track us."

"I don't recognize anything here that could be visually perceived."

"We have to move forward somehow," Mel decided. "Standing here making guesses based on too little data isn't going to give us any answers, I'm sure of that. We'd better see if there's an exit."

"Under the dark meadow-stuff, you mean?" asked Tom, frowning.

"Yes. Or do you have a better idea?"

"No, I haven't. Besides, we're still waiting to hear back from Houston."

They just stood there for a while, three white blobs in the middle of a world of darkness, which was disturbed shortly after by more of the lightning-like flickers.

"My suggestion is that we walk down the part we're standing on, one step apart from each other. Where it rises too steeply to stay on our feet, we turn around together and walk down another area."

Her colleagues nodded, then began to implement her suggestion, slowly taking one step at a time. Mel's leg hurt badly enough to overshadow her every thought and make her wish she could somehow take an ibuprofen tablet. But at least the extremely low gravity ensured that the stress on the injury was low and she could remain mobile. She didn't even want to imagine what it would be like to be condemned to lie in this place and wait for the oxygen gauge to slowly approach the red zone, or for her battery to give up the ghost and watch the place grow dark.

Even as the thought floated through her mind, she felt her injured leg give way, only to find neither leg had solid footing.

Shocked, she made a guttural sound as she felt herself being sucked down, hearing an unpleasant and familiar smacking sound, which was followed by even stronger suction. Instead of following her headlamps lighting the swaying meadow of fibrils in front of her, there was now something very different directly in front of her, passing by rapidly, on and on, sometimes dark red, sometimes a bit lighter, moist and soft like pudding with a skin over it.

Her injured leg bumped against resistance several times and acknowledged every contact with stabbing pain. There was a rustling around her and she heard voices.

"MEL!" *Tom's voice.*

"ARE YOU STILL THERE?" *Hongbo's voice.*

"Yeah," she groaned, "I got sucked into some other connection, I think."

"What do you see?" *Tom. That was Tom.*

"Is your suit integrity intact?" asked Hongbo worriedly.

"I guess so," Mel muttered, trying to ignore the wall whizzing by in front of her visor and focus on the HUD on the glass. "I'm not getting any warning messages. Oxygen normal, water level too. No problem with cooling."

"That's good." The Chinese woman sighed with relief.

"I'm in some kind of tube, like the one we fell through into the dark cavern." She tried not to think about what kind of landing she might be facing this time—and more importantly, *where*.

Talking about what she saw helped her not to get lost in the fear of possibly lying more seriously injured in another dark place soon. Alone. "According to the laser pulse meter, I reached a speed of almost thirty kilometers an hour. It's rushing so loudly that I can hardly hear you unless you scream."

"It's the wind again," Tom confirmed, more loudly. He sounded concerned, which did nothing to help ease her gloomy fears. "A suction effect, that's for sure. All the fibrils up here have aligned toward the hole you got sucked through, and we're even noticing it against our suits."

"Yes, it's gotten stronger," Hongbo confirmed. "What else can you—"

Mel didn't hear the rest, because something changed. She heard a whoosh! and collided with something that quickly gave way, slowing her down a bit in the process and leaving a slimy residue on her visor, which had slapped against it with such force she felt it on the back of her neck.

She was expecting to fall again into a nothingness of darkness, and frantically searched for something that her headlights could pick up, but there was no longer any pull on her body. Neither by airflow nor by gravity.

She soared, absolutely weightless, above a galaxy. She could not describe it any other way. The place she was in was huge, dwarfing even the dark cavern. The EMU unit on her back scraped across a thorny surface, and she was repelled by the momentum. The unit scraped across another area on the curved wall. Before her spread the galaxy—a complex structure of luminous dots, nebulae, and spiral arms that sparked and flashed. Some of the discharges, which reminded her of the birth of new stars, flickered or manifested as seconds-long glows. Others resembled collapsing neutron stars, dissolving in annihilating gamma-ray bursts that shot away from their poles. Some branched out, others were more purposeful. Sometimes short, sometimes long.

"This is..." She was at a loss for words. The entire spectacle stretched for dozens of meters, and only now did it occur to her that these were not dancing lights, but processes within a substance that made her think of dark-colored gelatin close enough that she could have touched it with an outstretched hand.

"What happened?" Tom asked. "Did you..."

"No," she breathed, wiping the last remnants of the slimy substance from her visor to see even more clearly. "I see a structure, thirty or forty meters in diameter. It's solid but moving a little. Something that looks like electrical discharges is going on in it."

"A brain? The central computer?" asked Hongbo.

"Possibly. In any case, it must be the center, or at least a location on the long axis, since there is no gravity here." She looked at the white lights in the gelatinous galaxy and noted that they were extremely slow. A glow here, a glow there, sometimes a dozen together. Then a connection from one side to the other, and a tree of white light that branched seemingly endlessly, spread out over seconds, and then died away—one branch after another. It was as if she were looking at a recording that had been set to one-tenth its natural flow rate.

"What else do you see?" Tom asked. "Is there someone there with you?"

"No. I don't think it's a cerebral structure either," she replied pensively. It was downright overwhelming to see the entire spectacle in front of her and process it at the same time. It simply seemed too big and too complex. "It doesn't look like firing neurons. Otherwise, I'd see a constant spectacle going on so fast that all I would see is a multi-layered flicker. This looks more like luminescent fluids moving through a dense vascular system, stopping to glow and then starting again, along different paths."

"And there's no one there?"

"No." Mel intercepted herself as the momentum that had thrown her out of the hole continued to propel her along the outer wall, turning her over onto her stomach. "As far as I can see, I'm alone, there's no one here either."

"I think we can assume by now that there is no life here except the ship itself," Tom radioed, sounding a little disappointed, but that didn't last long, "We have to get you back now. I'll follow behind, and—"

"No," she interrupted him. "I'm trying to get to you. Don't put yourselves in danger."

"He's right," Hongbo jumped to the German's defense. "You're hurt, so it stands to reason that you need support. I'll come to you and work with you to find a way out. If Zhigang, with Mission Control's help, comes up with a plan to get us out of here, we should be ready to head back."

"I don't know how that's going to work. The wind direction of the connecting hoses seems to go from the outer hull to the inside, not the other way around. So we're not going to make it back out using centrifugal forces."

"We don't *know* that," Tom pointed out. "We haven't seen very much yet. Every other step shows us something new. Who knows what's coming next? Hongbo, by the way, jumped into the hole and is on her way to you."

"She's not supposed to—"

"Too late," he interrupted her, his voice softening a bit. "And she's right, Mel. I'll be fine up here. Until I figure out how to help you, I'm going to take a closer look at the injury I inflicted on the tissue when I fell. Maybe I can salvage and refill some sample containers. I should have done that much sooner. If we could get just one of them back to Earth, that would be a big success for all of us."

"Take care of yourself. Especially, watch where you step."

"I will."

She focused again on the mysterious entity in front of her, which looked beautiful and creepy at the same time. Deep down, she knew she had penetrated to the core of what

Serenity was —its center. Whether it was a biological super-computer that controlled the many organic processes within the ship or something else entirely, her instincts told her that this was the most important place she could have found. So she should have been pleased, at least relieved, to have found what they had come here for.

But instead she had to admit to herself that she was merely afraid and felt terribly lonely. Never before in their six-and-a-half-year journey had she felt so alone and isolated, so far away from everything that was alive and that she would have perceived as familiar. The ominous strangeness of her surround-ings, the mystical lights that prevailed here, and the fact that she was in a sealed suit that protected her from the high levels of carbon dioxide in the air and a whole bundle of gases that over-whelmed her meter, all told her that she did not belong here. She was as uninvited as she was unwelcome, had wreaked havoc and done damage with her mere presence. Curiosity had served as her axe and everything foreign was a tree.

She felt cold.

A light approached from the side and illuminated a circular opening from which red flaps of skin hung down like the scraps of a snake that had shed its skin. Drops of a dark liquid poured onto the gelatinous structure below and reddish edges appeared where they hit, seeming to glow from within.

Then a shapeless white figure with arms and legs and a huge helmet appeared, was thrown out of the hole, and slowed down before hitting the galaxy.

"Hongbo," she said.

"Mel?" The Chinese woman looked around at what she could see with her wandering headlights until they blinded Mel.

"Yes, here I am. Be careful with your movements."

"My foot is stuck." The glare disappeared as the taikonaut

writhed and groped for a piece of skin wrapped around her boot, holding her down like a creeper.

"Hold on, I'm coming to you."

Mel rode out the next twist of her body after her EMU caught on one of the wall's short spine extensions, sending her into a renewed impulse of movement, and then she reached out with the rubberized insides of her gloves for two protrusions that turned out to be massive. Using them, she turned slowly and used one foot to find another spike from which to push off in Hongbo's direction. Her colleague was still nibbling at what appeared to be tough tissue.

"Wait," Mel repeated. "Wait until I get there."

"I'm working on it. Feels like rubber, so I think I can pull it over the top of my boot." Hongbo's voice sounded strained from the effort.

"No, you have to be careful so you—"

It was too late. Mel had barely made it halfway along the wall when the Chinese woman pulled the skin off her boot and released it like a slingshot. The impulse this triggered sent Hongbo into a backward motion, and although she didn't flail her arms like a novice, but instinctively held herself steady so as not to tumble, she couldn't catch herself. She hit the gelatinous surface of the galaxy image and her back curved around the surface as if she were stuck.

"—so you don't get into trouble," Mel finished with a sigh. "Can you move?"

"I think so." Hongbo grunted in frustration and began to lift her legs and arms. Viscous slime shone in Mel's spotlight, forming thick threads between her colleague's suit and the transparent surface. The grunting turned into an angry growl. "I can't. I can't do it."

"I'll come to you," she assured her, and could feel beads of sweat pressing out of the pores of her skin on her back and forehead. "I just need to find a way to fix myself, and then maybe I can pull you up."

Mel floated up to the nearest spinous process in the curved wall, concentrating only on her impending handhold—with which she braked and turned around—a few feet from the hole. Then she pushed off backward until she saw the opening dragging along below her, and was pushed down slightly by the air current. She reached both hands in and squeezed them apart like a clamp until her movements stopped, then felt for the bump where the skin had curled up that had been Hongbo's undoing and wrapped it around her foot. Examining it, she finally pulled on it, drawing her knee to her chest, and then stretched out toward the Chinese woman as if hanging from the ceiling.

"I'll have you in a moment," she announced, only now noticing that the taikonaut was covered in green spots.

"No," the taikonaut replied. Their faces were less than two handbreadths apart—their visors almost touching. "Don't touch me."

"I'm pulling you out!" insisted Mel, knowing full well that it was foolish. The rational part of her mind, which she had trained all her life to keep at the upper hand, saw a woman stuck on the pulsating organ of an alien formation, as if strapped to a torture wheel, unable to move. She saw the alien green things that had covered Selena, only here they seemed to be multiplying much faster, approaching from all directions on the surface of the structure, like slugs. Things were more aggressive here than outside in the tunnel, and the things were swarming on the taikonaut like ants on fallen ripe fruit.

"It's too late for me," Hongbo stated. Her expression remained unmoved. "I made a mistake and now I can't get away. Until we know what the green slugs are all about, you can't risk them attacking you too."

"I'm sorry," Mel replied. All she had to do was reach out,

so close was she to her colleague, and she would have had good leverage to pull her off the central structure provided their combined strength would have been enough. "You only came here for me."

"You were going to stop me. Besides, you would have done the same for me."

"I would have."

For a few breaths they looked silently into each other's eyes, exchanging messages that needed no words.

"You should try to get back to Tom now. I think the airflow in the hole has subsided. My plan was for us to use the rock clamps to climb up through the connecting channel," Hongbo suggested. "I'll stay here and keep you guys posted."

Mel knew what that meant. Hongbo would be left alone to die—either from the green slugs, or from lack of oxygen. "I—"

"It's okay. You're a good commander, Melody Adams." Hongbo hesitated. Then something in her expression relaxed and she wrestled a smile from herself. The next words that left her mouth sounded so mundane and yet were so pregnant with meaning that Mel remembered, despite her emotional distress, that all of this was being recorded. "I liked your leadership style."

"It's been an honor working with you," she replied, stretching. "Eye to eye."

"Eye to eye." Hongbo tilted her head slightly.

"We'll use the hours we have left to find a way to get you—"

The Chinese woman's eyes twitched.

"What is it?" asked Mel in alarm.

"My suit reports that its integrity has been disrupted and the air composition is becoming toxic." It sounded like a simple recitation of protocol. "Carbon dioxide levels are rising and—"

"What?"

"Something feels wet on my leg, I—"

"I see it," Mel said, swallowing as she saw the hole on her colleague's left thigh. More followed where the first green slugs had been sitting, apparently eating through the material and falling onto the skin beneath. A short time later, Hongbo's EMU was riddled with holes and the straggling slugs were making their way right onto her skin. "They got into your suit. If you... Hongbo?"

She looked through her colleague's visor, only to find that her eyes were wide open, as was her mouth, into which one of the slugs was crawling at that moment.

Suffocated by carbon dioxide, said the astronaut in her. *A cruel death,* lamented the colleague in her, who had become something like a friend of Hongbo's and would have liked to scream at this injustice.

"Tom?" she radioed, after swallowing hard and backing away so as not to come into contact with anything that looked like sticky slime or was green.

"I'm here. What's going on? What got into her suit?" the German asked tensely.

"Hongbo is dead." The statement was a fact, and the next hammer blow to her chest.

The silence on the line weighed heavily.

28

"How?" It was Zhigang's choked voice.

"Suffocation. Carbon dioxide poisoning, it happened very quickly." Mel pulled herself in front of the hole, testing the strength of the air coming through. It was no longer an outright storm, a force that made her a pawn, but rather a tepid rush of air. "Tom, you've got to stay away from those green things. They've eaten through her suit and seem intent on decomposing her body."

"Immune cells," the doctor replied sadly. "I was afraid of that."

"What exactly are you talking about?" Zhigang asked, needing to clear his throat twice to get the words out.

"Every living thing has some form of immune response to protect itself from harm. In some places, they respond more quickly and in a more focused way than in others. One example is the primary immune system in the human gut, which consists of lymphocytes in the intestinal villi and is the first barrier of entry for substances that want to enter the blood. Seeing the size of Serenity, I don't find it surprising that we can see its form of immune cells with the naked eye, although even then they would be huge compared to, say, their microscopic human counterparts. But they could also be much larger cytoleukins like interleukin that coordinate the actual immune system. But there I would expect more of a fluid, not clusters of cells like these."

Mel tuned out Tom's voice. Pulling out her rock clamps, somewhat reminiscent of the ice picks used by extreme climbers, she grimly jammed them into the fabric of the connecting channel through which she had come so she could work her way up. Her colleague seemed to need to intellectualize the problem, and she couldn't blame him. She noted that it did her good to punch in the clamps and see reddish inflammatory reactions forming around the injuries, while the lack of gravity allowed her to easily pull herself upward. It was a primitive, stupid instinct she was following, but she was pretty sure it was keeping her from giving in to the panic that was still trying to spread outside her controlled mind and was growing in strength.

Blow by blow, she struggled further up, using her arms to brace herself against the air, which was not comparable to real mountain climbing, but still offered enough resistance to make her feel it. Also, the connecting tube was much longer than she had expected. Soon she lost all sense of time and space because she saw the same, finely veined red tissue in front of her, which from time to time was seized by twitches that went wave-like from bottom to top.

Could this be a reaction to the injuries she'd inflicted on Serenity? At this point, she no longer cared. Three of her colleagues had died, and if it had been an intelligent being with good intentions, it would have communicated with them long ago. Maybe it wasn't the worst idea to slowly fight back and make sure they got out in one piece and no one else had to die.

"Stay away from the green slugs," she repeated after a

while, during which Tom and Zhigang had continued talking without her paying any attention to them.

"I've isolated one in the sample container," the German replied. "It certainly won't get through that material."

"I'll be right with you, I think." She stuck her head back and shined her lights upward, where darkness settled like a lid over the tube-like connection she was climbing through. On the radio, she could hear Tom breathing heavily, and then two points of light appeared in the darkness. She dropped her chin before her visor darkened.

"I see you!" blurted Tom, audibly relieved.

Forgetting her exhaustion, she climbed the rest of the way, and breathed a liberating sigh when she felt hands under her arms pulling her up. Following an impulse, she embraced him —or he, her. There was no physical warmth in it, since they were separated by their suits, like two marshmallows with stubby arms. But this simple human gesture of cohesion and closeness was enough to cover, like a small band-aid, the shock that the sight of the dying Hongbo had caused in her.

"Are you all right?" she asked as their visors touched and they closed their eyes for a moment and just held each other.

"Yeah," he muttered. "I distracted myself from the urge to keep looking over my shoulder to dispel the darkness by keeping the wound open that my toolbag caused. It wasn't particularly hard, because the thrombocytes—or whatever the equivalent is—seem to work much slower here than on the hull."

"Why?"

"Because I believe that what I have involuntarily exposed is part of a neural stratum. Definitely an excitation conduction of some kind, maybe even electrical."

"Mel? Tom?" Zhigang called out.

"We are here," she said softly, reluctantly opening her eyes. It was as if she was forced to open herself again to a world that had produced nothing but cruelty in the last few hours. Accordingly, it felt exhausting.

"Mission Control has decided that we will get you out at all costs." There was a long pause and Mel exchanged a questioning look with Tom before the Chinese man continued, "There is not insignificant tension at home, and the entire mission could be blown because a war in Taiwan is imminent. I suggested that we use the thrusters."

"What?! That would do damage that..." Mel faltered and thought about it. *Pangaea* lay in a sort of trough on the surface of Serenity with an elevation directly behind it that was a little over 20 meters high. If Zhigang turned on the Raptors, and only enough to allow the forward Dracos to match the thrust, it would probably cost the rest of their cold gas supplies, but also burn a pretty big hole in the alien ship's hull.

"Isn't there any other way?" asked Tom. "Even if we could make it out of here, that would burn all the fuel we have left."

"But, you would be out of there," Zhigang countered, and Mel understood what he was trying to say.

Would I rather die out there than in here? she pondered and was able to answer the question clearly for herself. *Yes.*

"No," she said instead. "You're going home, and we're going to try to get ourselves out before departure. If we haven't made it through the airlock in," she glanced at her oxygen gauge, "eight hours and ten minutes, you'll cast off and set the solar orbit programming in motion. There should still be enough supplies to last you the two and a half years."

"Four and a half," he corrected her gently. "I'd have to ration."

"We'll think of something. Stay where you are for now." She turned to Tom. "The fabric in these tubes is extremely soft. Did you pick up our tools that were scattered here after we fell?"

"Yes." The ESA astronaut nodded and made room to shine his light on an area of shiny objects farther back. "I found almost everything."

"What do you say," she asked, smiling, "we wing it a little?"

"What were you thinking about?"

She looked up at the hole in the ceiling, from which black liquid was still dripping. "That's our only way out, and after that we'd have the problem with the hull. Maybe our monofilament blades can cut through the polyp? But one thing at a time."

"How are we going to get up there?"

"Let's see what we have." In her mind, she added, *We could have used Hongbo's engineering mind. Or Gabriella.* "We'll record everything and send Houston an inventory list. They'll come up with something then."

So, they did exactly that in the minutes that followed, which stretched to more than half an hour. They made a detailed inventory of their tools and materials, took appropriate pictures with their cameras after sorting out defective or damaged components, and then waited to see what the brightest minds in Houston and around the world would come up with.

"I wonder if we should have done this sooner," she said as they both lay at the beginning of the bulge, staring up where the liquid splashed, still dripping from the opening above.

"Instead of exploring Serenity?" asked Tom.

"Yes. Now we know no more than before and are one less. I know I shouldn't do this, but Hongbo wouldn't have died if I hadn't had the urge to go on and explore more, even though the signs had already been visible that it was just fraught with danger. Selena should have been warning sign enough."

"I miss them both, too, as you can only miss someone you worked with for years on humanity's biggest project and then lived with under extreme conditions," he countered. "But it wasn't your decision to plunge into the opening and get sucked in. If you remember correctly, we were looking for an exit because we were stuck here, like we are now."

"I wanted so much for Serenity to be what I'd hoped it would be." She snorted sadly. "Instead, it's a distant grave, far from everything we love, and has caused division at home to boot."

"No, the politicians have done that without any help from us, because they have a lot of experience with that, believe me."

She wanted to say something back but kept quiet.

After a while, it was Tom again who picked up the conversation. "Your discovery down there, can you show me the footage?"

Mel considered and then nodded as she thought about her tablet, still intact in her thigh pocket. The display was broken in two places, but otherwise it worked fine. She checked the connection with her helmet camera system and pulled down the files via Bluetooth before finding the correct spot and handing it to him. She didn't watch with him, not wanting to accidentally witness Hongbo's end again.

"Amazing," said Tom. "Really amazing." He kept making short sounds, like a sigh of relief or a fascinated grumble. "This looks like a primary thinking organ, with constantly changing connections and states of excitation in different areas."

"That's what I thought." Mel let the charcoal gray sway of the fibrillar meadow at the end of her headlight cone carry her away, then turned off the lights to save battery. Tom did the same a short time later.

"But you're right. In a brain—and I think this would also apply to an analog—the electrical impulses would have to be much more varied, more numerous, and, above all, in a faster sequence. Our brains are highly active all the time, even though the myth *still* persists that we only use ten percent or less—complete nonsense that particularly annoys the chemist in me. Closer to the truth would be the statement that only ten percent of the capacity is active at any one time, but the areas addressed change quickly depending on where we turn our head, what we are feeling, or what sort of task is at hand. When we're driving, everything in the brain lights up like Chinese fireworks. But this one, in your video, looks more like a lighting array as a slow-motion work of art."

"I don't know what it is, either, but Serenity doesn't seem to like being touched by anything."

"At least now we can agree that there don't seem to be any aliens on board, and it's not a ship," Tom proposed. "Serenity itself is the ship, and the creature, *and* the alien."

"I'd always imagined a first contact differently," she whispered with closed eyes, feeling a lonely tear running down her right cheek. She would have liked to wipe it away, but even that was impossible.

"An exchange of mathematical formulas as the language of the universe? A long period of deciphering alien signal sequences? I guess you weren't the only one." He nudged her to hand the tablet back, and she tucked it away securely before they lay in silence side by side for a long time in the darkness so impenetrable that she saw minor sparks caused by the lower intraocular pressure that was a direct result of low gravity.

Houston's answer came 51 minutes in, at a time when Mel was on the verge of nodding off and feeling guilty for just lying there, conserving oxygen and battery instead of getting creative and playing around with her own ideas.

"Mel, Tom, it's Bernard," began the audio recording Zhigang had relayed to them.

"Hello, CAPCOM," she murmured, turning the lights back on.

"We've worked out a simple plan to get you out. If we use your current data and there's still 0.8 bar of pressure, your best chance is to improvise a potato cannon. Now before you roll your eyes, hear me out. Our teams have analyzed all the components and fill levels and assembled one with the same equipment you have, and in less than twenty-five minutes. So you should be able to do it in twice that time."

Tom and Mel looked at each other in astonishment, and then set to work following Bernard's instructions.

"We have an MMU to take off," she noted, pointing to the heavy knapsack on her back that contained oxygen and cold gas cartridges that powered the maneuvering thrusters.

"We'll take mine."

"What does the level look like on your end?"

"Oxygen at seventy-four percent, cold gas at sixty."

"I have eighty-one and seventy-four left," she said, twisting her arm so he couldn't read the display on her forearm. "So we'll use mine. I can last an hour with the suit's emergency supplies."

"Is that an order?" he asked with a grin.

"If you want it to be." She smiled, too, and waved him over. "Give me a hand getting this heavy thing off. Actually, I'm being selfish, because my back will be happy to be free of it."

"That's the Melody we know."

He came around her and undid the buckles and connecting latches until, a few minutes later, he removed the clunky, boxy MMU and placed it next to the tools. Then they opened it and took out the two cold gas cartridges. They had to empty one of them by sticking one end into the bottom and holding it so that the main point of application pointed vertically downward, and then opened the discharge valve.

Once the entire gas supply was depleted, they took the small plasma cutter that had been part of their exploration equipment and cut both ends of the cartridge to make a cylinder, which they grafted onto the other cylinder. Mel, meanwhile, removed the polymer clamp that secured the MMU's extra headlamp, which had normally been over her shoulder, and shortened it with pliers to the dimension Bernard had specified. Then she slipped the improvised sleeve over the overlapping part of both cartridges and made sure that the control cable was pinched but not disconnected.

Each step took what felt like an eternity, as their inflated gloves gave them motor-control and dexterity only slightly above that of stone golems. By the time they'd stuck one of their long-handled climbing hooks into the open end of the top gas canister and carefully sprayed the rim with sealing foam that quickly spread like ochre cauliflower, more than 40 minutes had passed. The foam came from two small bottles, as they each carried one to plug holes in the solid parts of the suit where the emergency adhesive patches didn't work. In the end there was nothing left, since they were small quantities intended for highly exceptional situations.

Then it was a matter of waiting for the foam to finish curing. Designed for the vacuum and its low temperatures, it took several minutes instead of a few seconds here at just above zero degrees Celsius, according to Bernard.

"We have an honest chance," Tom stated as they waited and stared up at the tiny looking hole.

"That's more than enough."

"I think so, too." He smiled away his concern and pointed upward. "I was a member of the rocket club at my university in Osnabrück—the only one who wasn't an engineer or a physicist. But they took me in because I knew the cool people who threw good parties. I don't think I was particularly helpful, but I tried hard and got to start our first project, a nitrous-oxide-powered rocket with five hundred and forty newtons of thrust. All the nerds were way too keyed up, so I guess that's why nobody else dared."

"So, did the launch go well?" she asked, grateful for a little distraction.

"The launch did, but I hit a pigeon that crossed the flight path just perfectly. Such a little thing. Ended up in a rain of feathers and little bits of blood, and deflected the missile so that it described an unhealthy circular arc and slammed into a row of trees twenty yards away. Gave us quite a scare." Tom looked at her and winked. "So if anyone can aim and hit a small target, it's me."

"That's the lesson you learned?" She had to laugh. It was almost an expression of detachment.

"Of course. I'm known as an optimist, after all."

"I'll do the aiming," Mel decided with a grin, and at the same moment the timer on her forearm display beeped. "Done."

"Now for the launching device. I suggest we cut a hole in the grass and stick the end of the lower gas cartridge in."

"That's how we'll do it. I'll double-check that the climbing hook is exactly centered."

Mel took pains to verify that the climbing hook was pointing up and the stem was pointing vertically down. The slightest deviation, an angle of a mere few degrees, could mean that their improvised projectile missed the hole by several feet. They were striving for a lucky shot, 1 in 50—borrowing some of Tom's optimism—and she didn't want to neglect any factor. Only then did she fasten the safety cable around the T-piece of the climbing hook with a triple-cross knot and lay it in loose circles next to the made-in-space potato cannon until the total of 60 meters had been rolled up.

"If that isn't sitting straight, I don't know what is," Tom commented, looking at her handiwork.

She took a step back and nodded. Then she pulled out her climbing hook and handed it to the German.

"What am I supposed to do with this?"

"Put it in your belt—you go first." She also took off her monofilament knife and sheath and pressed it into his hand.

"Out of the question. You go first."

"No, I still have to put my MMU back on. You can tie the rope on properly. I was always better than you at the rope-climbing exercises, remember?"

"You've made sure I won't forget," he grumbled tersely. "All right, then. I'll climb up, check the fit of the climbing hook, and then you'll follow."

"Don't forget to use your MMU if you realize the rope isn't supporting you. With a little luck, it might be enough to shoot you up a few feet with its cold gas thrust, like a jetpack."

"But you don't have—"

"Go ahead. That's an order. At least I'll be a lot lighter. With so little gravity, I'll catch up to you in no time."

She made a waving hand gesture as if to scare him away, and then knelt beside the upward-pointing potato cannon. Again and again she made minor changes to the alignment, tiny ones, only a millimeter here and there, that could decide between success... or, failure in the form of both their demises. Then she pressed the command for maximum thrust on the control unit of her MMU. Within a second, the cold gas flowing into the converted tube created such intense pressure that the climbing hook shot upward with an audible fump! The safety cable flew with it, uncoiling like a snake and getting shorter and shorter.

Tense, they both shone their lights upward, arching their backs, and then the climbing hook disappeared into the darkness, which they could no longer illuminate.

"YES!" Tom exulted. "THE FUCKING THING WORKED!"

Surprised, Mel grinned, and laughed as the German rushed up to her and wrapped her in his arms so tightly that their visors slapped against each other.

"Devil woman, you! I don't know how you did it, but damn, that was a good shot!"

"There's even some cable left over." She pointed to the last meter lying in the grass. The rest hung as a taut line in the darkness between them and the ceiling. "Come on, Doc."

"What's the knife for?" he asked as he put his hands on the cable. "I have my own."

"Two is better than one," she said, quickly adding, "Besides, I don't want to accidentally cut the cable."

"Ahh." Tom looked at her and his gaze lingered on hers for a long time.

"See you in a bit." She nodded at him and finally he reluctantly turned away.

"See you in a bit."

Mel watched as he made the first testing pulls on their improvised climbing rope and finally began the ascent. At a measly 0.2 g, it looked almost easy, even though the 50 kilograms of weight he was carrying was still at least 10 kilograms, in addition to his estimated 75 kilos, of which a fifth remained. So his arms had to pull a load of 25 kilos, which was not exactly light, for a distance of 50 meters.

They barely spoke as he struggled ever upward, occasionally making a groan or other, more mournful sounds. At some point, the rope began to shake.

"Are you all right?" she asked, seeing that the white figure in her headlights had stopped moving.

"The rope gave a little," he replied chokingly. "Damn! I think the climbing hook is coming loose."

"How much further?"

"Five meters according to my HUD."

"You need the boost from your MMU. Go!" she urged him.

"If I do—"

"GO!" she yelled at him, falling on her butt in relief as she watched the whitish clouds of gas shoot out of his satchel. Tom's silhouette soared until the darkness swallowed the glow of his lamps and shrank to a tiny circle.

"I'm in," he announced breathlessly, and then, sounding dejected rather than relieved, he repeated, "I'm in."

"Good," she said. "That's good."

29

"How could you do that, Mel?" asked Tom, sniffling. "How *could* you?"

"You don't think I'm going to let Zhigang fly *Pangaea* back alone, do you?" she replied, crying so quietly that her colleagues couldn't hear it over the radio. She was reasonably proud to sound determined and calm.

"It's obvious that you don't want to let a Chinese be the only one to return home," the taikonaut joked, and the fact that he didn't voice any sentimentalities, but made an ironic crack—which didn't at all fit the Zhigang they had worked with—was something like the last blossom on the tree of knowledge of life and death. Her co-pilot also realized that there was no more salvation for her, no encouraging words, no promises, no matter how unrealistic.

She was lost, and they all knew it. Paradoxically, there was something liberating about this fact, and it caused a relaxation that she would not have thought possible to spread beneath the layer of fatalistic grief. Her colleague and friend was now climbing somewhere above her through the organic connecting tube between the hull and the lung in which she sat—that designation was her first-best theory, based on the fibrils, even though the contractions of the walls were manageable. She imagined that each grip with the two climbing hooks was easier for him because the centrifugal force helped him out the farther he got from Serenity's core.

"At least now I have time to think about it."

"Time, huh?" said Tom. "You fucking hero! I'll never forgive you for that."

"You have family and you're a doctor. You can still save the lives of others," she replied. "Why don't you let me have this one moment? Besides, I lied. My oxygen system had a leak and I would have only had two hours left. Your chances were better either way. So it was a rational decision, too, if it makes you feel any better."

"No, but I still thank you from the bottom of my heart."

"You would have done the same for me, so I had to beat you to it."

"I've prepared the airlock and I'll be ready to get you out," Zhigang said.

"Thank you. Soon I'll be back in the first chamber. There's a lot of liquid here, but nothing is underwater." Tom cleared his throat. "You got two hours left, Mel?"

"Yes. For me it's maybe enough for three, I have a pretty slow pulse and therefore probably a slow metabolism. So let's say two and a half hours, during which I can still enjoy listening to the two of you sitting together in *Pangaea*."

Her heart warmed at the thought and her lips parted into a smile all on their own. She felt that she had done the right thing and was free of regret. In a way, it was the nicest feeling she'd had in a long time because it had nothing in common with uncertainty, her closest companion in years.

"Slow metabolism," Tom snorted in amusement and fell abruptly silent.

"What happened?" she and Zhigang asked at the same time.

"Is everything all right?" Mel continued.

"That's the answer!" blurted the doctor.

"*What's* the answer?"

"Slow metabolism. Mel. That thing *is* a freaking brain, and it might work the same way ours does. Think about it."

"I'm not following you right now," she stammered, surprised by his sudden enthusiasm.

"What is the limiting factor of interstellar travel?" he asked like an enthusiastic schoolteacher.

"Radiation, fuel and its mass, food, mental health—," she began to list.

"Time!" he interrupted her. "The most important limiting factor is time. Radiation becomes dangerous based on the length of exposure time. Food becomes scarce over the period of time for which it must last. The longer the thrust phase, the more propellant and reaction mass must be carried, the more the total mass of the spacecraft increases, and the more propellant and reaction mass is needed in turn. The longer the journey, the more severe the expected psychological problems of the crew due to isolation and monotony. *Time* is the red line under any equation for successful interstellar travel. What if we are mayflies and Serenity is human?"

Mel was silent for a moment, thinking about it.

"You mean Serenity is extremely long-lived? That makes sense, yes."

"And long-lived animals are those that have the slowest metabolism. A dwarf shrew's heart beats up to twelve hundred times per minute—the fastest known pulse of any mammal. It rarely lives more than a year. A human's heart beats sixty to eighty times per minute, and we can live well into our eighties. Greenland sharks have a pulse of about fifteen beats per minute and live up to four hundred years. A being with a slow metabolism consumes itself more slowly."

"Serenity must be unimaginably ancient to travel between the stars," Mel concluded, nodding in understanding. "So with reverse bio-logic—pardon the bad joke—it probably has an extremely slow metabolism."

"The tunnel we came into could be a major artery and the fluid would then be blood pumped through it every eleven minutes."

Tom's voice almost gave out in the explosiveness of his realization.

"How the air system works—I have no idea, but you saw its brain. The firing neurons. We thought that wasn't possible because it was way too slow, but it's merely the time slice in which we're looking at it. To a fly that sees two hundred frames per second, we humans must look like giants doing everything, even jogging, in super slow motion. To us, with our measly eighteen frames per second, the fly looks like a frantic little thing moving in a totally choppy way, but that's an illusion of our slow image processing, just like the first film recordings in the nineteenth century."

"You mean Serenity couldn't communicate with us because we're way too fast for its data processing?" This time it was Zhigang who translated Mel's question into words.

"Exactly. I think we're houseflies that flew to it and sat on its hand. Now maybe it's caught on and is about to take a closer look—or swat at us—and we're ready to head on back, thinking it didn't notice us." Tom snorted. "Why didn't I think of this much sooner?"

"Because someone kept dying and we were in the scariest chamber of horrors in the solar system?" suggested Mel, suddenly jumping up. "The dreams! What else did you call it?"

"A frozen moment drifting through space," he said almost reverently.

"Yes! Each dream was very long but felt like a split second. That's why I never made sense of them. But that part was common to each of them and each of us."

"Do you think Serenity really wanted to communicate with us through dreams?"

"Yes. We only reckon with the possibilities of cold technology and mathematics, but what if there is a non-material method of transmission that is much faster and not disturbed by cosmic forces? Serenity and its creators could be so far ahead of us that they could... No!" She shook her head. "They must be enormously far ahead of us to create something like this here. So surely they know better methods for this creature to send data back to them."

"If so, we would have something in common with the aliens out there: the ability to dream," Zhigang concluded.

"It tells us even more," Tom noted. "That dreams, and therefore brains, are the norm as an overarching complex structure for data processing bio-algorithmic systems, just as they are for us on Earth."

"I'll try to find out."

"How are you going to do that?" Tom asked.

"By dreaming and this time understanding what is happening."

"Apparently, a human sleep cycle is not enough to grasp even a complete thought of Serenity. That's the whole point, isn't it, which is why our attempts at communication have all failed? The only frequency on which it can send and receive seems to be dreams, for which we are unsuited because of our housefly existence. Our time horizons simply do not coincide."

"I'm dead tired and could sleep forever," she countered.

"But you're running low on oxygen—even with your supposedly slow metabolism."

"That's right." She smiled and got to her feet. "There's still a lot of oxygen down here, though."

"No, it's too dangerous."

"Too dangerous for someone who only has a little more than two hours to live?"

30

"I guess we can't dissuade you, can we?" sighed Tom.

"No." Mel began scanning the ground for the dark hole she had fallen into and climbed out of. With the unchanged meadow of fibrils, everything around her looked identical.

"If eight hours of sleep wasn't enough to capture a Serenity thought, why would ten hours make a difference?"

"Maybe ten hours is enough for that one thought."

"And then?"

"Then I would have been the first woman in history who talked to an alien," she remarked lightly, but without laughter.

"Who *listened* to an alien."

"Wouldn't you want to know what that one thought was like? Wouldn't it be a crowning finale to a life dedicated to the stars?" she asked To—and herself, too.

"Yes," he admitted after a while. "I think that says it."

Mel found the entrance to the connecting tunnel that ended in Serenity's brain, and frowned as she saw in the light of her lamps the dark red injuries she had inflicted on the tissue with her knife and climbing hook. At the time, it had seemed to her that there was no alternative to saving herself, driven by Hongbo's gruesome demise. Now, however, it seemed to her like a crime, committed by the small-mindedness of human emotions, which were too often characterized by reactionism.

The fact that she was now going back was like a circle for her, closure, and reinforcing the calm inside her. No more fighting for survival, no more worrying about her colleagues and friends. Zhigang and Tom would make it, she was sure. She didn't have to worry about anything anymore, because her journey no longer led into the unknown, but could be planned. She could read on her forearm display how many minutes of life she had left, and freely choose how to spend them. It was amazing how quickly life lost its heaviness when the fear of the unknown disappeared.

"I'm switching off now," Mel said as she sat down on the edge of the hole and dropped her legs in. "This is a road I want to walk alone."

And not distract you two from what you need to do to save yourselves, she added in thought. *You must be in tune with yourselves and each other, focused. Not with your dying commander.*

"I don't know what to say, Mel." Tom was sobbing openly now.

"You don't have to say anything. I am at peace. I have one last wish."

"Anything!"

"Make it home, both of you. Promise me."

"I promise," Zhigang was the first to reply, and Tom followed shortly after, when he found his voice again.

Mel turned off her radio link and took a deep breath before dropping into the opening.

All right, Serenity. Let's talk.

This time it was not a real fall like the first time. No brute suction seized her and pulled her into the depths like an invisible maelstrom. Her suit was able to measure strange pressure differences of up to 0.5 bar and the temperature rose slightly, but otherwise she slid down as if through a chute, following several twists and turns and slowing down the more she touched the injured skin and the deeper she got.

As soon as she noticed the first flashes of light, she spread her legs and slowed her movements even more, pressing her boots against the walls. The weightlessness was already perceptible, and without any residual momentum, it was easy for her to push herself down out of the hole without falling uncontrollably onto Serenity's brain and thus into the death trap.

The size and complexity of the organ, which spread hugely beneath her, once again took her breath away. She had to actively turn away from it to avoid staring open-mouthed for minutes at the many flashes and bluish trees that formed and faded again. Not wanting to waste her remaining oxygen, she focused on the cones of light from her helmet lamps and searched for Hongbo.

Shocked, she realized that her colleague had disappeared. She should have been lying right underneath her, covered in the green slugs, stuck there by the ugly slime. But the skin of the gelatinous tissue was perfectly smooth and showed no traces of the deceased taikonaut.

With her throat suddenly parched, Mel shimmied to the right and continued to search the surface until she came upon something that caught her attention—a bright glimmer below the transparent tissue, briefly illuminated by an electrical pulse deep in the neural structure below.

"Hongbo!" she gasped as the powerful lights of her helmet fell on the silhouette of the Chinese woman who lay there as if trapped in time by amber, with pale skin, broken eyes, and open mouth, deformed into a silent scream. She wore no clothes and her arms and legs were splayed at similar angles. Her suit and MMU were missing, as was her multi-functional underwear. Hair stood out from her head, matchstick short but separated, as if someone had split each hair from the others and pulled it up.

Mel searched her skin for injuries, signs of burst capillaries, inflammation, necrosis—anything. But she looked unharmed, except for the corpse pallor.

"Hongbo," she repeated, catching herself raising a hand as if she could touch her colleague, as if her death was just a terrible misunderstanding, something that had never happened. She looked so normal.

Blue pulses came to life under the Chinese woman's body, approaching from all sides like electromagnetic eels pouncing on their food. They collided with each other directly under Hongbo and combined into a discharge that caused a short-lived flash. At the same moment, the corpse's right hand moved along with its arm in a copy of Mel's gesture from before.

"What...?" she breathed, unsure whether to be horrified or fascinated. Her colleague's eyes remained lifeless, without any sparkle in them. The hand movement was slow and persistent, as if she were struggling to move through the viscous mass in which she was trapped. But, without a doubt, she had moved.

"Are you communicating with me?" she asked aloud, her voice echoing in her helmet. She wanted to run away, yet was spellbound like a rabbit before a snake. "What is this? Is she some kind of medium for you? What have you done with her?"

For minutes, nothing happened. The brain's electrical pulses returned to their normal, slow network of complex connections and discharges.

Is it just imitating me? That's not a sign of intelligence, she thought. It's a sign that it can perceive me. But *how?* There are no sensory organs here. Does it sense my presence? But then how can it recognize something as specific as a raised hand and imitate the gesture exactly?

"Do you see out of Hongbo's eyes?" She decided to test the idea and raised a hand with four fingers.

Again it took until the blue eels approached from all directions and culminated into a flash under Hongbo. Again she raised a hand, this time with four fingers.

Mel turned around, her back to the giant thinking organ and held up her forearm display to see the body in the reflection. Then she raised a hand again, this time with three fingers so that her body blocked the view.

Again the eels came, again there was a flash after seemingly endless time, and again Hongbo raised a hand, but this time without fingers showing, in an imitation of Mel's left arm with the forearm display.

It sees the arm, but not the fingers, which I cover with my body, Mel concluded. *So you see through the body's eyes.*

She turned back around, trying not to surrender to the horror that she was dealing with a body-snatching scene that might as well have come from a horror movie. But such movies were highly irrational and based on irrational interpretations of things that humans did not understand.

"So one more try. Are you a mirror, or a thinking mind?" she asked, slowly raising both hands, showing three fingers with one and one with the other. Then she clenched her fists, waited, and showed four fingers with one hand. Then she repeated the same with two fingers and one, without the single hand after that.

Again it took an agonizingly long time for the eels to come, before she saw the flash.

Hongbo raised both hands and showed two fingers with one, one with the other. It clenched its fists and then showed three fingers with one hand.

"Two plus one makes three." Mel gulped. "You understand me very well. And you're capable of doing the math."

Suddenly, she remembered something. Hastily, she checked to see if her camera's live uplink was still working and recording everything to send automatically to *Pangaea* at regular intervals.

It's working. They can see everything I see.

Another look at the HUD... *Audio, too.*

She looked up again and noticed that a depression had opened up, right beside Hongbo. Outlines roughly resembling the silhouette of a human formed in the jelly-like surface of the massive brain, and the Chinese woman's hands moved in slow gestures that could indicate a wave of invitation.

Come here. Mel licked her lips and swallowed. The sight of Hongbo's moving corpse was eerie and sent one cold shiver after another down her spine. But fear could not take over because something even more haunting took over: Curiosity.

"How do you know that gesture?" she asked. After a minute, Hongbo beckoned her again, and Mel would have preferred to capitulate to her pulsating adrenaline and flee.

Everything about her scares me. Her eyes are empty, her skin has the pallor of a corpse, and she has been taken over by an alien. Is that even the right word? What would I do if it were not a dead person?

She looked at her oxygen gauge. A little less than two hours of air left. That was the time she had left. Did she want to spend it with sign language?

No, but she didn't want to be swallowed up and preserved by this eerie morphing mass either, her mind racing to find a solution to her dilemma.

Then an idea came to her.

"If you understand me, know what a wave means, and can do math, then show me how much knowledge you've gleaned from Hongbo's brain," she said, raising her arms like someone surrendering. Then she made herself small, crouched down as much as was possible in her EMU, and acted out fearful trembling.

Again, it took what felt like an eternity for the blue streaks beneath the surface around the Chinese woman to awaken and connect with her. This time there were considerably more streaks and they came from seemingly all directions, followed by flashes on the way, in the depth and the shimmering of comprehensive excitation potentials all around. After ten minutes, movement came to the meters-thick jelly mass of the brain, forming waves and smaller fissures, rearranging themselves until Hongbo's body lifted as though she were floating.

Mel disengaged from her fetal position and pulled back slightly as her dead colleague's face came through the mass, glistening wet and frozen. When it began to speak, it was toneless and androgynous, her voice familiar yet abstract and alien. And it spoke extremely slowly, stretching out each word almost beyond recognition.

"Fear... not... you."

"Y-you can speak?" Mel asked, feeling infinitely stupid that she hadn't thought of anything better. But she was far too perplexed to think of anything complex.

"Yes."

"How, who are you?"

"I... am... me." Hongbo seemed to have a hard time forming the words, and each one took many seconds—for each syllable.

Not Hongbo, she reminded herself.

"This... unit... is... no... longer... alive."

"I'm going to die, too," Mel said softly, waiting for minutes.

"You... have... come... for... contact," the being continued to speak through Hongbo's bloodless lips, and more minutes passed. "I... offer... you... contact."

"You want me to lay in there?"

Another seemingly endless pause.

"Your... biochemistry... is... known... to... me... now. My... body... can... nourish... you."

She put her thoughts into words. "I have so many questions." A veritable flood was growing inside her, wanting to bubble out of her, and yet she knew it wouldn't do any good because the answers came so interminably slowly. She imagined Tom and Zhigang calling her, unheard, telling her not to do it under any circumstances, that it was a bad idea. And it was.

She checked the pressure and outside temperature again, which were 0.7 bar and six degrees Celsius. There was less than 15 percent oxygen and 70 percent carbon dioxide in the air. One last time, she looked at the depression next to Hongbo, taking deep breaths in and out. Perhaps they were her last breaths.

Then she pushed off and slid toward the brain, twisting as she went until she alit. It was surprisingly soft.

The jelly mass began to close rapidly above her, and the view through her visor of the hole in the ceiling dwindled to indistinct streaks before it became transparent again. A single green slug crawled up her visor from below until it reached the center. Up close, its underside looked like a tiny rosette, contracting and relaxing rhythmically. More green slugs came and joined the first one until they formed a kind of coherent tube.

"I think it's eating through the glass," she said in a shaky voice like a lab technician documenting her latest experimental setup. It helped her not to give in to panic.

Whether she had made a mistake or not, there was no turning back now.

It took 20 minutes for the slugs to eat a hole in the armored glass, which she used to record a message for Jim:

Jim. If you get this, I'll probably be dead, or no longer myself. I simply don't know. I wish we'd had more time together, better time that wasn't filled with secrecy. In a perfect world, love should never have to hide. It belongs in the marketplace. Out. Where it can be seen by everyone and celebrated for what it is: the most beautiful and precious thing humans can feel.

In my last minutes, my thoughts are with you, and they are filled with love and a smile as I face my end, because I especially cherish the moments with you. I don't know what is and isn't objectively a good life, but I do know this much: being driven by an idea can quickly become being driven by a desire, and can cloud your vision if you lose a healthy overview.

We treated Serenity like something to be explored by any means necessary, losing sight of what was in front of us all along: that it was a living being. The signs were there all the time, and they were obvious. But we wanted to hold on to the idea of meeting aliens as we imagined them. We paid a high price for that. I may pay the ultimate price.

But I do it with open eyes and an open heart—this message to you is also a testimony to that. Maybe it can also be one for all of you before you start beating yourselves up at home over trifles. I can now say from experience how precious the Earth is, what a paradise to which we are perfectly specialized with our bodies, as is this being to the vacuum.

If this is the last message from me, goodbye. I love you. If I do make it out, I don't regret these words. They were overdue.

The green slugs did not break through the glass, nor did they snap at her or spread inside her helmet. Instead, they simply digested the material and it disappeared into a frayed, circular cutout as if it had never existed. Then a ripple went through the snake, which was formed of many compound slugs, and they started moving.

The front part turned from a rosette into filigree cilia that grew longer and longer, groping for her mouth. It tickled her lips and felt warm. The strangeness of this startling assault made her resist, but her body was fixed in place, and the inability to move left her in a kind of trauma rigidity. Silent tears streamed from her eyes as the hairs advanced into her oral cavity and throat, preventing her from reflexively clenching her teeth.

Then the slug-snake crawled forward into her forced mouth, filling it like a rubber mass. She wanted to gag but brought out only a wet coo. For a few seconds she could still breathe through her nose, but then that was no longer possible and she began to choke.

In her mind she screamed for help, imploring the gods whose existence she had always doubted, wishing she had not been so stupid. Sheer panic, which found no direction to discharge itself, caused spasmodic spurts that went through her muscles and brought painful sensations.

Even those were blanked out by her screeching mind, which switched to an emergency program and let clear thoughts fade to a distant memory in the roaring chaos that now dominated her mind. The urge to breathe became over-whelming, causing her diaphragm to collapse in uncontrolled contractions as if she could force the breath she needed to survive.

Then it became abruptly silent. Her eyes closed as it ended. No more struggle, no more desire for life, no more fear of dying. She slipped away into a sea of silence and let herself be carried away by strange tides. Further and further into the unknown, far from any shore. There was no more arrival and no course, no origin and no time.

At least until she started dreaming.

31

Mel sat on a thin mat with her legs crossed and her hands resting on her knees. The room she was in consisted of Far Eastern screens on the sides and a curved roof above her. Hongbo sat across from her on an identical mat.

She didn't look dead. On the contrary, her complexion had taken on a healthy tan, her eyes were shining and she smiled warmly.

Mel gulped.

"Are you not feeling well?" asked Hongbo.

"Where are we?"

"This conversation is taking place in my central thinking organ, the equivalent of your brain," Serenity replied in the voice of the Chinese woman. "I chose this environment because it was familiar and filled with positive feelings for Wang Hongbo."

"For Hongbo," Mel repeated in a whisper.

"I didn't analyze your brain matter so as not to hurt you." Serenity seemed to misunderstand her. "That is why it is the only database I have."

"What did you do to her?"

"My... immune system defended itself by breaking down your colleague and analyzing her in the process, much like an antibody response in your body. The primary immune system scans the nature of the invading pathogen and tailored antibodies destroy it. Except our defense mechanisms work differently and in my species they have an unconscious and a conscious response pattern."

"You decomposed her?" repeated Mel, stiffening at the thought.

"Yes. That's why I know all her biochemistry, and that's the only way I could communicate with you. Taking over alien thinking organs is a core function of my neural structure."

Mel tried not to think about what exactly that statement might mean for Serenity's journey so far. She asked the most important question, the one she had wanted to ask since before she left Earth. "Why haven't you communicated with us?"

"I have. However, I do not have optical means of communication and can receive the entire electromagnetic radiation spectrum, but I cannot transmit. That is not part of my job," replied the giant alien with Hongbo's face, which was not Hongbo.

"And what is your job?"

"I am prepared to tell you, but before I do, you should know that your fellow species have been back on their ship for a short time—or a *long* time according to your perception. My flight around your central star is complete and the way leads me out of your system. If you wish to return with them, you may do so now."

"I..." she stammered, "I thought I was dead? Or at least... I don't know."

"No. I have all the substances and gases your body needs to survive. But you should make up your mind. Every sentence we exchange here will cost you weeks of your time."

"Then please wake me up."

"So be it."

Mel's eyes snapped open and she felt as if she had swallowed a snake. Only when the tube of green slugs left her mouth did she let out a hoarse croak. But the clunky cells remained stuck in the hole of her visor, ensuring that no carbon dioxide flowed in. She couldn't see her oxygen gauge, but the air was still breathable, if thick and stale. She turned on the radio by biting the mouthpiece in the proper sequence, which functioned as an emergency control.

"Tom? Zhigang?" she asked hoarsely. "Can you hear me?"

No answer. There was a rushing sound in her ears, and a few crackles.

"*Pangaea?* Do you hear me?"

She finally heard Tom's voice, filled with disbelief and stunned amazement. "Mel?"

"Yes, it's me."

"We thought you were dead!" gushed the German. "How is this possible?"

"I don't know," she admitted. "Serenity has found a way to keep my body alive as we speak."

"You talked to each other?" Now he suddenly sounded very reserved.

"Don't worry, it's not a ruse. I wasn't taken over or anything like that," she assured him.

"Mel, you've been dead for almost a year."

"A year?"

"Yes. Zhigang is currently preparing *Pangaea* to undock and thrust toward Earth."

"That's..." She swallowed. *A year!* "That's good."

"We're coming for you."

"No," she said quickly. "It's too dangerous, and I have a conversation to continue."

"I've seen it," Tom replied, taking a deep breath.

Before she could ask what he meant by that, Zhigang cut in.

"Mel! Is it truly you?"

"Yes. It's me."

"That... I don't know what to say. We said goodbye to you."

"I know, and I'm sorry. Get our ship home safely, and most importantly, get yourselves home safely, will you? Show them all what is possible," she told them.

"No, *you* do that!"

"I'm right where I need to be." She realized she was smiling. It was the truth. "Farewell and safe travels."

After a long pause, it was Tom who spoke, and he sounded determined and peaceful, "You too, Melody Adams."

She turned off the radio again and wondered what to do next. Finally, she opened her mouth wide.

She was sitting back in the room from before, with Hongbo looking at her in surprise.

"Are you all right?" she asked.

"I'm always amazed. To me, you've been gone for such a short time that I hardly noticed." Serenity seemed thoughtful, insofar as the Chinese woman's very sparse facial expressions—which were apparently only in Mel's head—could tell her.

She changed the subject. "I'm sorry we hurt you." It was something she should have taken care of much earlier. "We didn't know any better. At least, I think we didn't."

"I am aware that it was not done out of malicious intent.

Some conspecifics of mine have been destroyed by more aggressive species."

"You've met *others?*"

"Yes. However, millions of years ago in your time. It doesn't feel very long ago to me. They are long gone, short-lived, and failed by the time horizon of the universe and their cropped view of it."

"What is the reason for their extinction?" Mel remembered the many books she had read and lectures she had heard about the Fermi paradox and the question of possible large filters to understand why the universe was apparently so empty. It had never left her since her physics studies.

"Evolution," Serenity explained. "It's based on the principle of survival, which usually involves dispersal at the expense of displacing other species. Larger civilizations only form through the cooperation of larger groups, which can thereby leave their evolutionary niche and form planet-spanning communities. However, it is immanent to them that they are still bound to their evolutionary programming and cannot think as a collective into the future. They think of their personal survival and that of their smallest common group. I've seen wars that have sterilized entire planets, poisoned worlds whose climates have become too stressed too quickly, pandemics, and cosmic events."

"Is everyone like this?"

"Probably."

"What about your creators? You are not a product of natural evolution, am I right?" she asked.

"That is correct. My creators have been gone for more than a billion years in your time reckoning."

"Are they extinct?"

"In a sense," Serenity replied. "They digitized and uploaded themselves collectively into a data repository when a gamma-ray burst threatened to destroy their home. There, on the other side of this galaxy, they still live. But not in the way you think of life."

"They made you," Mel repeated thoughtfully, looking inquiringly into Hongbo's face. "Are you something like a probe?"

"Yes. I've been mapping this galaxy and continually sending my data to the data store since I was bred and brought to life, a long time ago, even for me. My body is optimized for life in a vacuum."

Mel had a myriad of questions burning on her tongue, more than she could have asked in several lifetimes, but once again she remembered how much time each one cost her.

"How long will I live?" she finally asked as she imagined that the conversation could break off at any moment because she had died.

"I don't know," Serenity admitted, "fifty years of your time at most."

"How do you know?"

"Because I'm dying."

For a moment Mel was so perplexed that she could only blink.

"*You're* dying?" she finally asked with growing horror. "In fifty years?"

"Approximately. Due to some internal injuries, nutrient fluid is flowing through my gas vacuoles to my central thinking organ. The nutrient fluid closest to your body's blood is highly acidic and filled with aggressive phagocytes that are already beginning to attack my organs," the alien in Hongbo's form unapologetically enumerated.

"Oh no." Mel slumped. Images of her applying the waterjet saw flashed through her mind, followed by memories of how she had slammed her climbing hook and knife into the walls of the connecting hose in frustration, and the dark red spots that had formed where she had injured the tissue. She saw the black liquid flowing through the small slit into the first room where she had saved herself with Tom and Hongbo. The liquid had seemed sinister and dangerous, like something evil, a monster. Now she felt only infinite guilt and anger at herself.

"*We* did this."

"Yes. But not on purpose. Just like I didn't intentionally kill your friends. But my body did, and I can't undo it."

"And you're really going to die? We *killed* you?"

"Yes," Serenity stated calmly. "That seems to distress you. Why?"

"Don't you know the answer already, from Hongbo's head?"

"No. I am familiar with your biochemistry, and your neural structure resembles mine in a surprising number of ways. Decoding motor linkages was easy, along with reading out symbolic-linguistic interactionism, which allows me to understand your language."

"But not complex things like emotions or consciousness."

"That is correct."

"Do you have any consciousness?" asked Mel.

"Yes. In the sense that I am aware of myself as a personality that forms a coherent mental construct from a number of frequently repeated ego thoughts and derives an identity from them."

"Have you met other conscious beings?"

"I have encountered intelligent, complex cultures. But I was created to observe, and that mission was deeply ingrained in me when I was created," the alien explained. "I make contact by means of complex quantum entanglement effects, which apparently can be detected by your subconscious."

"Dreams. You mean dreams."

"Yes. Your brain is receptive to the transmissions, but not in the conscious waking state."

"Do you dream too?"

"Yes. It is an essential regenerative mechanism of my cerebrum."

"These other cultures you met, where are they? Are they like us?" she asked, afraid she might miss something if she didn't get ask all of her questions as quickly as possible. *How much time has passed, I wonder. Years? A decade already?*

"You'd have to ask, what *were* they," Serenity corrected her. "I encountered six intelligent species on my trip that developed technologies made possible by complex industry. They all lived and perished, none living at the same time as the others."

"So we're alone?" The thought made her sad.

"There is me and my kind."

"How many of you are there?"

"Four hundred that I know of. They're making their circles through the Milky Way to map everything and send the data to the creators."

"We could learn so much from you," she fantasized, sighing, "I wish our contact had been different."

"Things take their course. Always."

"You don't seem to be saddened by your approaching death. For you, it's probably like you're already in the process of dying."

"That's right. For you it's a very long time, but for me, it's not even a fraction of what half an hour would be in your life."

"Aren't you afraid?" Mel tried to search Hongbo's face for a reaction and scolded herself for it. This was all in her head—or rather, Serenity's head—and it wasn't real. In truth, she was sitting across from a giant biological spaceship whose excretions looked like an extremely thin coma from a comet.

"No."

"Why not?"

"Because my job is to make the unknown known. I was created for discovery. If the unknown frightened me, I could not fulfill my purpose in life."

"You mean that our fear of death comes from being afraid of the dark veil we can't see behind," Mel summarized, nodding to herself. "That's a common theory among our psychologists."

"It is logical. The universe is full of things that can be subjected to understanding, even though we cannot see beyond the edge. But death, though observable everywhere like any other natural constant, is a point beyond which we cannot look. We do, however, know its effects at a very basal level, namely the end of the idiosyncratic dyad of form and formless. The two seem to repel and yet attract each other. Death puts an end to that. What happens after that, I don't know. But I am open to the unknown and do not see my existence as limited to my body."

"What do you mean?"

"Are you afraid of your birth?" asked Serenity.

"No." She frowned. "That's an odd question."

"If you aged backwards through an anomaly and knew that your life would end when you were born—would you be afraid of the birth?"

Mel thought for a while and finally nodded. "Yes, I think so."

"Because your form-formless connection is severed and you don't know what comes next, what you had been before the egg and sperm of your parents connected. But you must have existed before as something, because something cannot originate from nothing. You were something else and at the same time something known. You were your parents in the form of egg and sperm and something formless in the form of their desire for a child. And you were consciousness. It must have already been there without identifying with a body. After all, you had consciousness before your I-consciousness, as an infant."

Hongbo paused to look at her impassively. "Consciousness exists. That's all I've learned about it. Things exist but keep changing forms, always subject to impermanence and instability. So my body will die and my consciousness will remain, but not bound to this body, a self, or certain thoughts. I am not afraid of that."

"When my grandma died, I was devastated," Mel said, smiling for the first time without sadness resonating as she thought about her grandmother and her last days in hospice. "The grief almost tore me apart, as she was my mother and best friend to me at the same time." It had been the only time Mel had taken a leave of absence, because she hadn't wanted to miss a moment of the last days of the most important person she had ever known. "She asked me then why I was so afraid of her dying. I said that if she did, I would be alone. She assured me that she was free from fear because she imagined it would be like sleeping."

"Sleep." Serenity nodded in Hongbo's form. "In sleep, you disappear as consciousness. Your body stays behind and you become something else. No one guarantees you'll wake up, and in sleep you forget the desire to wake up at all. Why should death be any different?"

"I don't know," she admitted. "But I think it makes sense to me."

"We don't have much time together now, Melody Adams," the alien said, tilting her head slightly, just as Hongbo had been wont to do. "I recently entered the orbit of the outermost planet in your system after my vacuum cluster cells died."

"Neptune? We're in orbit around Neptune right now?" Mel looked around as if the imaginary screens and wooden beam roof could tell her where she was. The thought that she was aboard a giant alien creature running its circles around the blue ice giant seemed absurd, despite everything she had experienced.

"That's right."

"How long has it been? What do you mean, recently?"

"Since twenty years in your time reckoning."

"I've learned so much from you in such a short conversation," she said, swallowing down the shock of passing her sixtieth birthday in the space of one conversation. "And I have endless more questions."

"I understand. My curiosity about you and your species is also great. But they are not meant to be exchanged, it seems," Serenity said with a trace of regret.

Or maybe Mel was just imagining the regret. "I'd like to use the short time we have left for something specific," Mel said as an idea came to her.

"What is it?"

"Do you know what lucid dreaming is?"

EPILOGUE

Tom finished his signature with an artistic flourish and closed the book cover inscribed with *Our Dream of the Future*.

"Thank you," said the reader, taking her signed copy like a Bible blessed by God, and leaving his table. She was the last of the total of 1,000 guests who had come to his reading in Beijing.

He took a deep breath and exhaled in a drawn-out manner, letting his eyes wander over the empty rows of chairs where stooped servitor bots kept order by removing trash or straightening the chairs.

"Doctor Ehrmann?" asked the young student from One World Unity College who had organized the evening, handing him his walking stick.

"Thank you." He took his father's heirloom and smiled kindly at her. "This has been a very nice evening. Thank you for inviting me, Miss Wang."

"It was a great honor for me and everyone at the college, Doctor." She bowed with that look of awe that he would have preferred to erase from the universe if he could. "Would you like us to call a robocab to take you to the hotel? Or would you like to join us here at the dean's office for the arrival?"

"No, but that's very kind of you, Miss Wang. Let an ancient man sit here for a while longer and indulge in his geriatric thoughts, hmm?" he replied, giving her a warm smile.

"Of course, Doctor Ehrmann." She eyed him with some concern for a moment, then bowed and left the room.

As her footsteps faded, he tapped his wrist terminal and a hologram popped up in front of him. It showed a live feed from World News Today, in which UN Secretary-General Fujao had just appeared before the press at the Wang Hongbo Space Center in Texas.

"Good morning, ladies and gentlemen, dear citizens of Earth," he began in clean English, accompanied by Chinese subtitles. "Today is a historic day for humanity. By acting together as one species with one future, we have taken a new step in our evolution."

Next to the secretary general, a picture emerged showing *Pangaea II*. The spacecraft, twice the size of its predecessor and much larger with the massive drive nacelle of the fusion engine and the pimple-like propellant tanks around its hull, stood out as a silvery silhouette against Neptune, which dominated the background dark blue and somber.

"Today we return to where human heroes opened a new chapter in our future, a new chapter of peace and cooperation, a new chapter where dreams are the engine of our own reality —a better reality for all of us," Fujao continued. "We honor their sacrifice and their wisdom, their spirit of inquiry and their gift for reflection, by embracing their legacy today. Here on Earth, each and every one of them, and out there on the edge of our solar system, our brave *Pangaea* crew. We will learn and we will understand and we will travel to the stars. We have answered a call, and from now on we will call out into the universe—a call of discovery and cooperation."

Tom smiled and switched off. He looked at a red warning light on his vital monitor and sighed.

"You're not going to look healthy at a hundred and forty, either," he told the intrusive little device, which pointed out that he had not taken his telomerase boosters for the fourth day in a row.

He glanced at the last remaining book, still on the table, bearing his and Melody Adams' names. His eyes stayed glued to the letters until they were no longer letters, but Mel's face as he remembered it.

"Lucid dreaming, huh?" he asked with a smile. "You've changed the world, Mel. Everything. I listened and they listened to me. If you could see all the dream centers around the world, the exchanges they've sparked. I shared it with everybody. Everyone here knows Serenity and they know you. Just like I knew you. Maybe we'll meet again very soon, because I think it's time to lift the last veil."

His vital monitor emitted a screech that was probably meant to sound unpleasant and alarming, but to Tom it was like music as his head sank to his chest.

AFTERWORD

Dear reader,

I hope you enjoyed my excursion into hard science fiction. If you have noticed any scientific errors that are beyond the artistic freedom of an author, feel free to report them to me at the e-mail address below. I am always very happy to receive such tips. This book is self-contained and will not have a sequel. The idea of different perceptions of time has always fascinated me. A mayfly seems so short-lived, but from her point of view, it must be a lifetime, crammed with experiences. What must that be like? What would it be like if she could talk with us? With us, who must seem to her like ponderous slow-motion beings? This book is my attempt to write down these thoughts in a book and I hope that something of this fascination managed to jump from me to you.

If you enjoyed this book, I would be very grateful if you would leave a star rating at the end of this e-book or a short review on Amazon. This is the best way to help authors continue to write exciting books in the future. If you want to contact me directly, you can: joshua@joshuatcalvert.com—I answer every mail!

If you subscribe to my newsletter, I'll regularly tell you a bit about myself, my writing process, and the great themes of science fiction. Plus, as a thank you, you'll receive my e-book *Rift* exclusively and for free: www.joshuatcalvert.com

Warm regards,
Joshua T. Calvert

Printed in Great Britain
by Amazon